Fish Sunday Thinking

By

Alex Gilmore

Published 2005 by arima publishing

www.arimapublishing.com

ISBN 1-84549-031-2

Printed and bound in the United Kingdom

Typeset in Garamond 10/16

arima publishing
ASK House, Northgate Avenue
Bury St Edmunds, Suffolk IP32 6BB
t: (+44) 01284 700321

www.arimapublishing.com

To my loving family, the grandparents that inspired me and, most importantly, my soulmate.

Part One

Chapter One

Most days are work days

Most days, for most people, start in darkness. Quite often - more often than not - it's hard to tell where the nightmare ends and reality begins. Most days start with a sense of unease. Discomfort. Pain. Most days start with......morning.

Morning. One of the most chilling prospects in the English language. Right up there with power cuts during a World Cup final or a betrayed ex with a pair of scissors (God rest your soul, Mr Bobbitt).

Mornings are God's eternal plague on mankind. They are damp, dark, torrid affairs where comprehension, reason, and common sense have no place. Of course, this is primarily because comprehension, reason and common sense are late risers and are really not morning people.

Let's face it - mornings are not joyous occasions for anyone. No one wakes up, bounces out of bed and exclaims - "Oh good golly gosh - the morning - the morning is here and I feel as happy as a cloud over a meadow of golden daffodils". Well, no one that you should be associating yourself with in good company anyway.

No, mornings are a time of grunts, groans and yawns. A time where conversation is reduced to anything that can be communicated without the actual need for words to be exchanged. A time where people will only ask questions that can be conveyed by pointing at inanimate objects no further than a few inches from the end of their barely outstretched arms, and only then on the tacit understanding that the response must: a) be communicated by a small head movement either on the horizontal or vertical plane; and, b) must not involve the proposee making much effort in order to satisfy the terms of the proposal.

Mornings are not just a chore. They are not just annoying. They are totally without purpose, as if God really really didn't quite think the idea through.

It is no surprise that there is a correlation between the depressing nature of the occasion and the fact that most days are work days.

Lets be honest - the same sense of unease, pain and suffering doesn't happen at weekends. Of course not. For a start, weekends do not have mornings. Weekends begin at eleven a.m. and end at three p.m. on a Sunday when you realise that the party is over because its work tomorrow.

Whilst everyone accepts that mornings are dire, most people eventually get through the extreme inconvenience of them. This may be through the rejuvenating effects of their power shower/sandblaster; the fifteen cups of coffee they drink the moment they arrive at their desk; or, simply because their chosen career is so tedious that they can switch off until two in the afternoon anyway without anyone noticing or their productivity diminishing, for example train drivers, civil servants or politicians (oh come on! What do they actually do?!).

Denton Voyle, though, is not quite so fortunate.

For Denton, the pain, confusion and general dislike of the morning does not pass and, on occasion, the same feelings seep through into the early part of the afternoon.

For Denton Voyle, most mornings, on most days, take on a fairly familiar pattern.

For Denton Voyle, there is more than a passing dislike of mornings - there is an abhorrent detesting of them. Mornings encapsulate the week day, thereby reinforcing his reluctance to embrace working, which pretty much sums up his resentment at the prospect of a lifetime wasted at work.

And for Denton Voyle, the all too regular occurrence of the mindless din that is his alarm clock is too much of a painful reminder that his happy unconscious dreamlike state of ignorance and bliss is about to end, to be replaced by an unwanted wave of crashing pain, nausea and lethargy, as his regular hangover and work avoidance syndrome kick in in a symbiotic fashion.

Although whilst accepted that the mindless din of the alarm clock does tend to grate after a while (and often causes its owner to hit the snooze button with such vigour that it releases a satisfying sense of control over one's destiny), it can also motivate even the most lethargic of all individuals to bounce out of bed when they realise that: a) the damned thing has been going off intermittently for over half an hour, and; b) leaving it until eight o'clock to get out of bed is really not the way to endear yourself to your boss.

For Denton, this is the usual pattern.

They do say that muscles have memory. This is reassuring for a man in Denton's position - a man who has made it his life's work to systemically destroy the 100 billion (give or take) neurons in his brain through the regular consumption of alcohol. At least once the brain cells have gone, those muscles, honed over the years through lifting pint glasses, will help him work out such important matters as where he put the keys to his flat the night before.

But then again, perhaps even the memory in Denton's muscles has been affected over the years by the barrage of alcohol abuse. What other explanation could there be for the fact that during most mornings he would stumble through doorways, bouncing off door frames, walking straight into lampshades, low tables and unsuspecting briefcases, as if someone had reconstructed his room in the night, just a little bit too much to the right.

But then, if muscles have memory, why could they not remember how far to turn the taps of the shower on a morning and save Denton Voyle from the daily torment of being sliced in half from the freezing water and then steamed like a cabbage when he turned the tap slightly too far the other way.

And, just exactly what did cause mornings to be such a depressing affair? Was it the semi-permanent hangover? The monotony of it all? Or just simply the inherent, deep rooted pointlessness of his existence?

And what could signify the pointlessness of modern life more than ironing? And not just ironing itself, but ironing shirts for work. Each morning, Denton's reward for escaping the shower inferno with only third degree burns would be the prospect of ironing a shirt during which, he would spend the mandatory fifteen minutes cursing the man who invented the iron, and the man who invented the cotton shirt. Did they just never meet up to discuss their ideas before they started mass production? *"Hey! I've invented a heavy cotton creased shirt". "Hey! I've invented a steam iron." "Brilliant - well if you put my creased shirt and your steam iron together then we should get…hang on…wait a minute...humph…just getting the…almost...shit they don't work together at all. My God - this is a disaster." "I know". "Let us never talk of this again and everything will be fine." "You're right - perhaps no one will ever find out." "Very good. Crisis averted. Good day to you sir".*

Worse still. The man who invented the tie. What was he thinking? He was either drunk at the time or had had such a bad day that he was determined to make mankind suffer from that day forth. Maybe he'd just bought an iron and a shirt and was still feeling bitter. Either way, he had not given it the forethought it deserved.

With just enough time to make a decision on whether vomiting now would be the smart move or not, Denton would leave his flat, suited, booted and full of nurofen, filled with a sense of hangover-tempered despair each morning and make his way to a certain London law firm, where he spent his days slowly, slowly dying as a trainee solicitor.

Morning prompted afternoon, afternoon prompted evening, evening prompted morning, morning prompted the same old question. *The* Question. What on earth is this all for? Asking the Question prompted avoidance, avoidance prompted drinking, drinking prompted darkness.

Darkness, groan, temple based pain, followed darkness, groan, temple based pain just as wake, wash, mid hallway door frame collision followed wake, wash, mid hallway door frame collision. And day followed night and drinking followed work just as Denton's feet followed his swaying body as he stumbled his way home in some kind of never-ending circle of despair.

A constant waste of perfectly good oxygen.

Chapter Two

Weekends

It was June 2002.

The incessant drone happened again.

"God damn it," he mumbled to no one in particular. An aimless arm came crashing down onto the unsuspecting alarm clock which immediately ceased it's nagging - though not without the briefest of squeaks, as if to register its displeasure at the disproportionate attack.

"Just doing my job," it might complain if it weren't made entirely of plastic. Even then, it would probably have retorted in Taiwanese.

Denton stirred. "God damn it," he winced. He opened an eye causing himself obvious pain. The alarm clock flashed 7.20 with unnecessary glee.

He rolled back over. He lay still momentarily then stirred again. He sighed. Then rolled on to his back. He lay still and then without any warning swung his arms and legs violently causing him to kick and lash out at the bed.

"God damn it. God damn it. God damn it!" He exclaimed. "GOD DAMN IT! It's the sodding weekend!"

He stopped and lay still.

"Nope, it's no good," he cried. "I'm awake now."

Denton reluctantly rolled out of bed.

"I mean - it's not even the weekend - it's morning, so technically it's still Friday night."

And then the pain increased as the realisation dawned on him, "Oh Christ, its not even Saturday...it's Sunday. Bollocks."

With accentuated vigour, he pulled on his dressing gown. "Sodding muscle memory my arse - why couldn't you remember to sleep in?"

Denton stopped in full flow and almost doubled over in pain. The blood, which had previously been doing nothing more than proceeding as usual in the circular fashion that it had gotten used to in twenty three years and which it still enjoyed in spite of the predictability of it all - in the same way that dogs enjoy chasing their tail and women enjoy torturing men - suddenly found itself - all nine pints of it - in Denton's head, gasping for air. The room spun and his double vision doubled.

"Ow, ow" he winced. "Hangover." Inevitably, he collapsed back on to the bed.

"The weird thing," Denton would often say, on many occasions, and to no one in particular, "is that the weekend represents the only opportunity to lie in, so why is it that it is also the only time when you're wide awake at exactly the same time that your alarm clock would usually go off? Is it just that it is ingrained indelibly on your brain that mornings - whichever morning it happens to be - mean getting up early and going to work? It must be that you piss off your body so much by having to get up early every week day morning (despite the fact that it usually, and very amply, shows its annoyance by refusing to function properly until lunchtime) to such a degree that the failure to lie in on a weekend is its way of getting its own back. *"How do you like it?"* it might say, if it could. Which, fingers crossed, it can't."

"The thing is though, there is just no need for your body to react in this way. Every victory is a pyrrhic victory. It is blindingly obvious that co-operation on this point would be a win-win situation for both parties - you get a chance to sleep in and your body gets a chance to recuperate. But does it listen? No - it's completely irrational and unreasonable. Conclusive proof, I think you will agree, that every body is essentially female. Understand your body and you will understand women."

"Do 'Relate' do sessions for breakdowns in relations between you and yourself?"

"OK then Mr Liver - hello there the Kidney twins - I have a proposal - how about I just lie here for two or three hours and you just rest up. Sound like a good plan?"

"But *'oh, no'* your body protests, *'you pissed me off every day this week by making me get up early, so come on fat boy, get up now if you like it so much - don't let me stop you. I'm gonna release a whole load of chemicals into your blood stream to make you thoroughly awake and ensure that you properly enjoy the hangover symptoms to full effect. After all, you went to great lengths to get them, so let's not waste them now. Lie back, and enjoy as the blood pounds in your head, as the ache in your head takes hold and your stomach churns over the gunk that you poured into it last night, all in the name of being sociable......oh, and don't think that we forgot the dead pigeon that you saw fit to eat last night under the pretence of it being a "kebab". You'll be relieved to know that that is what the rotting flesh taste is in your mouth right now.'*

Denton slowly rose again to his feet. "Water," he gasped, "Need water."

He looked around in vain, trying to see where he might have placed a glass full of water last night, in an unprecedented act of forethought. "The pint glass full of water is.....as empty as it was when I neglected to fill it up last night. Oh God. I need some water. How do I fill a pint glass again?" he said, resisting the temptation to vomit on his duvet.

"And where are my specs? I can't see a thing without them!" complained Denton, spinning around on the spot trying to find his spectacles. One of the unspoken casualties of the computer age, Denton daily lamented the fact that he held more in common with Moley from *"The Wind in the Willows"* than he might perhaps have hoped he would at twenty-three. He felt sure that most of his peers felt the same way.

"Seriously, where are they?!" He said as his head throbbed causing him to feel and hear the blood passing through his ears. Not a particularly enjoyable experience, he had to admit.

"Do they have to be on the floor? Can they not be somewhere at head height so I don't have to bend down?" Due to the fact that all the blood in his body still seemed to be swimming around in his head, Denton was loathe to bend over for fear of his head falling off. Tentatively, he crouched down, supporting his head as if his neck had been replaced by a cocktail stick in the night. "There they are!" he exclaimed as he found them - noticeably relieved that he hadn't trodden them into the carpet.

Cautiously, he opened the bedroom door and stumbled forward into the dark corridor, though not before he had rebounded off the door frame, which he presumed had again been moved five centimetres to the right during the time he had been unconscious. He peered around, not entirely able to focus even with his glasses, on account of the fact that his eyes were stubbornly resisting his semi-formulated command to open. Somewhere in his brain was the message, *'Mind the hall table,"* which was just floating around, trying to hook up with the muscle section that dealt with such co-ordination matters. Having taken a wrong turn, the message never got there and instead Denton stumbled blindly into the table. At the same time, the message *'Why didn't someone down there remind me about the table, can't you see we have enough to worry about up here?"* shot off in the opposite direction, got equally lost and eventually found the *'Mind the table"* warning but only by the time that both had been consigned to the *'For the love of God, stop drinking"* message wasteland.

"Oww!" Denton found himself saying. He heard something tumble over and roll onto the carpet beneath. A wet foot and soggy boxers suggested to him that it was probably the vase of flowers.

Ridiculous, thought Denton, *Why would a flat that two guys share have a vase of flowers on the hall table? Bloody landladies. Yes, of course, we can all accept that flowers add that sense of homeliness to a place - but we're blokes! Entrusting us to look after stuff like this is quite frankly asking for trouble. And now I have a wet foot and something to clean up later. Brilliant.*

By now, Denton had completely lost the impetus to find water and was seriously contemplating ending the sham of his hungover life right now by commanding his brain to self-destruct. The banging headache and the soggy boxer shorts were not helping the situation at all.

And where the hell is the kitchen? Did they move that in the night too?

The combined nature of his banging headache, his upset stomach and his distinct sense of nausea had caused Denton to pretty much forget what the layout of his flat actually looked like.

What did I get up to last night? he contemplated. His brain was failing so utterly in trying to achieve even the most rudimentary of tasks that it really did not have the capability to start piecing together the fragments of memory to actually form a picture of where it was or what it was doing the night before. It did not dare send out another message to ask other parts of the Voyle anatomy if they knew for fear of losing another one. In fact, to be honest, recollection was pretty much the last item on the agenda for his brain. It was far too busy convening the *"surviving brain cells together"* meeting in which it struggled to understand why the membership numbers seemed to be decreasing exponentially on a daily basis. It briefly considered that the directions to the meeting had been unclear and that maybe the instruction that each brain cell "turn left at the sixth millionth synapses" had been just a little too vague.

Denton stumbled into another door frame.

"Ah, the kitchen," said Denton, with a certain sense of achievement, as he fumbled in the dark trying to find the cord to make the lights work. He knew it was there on account of the fact that he had hit it twice. But now it was flailing around and there was no way he could make some kind of co-ordinated effort to actually grip on to the blessed thing.

Forget it, he thought, *I don't need light, not now all the major components are here to aid me on the road to recovery; running cold water, the receptacle in my hand in which to deposit it; and, a semi-operational muscular action in my arm by which to deliver it to my mouth. And later, the key to the cure - the fry up! But, urgh, not yet though. Sorry stomach, I now realise it was a bit too soon to contemplate that. No, no please don't get up. I'll be good. Don't make me be ill - not in the kitchen sink. OK, truce - you don't contract now and I'll make sure I feed you every lunchtime this week - look the offer is on the table - peace? OK, that's better.*

So, simple job. Turn the tap. Water comes out. Glass catches water. Drink from glass. I can do that. Denton turned the tap. *No. No, apparently not,* thought Denton as the water cascaded from the tap and covered him in water across the whole of his mid-section.

Great, thought Denton, *Even soggier shorts. Brilliant. I swear someone has been messing with the pressure in this thing during the night. Well, fine, at least I'm slightly more alert after the impromptu shower.* Denton held the glass to his lips. *So now I'm drinking and…oh god, does that feel good? Wow, I never realised water could taste this good. Oh, God bless running water.*

Denton stopped gulping in order to catch up on some other essential activities such as breathing. He took long, deep breaths and placed his hands on the sink for support. He prayed that he would stop feeling sick soon.

Feeling exhausted, Denton thought now might be a good time to sit down. "Where's the living room?" He wondered out loud.

He ambled out of the kitchen and headed for the adjacent room. Pushing the door, he peered into the dimly lit room.

Ah, here's the living room, he thought, *except its more of Night of the Living Dead room. Is that my flatmate in there? Well, there's definitely something or someone sat on the sofa. It might still be pitch black on account of the pre-war curtains being drawn, but, yep - I can make out a figure.*

Undaunted, Denton entered the room and sat down on a sofa too small to be described as comfortable and too shabby to be considered aesthetically pleasing. It might have been described as 'homely' but only then in desperation and even then, in relative terms. There were two sofas, adjacent to each other and it was quite clear that there was definitely something on the other one. Whether it was human and alive was only confirmed in the broadest terms when the thing began to snore. In spite of this, Denton seemed to have had no qualms about turning the TV on.

This had the desired effect since it caused the thing to wake in a start. Denton's eyes adjusted to the bad light to the point where it was clear to make out the sofa. There sat a man, with short blonde spiky hair, small, slightly sticky out ears and small eyes perched behind metallic thin rimmed glasses. It was his flatmate, Randall. An intriguing feature about him was the fact that his head was just perceptibly smaller than it ought to be, as if, on a visit to deepest, darkest Africa, he had once crossed a headshrinker who had started to perform his ritual against him but had then thought better of it. Maybe there had been something on the TV that he just couldn't miss.

Clearly, Randall was asleep. He sat on the sofa with his arms folded and his head leaning to one side with his blonde hair ruffled and his glasses just slightly off kilter. For whatever reason he was wearing a frown upon his face.

On being disturbed, Randall moved from his starting position to wearing a slightly less puzzled but vaguely scared bunny rabbit expression on his face and then quickly opened his eyes, at which point he bolted upright as if trying in some way to demonstrate that he was awake the entire time.

"Ah…er," he bleated. His eyes darted as he looked around the room perhaps trying to figure out where he was. It was certainly obvious that some kind of natural instinct had just kicked in on account of the darkness since he was about to demonstrate how little his brain was actually functioning right now. His arms outstretched, he stood, yawning, "Well mate, I'm shattered. Time to call it a night, I think. I'll see you in the morning."

As he got up and began to walk away, Denton felt that it was only appropriate to point out the one flaw in Randall's otherwise logical deduction.

"Randall…"

"Yeah?"

"It *is* the morning."

"Really? Oh…right." Randall stopped, looked around the room one more time, perhaps looking for more proof than simply relying on Denton's word, he looked back at Denton "When did that happen?"

Denton thought momentarily about the implications of this question. Then stared at Randall with a look of almost desperation. "Pretty much the usual time, I think."

"Really?" asked Randall, almost as a natural reaction rather than because he doubted the truth of the matter.

"Yes. So it would have been somewhere between where beer ends and day begins." Denton nodded towards the sofa. "You passed out on the settee again."

"Oh, God damn it. Not again!" cursed Randall. Then the look of confusion was slowly replaced with one of annoyance, "Every time!" He was beginning to see the funny side of it until a dreadful feeling of realisation sunk in, causing his face with erupt with horror.

"Oh bollocks, it's Sunday isn't it."

"I'm not going to lie to you, Randall." said Denton sincerely, without taking his eyes off the TV.

"Bollocks" exclaimed Randall.

Denton could only agree with the point, which he considered was very well made.

Chapter Three

Sundays

Weekends are not so bad. At least the weekend offers some solace from the constant onslaught of the week day. They break the monotony of it all and make life more interesting. And if not interesting, then almost bearable.

Of course, the same is not true of Sundays. This is probably on the basis that Sundays are just big fat liars. I mean, they purport to be a part of the weekend but in reality they are definitely not. Sundays are just the façade that hides Monday. No more, no less.

And what is Sunday? Sunday is the reminder of the Question. The Question that we all ask in different forms. *Why am I here? What is it all for?* Or, more selfishly, *What am I doing here? Where am I going with my life? What the hell is going on?*

But the Answer doesn't come easily. In fact, in most cases, the Answer doesn't come at all. And so Sunday is also the reminder that you don't know the Answer. Which inevitably means Sunday takes on that sense of gloom on account of the fact that avoidance of the Question altogether is the only way to get through it all.

And what is Monday? Monday is a realisation of the fact that you do not know the Answer. Monday is the knowledge that you are not empowered to escape from the imprisonment of your own existence. Monday is just another instalment of your miserable working life.

Einstein said something once about equal and opposite reactions occurring in the same something. I don't know, it was in a film. Someone was floating in space and they threw a spanner and they went in the opposite direction from the spanner to safety. It was all very moving, though ultimately disappointing when the leading lady didn't get her kit off. Anyway, the point is that for every beacon of hope that is Friday, there must a harbinger of doom that is Sunday. Einstein said so.

"Now you must admit," Denton would say, given half a chance, "there is something inherently wrong with Sunday."

"The sun rises," Denton assumed, although he had never actually seen any proof of this, "and the sun sets in the same way, I'll grant you. The weather is the same on a Sunday as it is on any other day, with the exception that during the summer months, the sun will shine for as long as you are in the office only to be replaced by a monsoon the minute you leave the building. Like every day, birds don't sing in the City on a Sunday. OK some similarities, but, no, on the whole,

Sunday just isn't right."

"Maybe it's because Sundays are just Saturday's hangover. Maybe it is because they stand there hiding Monday. Or maybe it's because they are just so fucking pointless."

"Any way you look at it, there it is. Sunday. Sitting there all innocent and holier than thou, just goading you into doing fuck all, all day long, with its hollow promises of being the day of rest. You find yourself, in front of the TV not knowing why you're watching it, and you sit with that vague sense of dread that only comes from the realisation that, sooner or later, you *are* going to be watching Songs of Praise."

"And Songs of Praise - what is that all about? Why are the people in it so happy? It's Sunday. And what have they done by being at Church? Nothing. Absolutely sod all. In fact, all they've done is just delay the inevitable ironing that must occur at some point during the day."

"And don't get me started on ironing."

"I mean, no one will ever say, 'I tell you what, I'm glad it's Sunday. I've been looking forward to Sunday all week. Ooooh Sunday.' No. That simply never happens. OK, it's made more bearable by the fact that you might mow the lawn in the sunshine. That might be acceptable for an afternoon's entertainment. You might go for a stroll with your beloved down a country lane, in the autumn breeze and maybe, watch the dried brown leaves tumble past your feet, as you realise how lucky you are to be with such a beautiful woman. But unless you happen to find yourself stuck in the middle of a Mills and Boon novel, then you're unlikely to be in this position."

"In any event, these things do not happen when you live in the Barbican. Have you ever been to the Barbican? Well don't go and certainly do not go back, even if you live there. Not even if you live there and you just realised that you left the gas on. Don't go - claim on the insurance instead and set up home elsewhere. Somewhere green."

"Someone once told me that George Michael and Michael Caine had penthouses in the Barbican. Is this true? Why would they do that? I can only imagine that if they did, they did it in furtherance of their charitable work purely so that the lives of some poor unfortunates were saved by ensuring that they didn't have to waste their lives trapped in this monochrome nightmare."

"The Barbican. I mean, what happened? Did someone wake up one day and think, 'well, fuck me, I've got a fucking shed load of concrete - what am I meant to do with this? Well, I'll tell you one thing, all that greenery in the Barbican is going for a start!"

"Someone else told me that the Barbican was built by someone who thought it was a vision of the future. What? Were they drunk at the time? Were they on anti-depressants? Had they just read 1984 and thought 'Ooh, running out of time a bit, better get a move on otherwise Mr Orwell's vision just isn't going to come true at all.'"

"How could anyone believe that this was a vision of the future? We all joke that before colour TV was invented, everyone lived in black and white, but maybe it's not a joke, after all. Clearly someone did. I mean what kind of vision for the future is this? A future where the only colours that exist are sixteen variations of grey."

"The Barbican. You know Bill Bryson never wrote in his book on the hidden beauties of this once majestic land, *'Have you visited the Barbican? Well if you haven't, go now. Please, take my car.'* and there is a reason why he didn't.

"In fact, I dare you to go. Go to the Barbican. Go now. I dare you. Go, look up at those ridiculous towers since I'm positive that if you did you would say, *'wow, if only I had one million pounds, colour blindness and no sense of vertigo - then I'd know joy.'*"

"Yeah. Of course, you'd say that. Yeah. But no. You wouldn't."

"And don't start with the whole *'Oh, but London has many fine designated green areas, just waiting to be enjoyed.'* because we all know from Eastenders, these designated green areas are tiny squares of grass with the odd park bench where people go to sit, be miserable and contemplate taking their own life."

"And even if I did want to go to somewhere like Regent's Park or St James Park, which is so big and so green that you don't even notice the horse track around it, how would I get there? Certainly not by tube. There never seem to be services between the Barbican and the rest of the world on a weekend because there is always 'necessary work' to be done to the track. OK, but if that work is so necessary, how come you never see it being done on a week day?"

For Denton and Randall, in their largely empty and unfulfilled lives, Sundays and particularly Sunday afternoons, were a time when nothing much happened. A time for sitting. A time for catching up on the thoughts that you did not have time to concentrate on during the week.

Their rented flat was minimal. Minimally decorated. Minimally furnished. Minimally thought out and with minimal effort. It comprised of three bedrooms. One with an ensuite, one without an ensuite and one with hardly enough space to get a bed in, let alone an ensuite. One bathroom. One kitchen. One hall. One living room. Two beds. Two sofas. One TV. One stereo. One dining room table and three unfeasibly heavy dining room chairs.

It was in this context that Denton and Randall expended the minimal amount in its minimal upkeep. And to this end, since Sunday was the designated cleaning day, Denton and Randall largely spent most of the afternoon sat on their designated sofas.

Both unshowered, unshaved and unkempt. Denton with his large array of dark hair partially hiding his dark brown eyes, wearing his blue dressing gown and largely dried boxer shorts following the weekly vase mishap. Randall, on the other sofa, sporting a mop of blonde hair, his blue eyes sitting behind a pair of spectacles and also clad in a dressing gown, with this one being a faded bottle green. Both sat with pained expressions. The kind of expression you might expect to see on a six month old baby momentarily after it had taken great pleasure in ridding itself of the lunch that it had finally processed through its newly working digestive system without really taking into account the post-event discomfort of the procedure.

Both were sat staring at the television. On top of the television sat Denton's woollen monkey. A once proud figure that had come to symbolise all that was good and true about being reckless with money but which now was beginning to look a bit frayed around the edges. A woollen monkey which now for commercially sensitive reasons, people dare not even talk about. Poor little thing.

And all at once both Denton and Randall's head tilted in unison as they stared at Ragboy, the woollen monkey, and a beautiful idea dawned upon them.

Chapter Four

Things to do on a Sunday afternoon when you're not quite dead

"As with all good activities, this one was simple at its inception and, by its inevitable end, would no doubt be consumed with commercialism, complexity and tinged with a certain sorrow when no-one remembered how on earth it began."

The goal of the game appeared to be to observe how many attempts it would take to knock Ragboy from his lofty perch. Why either Randall or Denton thought that this was a good idea, or even a productive use of their time, was not entirely clear. However, it did give the Sunday paper another use, as they sat there decimating the small forest that was *the Sunday Times*.

"Bet you can't do it in five," challenged Randall, both he and Denton acutely aware of the implicit understanding that there was no actual prize on offer other than a sense of self satisfaction, which in itself would be pretty priceless.

"Fine. I accept that challenge. Look as I do it in one and thoroughly mock the ridiculous idea that it would take more. OK, so I'm just getting my eye in there. OK, well I was close that time. Shit. Is that our vase? Yeah, no, good point, why would we own a vase, must be the landlady's. OK, well at least the picture frame bounces more than the vase did. Oh, shit, sorry, was that your eye? Fine, well you do better then," said Denton, resigned to the fact that he had absolutely no hand to eye coordination.

"Ha ha. I will, and in fact, look at me as I hit....OK, the TV, but I was close. OK, so the window is not so close. But. OK, well, you laugh, but technically the window sill is closer. Yeah, no, the picture frame is a little further away. Ooh, look, I broke the vase again, who would have thought that was possible. YES! I've....hey! That's not fair. It hit him but he didn't fall."

"Hmmm," said Denton examining the balls of paper strewn across the carpet. "So we've made a lot of mess and yet have not actually accomplished what we wanted to," said Denton, scratching his chin, for effect, if nothing else.

Collective frowns all round did not help the situation and it dawned on Denton that Ragboy was looking particularly smug. "We'll get you sonny and....are you winking?"

"OK, well, how about if we use those wicker place mats instead - they're heavier than paper." There could be no faulting Randall's logic on this one.

"Mmm, no, you've got a point there. OK, although you realise that this means getting up don't you!?"

"You're right," frowned Randall, knowing that there was one flaw; he had not built in to his plan the correlation between the idea of using wicker place mats with the fact that he would have to actually use physical effort in order to stand up and get them.

"Well, I can't do it….my spine congealed into jelly during the night."

"Yeah, no….mine too."

"OK, well, whoever falls forward the least has to collect the place mats. No, wait, hang on, actually there is one just here on the floor. Hey, look how well they fly - right out of the window. Hang on. Did you open the window?"

"Well, it was getting hot in here." said Denton, suddenly stood by the window. "So, now I'm up, I might as well get some more mats."

"This is a ridiculous way to spend a Sunday afternoon. You realise that don't you?"

"Yeah, well. What else are you going to do on a Sunday?"

"Yeah. You've got a point."

Much inept wicker Frisbee throwing later and they had managed to knock Ragboy off the TV five times, much to his silent but obvious annoyance. Unfortunately, this was more indicative of their aim than the amount of time that they had spent in this pursuit, which was considerable in itself.

"Is it me, or is Ragboy starting to look forlorn?" asked Denton.

Randall squinted and slightly tilted his head, "Yeah, it's like a cross between pain and puzzlement, as if he might yelp 'Why?' in between being pelted. You know what? I think that this game is a bit unfair. He needs armour."

"Yeah!" said Denton with enthusiasm. Now, why on earth would Denton think that Randall's suggestion was perfectly logical?

Several metres of kitchen foil later and it was not so much Ragboy the Monkey as Ragboy the Mongol Warrior, decked resplendent in kitchen foil body armour, a kitchen foil wrapped funnel upside down on his head, a pan lid as a shield and a fuck off big kitchen knife in his little woollen mitts.

"Now….he's prepared," said Randall, beginning to think that the result did not justify the considerable inflammation of his hung over condition that the process necessitated. "OK, maybe it was worth it," he said, "Look at him - he's all kick-ass."

And then the wicker Frisbee began to lose its effect, he just kept batting the damned things away with his bloody great kitchen knife.

"I knew we shouldn't have given him the knife!" cursed Randall

Ragboy just sat there looking silently smug, bordering on cocky.

"Alright, Ragboy, don't get on your woollen high horse, we can quite easily remove you from all that stuff you know. And remember this, we'll definitely have to come tea time. We'll need that pan lid. Yeah, not looking so smug now are we, little one?" said Denton.

"You know what we need? A gun." began Randall. It was nice to see that the brief military training in the TA had not been lost altogether.

A look of anguish flashed across Ragboy's face.

Intrigued, Denton ventured, "How?" Of course, any normal person would have probably just have asked, "Why?" but this point somehow eluded him.

"Ah, ha!" said Randall, his finger shot up in delight as a smile exploded across his totally unprepared face.

Twenty seconds later, the internet was beckoning. Well, at least, it would have been if they had been featuring in some cheesy internet service provider advert, but since this was the real world you should of course read minutes for seconds.

"Never underestimate the power of the internet," chirped Randall.

"Websites with BB guns?"

"But no ordinary BB guns, look at these bad boy BB's firing a hundred BB's a minute."

In horror, Denton read a testimony, *"I tried it out on a CD stapled to the wall and in two minutes, it was obliterated."* He looked at Ragboy and took a double take, "Is he…Is Ragboy shaking?"

Randall looked up casually and looked back at the computer. "Yes. But then he has good reason to be. These things are semi-automatic."

Suddenly a vision entered Denton's head of Ragboy on top of the TV, blind-folded with a cigarette in his mouth, whilst in the distance a lonely trumpet sounded and a female…er…monkey stood weeping, perhaps for her soon-to-be lost love. Seconds later, after the rattling but all too brief sound of shots had rung out, stuffing briefly filled the air before gently floating back sombrely to the ground."

"No, NO!" said Denton shaking his head to dispel the awful vision, "I cannot let you do that. A man, in good conscience, should never allow anyone to fire a semi-automatic weapon at his monkey. I won't let it happen! We'll just stick to wicker Frisbees. No one ever got hurt with those."

You know there are times when people should really think about the full implications of what they have just said before they say them. There are also times when people should watch their aim. And, you know, invariably there are also times when strangers should not walk past open windows.

It was after the screech of pain came flooding through the net curtains that they realised it was time to stop the game. And probably to move addresses. Perhaps also to consider a change of identity.

Chapter Five

Monday mornings sometimes come without warning

Monday came, as it usually did, right around the time when Sunday stopped and slightly before the time when Denton's alarm clock did that whole annoying bleeping thing.

God, I wish it wouldn't do that, thought Denton. But it did anyway.

"Fine… fine… I'm up… you happy now alarm clock?… Feel like you've accomplished something worthwhile?" said Denton as he bounced/fell out of bed. "Well, you just enjoy it while you can - yeah - you enjoy that smugness while the sun shines buddy because one day I'll die and then we'll see who's sorry. Yeah. No answer for that have you? No."

From outside of the door came an equally tired voice.

"You talking to the alarm clock again?"

Denton, both at one and the same time, with a scared and yet accusatory face, peered at the wooden panelling and frowned. He edged up to it and tentatively gave it a prod. *How did the door, renowned for being an inanimate object, do that?* he thought.

Now, to Denton, Mondays could only mean one thing - work.

"It is universally accepted that," he might say, "Monday mornings mean the end of the weekend and the commencement of the excruciating return to the grindstone. Time to step back into the shackles and fasten up that ball and chain. And you would be surprised just how many people become resentful about that. I mean, what? Did it come as a big surprise to them? Do couples nudge each other in bed on a Monday morning and say:

Female: "Honey, I think it's Monday." Male: "Yeah, so? Leave me alone woman, I'm trying to sleep." Female: "Yes, but it's the start of the week and we have to go to work." Male bolts upright and turns to female, "Oh, you're joking, aren't you?!?"

Surely, this doesn't happen. So why is it then that on Monday morning more than any other time, people seem to meander through the City of London, absentmindedly kicking stones, hands in pockets, as if they might be muttering to themselves, *"Fricking Monday, no one told me that meant I had to go to work, mumble, mumble, mumble."*

And then there are those people who, instead of kicking stones, will wander through the City reading a book. Yes, that's right, reading a book. They're actually reading while they walk. What is that about? Are these people in denial? Are they wandering around saying, *"Its not Monday, I'm not walking to work, I'm at home in bed reading my book and that isn't a juggernaut hurtling towards me."* Well wake up buddy, it is! The trouble is, they never get hit by the juggernaut and that makes me resentful. If they can miss fucking big juggernauts, how come they can't miss me when they walk past? I'm not a big guy. I'm quite thin but, oh no, each and every time, they manage to walk straight into me."

"And explain this. Why is it that each and every morning, as I make my way toward Liverpool Street station from Moorgate, every other bugger is walking in the opposite direction? More infuriatingly, why do they walk as if they have right of way? It's a pavement. Just because I work near Liverpool Street, why do I have to walk in the gutter to get by? Of course, if it was that simple to remedy the situation I would gladly walk in the gutter to avoid being barged into - but would this solve the problem? No. No, because in the gutter, you then have to deal with the bloody cyclists. Big bloody brain-dead cyclists. Well, I need not say any more about them. No one likes cyclists. Anywhere. Ever. They just get in the bleeding way. And they treat the place as if they have right of way whether they're riding on the road or the pavement. Well guess what, cyclists? You don't! There are pedestrians around! Why don't you just bloody walk instead? If God intended us to ride around on bikes he would have installed little hooters on the end of our noses to warn people that we were coming. And that annoys me. God damn bloody little tinny efforts that cyclists have. *Briiing briiing. Briiing Briiing. 'Why did you not step aside on hearing my tootling, pedestrian?'* Well, one, I can't move over anymore without being in a puddle and two, BECAUSE YOUR BELL IS TOO FUCKING QUIET."

It was on account of his exposure to this generally anti-social behaviour by cyclists and pedestrians, both of the book reading and sauntering variety, that Denton and also Randall had decided that Parliament's next task should be to legalise the execution of anyone, by the medium of a magnum handgun, where they were guilty of such anti-social behaviour anywhere within the City Square mile.

"I mean, why? Why do people saunter in the City on their way to work? Why? Are you a tourist? No. Because there isn't anything even remotely 'touristy' to see between Moorgate and Liverpool Street. It's a financial district. So why saunter? What? Have you got nothing better to do, buddy than wander around aimlessly? Can't remember where you work? Oh well, you can't be that important then. Ergo, you won't be missed. Ergo…boom. No more sauntering. No downside… Well maybe the increase in dry cleaning bills for the executioner but hey - shit happens."

" 'Shit happens'. What a crap expression. 'Shit happens'. The shit hits the fan. Shit for brains. Shitzus. Tottenham Hotspurs. How have all these things full of shit managed to pervade our lives?"

Another problem for Denton was the fact that on Mondays he was always just a tad grumpier than he usually was. Probably on account of the fact that Monday was one of those rare occasions when he would never have a hangover to bring with him into work. Denton's theory was that the lack of hangover simply confused his body too much.

Of course, without the usual misery inducing feelings of a hangover to nurse, Denton was also more acutely aware on a Monday more than at any other time of the shakes which he seemed to have acquired. He did wonder whether the shakes where nothing more than a manifestation of the confusion that his body was feeling at not having to process all that alcohol. Did his organs worry themselves silly in anticipation of the onslaught and then, on realising that no such onslaught was forthcoming, simply vibrate in anger at the unnecessary stress and anguish that he had caused them?

This puzzled Denton, but not as much as the reaction he got from people who saw his hands shake. Now, in this day and age there is now a taboo associated with pointing out other people's imperfections to them. In the Victorian age it was quite right and proper to go up to a deformed person and remark *"Good God, man - you look like an elephant, what? Pull yourself together,"* in order to overcome the embarrassment and discomfort of the observer. They might also consider putting a doily or drape over the offending article to ensure no other normal member of society suffered the same visual discomfort. Nowadays of course, people think it more appropriate to go out of their way to ignore the problem. *"I don't see a wheelchair - I see a man with a more advantageous centre of gravity".* Conventions change, but the end result is the same. People do not know how to cope with people who are different to them.

So what made Denton more than a little perturbed then was the fact that it was in that context that he found it so remarkable when people had absolutely no qualms in regularly pointing out his shakes to him. Did they think they were being helpful? *"Denton, do you know you're dribbling water everywhere when you drink from that plastic cup? Yeah, no you are."* Or did they think that if they simply alerted Denton to the fact, then he would be able to do something about it. *"Denton. Denton! You're shaking again. Come on son, we've talked about this before. Stop now."*

"I mean, if I had a lisp due to an overly enlarged tongue or a stammer - would people be so quick to point that out? Would they say *"do you know that it has taken you fifteen minutes to finish that sentence and, what's more annoying, is the fact that I finished it for you twice but you still kept going?"* Would they say, *"you do know there's no 'thh' in something, its not thhomething...you know that right?"* No. These things do not happen. So why do people draw attention to the shakes?"

"Yes, I know that I shake. I drink a lot. Numbness is a good thing. You should try drinking once in a while, Thhtanley - might get rid of that ridiculous lisp. And you, 'half sentence Henry'."

"B...bb...bbbb...bbbbb..." Henry might protest.

"Oh shut up, Henry, I haven't got time to wait for the end of that sentence. I've got a bus to catch."

"See - that's just mean. So if I can recognise that, why can't they?"

So anyway, Monday.

"God, are we still on Monday? It's taking a bloody long time to get to the part where the Spurs hit the fan. Anyway, I'm sure we'll get there soon enough.

Thhoon enough. See - it's just not funny."

Denton continued on his way into work - slaloming between the saunterers, dodging the oncoming traffic and trying, where possible, to clip anyone walking and reading at the same time, on the back of the leg with his briefcase. As he did so, a thought struck him, and with it came a sinking feeling. *Either I've forgotten something or something important is happening at work today.* He glanced down. *Well, I've remembered to put my trousers on, so it can't be that. My suit jacket matches my trousers. So what is it? Mmmm.*

Monday may have been a big day for Denton, presumably in no small way, on account of the fact that he was going into work with all his major functions working, but for his boss, Colin Hooley, it was bigger than big. It was probably no overstatement to say that it was huge. And Colin didn't do huge, he didn't like huge and he didn't understand why other people liked huge, as his wife would no doubt testify. Oh yes. Today was certainly a day when Colin needed everything to go in its usual clockwork way. Everything had to go smoothly. There could be mistakes. No balls up. No cock up. There could be none of this. And his wife would also no doubt testify that this was usual.

But then, as Colin Hooley knew only too well, and if he didn't then he really should have, sometimes life does not exactly play by the rules. If you work hard, if you know when to be subservient, when to be masterful. If you know who is the pigeon and who is the pavement. If you know who to respect and who to ignore. If you value your family and if you want only to provide for them, above all else, then life will play fair. Right? Right?

However. Breaking down on a motorway, getting out of your usually reliable estate, pulled up on the hard shoulder, whilst other cars whizzed past you, on the one day when God in heaven and all his angels needed to be lined up on the steps to St Peter's gate, really, really, really was a sign that maybe, just maybe, Life had absolutely no idea of how to play fair.

Of course, what gave it away, as an absolute cert that Life had pretty much given up on following the 'fair play rule book' and had moved on to 'how I get my kicks out of your misfortune' was the fact that Colin also had two black eyes, a neck brace, 'Simply as a precaution, Mr Hooley', and a suspected broken nose on the one day when he really, really had to impress upon his biggest client that he was in charge of absolutely everything including, but not limited to the universe; Hades; Mount Olympus and the map revealing the location of Atlantis. The fact that Colin clearly was not even in charge of his own timekeeping was, to him, the clearest evidence that he had really pissed Life off in a big way. Maybe he'd forgotten an anniversary or something. Maybe he should send it flowers and a big box of chocolates to cheer it up.

Mind you, Colin might have thought that he had it bad, but then he didn't have to deal with the pedestrians, like Denton did. *You know, it's seriously beginning to annoy me now. The whole inability of people to walk normally on a Monday morning,* he thought as he weaved in and out of people. *And what is it with people this morning? Did I become positively charged in the night at roughly the same time that everyone else became metallic? What is with the whole walking in to me thing that people keep doing? I'm walking in a straight line - how are they getting confused about the direction that I'm taking? It's a straight line -* A STRAIGHT LINE.

Look, here comes one now. Head down. What's he thinking?:

Pedestrian: "It got me again, the whole Monday thing. I swear she's wrong about me having to go into work. I swear that I didn't last week. Ok, so there's a guy coming towards me. It looks like he's walking in a straight line and that our paths will not intersect. But then. Hang on a minute. That can't be right. Must be a mistake. Can't be that simple. He must be about to change direction. Got caught out by the whole Monday thing but I won't let this beat me…so I'll just veer out into his path in a bid to avoid him and…"

Oh yes. Well done buddy. You are officially number twelve to barge into me this morning. What is wrong with people? Definitely time to get out the magnum. Oh, look! There's Mrs 'Lets-Read-Along-The-Way'. A regular on this route. Always the same. Am not convinced that she is getting any further with that book. And what's this? Guy with head down. Where's he going? Could be going anywhere. And. And. And there it is. Straight into my shoulder. Brilliant. I swear one day that the magnum is coming out with me.

Colin could quite happily have done with a magnum himself at this point, although it most probably would have been to use on himself. His car was still not working and the Green Flag was still on the way.

Get out of the way, simpleton, thought Denton as he dodged yet more people, *Magnum, magnum Oooh yes, Magnum for you too.* Of course, whilst Monday, was without doubt, the worst day of the week, it did have one redeeming feature. It was the single furthest point from Sunday, which could only be a good thing. At this point now, the boredom of Sunday afternoon seemed like a million miles away.

The reality of the situation, though, was that Sunday was not that far away at all. Sunday was right around the corner. "Do you know why each year feels as if it's shorter than the last?" Denton would often say, when pushed. "Do you know why it's June now but yesterday was September. Do you know why that is?" No, was usually the response and usually from some blonde that Denton didn't know and never would and who was, no doubt, seriously contemplating never speaking to her friend again for going to the toilet without her. "Routine."

"When you were young, every day was new and exciting. Every day was different or had the illusion of it. Seconds lasted minutes. Minutes lasted hours. Days lasted months. Months were eternal." At which point, he might slug on his bottle of Asahi and take an all too obvious school-boy glance down her top. "You'd wake up refreshed and say 'yeah momma, this day was made for me. The sun is shining in a way that it has never shined before. Those birds, why I reckon that the angels themselves came down to sing me a song. Now, go into the kitchen and get me some rusks, I'm-a-hungry. Go ya big assed bitch. Yeah!' Or in any event, words to that effect." She would probably have stormed off at that point, having concluded that starting up a new circle of friends might turn out to be the best thing that ever happened to her.

"But now, you're older. Things are different. Now, before you know where you are, you find yourself stood in the shower, washing the same parts, trying to figure out where the hell belly button fluff comes from, and why it's always blue. Then, before you realise it, you're on the way to work, blowing someone's head off with a magnum. Then you're at the lift and even though you say hello to him everyday, the door man still does not even give the merest hint of recognition. And then it dawns on you. You're stood at the sink, in the tiniest closet barely capable of being called a 'kitchen' (or in some parts, a 'galley', although God only knows why - this isn't a bloody ship, Jim Bob and no, Mr Senior Partner, sir, you're no bleeding Captain. Though if you were, you'd be Captain Bligh and I reserve the right to try to depose you at some point in the future).

You're stood at the sink and what are you doing? You're making a cup of coffee again. The same old cup of coffee, every day. Open dishwasher door. Remove cup that doesn't belong to you but hopefully doesn't belong to anyone else either. Formally adopt cup. Find solitary teaspoon in drawer. Wonder where others are. Do people eat them? Is the cleaner selling them off at a premium to some unsuspecting tourists? You wipe clean inexplicable mark off said spoon. You open Land of the Giant sized coffee tin and momentarily wonder what it would be like to be a midget. You get two sachets of brown sugar from the cupboard. You wonder where the word sachet comes from. You wonder if it's French. You wonder whether naming someone Sacha Distell borders on child abuse. You rip the tops off, possibly imagining the sachets to be the head of an ex-girlfriend and if not, the heads of people previously magnumed on the way over. Add milk. Add hot water from hot water tank which probably contains a dead pigeon or two. Burn hand on hot water even though you had been extra, extra careful having read the 'Caution! Hot!' label and understood its implications a thousand times over. Stir. There it is. 'See you later boys', you might say to absolutely no one."

"And there it is. That's how you find yourself on Monday, then its Tuesday. Wednesday came from no where. Thursday pops around for a quick chat. Friday's there - look at him go. Saturday - hey! Is that a new haircut? Nice. Then, lo and behold! Sunday rears its ugly head. *'Wish he'd wait until he was invited before he just showed up on our door step,'* you might lament. *'Told you we should have pretended like we weren't at home.'*

At this point, in an all together different part of London, Colin would happily have at least checked out the prices in the selling section of 'Loot' in order to see, for curiosity's sake, just exactly what the going rate was that one could get for a one-family-owned Grandmother these days, if, of course, her sale would have meant that he enjoyed his familiar routine.

In frustration, Colin kicked the car as hard as he could with a suspected broken nose, two black eyes and a neck brace. The car still wouldn't start.

Today was a big day for Colin. Today, one of the firm's biggest clients, and certainly Colin's biggest contact, Mr C. Muftny, was due to have a full and frank meeting with Colin about what the firm could do for him following the recent balls up on a deal that Colin had done for him. Mr C. Muftny was not impressed when he was left with a whole load of egg on his face following the collapsed takeover of a large dairy distributor. Oh yes, a whole lot of egg…milk…and three types of cheese. This, combined with the fact that Colin was currently applying for partnership at the firm and, having been turned down once before, was heavily relying upon the fact that he had not only introduced Mr C. Muftny to the firm but had also ensured that good relations were kept with his company, Accumulative Holdings Limited, which currently provided a huge raft of work for the Employment, Commercial and Dispute Resolution departments, to carry him through to get the nod from the other partners. As a result, this really wasn't the best of days to be late into work.

And as Colin sat with his head in his hands, a good few miles from work, waiting for the nice Green Flag man to cease and desist the head scratching that had kept him occupied for the previous fifteen minutes, Mr C. Muftny was becoming increasingly frustrated by the fact that the only service he was getting from the firm was limited to a seemingly never ending supply of bad coffee and limp biscuits. This was ferried to him at regular intervals as he sat in the spacious reception at the firm as if someone, somewhere, thought that his increasing frustration would be dampened by the barrage of caffeinated fluid and digestives. And as he sat there, battling to keep his ample frame on the inexplicably uncomfortable mock leather seats, awkwardly moving with a constant pained and irritated expression, he could only marvel at exactly why the decision had been taken to decorate the reception with such ill-advised colours. In fact, the chair was so uncomfortable that it forced him to fidget around on his seat. Being a heavy man on a leather seat inevitably caused awkward noises to emanate from somewhere too close to his backside. It did not help that his cheap and scratchy suit was beginning to irritate him. As he itched, he felt something in his pocket. Reaching inside, he pulled out a business card, which caused him to smile and raise his eyebrows. It was the business card of the rather attractive, and certainly well-endowed, blonde girl who he had met the other week at a law seminar somewhere out of town and had thought of semi-constantly ever since in both a professional and not so professional context.

She probably did not know the law any better than Colin - if she knew any at all - but she certainly looked good in a suit and no doubt looked even better without one. The more Mr C. Muftny thought about it, the more he felt comfortable about the idea of spending two hundred pounds an hour for this woman to give him legal advice, tending to his every need. He relaxed back into his chair as he imagined the white frilly-edged shirt that she had worn during that day. He could still remember the musky scent she had been wearing and the glossy, inviting lips. From where he had stood he had been in the perfect position to observe as she lent forward, causing the two flaps of the shirt to move apart slightly exposing a cheeky mole on part of her cleavage. At one point she had knelt down in her tight skirt to place a glass of wine by her exquisite feet, which resulted in most of her chest being exposed to him so that he could see a lacy white bra. She had looked up, caught him looking and given him a devilish grin. Oh, she wanted him alright, he knew it. Oh yes. Two hundred pounds an hour for a few one on one sessions with her would be most agreeable.

He suddenly shook the thought from his head. What on earth was he doing wasting his time with Hooley? Incompetent little shyster. Did he not realise how big a client he was? She would appreciate him. She would realise just how big he was. He smiled and his eyes glazed over. And she had the nicest long tanned legs, the kind he would just love to have wrapped around him. What would she do to have him as a client? How far would she go? Dinner, at least. Then maybe a hotel room. That sexy, cheeky little mouth wrapped right around his...

Suddenly he remembered where he was. He had gotten a little too comfortable. He would wait five minutes until he was 'composed' again and if Hooley hadn't showed up, he would go straight to her office. Did she know the law though? Probably not. Women like that did not get to the top on their brains but she was probably well supervised by someone who did know what they were doing. Four minutes forty seven seconds until he made his way to her office, he thought......

This was not a good day for Colin. It certainly looked like it may get better, especially as the Green Flag guy took only twenty minutes to turn up and then only five minutes to diagnose the problem. Of course, the car would need a major part at a cost of, probably, hundreds but Colin did not mind since at least the guy would be able to tow his car to work. Oh yes, it was all starting to look rosy again. Well, that was until, after what seemed an age to attach Colin's car to the recovery van, the recovery van refused to start.

"Ah, that's not good is it?" said the driver, sheepishly, trying to make light of the situation. He soon realised that this was not the time for humour when he caught a glimpse of Colin's pained scowl as he turned from the waist to glare at him.

"I do not know," said Colin, tersely, "You are the mechanic."

The Green Flag guy laughed nervously.

"And you can fix it, right?"

A simple enough question which of course was greeted with a simple enough answer and, of course, Colin believed the guy when he replied yes. He did for the first twenty minutes, at any rate. After the second twenty, he had his doubts. And of course by the third twenty, during a long telephone conversation between the Green Flag guy and someone else, he began to appreciate that the simple answer he was looking for was still a simple answer, but just happened to be the complete opposite of the one that he would have liked.

"By the way," asked the Green Flag guy as he returned to the driver's seat, "I just wanted to ask - what happened to you?" Colin sighed. *Oh yes, the brace,* he thought. *People probably would notice. It was naïve to think that they wouldn't ask questions. Why did people always have to ask?* Today would be a very long day. They sat in silence and waited for the recovery vehicle's recovery vehicle to arrive.

It was 10.30 am and Denton was back at his desk having made his second coffee of the day. He was on the phone, being slowly brainwashed by the incessant xylophone music being played down the handset. He stared at the desk with a look somewhere between abject horror and terminal boredom. He was convinced he could feel part of his brain seeping out of his ear. Life could not get any worse.

"I'm sorry but all our operators are busy right now. Your call is important to us. Please stay on the line or press one to leave a message...."

Maybe it could. *What is the point of leaving of a message,* he thought. *You won't listen to it and even if you do, you won't return my call.* The time for pressing 'one' passed and the incessant music returned.

Denton managed to drag his unwilling eyes, which were asleep even if the rest of his body was not, over to his monitor. An e-mail had arrived. Denton lay back in his chair, craned his neck so that he could grip the phone and looked over to his screen. He could imagine his display screen equipment assessor going spare at him for adopting such a pose. No doubt she would suggest that he put his phone on loudspeaker, replace the handset and turn his chair to the screen if he wanted to use his computer, with his back straight and arms horizontal with the floor.

"Yeah, right. The chair is too low and doesn't turn. The screen doesn't have a radiation filter and causes me to get horrendous headaches. My arms ache from typing. My hands hurt. And I can't put the phone on loudspeaker because the partner in the next office/podule along from me will only wander in and say, *"Is that call necessary? I'm trying to think in here!"* Luckily though, I have filled in form 27(2) (b) which I filed at window 14 on the seventh day of the moon when Venus was in the house of Aquarius and Mars' two moons were aligned with Uranus. If I hadn't done that then I would have had to have waited four months for the next part of my DSE assessment - the part where they actually replace and improve the stuff I've complained about. As it is, I've only had to wait two months and have been promised that the stuff I need will be here just as soon as they've had chance to order it. Of course when I asked when it would be ordered I was greeted with *"I'm very busy, you know? Can't you see I'm busy? I have so much to do. You don't know how lucky you are!"* Sorry. I'm just part of the fee-earning team. We only bring the money in. Sorry, I should have remembered my place."

"The thing is about being a trainee solicitor - it's all about embracing challenges. You read the brochures - *"Those that do not enjoy challenges need not apply".* Which is all very well and good, and who wouldn't apply? Have you seen the salaries that trainee solicitors get paid to work in large commercial firms? Fantastic. The firm pays for law school, gives you a grant to live on while you are there and then they pay you a fantastic salary for two years whilst you're still learning and not expected to know anything. Brilliant. Who cares about the challenges? Think of the money! I'll worry about the challenges later once I've got my foot in the door!!"

"Yeah."

"If you ever contemplate a career in the law," Denton would often preach, usually whilst perched at a bar, "And money is the key motivation, then for the love of God, do not do it! Find something else to do. There are much better (and more profitable) ways to make money."

"For a start, '*Challenges*'. Let me run you through a couple of the '*Challenges*' that you will need to overcome. First challenge. No secretary will do your work for you. This is a challenge because every fee-earner charges time to a client by units. Units are a measure of time. One unit equals six minutes. Ten units to an hour. The basic rule is that for a simple letter, you can only charge a client one unit of time. So, for every letter you send you have to have finished it within six minutes. The challenge, therefore, is, in order to complete a letter within six minutes do you a) type it yourself, which depending on your typing speed is likely to take longer than six minutes and will mean that the additional time cannot be recorded which will no doubt cause some irate partner to ask you what you've been doing all day long; b) take one minute dictating the letter including all the relevant details such as the postal address, reference details for both parties, date, subject heading and signature block so that a secretary need not have to waste time searching the file for the relevant information but simply bang out the letter, then spend five minutes trying to persuade a secretary to type the letter and find that the only one who will co-operate is the one who is so utterly useless that no one else will use her so she always has capacity, then spend twenty minutes amending, re-amending and finally throttling that same secretary because she just keeps making the same mistakes or c) don't write the letter then deny all knowledge of anyone ever asking you to do the task in the first place. Challenge.

Second challenge. Becoming an expert in how to repair the photocopier. The photocopier is always, always, always guaranteed to break down just when you need it the most. In law, there is an inordinate amount of paperwork involved. Sometimes lots of people all need to see the same piece of paper and rather than just take your word for it about what the damned things say, they are nine times out of ten, insistent on holding a copy in their grubby little palm before they will play ball. As a result, there is always photocopying to be done. As a general rule: no one likes photocopying. Most solicitors will either try to palm it off on their secretary or the trainee in their department. Since most solicitors know which way their bread is buttered and, more particularly, which out of the two of these candidates will cease to do their typing if annoyed, angry or, in some cases, even disturbed, then there really is no contest. The trainee does the photocopying.

Inextricably linked to the fact that the photocopier will always break down just before you really, really, really need it are several other little quirky occurrences. One, when you need the photocopier there is always a queue. Two, in front of you at the queue will be the needle-nosed librarian for whom smiling is strictly prohibited during office hours, someone from Personnel and finally someone from the Quality Control Department or some other such "what-the-fuck-do-you-contribute-to-the-organisation?" person who just has to photocopy this weeks crossword from Woman's Weekly about fifty million times. Three, the photocopier will work just fine for them. Four, just moments before your document gets shredded, the fuse in the plug blows and the toner cartridge explodes spraying a fine mist of black shit up your nice clean YSL shirt, you will hear your boss' dulcet tones echoing down the corridor *'Have you finished that photocopying? I need it now!'* Challenge.

Third challenge. Understanding the work that the support units do. This is especially important since at most points during your training contract, you'll be doing their work on a daily basis. First, secretarial work. Every trainee soon needs to come to terms with the fact that they spent three years at university and one year at law school, studying hard to remember facts, *ratio decendi* and *obiter dicta* just so that they could have their boss dictate letters on to their voicemail at six o'clock in the evening when their secretaries had buggered off home for the night. *'This letter needs doing now. If you have any problems, come see me. I'm in my office next door. I trust that I have made myself clear enough though so there really is no need to come and see me. Just type up the damned thing and send it.'* Which would be fine if the rest of message didn't sound like *'Cuuuoldd duuuu ltter too derrrrr smllllls at uniiiiiii hhhhheerh mmemmememe'.* Challenge.

You also have to appreciate that: The library couldn't possibly photocopy a case or find a book for you. They are far too busy. Anyway, it's not in their job description; the secretaries couldn't possibly type up your dictation. It's not in their job description; Reprographics couldn't possibly do all that photocopying for you. It's not in their job description; Partners couldn't possibly take the time to give you the right instructions. They're too busy staring out of the window thinking of their Porsches.

Fourth challenge. Becoming a computer technician. When the computer inevitably goes wrong and starts to do stuff that you never asked it to do or not save things that you really, really, really did ask it to do, then its time to get the experts in. Its time to dig out the internal telephone directory (or invariably press the number one button quick dial on your phone). "Right," you will say. "I'm having *this* problem and *this* message keeps appearing - what do I do, Mr More-expensive-by-the-hour-than-me?"... "Yeah, OK... Well, have you tried turning it off and turning it back on again?" Ah yes, I should have known, the cure-all solution and for this we pay you £150 an hour to be on standby? Are you in the pub when you give me this 'advice'? Seriously, you might as well be. In fact, you ought to be. At least I would like you more or, in any event, cancel the contract that I've taken out to have you killed in your sleep by a Magnum at point blank range.

Fifth challenge. Honing your skills as passive counsellor. Every secretary in every department has a boyfriend called Gary/Dave/Steve/Andy with whom she has problems with, mainly on account of (i) Gary/Dave/Steve/Andy sleeping with her best-mate/Mum/Dad/sister/all-of-them; (ii) Gary/Dave/Steve/Andy not understanding that even though he is a monkey and can't even turn on a computer, he still thinks that he can get their last minute dot com holiday to Ibiza for less than £200 and, therefore, the fact that she paid £200 means she's stupid and/or fat; (iii) Gary/Dave/Steve/Andy had a go at her best-mate/Mum/Dad/sister/all-of-them at the weekend in a pub/dodgy club/living room/all of them; (iv) Gary/Dave/Steve/Andy has gone on holiday with his best mate(s) Gary/Dave/Steve/Andy and ended up shagging Sharon/Gary/Dave/Steve/Andy or on a particularly bad weekend (v) Gary/Dave/Steve/Andy had a fight/shag/holiday with her best-mate/Mum/Dad/sister/Sharon/Gary/Dave/Steve/Andy/all-of-them all in one weekend all because he said she looked stupid/fat/ugly in her bikini/suit/dressing gown. The only way for her to now get through Monday/Tuesday/Wednesday/Thursday/Friday is to talk exceptionally loudly about this delicate problem with all the other secretaries and much to the obvious annoyance of everyone else. You therefore need to get up to speed almost at once to deal with the fact that you will be expected to perform the functions of a trainee solicitor whilst being subjected to this constant barrage of nonsense as if you were living your life in the pages of Hello/OK/Bella/Women's Weekly (is that still on the go?) with no prospect of ever escaping, and at all times remembering that the secretary is too busy to do your work. Challenge.

Sixth challenge. Dealing with your supervising partner. You also need to quickly understand that the partner who supervises you is likely to have qualified at the time when to be a solicitor you only needed to collect twelve tokens from the back of a rice krispies packet. He is, therefore, unlikely to have been to a good university or any university at all. He certainly will not understand complex notions such as what the law actually is. He will not be able to work a computer. His wife will be on the verge of leaving him. He will have two, sometimes three, mistresses on the go and so will expect you to cover for him (usually because his secretary is one of his mistresses). He will be a workaholic but usually because he is too inefficient to do his work between nine to five. He will expect you not to have a social life and, if you do, not to brag about it. If you're male, he will expect you to be as lecherous as him. If you're female, he will expect you to have blonde hair, big tits, wear tight fitting or low cut tops and to ask him questions no more complex than "*would you like to fuck me?*" The challenge is to live up to this expectation and not deviate from it. He does not want smart alec twats who can embarrass him in front of clients by understanding complex areas of law in meetings when he doesn't. He does not want someone who doesn't laugh at his jokes and he certainly does not want flat-chested lesbians in the office looking intelligent. He will also expect you to know, at all times, just exactly how important he is and just how lucky you are to be in his presence. He will not appreciate being told that he is a balding, middle aged tosser whose obvious lack of control over the course of his life in either the workplace or at home is blindingly obvious by the pathetic way he conducts his meaningless life.

Seventh and final challenge. Recognising that your job might also involve anything that is (i) irrelevant to your job description; (ii) is something for which you are incredibly over qualified; (iii) is so mind numbingly pointless and boring that you seriously have to question just exactly what it was that you did to get God all riled up like this, and (iv) you have to do it even though you have the hangover from hell that you really promised yourself yesterday that you would not get today.

In order to get through these challenges it is always useful to chant a few mantras to keep you sane. Here are just a few: *"There is no place for humour in the workplace, there is no place for humour in the workplace", "I am not a human being, I am a set of three letter fee earner initials, I am not a human being, I am a set of three letter fee earner initials", "My place is in the office, not the home, my place is in the office, not the home", "My firm is my wife, I shall be faithful to the firm. My firm is my wife, I shall be faithful to the firm."* Of course chanting these mantras won't help you but if anyone important hears you they will instantly recognise that you are still willing to be a very small cog in a very mindless machine and they will be happier as a result. Demonstrating that you have not lost the faith is the only way to get by without being culled.

Of course, for Denton, embracing challenges is what he lives for. The regular challenge that Denton likes to set himself is to see if he can get through the working day with a stinking hangover without a) throwing up; b) falling asleep; c) getting caught doing a) or b); or d) being caught asleep in a toilet having just thrown up.

The other challenge, which he was getting pretty good at, was to give the impression that he was in control, on top of matters and working hard, when in reality he was sat at his desk, staring at the same coffee stain on the desk that he had been staring at for the past twenty minutes. In order to succeed in this challenge he did need to ensure that he did not have anyone in an even remote position of responsibility come near his desk otherwise they would be able to see that actually Denton was doing sod all, looked so white underneath his mop of dark floppy hair that he was almost transparent and reeked so much of alcohol that placing naked flames nearby was a seriously bad idea.

In fairness though, Denton had stated his love of challenges on his application form, so it wasn't as if he had misled his employer in any way. He had also indicated that he was 'well motivated' and enjoyed 'problem solving'. These representations must have come as the result of a typographical error since it really should have read 'well oiled' and has a 'problem with solvency'. The ridiculous photograph should also have been a giveaway that this guy would always be stretching the phrase 'professional' since it quite clearly showed the image of a man with unkempt brown hair and a semi-permanent expression of looking lost and generally out of touch with the world around him.

Unfortunately this photo had been taken during Denton's university life where he was young, innocent and really not quite ready for the world. Today was a different matter. Innocence had given way to cynicism. Optimism to despair. Enthusiasm to belligerence. As a result Denton's day to day existence did not really encapsulate the professionalism that he ought to maintain. But who could blame him for this turnabout? He started out well enough, working hard, forsaking alcohol and women for the possibility of success. But it all went sour when he realised that being successful is not a game played with any discernable rules. Those that get ahead are not always those that work the hardest. They are not always those that are the brightest. Those that get ahead - get ahead, without anyone really understanding why. If the same thing happened again, the same result would not necessarily occur. This realisation came to Denton right around the time when he realised that being a trainee solicitor was not all it was cracked up to be. For a start, most people seemed to regard having a trainee around in the same way they might imagine having a monkey in the office. Stick them in a room, give them a banana and just hope that they don't produce too much shit.

Then there was the unspoken hierarchy that every department seemed to have. This should have been perfectly reasonable. Naturally, he was fine with the idea of partners being at the top, then associate solicitors, then assistant solicitors from the most qualified to the newly qualified. He then expected trainee solicitors to fit in there. What he was not expecting was to find the secretaries, members of Personnel, the photocopier, the lad from the mail room and the contract service cleaners to all be ahead of him in the pecking order. This was especially due to the fact that three of the cleaners did not even speak English and one of them had only been in the country for three days.

What made it worse was the fact that Denton had initially felt like he was contributing to the firm. He felt proud of the fact that the fees he generated always out-measured the salary he was paid on a monthly basis. It was, therefore, a bit of pain in the ass when you were up to your eyes in work and a three year qualified, who really should have known better, would come into the room to say, 'You're not too busy to just put the kettle on are you?' 'Of course not,' Denton would like to have replied. 'I've been here since 5am, I've worked until 10pm every night this week. And during all that time I've just been sat on my hands waiting for someone to ask me to put the kettle on.' His frustration was increased by the knowledge that he knew the law just as well as the next man but, in the absence of the much coveted practising certificate, etiquette and conduct rules prevented him from telling anyone exactly what that legal answer was.

It was on the basis of these events that Denton's ambition slowly fell away, which was why he now found himself still sat at his desk, still with a phone cradled under his ear but now listening to 'Ticket to ride' being played by what must have been a tone deaf hamster with a limp running up and down a Casio keyboard. He put the phone down in frustration. What was the point?

And Mondays just did not help motivate him into thinking any differently. Neither did the arrival of Dom Peasgood at his door.

"Morning Denton, how was your weekend? Was it good? Did you enjoy it?"

Ah, thought Denton, *Another challenge that I neglected to mention earlier. You have to be able to deal with other trainee solicitors. You have to bear in mind that a training contract at a law firm is fixed over two years. There is no obligation at the end of it for you to stay at the firm. Neither, however is there any obligation for the firm to retain you. For many trainees this is not an issue. You work hard and you hope the firm will notice the hard work you put in and want to keep you on. For some trainees, being good enough at the job is not something that they can rely on to keep them in work, especially when you're as average as Dom. Therefore, you need to rely upon personality to get you noticed above others. This was also a sore point for Dom. He didn't really have any. Well, that's not entirely true. He did. But he did in the same way that a lap dog has personality. And of course, some people like lap dogs, they think that they are cute. They think that they are nice to have around. Other people just think of them as being harmless. I, on the other hand, can't stand them, or their inane whining.*

Dom stood in the doorway waiting for an answer with an inane smile on his face, his eyes all lit up expectedly.

Trainees, like Dom, have got it into their head that the key thing to securing a job is taking an interest in people. This is how to show that you're a team player.

"It was awful Dom. Truly awful. It could not have gone any worse." replied Denton.

"Did you see the football?"

"No."

"Did you see the Golf? Did you see the Rugby? What did you think about that thing in the newspaper about that girl from the Telly and chocolate sauce?"

"I didn't see that story, Dom."

This is not a bad game plan on Dom's part but one with a slight flaw, thought Denton *If you are going to take an interest in someone's life, actually listen to the answer that they give before moving onto the next question. It will give you some information about that person so that you can ask a question that is actually relevant to what they are saying.*

He stood there looking like a rabbit caught in headlights for what seemed an eternity during which time neither of them spoke. Then, eventually he said, "OK, see you later!" and left.

A new e-mail arrived causing Denton to wake from his Dom-induced hypnotic state. It may also have caused him to cluck like a chicken.

An e-mail, thought Denton, *Fantastic. Finally something to lift the monotony.*

Eagerly he opened it up.

"Oh, bollocks," he said, unable to contain his disappointment. "It's from Colin Hooley - I've been summoned."

He stood, pulled on his suit jacket and approached the pool of secretaries outside his office with much trepidation.

"Just off to see Colin then, Cheryl," said Denton to the secretary who had been designated 'the trainee's secretary' and who was still annoyed about it.

She stopped typing and glared at him.

"OK then, I'll take those calls for you and send that urgent fax for you in your absence," she didn't say, as she sat there stony faced chewing gum.

Cows don't chew that much. And most of them look better.

"If anyone is desperately trying to get hold of me, can you ring Colin's secretary so that she can let me know?" Denton said as he began wandering the down the corridor, reaching the connecting door between his section of corridor and Colin's. "Assuming you know how to," he muttered from this safe distance.

"I'm sure we'll cope," he just heard Cheryl say in her best sarcastic tones. He could imagine that she was still glaring in his direction now as he approached Colin's office, in front of which sat Colin's dutiful secretary, Gladys. A real secretary. The kind of old school dear who thought it a real privilege to work for someone as senior as Colin. Bless her.

For a reason which he could not quite explain or understand, Denton's stomach had sunk on the way from his room to Colin's. Getting a summons from your daily supervisor caused him a great deal of concern. That, added to the ominous feeling he already had about today, made Denton think that going into this room was going to be a life changing experience. It would probably involve a bollocking at some point as well.

Denton was suddenly reminded of a conversation he had had with Billy one particularly drunken week day night. Billy was an old university friend.

Denton stood near Colin's office, contemplating whether the reflection he could see on the door was caused by Colin's curious bald patch. Curious on account of the fact that Colin had the curliest, thickest, bushiest, wiry mass of hair that Denton had ever seen, which made it odd that he should have a perfect bald patch the size of a fried egg on the crown of his bonce. Denton took a step closer. It was instantly apparent that Colin was on the phone.

Denton could almost still taste the beer in his mouth as he recalled the conversation with Billy. "Colin's effectively my boss. He's my daily supervisor and pretty much tells me what to do."

Denton slowly edged towards the door of the office where he was almost blinded by the shine. *Does he wax that bad boy or what?* thought Denton. Colin was looking down at the desk whilst talking into his phone.

"You see, Colin's pretty boring," said Denton, probably slurring his words and sloshing his bottle of Staropramen around, 'Colin's middle aged. Colin's about forty-five. I believe he has a son of, perhaps, thirteen years. Colin has a wife of, perhaps, a little longer. Colin's very, very dull. Colin's..." Denton's thought process was suddenly interrupted as he walked fully into the room ...wearing *a neck brace!?!* He thought.

Denton could not help but look confused. It was a natural reaction on seeing a man, who unashamedly had several crossword competition certificates proudly adorning his walls, with a neck brace, two black eyes and, if Denton wasn't too mistaken, a suspected broken nose. Colin did not strike Denton as much of a risk taker. How on earth had he got all that?

This vision of one man's pain and turmoil was heightened by the fact that Colin's conversation was not going well, judging by the pinkness in his cheeks. Denton hovered at the door but not so much so that he was in Colin's personal space but more so that Colin could see the promptness with which Denton had dealt with his request having read the e-mail. Colin didn't acknowledge Denton's presence and so Denton quickly resumed his previous thought.

"In fact, he's so boring that his nickname around the office is 'the Crowbar' on account of the fact that if you spend any considerable length of time talking to him your head starts to pound very much like you had been hit, well, you get the rest."

Denton suddenly had another thought. Was it really so wise for him to turn up so promptly? Did it not just convey the idea that he did not have enough to do? Did it suggest that he just sat around all day waiting for people to e-mail him? Of course, that was perfectly true but he would rather that his boss did not know that.

It was clear though that Colin had more pressing matters on his mind than whether his trainee was spending his training contract reading e-mails.

"Clive... but Clive ...well if I could just interrupt you for a minute... well, yes I appreciate that," he said, "but I don't really understand what you're saying to me here, Clive... well, yes, I understand that, but I don't understand why... yes... no... no, I hear you, you're considering... well that's good... it's always good to see what our competitors can offer, it keeps us compete... yes, I know her... yes, I'm sure she is, but Clive let me reassure you that we can... how much?... well Clive, you know quality is something you can't put a price on...."

Denton, though, was not paying much attention to what Colin was saying. "Will that go in my appraisal? Spends too much time reading his e-mails?" wondered Denton, "I mean it's not always my fault. Some of them are very important. Like the one from the post room this morning. '*Vermin Holwash solicitors have received a fax of twenty four blank pages from someone and would like to speak with the sender.*'"

"...yes I do know she is...but let me assure you that our level of quality is second to none," Colin pulled the phone away from his ear as Mr C. Muftny screamed, "Ok, well, there was that time, admittedly. Yes, but it was a simple typo and could have happened to anyone, you know....yes I appreciate that Mr Gunt won't do business with you ever again. Yes, nor will Mr Vulva.....sorry....yes, Valva....sorry. Yes. Yes, well I'm sure she wouldn't make that mistake...."

"To which Randall had replied... '*I sent it. They said they were running out of paper over there, so I told them I would fax over a ream of five hundred pages so I don't know why they're complaining now.*' to which I added '*well maybe they're just ringing to find out what happened to the other 476 pages.*' Genius."

"But Clive," protested Colin, pulling at his neck brace, his face getting redder and redder. "Clive! Clive! Oh for God's sake! SHE'S JUST A BRAINLESS BLONDE BIG-TITTED FREAK!..." and with that he slammed the phone down. Sweat poured from his brow and finally he looked up to notice a very concerned looking Denton doing his best rabbit-trapped-in-headlights face. Colin adjusted his tie and coughed nervously.

Where did he learn charm like that? Is this how we keep clients? Maybe I should have brought a pen and paper… thought Denton.

"Colin…I…is this a bad time?" said Denton verbalising the blindingly obvious. He hoped that Colin would look for the positive in his comment and perhaps acknowledge Denton's observational skills.

"Denton. Hi. Thanks for responding to the e-mail. Just give me a second. Come in and sit down, while I get a glass of water or something."

Denton sat down. Awkwardly Colin got up, keeping his neck and back straight, and moved across the room like the world's least convincing robot. His phone began to ring.

"Gladys, can you get that?" he asked as he put one hand on his office door and began to close it. "I don't want to be disturbed."

"Yes, I'll get that," Gladys dutifully replied.

"You wanted to see me, Colin." said Denton, feeling slightly awkward.

"No, I'm sorry, he cannot be disturbed right now, he's in a meeting. Can I take a message?" said Gladys.

"Yes, that's right Denton, I've cleared a space in my diary for you this morning - it's your mid-seat appraisal. I trust that you have had time to complete your appraisal form."

Oh bollocks! thought Denton, *Is that today? Shit. Damn you electronic calendar! You were supposed to warn me in good time for this event so that I could prepare something! I am so pouring coffee over you when I get back! Oh yes.*

Colin started to close the door to his office. "Oh, is that you, Mrs Hooley? Yes, I can take a message." said Gladys

"Yes, well as you know, Colin, I have been very busy lately what with the deals we've had on."

"…is it a message from the Police?…" asked Gladys. Denton sat and wondered - how long does it take to close a door, Hooley?

"Of course… I fully… " Hooley whipped round his head as he spoke (to the extent that the neck brace would allow) distracted by the conversation going on behind him - "Is that my wife, Gladys?"

Well, I've certainly never seen a man with a collar turn that quickly, thought Denton.

"…I mean, I've been heavily involved in Project Bluefish. Project Makepeace, not to mention Project Dempsey…" Denton continued undaunted, even though Colin's concentration had clearly deserted him.

"…well, you know, I thought they might be trying to contact him. You know. After the accident…it looks terrible…" Gladys continued.

"…just tell her, I'll call back, Gladys," said Colin, slightly raising his voice and generally looking a tad agitated. Denton looked up momentarily. *He's not buying this at all…* he thought, and looked back down at his own feet again.

"…and then Project Deep throat has taken up a considerable amount of time you know…"

"…I mean his eyes are all swollen like that…" said Gladys.

"…just tell her I'll call back Gladys…" said Colin, now clearly agitated.

"…especially after the incident with the photocopier. I'm sure you heard what happened to Peter. I don't think he's worn that tie since you know…"

"…his neck is in that poor brace…"

"…Gladys! Can you hear me, put the phone down!" commanded Colin in a very un-commanding manner.

"…he's in therapy, I understand. They never did get that ink stain out…"

"…of course, the other girls think that he's a hero…"

"…we don't pay you to talk all day…"

"…or fully mend the photocopier. You can still see Peter's terrified image on the screen if you look hard enough…"

"…well, you know, after saving that child…"

"…we especially do not pay you to talk to my wife…"

"…so you see…"

"…from that burning car…you know, after the car accident? I mean, there was a car accident, wasn't there?" Doubt now crept into Gladys' mind.

"…Give it here!" screamed Colin as he hurled himself across the corridor towards Gladys. "Look, let me speak to her - NOW!" They wrestled for the phone.

…which must have caused someone to press the hands free button.

"…No, Gladys, dear - he injured himself after showing off on our teenage son's BMX…"

Perhaps the entire corridor suddenly went deathly quiet. Even phones that were previously ringing and printers previously printing seemed to stop all at once. But only for a moment. Then came the furious sound of typing as every one tried to scoop the exclusive.

Colin finally shut the door and sat down.

Neither of them spoke for a second.

Eventually, Colin looked up. "Yes, thank you, Denton. That will be all."

"…Oh…ok…" said Denton. *That was weird,* he thought, *why didn't that happen every time I forgot to do some work?*

Denton returned to his desk to discover a couple of new e-mails. Nothing exciting on the face of it. One from the facilities team. One from Randall.

Denton opened the one from the facilities team. It was addressed to PC Users All. "Could I please remind everyone that the propelling pencils in the meeting rooms are for clients only. It has come to my attention that several pots of these pencils have gone missing. You are reminded that the unauthorised removal of pencils from the meeting rooms is treated by the partnership as theft and disciplinary action resulting in summary dismissal may occur as a result, Signed, the head of facilities, Mrs R.V.G Braithwaite."

Mmm, thought Denton. *Well, this is a quality establishment that I work for isn't it!?! Which kind of law firm, with a turnover the size of Manchester United's, classes the removal of pencils from the meeting room as theft? Why on earth would anyone want to work here?* He quickly glanced around at his desk and noticed that he had three propelling pencils dotted about. Suddenly, he felt very guilty, and grabbed them, stuffing them into his top desk drawer. He reached for his coffee cup before realising just in time that it was cold. *Lucky escape,* he thought and wandered over to the kitchen to make himself a fresh one. All along the corridor he could see people looking at each other with the same guilty expression, casually hiding propelling pencils.

"The facilities team are in charge of everything from photocopying to the post room to the cafeteria to site management. The day to day running of it is generally very smooth and hassle free since the people who do the photocopying, posting and run the cafeteria are genuinely nice people. However, the same cannot be said for their manager, the Head of Facilities. The thing about the Head of Facilities is that they generally tend to be completely unqualified in everything, know pretty much nothing about the work that solicitors do, and are labouring under the misapprehension that they are important people. To put them into context. Remember how smug really bad head teachers always appear? They always act as if they are in some way at the top of the food chain looking down on everyone else. Remember how irritating they can be? Now imagine feeling that level of contempt for someone who is less qualified, less intelligent, less capable, less motivated, less adaptable, less imaginative and generally, barely more significant in the whole scheme of things than an amoeba. That's pretty much them. And they're fat. You should now understand why pretty much the whole of the firm despises them but no one can be bothered to do anything about it. They're just well hidden enough for you not to have to see them on a daily basis but when they do appear, they send e-mails like the pencil one, which reminds you of their utterly meaningless existence and how you want to assist them to end it."

"Unfortunately though, the senior partner invariably loves her and considers her irreplaceable. According to him, we must treat her as an extremely important person since it is really hard to get hold of people like this. Presumably, he means this in the same way that the American's regard Osama Bin Laden as an important person."

But in some ways, Denton regarded it as quite reassuring that it was hard to find these kind of people to fill this position. "Heaven help society if there were an abundance of these vile little people just running around causing the decent human beings such irritation."

Hell is filled with facilities managers, and Charles Manson. Well, assuming there is room for him. He is by no means guaranteed a spot ahead of them.

Denton returned to his desk, having made a fresh cup of coffee. Much to his obvious horror, there were now fifteen e-mails in his inbox, each with the heading of 'tonight' and all from Randall, Billy and another university friend, Winston, who had a tendency to fall asleep at the most inappropriate of moments. Whilst Denton had wasted time thinking about those bloody facilities managers, he had missed out on an e-mail exchange bonanza.

"E-mail war is a fantastic thing, but it does not happen all that often, so when it does, it must be cherished," Denton might explain to anyone he thought too stupid to understand the concept - except facilities managers, just in case it distracted them too much from throwing themselves off the top of the building. Not that he would want any facilities manager to actually throw themselves off the top of the building. It would just be a complete waste of concrete to have to repair the pavement below. "Basically, what happens is someone sends an e-mail which causes practically everyone on the recipient list to reply and reply and reply until no-one can reply any more. The reasons for replying are many and varied. Much of the best fun was to be had in picking on other people's e-mails, sharing their errors with the group or selected people in the group and systemically mocking them for it. It may be that the original sender has made a massive mistake somewhere in their e-mail. Maybe it was a spelling mistake. Maybe they inadvertently sent it to the wrong person. Or maybe, just maybe, they likened the managing partner to a giant cock. Who knows? But as soon as it happens, you just sit back and wait for the myriad of funny spin-off lines that people feel the uncontrollable urge to get off their chests. The ultimate hope is that the result will be that you have on paper, your very own comedy sketch with every reply crafted from the heart. Of course, this is very rare, mostly because some twonk will ruin it by putting down the first blindingly obvious line that comes into their tiny little head. For example, in the above doomsday scenario replying as quickly as possible *'He said cock! John just called the managing partner a cock! A cock!'*, which really just ruins it for everyone."

"Of all the e-mail wars that I have had the privilege to be involved in, the very best one occurred between me and another trainee called James," contemplated Denton. "It may not sound like much, but we actually managed to hold an entire conversation across 12 e-mails referring to all of the James Bond films. I know what you're thinking and, of course, you're right. We are geniuses. Ok. You might not be thinking that. But we do deserve some recognition - it was bloody hard. OK, well you try to hold a conversation and get the word 'Moonraker' in. Yeah, not feeling so clever now, are we big guy."

"But then, in the present context, coming into an e-mail war this late in the game would only be heartbreaking. All the best lines would have gone causing each e-mail to take on a 'for your information only' subtext. In fact, having to read through it now would be like surveying the scene of a disaster. Too many 'what ifs'."

Denton opened up the original e-mail from Randall. It was addressed to him and Billy.

"Afternoon Guys, am having a really bad day at the office. The photocopier is broken and no one in my department will accept that it is not my job to fix it. I have dictated three massively urgent letters but none of the secretaries have capacity to type them, even though as we speak I can hear one of them talking really loudly about her boyfriend shagging either her sister or a dog. Dunno can't quite tell which. It's either *'Ar Sadie'* or Alsatian. Anyway, point is, I need a pick-me-up, any of you fancy a BC tonight?"

Fantastic idea, thought Denton, *A BC. I'm up for that.*

"Of course, a BC is a not very well hidden code for a bar crawl. Everyone discussing the prospect of one should abbreviate in this way. I wouldn't recommend spelling out in too much detail on your employers e-mail account all of the many and varied ways that you are intending to get absolutely shit-faced on a school night, just in case they find out, or more likely, in case they monitor the use of words such as 'bar' where in close proximity to 'crawl'. Bar crawls are fantastic, though ultimately largely messy affairs that hark back to the days when you were a care free student, you had no money and alcohol was the only thing to get you through the increasingly pressurised university life where a 2:1 is a must have and a job at the end of it is essential or else you're just never going to pay off that student debt. Of course, once you actually get the job, you realise that alcohol is still the only thing that can get you the pressures of life and that you would have been better off doing that Archaeology degree, remaining at University as a lecturer, and at least, *trying* to become Indiana Jones."

To this Billy had responded, "Is it ok if Badger comes along?"

Randall had responded "Yeah, sure." He had then, only moments later, sent just Denton an e-mail, which read "Who's Badger?"

Ah, Badger, thought Denton. *Badger was Winston's nickname from University. The thing about Badger was that he was the type of guy who could have been referred to by a whole spectrum of nicknames. The reason that he wasn't was probably due to the fact that there were just too many to choose from. It was likely that different sets of friends referred to him by completely different names. Badger had a list of ailments as long as your arm. When he was born, something went horribly wrong.*

I can't quite remember the story, it could have been something to do with forceps being used inappropriately or him being attacked by a Jack Russell. Anyway, either way, the result was that Badger's right ear was disproportionately sized to his left ear. As a result, he now had the kind of ear that you might expect to see on a small child. Women referred to his right ear as being 'cute'. God knows the left one wasn't. Like so many of us, Badger had started to have 'issues' with wiry hair and a huge tuft of it had sprouted on his left ear. It wasn't a pretty sight. No one seemed to know whether his baby ear had affected his hearing. Perhaps no one had thought to ask. As a result, no one was ever certain whether Badger was slightly deaf in one ear and he wasn't much help in furthering anyone's understanding since he didn't have any point of reference to know the difference. Just to be on the safe side, most people stayed on Badger's left hand side, even if it did mean you had to stare at the tuft. Denton shivered just thinking about it.

As if that wasn't enough, Badger's eyesight was useless. Perhaps it was due to all that time living in dens, foraging for food in the dark. Anyway, he was as blind as a bat, too blind for contact lenses, and insisted on wearing these hideously huge tortoiseshell rimmed spectacles which were about four times larger than they really should have been. As a result, it had the effect of magnifying the size of his eyes to anyone who looked at him straight on. In some ways, this detracted from the whole ear imbalance thing so it wasn't a bad thing. The big eye thing also helped Badger with the ladies. He looked permanently lost and they all wanted to mother him because of it. Well, at least they did until they noticed the tuft. Denton shivered again.

As if that wasn't enough, poor Badger had an allergy to spinach. Naturally he stayed away from it now, but when he had first eaten it, it had caused his lips to swell up and they hadn't really ever recovered. Everyone's favourite game at University was to play 'hide spinach in Badger's food', which caused his lips to swell to colossal proportions. Of course he needed to be taken to Hospital, but as long as you got him there just before his oesophagus completely closed up, it was fine.

But perhaps, the most noticeable, and unfortunate ailment to hit Badger had come shortly before he even arrived at University. He had become so stressed out during his A-levels that it had caused his hair to go grey in places. If it had just been generally all over that would probably have been ok. This was not the case for Badger, who had two stripes of grey, almost white hair, down the sides of his head and a distinctive triangle of white hair just at the tip of his widow's peak.

Finally, the real kick in the balls for Badger was the fact that he had a habit of just falling asleep suddenly and for no apparent reason, and no one really understood why.

Randall obviously wasn't too fussed about who Badger was because the e-mails had continued after that one.

"Anyway, I'm up for that." Billy had replied. "Have copied in Badger just in case he wants to come out too. If he can stay awake long enough. Am broke but am having an equally bad day in the office. Am working part-time this week as a bank teller. Why do people take it out on me just because they have no money in their bank account? I didn't spend it for them."

"Are you sure?" replied Randall. "I mean, I've seen your flat in Clapham. It would certainly explain a lot if you had."

"Would also explain the wads of cash tucked underneath your be...," said Winston, presumably falling unconscious onto the send button before being able to complete his witty response. Denton suddenly got a mental image of Winston face down on a keyboard in the computer room at the library as those around him looked on awkwardly while he drooled onto the keys.

And so it went on.

No more e-mails followed after that and Denton could not help but feel cheated for the rest of the afternoon.

It was approaching five o'clock. A critical part of any day. A time when someone might come into your room and ruin your entire evening by saying, "Urgent job has come in. Need your help. What do you mean, you've booked tickets for the Opera and you're going with the hot girl from accounts? I don't care if you've waited six months for this - I've got photocopying that needs doing! Get your sorry ass in my room and start doing it! Oh, and just for your insolence, you can paginate those seventeen bundles that are there as well."

It was for this reason that Denton implemented his much admired diversion tactic. He found as many papers as he possibly could and spread them all over his desk. He then made a fresh cup of coffee, but using cold water instead of hot and left it on his desk. Then he ruffled his hair and sat at his desk with his head in both hands.

At five twenty, the big Hooley wandered into his room.

"Denton, I just need you to..." he stopped and looked at the state of

Denton's desk, "Oh…how are you fixed for work, Denton?"

"Well, I'm not at capacity yet, but I guess I'm pretty near. If you've got something urgent then I'm sure that I could help." And with this he took a sip from his cup of coffee.

"Well, that's very helpful of you…"

Before he could finish, Denton spat his coffee back into the cup, "Urgh, its gone cold! Have had my head down constantly, didn't realise how long it had been since I made it."

Colin paused. "No, it's alright Denton, this can wait. You are far too busy."

"I suppose that I am. Well, if you're sure. Thanks, Colin. I really appreciate that."

*****

"Right," said Denton as he raced out of the lift with Randall about twenty seconds later, "First, we go to the pub around the corner from work…'Night, Brian."

"Good night, Brian," echoed Randall.

"Oh…'Night lads," said Brian the security guard, stood next to a vase of poorly arranged flowers. Obviously, he was not about to rearrange them. Not at all. Not even slightly.

"…while we wait for Billy and Badger to meet us. Now let us be clear. We are staying for one and only one. I am not going to end up stood in a bar full of fucking lawyers all night long. It will just be embarrassing."

"Agreed," said Randall. "Although, you do realise that you say that every time we go out drinking."

"What?" said Denton stopping momentarily. "No, I don't." They started walking again. "Then we'll move on to Shoreditch, as agreed, starting off in Dragon bar."

Randall and Denton arrived at the pub around the corner, through the mock Tudor door, over the mock Tudor floorboards and headed straight to the mock Tudor bar.

"What'll it be lads?" said the mock Tudor bar man.

"Two pints of Grolsch, please," said Randall. They wandered over to a corner of the bar, where they were conspicuous enough not to be seen but still able to see who was coming in.

"God, I hate this place," said Denton.

"Yeah, I know," said Randall. "Anything interesting happen at work today?"

"Yeah, I had my mid-seat appraisal."

"Oh right, how was that?"

"Yeah, fine. He didn't say much so I must be doing ok. "

"Good."

"Oh my God," said Denton looking at the door. "My supervisor has just turned up. Quick, finish your pint!"

"Which one is he?" asked Randall, as he tried to buy himself some time to psyche himself up for the ordeal of downing one whole pint of the most gaseous lager he had ever consumed.

"The one with the neck brace, two black eyes and a suspected broken nose. Drink up."

"God, what happened to him?" said Randall, still not quite ready for the ordeal.

"Marriage. Quick, drink up."

"Why the rush?" gasped Randall, a half pint later.

"Why? Because at 5.27pm I told him that I was swamped with work. It is now 5.38pm. Somehow I don't think he is going to believe that I was quite as busy as I may have made out."

"Good point. OK, we'd better drink up. If he finds out, it'll blow your cover for the entire week." said Randall, trying to string out the sentence to give his stomach enough time to clear the gas to make way for the remaining quarter.

"I know, quick, we'll take the back exit."

Denton and Randall quickly made their escape and wandered around the back of the pub, on the road to Shoreditch freedom.

"Slight change of plan," said Denton as he telephoned Billy, "We'll meet you in Shoreditch instead."

The first bar in the Shoreditch adventure was Dragon Bar. Dragon Bar was a good place to start since it really summed up the whole Shoreditch scene. Dark walls, battered furniture, bizarre artwork and banging tunes. Unfortunately, as with all the top Shoreditch bars, it was a victim of its own success since it tended to be crammed to the rafters with a diverse population of clientele, who often bordered on the bizarre. Retro-pink-topped mohicans, bomber jackets, slashed light blue denim, white man afro's, thick-rimmed tortoiseshell glasses, 1950's American high school jackets, patterned shirts, print shirts, plain shirts, non-crease, creased, flowered, paisley, named, unnamed shirts, this was a place where suits did not really stand out since there was nothing to stand out against. But the price of such a diverse range was nowhere to sit, dripping wet walls and a queue four deep to get to the bar. Definitely not somewhere to go if you wanted to hang around.

Billy and Badger arrived.

"Gentlemen. Nice of you to turn up," said Denton.

"Yeah, I know we're a bit late. Got caught up on the tube. Hi, Randall," said Billy. "You've met Badger before haven't you?"

"Yeah," said Randall. "A couple of times now."

"What you having?" asked Denton.

"Erm, just a Bud please."

"Yeah, Bud." said Winston.

Denton disappeared into the mass of people never to be seen again. Billy followed and was later eaten by crocodiles as he attempted to escape having given up the search for Denton days before.

Even though the walls were vibrating with noise, an awkward silence descended.

"So, Winston," asked Randall, "I don't think I've ever asked you this before, what do you do?"

"Well, I don't really have a job. Never found my calling. Have been looking though since I left Uni."

"Oh, OK. You working at the moment?" said Randall, looking at Winston and hoping for inspiration on what to say in response to whatever he was about to say.

"Yeah, kind of. I work as a night time security guard at a local warehouse."

"Oh, OK," Randall suddenly realised that his conversational skills were now going to take a severe testing. He looked at Winston, who just smiled awkwardly back at him. "What's that like?" A test which they would obviously fail.

"Yeah, fine."

"Good." said Randall nodding. "Good. Gooooood." He nodded again, "Good."

Nervously, he chugged back the rest of his pint. All three thirds of it.

Winston looked towards the crowd, hoping to see Billy and Denton returning but couldn't see either of them. Neither could the helicopters circling above them, search lights flashing about amongst the noise of loudhailers. "Denton, Billy, can you hear me? Are you still alive?"

Suddenly a flash of inspiration hit Winston. "Do you know Brian who works at your place as a security guard??"

"Yeah! Yes! Yes, I do!" said Randall, falling over himself to reply, thrilled and shocked in equal measures that they might suddenly have a common ground, a theme, a conversational piece to wile away the next three hours whilst Denton and Billy battled back through the dense undergrowth, employing guerrilla tactics in order to emerge unscathed by the experience with a couple of buds, two pints of Kingfisher and hopefully a bag or two of flame grilled steak flavoured McCoy's to keep them going. There was nothing to fear now that they could talk for ages about their new common friend, Brian. Lovely Brian. Well done, Brian.

"Yeah," said Badger. "He works for the same agency that I do. Seen him around a lot."

"Really?" asked Randall, not as a serious question but more to give Badger the opportunity to expand upon what he had just said to give Randall enough material to draw out a conversation about a man he barely knew.

"Yeah. He seems like a nice guy. Very tidy."

Bollocks, thought Randall. *I know bugger all about Brian. What am I meant to say?*

"Yes," he replied, unable to disguise the sense of anti-climax that he now felt. "Yes, very tidy."

"Isn't he?" nodded Badger.

"Yes," replied Randall. "Yes, he is."

A short while later, all four of them found themselves in Grand Central, which was a stylish bar. Very spacious. Not that they were too bothered about that.

"The problem with the law," Denton found himself saying, "is that it is too expensive to apply. Access to justice is being cut back all the time. I mean think about what we do and how much we charge. It is prohibitively expensive for the every day person."

"Yes, but we do not attract the every day person, do we?" said Randall. "I mean, our clients tend to be big companies, or at the very least, medium sized companies."

"Exactly," said Denton slurping a bottle of Tiger. "That's my point."

"You lost me." said Randall knocking back a San Miguel.

Billy looked on, slightly lost by it all.

"We do not attract the every day person. Do you not think that there is something fundamentally wrong with that? I mean look at us as a case study. We went to two of the best Universities in the country. We did really well and came high up in our year..."

"Yeah..." said Randall, wondering where this was going.

"And when it came to choosing a law firm, would you have ever considered working for a high street firm?"

"Well...no."

"And why was that?"

"Well, because I could not afford law school fees so I had to join a firm that would sponsor me through."

"Exactly, and the only firms that would pay your law school fees and give you a sum of money for maintenance are the big firms. The little firms cannot compete."

"What's your point, Denton?"

"My point is that I get the impression that, in the old days, the distinction of whether to work for a high street firm or a commercial firm was not based entirely on remuneration. People who chose to be high street lawyers did so because they felt morally bound to do so."

"But surely those people still exist today and will become high street lawyers if they want to," added Billy.

"Perhaps," conceded Denton, "Perhaps. But the situation now must surely be different. I mean what price principles. Think about it. University itself is expensive. Ridiculously expensive. Do you know that they say it costs £10,000 to go through University? Add that to the price of law school, £5,000 in fees alone, plus maintenance. I mean, you could easily be in debt to the tune of £20,000 before you even start work. And then you have to make a choice as to which firm you want to work for? High street or commercial? High street, where you might start on £13,000 or less. Commercial, where you probably start on £20,000 plus recoup the money that you spent on law school fees. What price principles?"

"Yes, but there is no shortage of people entering the law. Smaller firms, high street firms will always be able to recruit," said Randall.

"Yes, that's true. But that's also the point that I am making," added Denton. "Who will high street firms be recruiting? This might seem unfair but I can easily imagine that it will be the people who might have been unable to enter the law higher up in the food chain. I mean, if you've forked out £15,000 to £20,000 trying to become a solicitor and you have not got a job at the end of Law School, are you just going to give up or will you simply take a job anywhere?"

"It depends," said Randall. "I mean, you still need to be able to be a certain type of person to work at a law firm. I did work experience in a high street firm. The kind of shit that they have to put up with day in day out makes our job look like first prize in the Times crossword puzzle."

"Is that the quick one or the other one?" asked Billy.

"But, in some ways, that adds to my point," continued Denton. "That means that you might get a candidate who is technically not that gifted, struggles through a lowly regarded university and law school, who is unable to get a job at the end of it, so applies to his local law firm. He gets in, but hates the work and hates his clients. However, he needs the job because he needs to pay off his massive debts and this is the only thing he's qualified for. Now. Imagine this. You are someone who has walked off the street and you need a solicitor. He's inept, he's miserable and he's really not that interested in how you feel. And yet, you're still having to pay him your hard earned cash, which you resent, just to try to get some justice. Hardly fair, is it? Is this access to justice for all? Imagine, it's a personal injury claim and this guy acts for the claimant. More likely than not it will be a firm like ours that acts for the Defendant insurance company. All you need is a clever girl like that trainee in your department, Randall. Delia is it?"

"M'dunno. Which one is she? The really fit one or the hyper-efficient one?" asked Randall to no one in particular.

Denton paused. "The one that does not have big tits and blonde hair, but does know what she is doing."

"Yeah, that's Delia. Yeah she is good," said Randall, lamentably. "But her tits are crap."

"OK, imagine her acting for the insurance company, eager to impress, motivated, organised. What chance does the Claimant have?"

"Yes, but if you have a good claim then surely it does not matter how super efficient the Defendant's solicitor is. Right?" asked Billy.

"No," said Denton. "Yes, you might have a good claim for establishing liability. It might be a clear-cut case. But. What about quantum? Essentially quantum, especially in a personal injury claim, is a question of negotiation. Delia is a good negotiator. Our man in the high street is not. The outcome is likely to be that the level of quantum will be the minimum amount that Delia's client can get away with paying."

"OK," said Randall.

"Now, I said before that I was using our guy as a 'what if' example. Taking it further, what if there are a lot of people like him. In five or ten year's time, how many people will there be out there like him??"

"But then, you're assuming that the people who work for the little firm are not that good, which they might not be. You're forgetting that there are also people like us working for the big boys who are out on a BC on a Monday."

"But we're different," said Denton. "I mean, would we be out drinking if we still couldn't do our job just as well the next morning. I can do my job with a hangover. That's part of the problem. I can do it stood on my head if necessary. We don't make decisions. We process. We make sure that something comes in at one end and goes out the other. The point that I am making is that in the ordinary scale of things, whenever someone wants access to justice you have the common man on the Clapham omnibus taking on the big company. Think about personal injury claims against the conglomerate. Product liability claims against the pharmaceuticals. We're talking about a man with little or no money against the Company with seemingly endless reserves. There's a disparity there before you even consider the lawyers. Then think about the type of lawyer that they can afford. The big Company gets in Clifford Chance. The little man has limited access to legal aid. He gets one solicitor from 'Norfolk and Chance'. But in the big firms, there is very rarely just one person working on a case. Typically, we come in teams of ten. That's one average, technically stunted solicitor against ten high-profile, well greased super solicitors. Then think about the facilities that a firm like ours has: fast computers; secretaries; librarians; photocopiers; couriers; professional support lawyers, against your small firm with one secretary and a typewriter. They probably do not even have propelling pencils. Ten Delia's against a Badger. Game over."

Denton nodded toward Winston who was asleep, face down on the table. He slurped back on his bottle with a satisfied smile on his face. Billy and Randall paused.

"Are you in love with Delia or something?" asked Randall.

Bluu was another bar that fitted in well around Shoreditch. How could it not? It had a choice between corduroy or leather sofas. What more could anyone ask for?

"But politics has a huge role to play," said Billy, knocking back a Kingfisher. "I mean, if the Government was more interested in making sure that people got access to decent legal support, then they would invest more heavily in ensuring that good solicitors worked for high street firms."

"Yes," said Denton chugging away at a bottle of Asahi, "I mean what young lawyers need is the incentive to work at a high street firm. Not just financially though, they also have to feel like they're not failing by working for one. End the stereotype of working for a high street firm as equating to a failure to do well in the law."

"Yeah," said Randall. "I agree with that. I mean, I really enjoyed my course on the law of torts at University. It was really interesting. But then to work at firms that do the really interesting law, you need to work for one that specialises in doing group actions or something."

"Yes, but you're missing the point though, aren't you." said Denton. "I mean, we get interested in the more complicated stuff which is why a firm like ours is good to work for. But the ordinary person does not have interesting litigation pending all the time. They have small stuff. They might be someone who is a sole trader dealing with someone who breaches a contract. They might be someone who just needs advice on a will. Do you know how many people don't have a will?"

"No," said Randall, "Do you?"

"No. But you've done Intestacy. You know what happens to people's money when they die without a will."

"Yeah, I know."

"But then surely the good people will leave a little law firm anyway, won't they? Especially if they're dealing with simple situations?" said Billy. "Is it my round?"

"Yes." said Denton. "I'll have another Asahi."

"Randall?"

"Erm. A pint of Stella," said Randall, taking a moment to ponder the complexities of the request.

"Right," said Billy as he concentrated all his efforts into attracting the barman's attention and briefly lamented his own lack of tits to assist him in the process.

"Maybe we should adopt a system more akin to America's."

"No way," said an animated Randall. "No way."

"Yeah, but think about it. No one loses out, do they? I mean the solicitors are more incentivised. The clients get bigger pay outs and its only insurance companies that lose out."

"Yeah, but then premiums take a hike."

"Yeah but only the premiums that the companies pay."

"Here you go," said Billy as he returned with more beer.

"Well," said Billy, "I reckon that the Government should put more money into legal aid and it should get this money by cutting its investment in all things military."

Where did that come from? thought Randall and Denton at one and the same time.

Next up was Liquid. Denton had no idea how he had got there. He did not really remember leaving the last place. Now, Liquid is not in the Guinness Book of Records. But it really should be. It must surely be the world's tiniest bar. It's as if someone went round to their grandma's for tea one day, got bored, removed all the doilies, trapped grandma in the cellar, ripped out the front room and put a bar in there instead. The result was a top notch joint with restricted breathing space.

"Well, I disagree," said Denton, trying to extract his elbow that was trapped between two people stood behind him.

"Why?" asked Randall trying not to use the person behind as a back rest.

"Why?" repeated Denton in astonishment. "Why?"

"Yeah, why?" joined in Billy, whose feet had become trapped between the left foot of the guy behind and Randall's right foot.

"Why?" asked Denton, rocking slightly as he stood.

"Yeah, why?" said Billy and Randall in unison.

"I don't need to explain myself to you," said Denton.

"Yes, you do," said Randall.

"I don't."

"You do," concurred Billy.

"No. No, I do not."

"You do," said Randall.

"Well, it's because….it's because. No, I do not. I am entitled to my opinion on its own without justifi…..justifici….reason."

"No, you're not," said Randall. "Why do you disagree?"

"Well, I mean it's obvious, isn't it."

"No, it's not, why?" asked Billy.

"…because I do not think that Britney Spears *is* fitter than Christina."

Denton looked up and realised that he was now in bar Smersh, still in Shoreditch. Bar Smersh is great. It's tiny and you could quite easily miss it, since it is located down a back street somewhere. Like all great bars, it's underground, dimly lit and features loads of Russian propaganda-esque posters. Not that Denton or Billy could actually focus on any of them at this stage in the proceedings. Both were sat on hard wooden stools next to the bar where a barman was on hand just in case, for whatever reason, they thought that it would be a good idea to get another one in. "I wish that I was a student again," the bar man may have been thinking as he looked at them, nodding his head gently in time to the banging music in the background.

"The thing is Billy…," Denton paused and tried desperately hard to focus, "…women are pretty much evil. I mean, they're not. But they really are."

"Yeah," nodded Billy, clinging to the bar for dear life.

Denton looked around, his head slightly bouncing as he did so, much as if he were a *Thunderbird*. He paused. He looked around again. He paused.

"Where's Randall?"

"Yeah," nodded Billy, positive that the floor had opened up and that he would be sucked in at any moment if he let go of the bar.

"I mean, they're not evil. But you just can't win. They want attention. They want devotion, which is like, what is that about…?" He continued no longer actually looking at or indeed focusing on, anyone.

"Yeah."

"But then they complain that you're being too, what's the word…."

"Yeah….."

"Cling…clinging," Denton paused and frowned."….clinglyingly. Yeah, kerlinglyingly."

"Right."

"Oh, here's Randall. Randall. No, Randall, we're here. No, over here." Randall couldn't hear him. Or, apparently, see them. In all likelihood, he could probably no longer see at all.

"Hello!" exclaimed Randall when he eventually found them, putting his arm around both with a big grin on his face, "I've just been sick" he declared in an almost valedictory way.

"Yeah," agreed Billy to absolutely no one.

"I was just telling Billy, women are evil."

"Evil," affirmed Randall.

"Yeah."

"I mean, you just can't win."

"Can't win," repeated Randall, shaking his head with a big grin on his face, hanging on to Billy and Denton to avoid falling flat on the floor.

"No, I mean, no. You try but then they just leave you. They say you don't…you're not in touch with your femininininity…so you try to and you realise you love them and they they…"

"Femnity?" asked Randall, confused, his head bobbing up and down as if it was an empty coconut shell on a stick.

"….leave. For another woman or something. Fucking lesbian."

"Yeah," said Billy, gripping the bar until his knuckles went white.

"Lesbian," said Denton. "Hey, where's Badger?"

"Dunno," said Randall, trying in vain to mount a stool but failing, mainly because he was aiming in the wrong place, "think that we left him asleep somewhere about three bars back."

"Oh."

"Yeah."

"I was sick. Cleaned it up though."

"Bitch. God, I hate her, fucking lesbian."

"Yeah."

"More drinks?" asked Randall.

Chapter Six

It was morning again and so Denton thought it only right that he should open his eyes. He had that sense of guilt, bordering on paranoia. That sense of confusion and a banging headache. It could mean only one thing, that his old friend, little Miss Hangover was here.

Brilliant. What day is this? thought Denton. *Saturday. It has to be,* he concluded on the basis that the alarm clock was sitting there looking quite sheepish. *Oh yes, not so clever now are we, Mr Alarm Clock. Not now Daddy decided to switch the alarm off. That's right, and one day, I'll send you into retirement. Right around the time when I get there myself.* A sense of perspective and a feeling of peaceful reflection had dawned upon Denton Voyle. The weekend had arrived, unfortunately not on its own since it had been accompanied by those gate crashing jokers: Nausea and Migraine.

Reluctantly, he slowly left his bed and, predictably, hit the table in the hall causing the vase of flowers to topple over.

Seriously, why do we have a vase of flowers on the hall table? And who keeps refilling it with water? he thought with a certain sense of annoyance at the inconvenience bestowed upon him.

Eventually, he relocated the lounge, which had customarily been demolished in the night and rebuilt in a different place. He put the TV on. Randall woke with a start. He briefly checked to see if Denton had noticed and glanced at his watch.

"Well, its 10.45. I had better go to bed. Thanks for a great night though." He stood up and yawned.

"Randall…"

"Yeah?" He glanced at his watch and then with a dawning sense of realisation, "Yeah, no. I've done it again, haven't I?"

Just to confirm, he moved across the room and opened the curtains. Light cascaded across the living room.

"Anyway," Denton pondered, picking up on something Randall had said before, "How do you know that you had a good night?"

"Huh?" Randall frowned, "Well, I …dunno…"

"Where did we go?"

"Erm, Fluid, I think."

"No… that wasn't last night, that was the other night when we suddenly became enamoured with the notion that we didn't need food to survive on at all, but rather, in the alternative, we could get all the nutrients that we needed to survive from vodka on account of the potato."

"Oh yeah," Randall smiled, "Erm..." and then that all too familiar look of horror descended again, "...oh, hang on...we went to Fluid on Friday night after work. If that wasn't last night...then that can only mean one thing...oh God...it's Sunday, isn't it?!"

Randall shook a fist in the air, and Denton was only half sure he was joking, "Seriously, God, why do you keep doing this to us? What happened to all the other days? Did you just miss them out this week? I don't remember Tuesday at all. I miss Tuesday. Bring back Tuesday this instant!!"

"Bollocks... we really ought to get to the bottom of this whole Sunday thing, you know that don't you?" Denton said looking at Randall's down-turned face that was quite obviously still manifesting signs of mourning. Damn, that guy really did like Tuesday.

"Yes," said Randall, fisting one hand into the palm of the other, "I want to know how it keeps happening..." finger flapping in the air, "...and who is responsible."

"Perhaps we can magnum them as well." said Denton.

Randall stroked his chin. "Mmm. Perhaps we can..."

Chapter Seven

Ironing

"You know, the song is wrong. It is not war at all. It's ironing. What is it good for?" mused Denton, stood behind an ironing board, with an iron in his hand. "It is a little known fact that eastern mysticism recognises ironing as one of the most truly evil things that exists on the planet. The Devil is an iron. OK, you don't believe me, but ask yourself this then, why is Hades so hot? Well, it's because someone left the iron on down there. Its true, Satan is the Widow Twankie of the Underworld. You never see pictures of Beelzebub in a creased shirt do you? No. It's because he's too fucking hot from all the ironing - those creases just drop right out. Don't bother going to a sauna for a quick steam, just do the ironing for an hour. Save yourself a fortune!"

"Ironing just epitomises the waste of time that Sunday afternoons represent. After all, Sunday afternoons are pointless, really pointless. What are they there for? Ironing. And not much else. *'I know how to round off the perfect day - I will iron. There, that'll cheer me up'.* "

"And what exactly does ironing accomplish? Nothing. Absolutely nothing. It never solved anything. World leaders do not get together in the Middle East and encourage Israel to iron a few Palestinian shirts to sort things out. No. In Parliament, MP's will not say *'on the question of Ireland, sir, I wanted to enquire what the Right Honourable Iron thinks is the way forward'.*"

"It never achieved anything. The Nobel peace prize - ever won by an iron? No. OK, well maybe if it did solve the Middle East problem and address the Irish question, then yes, maybe in those circumstances, it might win. But at the moment, at least, no."

"It never created anything. No newspaper ever ran the headline *'Iron spawns another iron...which spawns more irons....which spawns a toaster...'* No. That never happened either. Well, maybe in America.

"Of course, it never hurt anyone either. *'Man held as hostage by iron - demands better ironing board covers or it'll shoot'.* No, that doesn't happen either, although my brother once got his fingers ironed once. Well he deserved it. Well, no, he didn't. Well maybe. We'll agree to disagree - anyway the point is that it was an accident and it's no good still telling mum it wasn't. She didn't believe you then and she won't now eighteen years later. Anyway, as I said, he deserved it."

"Ironing is just one of the most pointless and thankless tasks imaginable. For example, no one will come running up to you in the street and say *'Oh my God!*

Did you iron that shirt yourself? Wow, that's amazing! You're really talented. I just love what you've done with the cuffs.' So why bother? Know why? Well, I'll tell you why. Social convention. If people did not get so fussy (and by people, I mean women - and you know that's true - when did a man ever say *'oh, I could not possibly go out in this. The creases are not perpendicular to each other and the smell of summer meadows has already started to fade')* then no one would have to iron."

"There is just no pride or satisfaction to be had from ironing. There is no skill to it. No one will ever go to night school to learn the craft. You will never hear any teacher address a classroom of eager students and say, *'Yes. Well the untrained ironer is likely to steam too frequently, but in order to be a professional you must learn moderation in your steamage - let the steamage flow through you.'* You will never see art critics viewing an ironed shirt in a gallery, and, with glasses arm in mouth, ponder what angst, what strife, the artist went through to really get those creases out of his 100% cotton white shirt. *'Ah yes, a fine specimen here from the early Voyle dynasty'* is a phrase that will never be uttered with pomposity around my framed masterpiece. Well, not unless Tracey Emin gets her way."

"No, ironing is not interesting and it holds no aesthetic value. Neither is it a spectator sport. Even Grandstand would think twice before showing it. Well, maybe not. They'd only show it if the World Twiddly-Winks Championship had been cancelled at late notice or something."

"Ah, yes, up steps Randall Leaver to the board. Clive, playing with a lot of confidence at the moment isn't he?"

"That's right Bryan, he is the ironing man of the moment. You pick up any Pro-Ironing magazine and you'll see his face on the front of it, and of course, he is certainly the one that the crowd have come to see. He's quick, he strong and he puts a lovely crease in down the back of his trousers."

"Yes, and of course, he's the young pretender to Denton Voyle's crown. A quick glance at the World Ironing Leader Board will show you that he is only a couple of loads behind Voyle now and certainly looking to out-iron his former master this afternoon. How do you think the pressure will affect him in this hot and humid living room?"

"Well, of course, that is a factor. It is well known in the ironing circle that he much prefers to iron in the kitchen, but due to record crowd attendances, there just isn't room, especially with the Sunday roast already on. I mean this place really is packed today, there really isn't any more room left on this sofa."

"That's right and, oh, well it looks as if Randall has won the toss, he's going to be ironing first. He steps up, plugs his preferred iron in. Just checking the temperature setting, and oh! Oh my word, the crowd like that trickery, he twisted the dial around to the preferred setting by clicking his fingers and catching the dial. Oh the sublime cheekiness of it! That's what the crowd came for! This boy is really showing some flair here. And a sly smile on Voyle's face there - yes - I think he appreciated that."

"Yes, that one was a crowd pleaser all right. Let's look at it again on the slow motion replay - yes, right there, just clips the outside of the dial with the returning finger - genius."

"Just waiting for the referee now to approve the temperature. Yes, there's the nod that gives

us the all clear. Happy enough that the iron is at the correct European setting. And of course, it has been a good few years now since that ruling came in following the infamous incident when Rowenta got deducted three shirts and a jumper for using a wall paper steamer disguised as an iron."

"Well, that's what happens, Bryan, when these famous ironers are allowed to endorse their own irons."

"Quite. And here we are now. Quick flex of the neck muscles. Shoulders rolled. Rounding the head. He steps up to the ironing basket - as soon as he selects the shirt the referee will begin the clock. And. And. And, we're off - he's whisked that easy iron shirt straight out of the basket, on to the board, twisting it in the air, and oh my word! He's....Clive. Clive. He's starting with the back panel first?!"

"Oh! Remarkable Bryan."

"And he's on to the front panel now, skirting around those buttons like a pro, in and out. Flips it around, on to the other front panel and then yanks it off for those hard to reach shoulder pieces......."

"No. That just does not happen."

"Another Sunday in front of the ironing board. Another Sunday bored rigid. Another Sunday wasted to recover from all the week's excesses."

"Pointless. Utterly pointless. Another waste of perfectly good oxygen."

Chapter Eight

Tuesday - Why?

Beep beep beep beep.

"No. NO! It positively can not be morning."

Beep beep beep beep.

"Please, no, for the love of God, it really can not be morning already," pleaded Denton.

Beep beep beep beep.

"Oh God, I really hate you, alarm clock. You know that, don't you?"

Beep beep beep beep.

"One of these days, seriously I'm going to take pleasure in totally destroying you with a big hammer."

Wisely, his alarm clock decided to stop beeping in such a smug way and reflected on whether it was appropriate to beep so deliberately in future.

Reluctantly, Denton got up, put on his blue towelling dressing gown and wandered aimlessly in the general direction of his bathroom. With eyes partially stuck together, he vaguely made out the shape of Randall wearing his green towelling dressing gown, wandering aimlessly in the general direction of his own bathroom.

"Morning," mumbled Denton.

"Yeah," mumbled Randall.

God, I feel like shit today, thought Denton, as he battled in his usual way with the taps for the shower, eventually giving up and settling on a temperature reminiscent of a former girlfriend in the bedroom - slightly warmer than cold but not really doing a lot to get him really hot. *I'm sure that drinking was involved at some point, but I'm not entirely sure when. Or where. Or why? Oh well, it will probably dawn on me at some point.*

"You drink too much then last night?" said Randall as he and Denton walked into work. "Magnum!" he said as another sauntering pointless member of public got in their collective way.

"Well, it's hard to say since I don't really remember. I remember drinking with Billy." said Denton. "Magnum," he said as another supposed commuter reading a book got in his way.

"So you don't remember telephoning me for directions then on your way home?"

A flash of memory was triggered in Denton's mind, closely followed by a tinge of paranoia, "Maybe. What did I say?"

"Well, you got lost somewhere near St Paul's. I know this since when I asked you what you could see, you said, '*A big dome thing.*'"

"Oh....but you got me home after that, right?"

"Well, that still did not really narrow it down that much so I asked you if you could see any signs."

"...and could I?"

"Yes. Only this sign wasn't as helpful as it might have been."

"Well. What did it say?"

"No parking at any time."

"Oh," said Denton. He vaguely remembered that. "Magnum," he said as they neared work.

"Now the thing about Tuesday is, it's a real non-day," Denton would often muse, "I mean, what is it really for? Wednesday, now Wednesday is the beacon of hope, the point where despair starts to fall away. Wednesday is the point at which you can say, 'I'm half way there!' Thursday, well Thursday is the night when you can say, 'thank fuck it's Friday tomorrow, let's go out to celebrate'. Friday, I don't think I need to spell out just how wonderful Friday is. Saturday, likewise, needs no introduction. Sunday, of course, is the old enemy that someone really should put down. Monday - dreadful, utterly dreadful, but then at least you expect that - but still worthy of a drink after work to celebrate getting through it. But Tuesday though, what's that about?"

Randall and Denton had by now shot most of London's commuters, which while justified on each occasion, was none the less likely to cause the road sweepers long delays in getting their jobs done.

Just when they thought the morning could not get any more irritating, Dom appeared. It was the kind of omen that suggested your bad day was about to get a whole lot worse.

"Christ," muttered Denton as Dom shuffled towards them from the opposite direction.

He stopped and faced them - preventing them from carrying on any further. They could see the office but to their horror it became apparent that they could not reach it without getting past him first. Reminiscent of old Cowboy movies, it was the kind of Western showdown that you really did not need that early in the morning.

"Hello Denton."

"Hello Dom."

"Hello Randall."

"Morning Dom."

He stood there with a god awful smile on his face, his big bright eyes all lit up. No one said anything for about an age as all the other commuters wandered past.

And just as Denton was about to comment on the fact that they really should carry on walking to the office, especially as all three of them were heading in that direction, Dom broke the silence.

"How was your weekend?"

"What?"

He shuffled on the spot awkwardly, his satchel bouncing as he did so.

"How was your weekend?"

"Fine. OK. Christ, Dom, I don't remember - it's Tuesday!"

"I wasn't in yesterday." said Dom, as if that was some sort of acceptable justification.

Denton and Randall continued walking past Dom as he desperately tried to think of another question.

They reached the main door to the building and there, as always, was Brian the ever-friendly security guard holding open the door for them.

"Morning Denton, morning Randall - how are you both this morning?"

Don't you start! thought Denton. "Fine thanks Brian."

"Alright ta," said Randall.

They wandered through to the lift and it was just possible to hear *How was your weekend Brian?* as, mercifully, the lift doors shut.

"Now Brian is an odd mix really," Denton had told Billy as they sat in Detroit bar near Covent Garden, "and don't get me wrong, I mean that in a really nice way. He's always smiling, he's always polite, he's very friendly and he asks questions which show that he is taking an interest in you. To be honest I have no idea how he does it. It's weird and remarkable all at the same time."

"Yeah, I know Brian. He works for the same agency that Badger does. Seems like a nice guy. Very tidy."

"Isn't he though?!" remarked Denton.

Denton and Billy were sat on oversized bar stools next to the highly polished chrome bar, casually trying to eye up the extremely fit bar girl. Without being too obvious, they were staring into the mirror behind the bar as she leant over the table behind them. Of course both 'casually' and 'without being obvious' should be taken in its loosest context here. In fact, the word 'casually' is used in the same way that every guy thinks he's sitting 'casually' after five pints of lager. In reality, its not so much 'casual' but more, well, slimy. And of course though they thought they were 'not being obvious', they were, but this bar maid had had many years experience of guys 'casually' looking down her top. She wasn't even that bothered about it as long as they didn't go any further. After all, they were nice breasts, why shouldn't other people enjoy them?

Neither Denton nor Billy did much to dispel her theory that all men were the same. Denton and Billy just hoped that the intense darkness of Detroit did enough to stop other people noticing them peering. It probably did. Detroit bar is great for that. The place is basically underground, containing pockets of earth coloured vacuous caverns, which look as if someone had dug them out using their own hands. In essence, Detroit is what would happen if an ant, who had been hit by a large dose of radiation that had caused it to mutate into the size of a regular man, suddenly decided to open up his own trendy bar in central

London.

There was a brief interlude whilst Billy did his business.

"You big poof!" jeered a semi-drunken Billy, as he returned to his stool at the bar and in relation to a comment that Denton had made about fifteen minutes ago.

"What? Oh, about Brian. Yeah, no I don't mean it like that, Tapman," snapped Denton. "I mean, he seems totally at ease with his own existence. It's like he has found his calling and really enjoys life. Why is that?"

"Got me. I still can't find a job, even though I have a degree. OK, it's not the best but a third still counts as a degree, you know." said Billy, suddenly defensive.

"Yeah, I know." said Denton, trying to appease him.

"I just don't feel like I'm in control at all," he burped. "And to make matters worse, I think Happy is really upset with me for some reason, he's really off his food."

Denton looked at Billy with a face full of scorn. "Tapman, he's a fish. Fish do not have feelings."

"Uuuuuooohh yes they do," said Billy, clutching onto his bottle of Peroni like it was a support to prevent him slipping off his bar stool. "Now, if you'll excuse me, all this talk of water is making me need the loo."

"Jesus, Tapman, you've just been. What is your problem!?!?"

"Don't start on the weak bladder thing. It's a blessing and a curse - sign of a healthy bladder, you know. Now, get more drink while I make some room."

"You got much on today?" asked Randall, completely disturbing Denton's recollections, which were just beginning to return to him.

"Yeah, well, a little bit of research, which I must find time to fit in between my busy schedule of photocopying and e-mailing. Where shall we go drinking tonight?" asked Denton.

"Erm, dunno. Dust? We haven't been there for a while."

"Yeah, ok," replied Randall.

"How you getting on with the other trainee that you're sat with?" asked Denton as he checked his hair in the mirrored wall of the lift. "What's her name?" he said coyly.

"What Delia? I thought you knew her name," said Randall as he stopped picking at his teeth to answer the question. He looked at Denton.

"No, I don't know her name," said Denton. "What made you think I did?" he asked with almost genuine indignity.

"Denton, you talked about her non stop for twenty minutes the other night."

"Oh," said Denton. "Are you sure?" He asked, but only in a half convincing manner.

"Yeah, anyway, she's not too bad," said Randall, deciding that he had had enough fun, wanting to move the conversation along. He returned to looking in the mirror to examine his neck for razor rash. "I like her. She's a bit bossy, but other than that, she's alright. Sometimes she's even funny."

"Now, lets not go too far there, Randall," said Denton as his eyes darted across to Randall, "I've had conversations with her before and at no point did I laugh. In fact, I don't really recall thinking anything other than wondering if anyone would mind if I strangled her there and then."

"Well, there is that." said Randall as they both stopped preening, turned around and waited for the lift doors to open.

"So what is it with you and this Delia girl then, Denton?" asked Billy as he returned from his ablutions in Detroit bar. "You fancy her or something?"

"No. No. Definitely not. No. Well." He paused for that second too long, "No, definitely no. No. Why? Why do you ask? Don't get me wrong, she's nice. She seems nice. I haven't really spoken to her. No. If anything she bugs me."

"I think you see her as a threat and a challenge."

"What? No. What?"

"Well, the threat is, you do not like her because she is doing a good job in the ways that you hoped you'd be doing a good job at work. I still remember the conversations we had at Uni, in your room. You always wanted to be a respected solicitor, getting recognition for doing a good job." He stared at his bottle, slowly lifting off the label, whilst Denton stared at him agog. "The challenge is, you want to be better than her and show people that you're better than her, but that would conflict with your whole 'this job is a waste of time' philosophy. That's the challenge."

Denton stared at Billy for a moment more. You could tell the situation was serious when Denton stared at Billy. Staring at Billy was not something that people chose to do without a really good reason. This was mainly due to the fact that Billy was not what you would call a pretty boy. For a start there were the goofy ears, then the squinty, pee-hole eyes that sat deep in his skull. Then there was the freckly skin which covered his gaunt face and was concentrated around his cheeks like blusher. Then there was the overly enlarged forehead, which was heightened by the slightly receding hair line, which was masked by the ginger hair that adorned it. Seriously, Billy really was not a guy to be stared at. Not even for a minute. Not even for a fraction of minute. Seriously. If you looked at him for too long, you would find yourself saying, *'God, what am I doing? If I carry on staring for much longer there is a real risk I will burn this image into my retina and take it with me to the grave. Oh God, my eyes - my beautiful eyes!'*

"You know, this is one of the reasons that I do not like drinking with you. Normal people get drunk and go stupid. You get drunk and then start coming out with insightful comments. Thank God I'll be too hung over in the morning to really remember this part."

Billy chuckled in an inane drunken way.

"And that is not an admission by the way. I definitely do not fancy her. I may be a little intrigued but it's no more than that. And yes, it does bug me when people do the job better than me. Well, it's not even that. It's the way she speaks to me. The way she holds herself. It bugs me that she just thinks she can do the job better than I can."

"That's the problem, though, isn't it? The fact is, she might be as good as you. If not better."

Denton turned and looked at Billy, as any man would who'd just run out of steam. "Oh…" He looked away and saw Randall enter the bar and wander over.

"Oh…go to the toilet why don't you, Tapman." But it was too late, he was already on his way.

"Alright Randall," said Billy as he cantered to the toilet.

"Hey Billy," said Randall, as he walked up to the bar and vaulted on to a bar stool, slightly self-impressed by the fact that he had managed to stay on and not fall straight back off again.

"Evening Randall," said a slightly deflated Denton as he thoughtfully slugged away at his bottle of Tiger.

"Hey." said Randall. "You look like you were having an interesting conversation."

"Yeah," said Denton, thinking as he chugged. "You just finished work?"

"Yeah, someone needed some photocopying done. Anyway, I can tell you were losing that debate. You always call him Tapman when you're losing."

"Do not." said Denton, safe in the knowledge that he did.

"Anyway," said Randall. "Why do you call him Tapman?"

"Who, Billy? Well, that's because he's Billy 'the Tapman' Yeovil," said Denton. "It's from University. I can't remember who came up with it but he got it early on. He always got teased by the others. I even teased him myself. He's essentially a really nice guy. A little geeky perhaps, but his heart is in the right place."

Denton swigged on his beer.

Then there was silence. It was obvious to Randall that Denton had reached the stage in the evening where he was the only one who thought he was making sense.

"Denton?" asked Randall of the vacant Denton.

"Yeah?"

"Why is he called Tapman?"

"Oh, right! Yeah, well it's on account of the fact that he always needs the toilet. Usually after every pint when he's drinking and often, when he's not, at times when it's really inconvenient. We used to say it was like he had it on tap. Tapman. Get it? You want a drink?"

"Yeah. Michelob please. So what is Billy doing this week?"

"Good idea. I'll get one too." he said. "Can I get three Michelobs please?" he said, trying to charm the bar girl. Bearing in mind he was sat 'casually', he probably wasn't succeeding. "Not a lot, I would imagine," he said, turning back to Randall. "Trouble is with Billy, like all of us, he hasn't got a clue what he wants to do with his life. But, unlike most of us, he got a third so can't even use that to give him a steer in any particular direction. He's been gone a long time, hasn't he?" said Denton suddenly frowning. "Anyway, he just floats around from one job to the next in the hope that one day he will find one that he enjoys. Oddly enough though, he's never short of money. His Dad was a City broker, have I told you this already?" He frowned in Randall's general direction.

"No, I don't think so, I mean I know he lives in that flat in Clapham. I always did wonder where he got all that money from. That flat must be worth a fortune. Cheers," he said lifting up the newly arrived bottle of beer.

"Yeah, well his Dad was a City broker. Died of a heart attack. Shortly before falling off the top of his office block. Poor guy had gone up there to kill himself but suffered from vertigo and they reckon the shock of it all on his weak heart just finished him off."

"That's awful." said Randall, suddenly losing his appetite for his beer.

"Yeah. Quite tragically, he was quite a large man and took out four pedestrians as he hit the ground."

"Oh God."

"Yeah, one of them was Billy's mum. She was only passing by at the time, on her way to Leadenhall indoor market. Weird how these things work out, isn't it?"

Randall sat in stunned silence, while Denton took another slurp of beer.

"There must be a queue for the toilet. Billy can't go under pressure. He'll be queuing for a cubicle. Anyway. He bought the flat with the inheritance money. Owns it outright. Now all he has is his pet goldfish. And his flat mate, Winston, I suppose." Denton turned with a frown towards Randall, "You know Badger?" They both looked across the bar at the guy slumped over it, unconscious, with his face stuck to a napkin.

"Yeah, well, no not really. I have met him on several occasions though but I couldn't say I know him."

"Yeah," agreed Denton. "That's probably true for all of us, but then he's harmless. We just let him come along for the ride."

"Anyway, Denton, I can only stay for one. I have a really busy day tomorrow and I want to get an early start."

"OK." Denton frowned. "What day is it tomorrow?"

"Tuesday."

Denton turned away. "So this is what I did last night. No wonder you were crabby about me phoning you in three hours time to say that I was lost. You were probably asleep. Must make a mental note to save time by looking out for signs to help you direct me home."

Chapter Nine

Denton lay there, partially unconscious, partially blind and mostly paralysed.

Slowly, he came to. It was dark, as it usually was around this time. But there was something different. Number one was the fact that there was someone else in his bed. Number two was the fact that she was naked. Number three was the fact that, from the blurred and squinty outline, she looked incredibly similar to a secretary who worked on a different floor to him. Number four was the fact that she was staring at him with a smile.

"Morning, tiger. How are you this morning?" She said, as she got up and moved towards the door.

"I'm just fine, thanks," he said, or at least that was what he was trying to say but instead it no doubt sounded like, "Mmmmm mnphph hphpg."

Number five, which was probably the biggest issue for him to come to terms with was the fact that she wasn't alone since there was the distinct sound of another woman moving around on the floor. It was at this point that Denton, whilst not entirely sure when or how these women had gotten into his bed, thought it would be only polite if he could at least remember their names.

The First Secretary bent over and stroked the other girl's hair, who appeared to be totally half asleep but still acknowledged her with a broad smile and a giggle. She also looked liked a secretary from work. She opened her eyes and gazed up at First Secretary, then looked at Denton and giggled again, messing with her long blonde hair as she did so. Secretary Number Two got up and stretched to reveal that whilst she was wearing more clothes than the first this was limited to a black thong. The First Secretary took her hand and led her to the bathroom.

And if that wasn't enough, the biggest surprise was…

"Oh, fuck. Its Sunday again, isn't it?! Is it?" He mumbled to himself.

Denton lay there, his head pounding as if it really might just explode at any second. The lower half of his upper body ached as if his stomach had been playing Twister in the night with his liver and kidneys.

"Need clarification." he said as he rolled himself slowly to the edge of the bed.

"Fuck. Fuck," was about the only thing he could say and even then he was saying so to distract himself from the immense and constant pain he felt. He heard giggling from the bathroom and the sound of the shower running. "Hey Denton," shouted one of them, "You coming?"

"Go away." mumbled Denton in a feeble voice. "Let me die in peace."

He stumbled out of bed, on to his feet and searched for his dressing gown in the chaotic mess of pants, bras and trousers. He found it beneath a feather bower and a pair of Devil's horns.

What happened here? he thought, as he tried to fathom out how on earth he had come to be sharing a bedroom with two pretty attractive women. From his present state, he was supremely confident that he neither had been nor was in any way capable of being able to do anything remotely interesting or mutually gratifying with either of them, let alone both, so what happened?

He stumbled into the living room, where he found Randall asleep on the sofa, bolt upright with a third secretary lying on his lap. As usual, Randall was sat with his arms folded and head slightly tilted. You might call this surprise number six. By this stage Denton was beginning to wonder if this was just one big hallucination.

"RANDALL!"

"What?" said Randall waking with a start. Randall looked around and then, on looking down to his lap, briefly shrieked. From the confused, bordering on terrified look in his eye, Denton concluded that Randall was as clueless as he was on how this whole thing had happened.

"Randall, what day is it today?" he asked, holding onto his head for fear it may fall off if unattended.

"Sunday." and then looking around the room, with a frown on his face, "I think. I'm very confused."

Denton sighed. "I thought as much," he muttered. "How can it be Sunday again so suddenly? Why isn't more warning provided that it's on its way?" He looked at Randall decisively. "Right. That's it. Just forget it. There have been too many surprises this morning as it is. I'm going back to bed. Let me know when it's Monday again, will you?"

And with that he returned to his room, threw a pile of clothes out into the corridor, slammed the door, and went back to sleep.

Chapter Ten

The shining beacon of hope that is Wednesday

I'm making coffee again, anyone else notice that? thought Denton. If only he could say these things out loud. Sure, there was a risk that people would think him insane, but then there was also the chance that someone might look at him and say, *"Yeah, so am I. I swear that I was in bed five minutes ago, how did this happen?"*

So today is the shining beacon of hope that I like to call Wednesday, thought Denton, *which means that the weekend is not far away.* He sat down with his coffee and returned to the important job of bundling a bible of documents together.

"Bundling Bibles," Denton would explain to anyone who might listen, "is both a difficult and easy task at one and the same time. Bibles are used in all corporate transactions. They are a collection of all the documents that form the transaction. The idea is that anyone could pick up the bible and know exactly what had been sold, when and to whom. When a company is bought or sold, there are invariably reams and reams of documents that need to be signed. You would be surprised just how much paperwork even the smallest deal can generate. The most important document is usually the sale and purchase agreement since this is the one that orchestrates the entire deal. The clauses within it set out in detail the basic information, such as parties to the deal, the price, etc, but also more complicated provisions such as all the conditions that must take place before the matter can be concluded. Once these are in place and have been properly signed and dated the deal is done and everything that everyone wanted to do has been achieved."

Denton picked up a piece of paper and hole punched it.

"For everyone else, this is the point at which the fee-earning and to be frank the interest levels drop off. However, the work is not yet done. For example, there are forms that need to be filed at Companies House or the Land Registry and, more importantly, a bundle needs to be made of all the documents that make up the deal, which is called the 'Bible'. I do not know why it's called that, but it is."

Denton placed the paper in an A4 lever arch file and turned the page over, inserting a white page divider.

"Now, this may seem like an easy task since it involves the following process. First, take photocopies of the originals. Two, place the documents in lever arch files with dividers between the documents. Three, prepare an index that indicates what documents are in each file."

He turned the page over. A figure suddenly appears at the door. It was the partner who was in charge of the deal.

"Denton," she said holding sixteen pieces of paper in her hand.

"This index…."

Sixteen pieces of paper that I have spent every day for the last week typing up, thought Denton.

"…it's…"

Sixteen pieces of paper that took an age to write because I had to go through all these sodding documents and work out what each and every one of them did… thought Denton.

"…well, it's…"

…which would have been a lot easier had I been more heavily involved in the deal from the start and had the purpose of all these bits of paper explained to me rather than you treating me like the office tea boy… thought Denton.

"…it's wrong. It's all wrong."

…yeah there it is. Now that is job satisfaction. It feels really great to be praised after putting the hours in… thought Denton.

"Any particular reason why it's wrong?" ventured Denton.

"…well, it's just all in the wrong order, its just wrong…"

Well how helpful, thought Denton, *I'm so sorry, how remiss of me. Well, I'll stop pratting around now shall I and put it in the right order, which is of course, so blindingly obvious to someone who has never done a deal like this before and has no idea what these documents actually do in practice. Of course, how simple, I'll just put them in the right order then.*

Denton stopped adding the documents to the five volumes that he had already completed and looked grimly at the remaining high stack of so far unallocated documents.

"I do apologise. I shall come up with a new one," he said.

"Yes. And quickly as well, Voyle, I want this out by the end of the week, OK?"

"Of course," said Denton as he thought, *with clear instructions like that on how to rectify the problem, why wouldn't it go out that soon.*

The female partner moved towards the door. "Oh, and to speed up the process, I'm allocating a trainee from a different department to help you."

Please God, do not let it be Dom Peasgood. Please. I could not bear the questions, the relentless questions.

"I'm allocating Delia Longuerait to assist you from the Banking department, you should liaise with her for the best time to begin. I suggest you book out a meeting room for the day and sit with her until the job is done."

Oh God, thought Denton, *purgatory is finally upon me.*

The partner left. *Now, the dilemma is, do I work solid on getting the index right, then show the partner and leave the file as it is, by which time the job will only be half done. Or do I do the index again and re-arrange the file to match then show the partner, which will either be completely right or completely wrong again,* thought Denton.

"Hi," came the prissy and some might say, annoying, voice of Delia

Longuerait. *Or should I just leave them as they are and bat Delia over the head with them,* thought Denton as out loud he said, "Oh hi, Delia, just got the message that you were coming down, haven't had chance to book a room yet, allow me…"

"It's alright Denton, I sorted it out before I came down, I sent you a meeting request by e-mail. If you check your inbox you'll see that we're in room 5.15."

Damn it, this girl was good. What was it that Billy had said? thought Denton as he picked up the files, probably to gauge its weight to estimate how much pain it would cause Delia when he hit her with it.

"Shall we go?" asked Delia as she started to walk off to the lift, leaving Denton behind to pick up all the papers.

"Certainly," came the reply that she never heard.

In the room, Denton was his usual calm and composed self, whilst he made himself comfortable in his cedar/salmon pink lining combination chair, hot from MFI, surrounded by salmon pink and turquoise wallpaper in a room barely big enough for the files themselves let alone the files, a round table (also in cedar), three chairs, Denton, Delia and their respective egos.

As Delia spoke, or more rather dictated, Denton sat with something resembling a polite smile whilst he snapped several pencils under the table, which made a satisfying crack.

"Now," she said with that unmistakable air of smugness, "I understand that you have been experiencing a few difficulties with the index on Project Deepthroat, Denton." She sat with an incredibly straight back, which pushed out (without accentuating) her small pancake breasts that were neatly hidden beneath a white blouse and a cream cardigan. Her chin was permanently held high and her head perfectly straight. Her straight blonde hair was tied back in a plaited pony tail which hung in a straight line to the middle of her back. Her arms were bent neatly at ninety degrees to the table and in front of her sat a clean, crisp pad of paper and two black pens sat perpendicular to it. Her green eyes looked straight at, and pretty much through Denton who sat, slouched in his chair, opposite.

God, I hate her, thought Denton. *Everything about her is so bloody straight and by the book. She looks like a model for the Correct Posture Society. You could balance books on her head. Of course, if we get any more papers in here we might need to. Oh God, there she goes rabbitting away about what a bible does. Yes, dear, I know what they do. Now she's adopted her best condescending voice and is explaining the purpose of an ERISA letter and how the investment loan notes work. I'm not listening, sweetheart, so you might as well not bother. God, I hate her and her prissy voice and her long hair, and her big green eyes and her shiny, full, inviting lips and ….urgh. What am I thinking?*

Denton shook his head, without really thinking about it. Delia stopped. "Do you disagree?" she said.

"No. No," he said quickly. "Please, carry on."

Phew, got away with that, he thought. Anyway, deals. Deals work like this. Typically Company A wants to take over Company B, which might be for any number of reasons. Company B might have lots of cash in it. Company B might have one massive customer or client that Company A wants for itself. Company B might have a goodwill factor that Company A would like to use, for example, everyone knows and trusts Coca Cola, but not everyone has heard of Company A's Brand X. Now, and this would never happen, if Company A made a really good orange fizzy drink which tasted great but no one had heard of it, let's call it Timmy's Goodtime Orange, Company A could spend a fortune on advertising trying to convince Joe Public that Timmy's was the drink for him. But what if Company A could get the goodwill associated with Coca Cola behind it? Then everyone would instantly know it and you wouldn't have to spend half the advertising costs to get it bought by Joe Public at all. People would consume it simply because of the name. Not many are likely to touch Jimmy's Goodtime Orange whereas Coca Cola Orange - *"Are you kidding? I love that stuff!"* You see? Fanta. Ridiculous name, but it has the Coca Cola name behind it. Bet you drink that, don't you Delia. Oh yes, bet you like that, don't you, bitch? Oh yes…what am I doing?

So. Deals. So Company A wants to buy Company B but in order to do so, Company A has to be convinced that Company B is worth buying and also that Company B doesn't have lots of little expensive surprises that Company A could do without inheriting.

This is where we come in. We, as solicitors, will take a look at everything associated with the company (often, so will the accountants but there is no need to lower the tone of the conversation by introducing them at this point). This is called Due Diligence. How many machines has Company B got? How many workers? What state of disrepair are they in? The machines that is. Not the workers. Any litigation pending? Heath and Safety Executive been snooping around here lately?

And so on. This takes a long time and at the end of this process, Company A may decide that it really does not want to buy this Company B on account of the fact that all the machines are at the point of breaking down, the workers are striking over the pittance they get paid, consumers are suing on account of the impotence associated with drinking high quantities of the soft drinks Company B already makes and the waste products produced by making this stuff are poured away directly on to the site which now has more than a passing resemblance to Chernobyl.

It is because this might happen that neither Company A nor Company B is likely to want anyone to know about this deal before it is completed. Company A is unlikely to want anyone to know that it is interested in buying this company and Company B is unlikely to want its competitors to be able to take advantage of the mess that it is in. Therefore, both parties will sign up to a confidentiality agreement before the matter starts, ensuring that neither the parties nor their advisors will mention the prospect of the deal to anyone. As a result, we don't describe deals using real names, hence names like Project Albatross, which might signify a really big job. Project Phoenix might signify a deal involving the purchase of a company that is bought when moribund with the intention of improving its health.

"…so," said Delia, slamming a file down on the desk, "that's essentially what Project Deepthroat was all about. Now, shall we get started on the bible?"

Yeah. No, thought Denton, *I have no idea why this is called Deepthroat. I think that it was the Americans who named it. They're usually responsible for that kind of ridiculous name.*

Many hours later they were still there, shut up in that box room. Much had been accomplished, mainly due to Delia instructing Denton on what, from past experience, was the 'correct' approach.

Now, let's just dispel a myth here, thought Denton as he reflected on Delia's 'correct approach', *There is no correct way to compile a bible and as a simple deduction in logic, there is also no wrong way to compile a bundle either. As a result, the method that Delia was advocating was simply how she would do it.* Whether this would later tie in to what Denton's partner wanted would be another matter, though he suspected that the fact Delia had been brought in at all largely confirmed that whatever she did would be the correct way.

"We should probably rearrange this index entirely so that all the banking documents go into one volume, all the investment documents into another and then all the Companies House forms, board minutes, etc, into another," said Delia. "Would you agree Denton?"

Would it matter if I didn't? thought Denton.

"Yes, I agree," said Denton out loud. "After all, that's why I pretty much arranged them that way myself." he said in his own head.

"Now don't worry Denton, this re-arrangement is no reflection on your capabilities. I think that Felicia asked me to come and assist you simply because I have experience of putting together a difficult bible like this one from the time when I was in your seat," said Delia. The prissy voice was not helping if it really was her intention not to be massively condescending.

Felicia? thought Denton. *Jesus, Delia, there really is no kudos in being able to do this shit. It's a bollocks job. God you annoy me. I could do this myself if I didn't find it so immensely boring. It's a nothing task.*

Delia continued to drone on. "Yeah, yeah," said Denton.

"I beg your pardon?" retorted Delia.

Shit, thought Denton, *I thought I said that in my head.*

"Erm…yeahhhh, yeah. Just…er…agreeing with you there Delia," said Denton, slightly embarrassed.

"Oh," said Delia, "I see. Well, anyway, this is the way that I think we should do it but feel free to disagree."

Oooh, now there was a trap if ever I saw one, thought Denton, and whilst his mischievous side had been in overload throughout their incarceration, his professional side got the better of him. "I agree entirely," he lied.

"That was close," said Denton.

"What?" said Delia.

"Damn it!" exclaimed Denton.

Meanwhile and probably at the same time, Winston 'Badger' Thurlgood was sat in a doctor's waiting room.

I am not enjoying this experience, thought Badger, *everyone in this room has something wrong with them. Whatever they have, I don't want it.* He looked around, distrustful of all sat near him as he tried, where possible, to shrink back from everyone. As if on cue, the man next to him starting coughing violently, causing Badger to flinch and sneer with a pained expression. As the man finished, Badger could only glare at him, his face a picture of disgust. *I'd have been better off at home,* thought Badger, *why didn't I just stay in bed. I cannot believe that Billy persuaded me to come here.*

Suddenly a man came into the fore and, with a suitably dramatic and booming voice, he said, "Mr Winston Thurlgood please."

"That's me," said Badger, also holding a hand aloft, without really knowing why - as if this action was the back-up device to alert the doctor to his location in case the primary device of speaking out loud failed to do so.

The doctor led Badger into a room, which was small, had a bed up against one wall, and was hideously decorated in pastel colours perhaps in some desperate bid to make the room appear more soothing. On the walls were pictures of small children of various ages but they all appeared to be of the same couple of kids a few years apart from each other. It was probably a safe bet that they were his. Well, either that or he was stalking them and seemed to be comfortable enough with this to share it with all his patients. *Well, trust is a two way thing,* thought Badger, *maybe this admission is designed to put me at my ease.*

"Mr Thurlgood?" boomed the voice of his doctor, who could have been James Earl Jones (You know, the voice of Darth Vader in Star Wars. He was in other things too. Big deep booming voice, terrifying really).

For the last time, I don't know the location of the secret rebel base, thought Badger. "Yes," he said out loud, slightly startled.

"I asked what was wrong, Mr Thurlgood," said the doctor. *What was his name again?* thought Winston.

"Sorry, miles away there. Well, I've been having the same problem Dr…" quick flash at the practising certificate, "Bloomthorpe," said Badger, proud of his good recovery. "It's like this doctor: I keep falling asleep, all the time and no matter how much sleep I get during the day, I keep finding myself asleep even when I don't really feel tired."

"I see." said Dr Bloomthorpe in a manner that suggested he didn't. He leaned over and looked into Badger's eyes, pulling briefly at his bottom eye lids. Suddenly he shone a bright light into them, causing Badger to yelp. Then he leaned further in, to the point where Badger feared he was about to be kissed.

"Mmm," he said suddenly pulling away. He pondered, then scribbled something illegible down on a piece of paper.

"What is it, Doctor? Are you writing down a prescription?"

"What?" said the Doctor, suddenly distracted from his thoughts. "Oh, that? No, I suddenly remembered *'Friends'* is on tonight. I haven't set the tape recorder. Must remind Mrs Bloomthorpe."

Winston was more than a little disheartened.

Dr Bloomthorpe returned to his patient.

"Tell me, Mr Thurlgood, what is your diet like?"

"Erm, varied." said Badger, after much thought. And of course he wasn't lying. It was varied. Do you know how many different types of takeaway places there are in Clapham?

"And do you do much exercise?"

"Yes," said Badger. *To pick up the takeaways,* he thought.

Dr Bloomthorpe wrote down something else. "And what do you do for a living?"

"Well, I work as a night watch man at the moment at a warehouse. You know, it's not much, it's just a part time job. I'm hoping to get something more substantial soon, you know, I've been to university and everything, I just need to kick start my career."

"I'm not here to judge, Mr Thurlgood, I don't need a copy of your CV."

Badger now regretted the fifty pence he had spent making copies of it at the library, in readiness.

"And what would you like your career to be in?"

"Well. That's the part I need to kick start." said Badger sheepishly.

"Like I said, Mr Thurlgood, I'm not here to judge." *Blooming layabout students!*

He wrote down something else.

"Is it serious, Doctor."

"Tell me, Mr Thurlgood, have you suffered from this problem for long?"

"Well, yes, I have actually Doctor, at university it was referred to as the 'Thurlgood effect'. I would miss lectures through being asleep and would then fall asleep in the lectures that I did attend. Of course, being at university, no one really noticed since everyone pretty much did the same."

"I see," Dr Bloomthorpe removed his stethoscope from Badger's chest and looked at him one more time. He frowned and adopted an even more serious tone. "Son, is there any history of narcolepsy in your family?"

"No, Dr Bloomthorpe. To my knowledge no one has been involved in drugs at all in my family," said Badger in a manner sufficiently serious enough to convince the doctor that he was not kidding.

"No, not narcotics, Mr Thurlgood, narcolepsy. It's a condition whereby people fall asleep at short notice or for no apparent reason. Now, I can't say you've definitely got this without running more tests, it may be that you just need to do more exercise or eat more iron, but I think that you should at least be aware of the problem."

"Oh God," said Badger, "Is it life threatening?"

"Well, only if you were to fall asleep crossing the road as the number 17 bus came around the corner," chuckled Dr Bloomthorpe. This was the laugh that gave Badger the same chill that Darth Vader might if he were laughing in his face. He noticeably shrank back into his chair.

"I'm sorry, that was inappropriate," said Dr Bloomthorpe, wiping a tear from his eye. "My wife said I should use more humour at work in order to relieve the stress of it all."

"Oh," said Badger, slightly confused. "Is it working?"

"No. Not really," he said, shaking his head lamentably. "Mr Thurlgood, please take this leaflet on the subject and maybe check out if there are any Narcolepsy meetings happening in your area." He handed Badger a leaflet entitled *'You are not a freak, you are different and sometimes different is good'*. "It might be worthwhile going along and talking to a few people. In the meantime get some exercise and make sure that your iron intake is high. I'd like to see you again in three weeks if the problem persists."

An egg timer rang. Dr Bloomthorpe got up and walked to the door, holding it open.

"Thank you, Doctor," said Badger, sensing now was a good time to leave.

"Oh, and Mr Thurlgood," said Dr Bloomthorpe as Badger walked away from him, "don't drive your car anywhere near where I live, ok?"

Badger looked away in a moment of confusion, then looked at Dr Bloomthorpe, then nodded enthusiastically before walking away in confusion.

Dr Bloomthorpe, closed the door again. "Why do I listen to my wife?" he said, shaking his head, as he returned to his desk.

*****

Back in the cell, Denton was metaphorically beating his head against a brick wall, which, whilst being a lot less painful than the real thing, was in no way as satisfying.

"I'm sorry, Denton, but you're wrong, it simply does not go there," said a defiant Delia.

"OK," said Denton thinking, *Why do people insist on telling me where it doesn't go without giving me the benefit of informing me where it does go.* "Where should it go then?" he asked.

"Here," said Delia, literally moving the document one place forward.

"Fine," said Denton, he was sure she would have some complex explanation as to why but he really could not be bothered with that right now. Five hours. Five hours they had been sat in this god awful room. And what had they accomplished, really? Yes, the bible was nearly now complete but seriously - was it really any different to the way that Denton had done it originally?

"Nearly home time," said Denton.

"What? What do you mean?" said Delia, momentarily distracted and obviously not best pleased about it.

"Nearly time to go home?" said Denton, not entirely convinced that what he said originally required expansion.

"Yes. Of course."

"You doing anything tonight Delia?" It seemed only right to enquire even if he wasn't entirely bothered.

"Er. Well, you know," said Delia slightly sheepishly, "Nothing much."

Interesting, thought Denton, *what's the deal here? Why has the ice maiden suddenly gone quiet?*

"You?" asked Delia coyly.

Whoa, thought Denton. *Where did that broadside come from? Why has she any interest in what I'm doing tonight?*

"Will probably go out for a few cheekies after work, nothing special, I mean it is Wednesday, so it would only be right to celebrate," he said.

"Oh…" said Delia.

"Will probably just be me, Randall and a couple of my old university friends, if you're interested in coming…" Denton suddenly realised what he had said. *Was that intentional?* he thought.

Suddenly the temperature in the room shot up by a couple of degrees and the ice maiden was definitely thawing. She was thinking about it, he could tell. And for some strange reason, Denton could not work out if that was a bad thing or not. Before he could work that out, she shook her head as if shaking the idea from her thoughts altogether. "No thank you," she said, concentrating on placing paper in the Bible. "Maybe some other time."

Denton returned to pushing pieces of paper around the place. He was too engrossed by that and what had just happened to notice Delia glance at him.

"Interesting," said Denton, hours later in Vic Naylor's bar.

"What is?" said Randall. Both of them were sat around a table that boasted a marble top. The semi-circular seat stretched around the table and was covered in almost bright red leather that contrasted in a distinct but not unpleasant way with the dark brown wooden panelling on the wall. From the speakers came the sound of drum and bass, not loud enough to be classified as ear piercing, but certainly getting there.

Vic Naylor's was a good bar, but it was very narrow. On a weekday this was fine since not many people would be there and since the bar was so close to the seats, you could usually get served just by shouting in the barman's direction. Of course, shouting on its own wouldn't work on account of the music, so it was more a mix of shouting and gesturing, with the emphasis on gesturing. And of course, this was fine if you just wanted a couple of beers since it was just a case of pointing at the empty bottle in your hand and sticking your thumbs up. If you had a girl with you, you really had to think twice about the appropriateness or otherwise of this method when what she wanted was a 'sex on the beach' cocktail.

"Delia. I do not get her at all."

"What?" said Randall, shouting to be heard. "Oh, Delia?" There was a two second time delay between the message reaching his ear, battling past the lingering sound waves which were dawdling at the entrance, and getting to his brain. "Yeah, I don't either."

"What? Oh yeah. Right." said Denton.

"I mean, sometimes she will sit there at work…" Randall said - he appreciated that this was not a full sentence but saw no sense in having an entire string of words, with a verb chucked in as well, just getting tangled up around

Denton's lughole. Far better to do it in bite size pieces. "And snap at me…for not doing something correctly…"

Denton nodded.

"As if she wrote the book on it…which really winds me up…" continued Randall.

"Damned right," said Denton.

"But then there will be a moment…and just a moment mind…when she seems…"

Denton waited for Randall to finish.

"…"

Then he realised that Randall didn't actually know how to finish the sentence.

"Normal?" he suggested.

"Yeah," said Randall, "and almost fragile."

"Yeah, I agree." yelled Denton, the veins popping out of his neck. "Maybe - in reality - she's actually quite a nice girl - and it's all an act - the whole professional thing."

Randall nodded. "I THINK YOU'RE RIGHT" he shouted, then realised that the music had stopped. Everyone would have stared, had there been more than the three of them in there. The barman merely glanced up, he'd seen drunken men shouting a thousand times before - it was nothing new to him. He was confident that he would see it a thousand times again. Maybe he would pay more attention to it then.

"It…errr…it doesn't work though," said Randall, slightly embarrassed at being caught out. "It just comes across as annoying."

"You know what," said Denton slurping on a Michelob, "I think her problem is that, well, you know that expression, 'you can't kid a kidder?'"

"Yeah," nodded Randall, knocking back the remains of a San Miguel.

"Well it works the same way in a law firm. Don't go overboard on the professionalism in front of professionals, it just pisses them off. It's like when you hear someone give a really bad rendition of the law - which you know they heard from a bloke down the pub who had read it in the Sun - in order to tell you that what you are doing - whatever that is - is against the law. It's really irritating."

"Yeah, you're right." suddenly Randall looked around. "Is Billy ever coming back from the toilet? He's been gone hours."

"Seemingly not, there must be a queue and he's waiting for a cubicle to free up," said Denton. Suddenly there was a noise as Badger fell forward and banged his head on the marble worktop. Randall and Denton looked across at him as he lay there, his glasses askew and his deformed little ear pointing upwards.

"Must be a real blast in their household," said Denton as he and Randall both finished their drinks and left the bar.

Chapter Eleven

"Oh you are kidding me, right?"

"Nope," said Randall.

"You absolutely have to be." said Denton in disbelief, "Seriously, you must be."

"I'm not, I've checked three times, its correct," replied Randall.

"But how?" asked Denton, the disbelief now causing his voice to waiver.

"I have no idea, but I'm telling you it *is* Sunday."

"Seriously, it cannot be. It was Wednesday yesterday. It was. You've stolen my weekend. Give it back, it's not funny anymore."

"I know, Denton, I know," said Randall in a soothing voice, trying to comfort Denton by placing a manly hand on his not-so-manly shoulder.

They both sat down on their respective sofas in a state of pure confusion.

"Damn," was all Denton could manage.

"We could always go to church, Denton," ventured Randall with a straight face. Seconds later they both burst out laughing.

"I don't know why," said Denton, wiping a tear from his eye, "but that is still a good one."

Meanwhile, in church, God fearing folk were sat crapping their pants as the vicar continued to advise them that their current life destination was an unlimited stay at the House of Hades unless they repented now. Of course, a few of the braver ones sat there slightly peeved on the basis that they felt they had already repented by their mere presence alone. Others, of an even braver nature, were slightly aggrieved and agitated and wondered why they should continue to pay the entrance fee each week only to be berated in this way when actually they were doing nothing wrong in their lives to deserve this.

"Beware," moaned the vicar. "Beware the dark side."

Oh my goodness, I'm in a scene from Star Wars, thought the bravest of them all who had now reached the point where he refused to leave his sarcasm at the door anymore, tied by a leash, but was actively encouraging it to come in with him and share his pew.

"Satan. Satan is always ready to pounce, my flock of sheep, and I would encourage you all to ask the question, 'Am I doing enough to ward him off? Am I really thinking without sin?' Because we are all sinful my children…."

Seriously, is this entirely necessary? thought the Rebel, *I mean, I work hard all week. I pay my taxes regularly. I married a virgin. I'll die feeling like a virgin, or in any event, an unsatisfied man. I give regularly to charities. I read the bloomin' bible for all the good it does me, and I still get this lecture?! What more do I have to do?*

"...sinful. Oh yes, we all think evil, sinful thoughts..."

I mean, what it boils down to is, I'm miserable. I'm 63 years old. I'm sexually frustrated and I have been for nearly thirty years now. I have to look at Mrs Urmenthine's increasingly ugly face every morning and listen to her complain about her corns, which I might add are really, really grim, and I put up with all this just to get to heaven?

"...and it is wrong, my children, wrong to think of each other this way..."

Well, I will tell you one thing, matey, thought Mr Urmenthine, *there had better be plenty of fit, young, nubile women up there otherwise I shall be spending most of eternity at the complaints desk.*

"...it is wrong to want to enjoy the pleasures of the flesh..."

Oh, are you still talking? thought Mr Urmenthine, casually looking around to observe the other parishioners who seemed to be nodding along with the vicar like those dogs in the back of cars that you see from time to time, and if you're really unlucky, you see in those TV advertisements made by talent-less people. *No one is actually listening there Vicar, they are all in some sort of hypnotic trance. In fact, they're pretty much all old aged pensioners who have come for the free heating, or else are brainwashed students who have come to rebel against their parents' liberal free love attitude.*

"...and the spanking..."

What? thought Mr Urmenthine, suddenly paying attention. He looked around in a more obvious manner, *did anyone else just hear that?*

"...repent my evil herd of sinners, repent and chastise yourselves of your evil ways forthwith..."

Mr Urmenthine returned to his previous position, *what is wrong with this guy? Is anyone else actually taking this in?*

"...now my flock, let us sing hymn number 432 while I return to my vestry to chastise myself. Come now, young Tanya, help me with my chastisement." said the vicar as he led what appeared to be a very well endowed sixteen year old chorister back to the vestry with him. "Oh, yes..." he appeared to mumble as he went.

"What?" said Mr Urmenthine.

When the singing had stopped, the parishioners ascended en masse. "You hear that?" said Mr Urmenthine as he turned to Brian, who was sat next to him.

"Sorry, Mr Urmenthine, what?" said Brian, as he returned to earth from his self-induced daze, "I wasn't really listening."

"Oh, it doesn't matter. Forget it, Brian."

"Ooh, is that Brian?" said Mrs Urmenthine leaning across Mr Urmenthine who seemed less than pleased by the invasion of his personal space. His hands leapt into the air as if a cat had just jumped onto his lap.

"Oh, look who woke up." said Mr Urmenthine in despair.

"Hello, Mrs Urmenthine," said Brian

"Oooh, Brian, the flowers look lovely today," said Mrs Urmenthine.

Brian looked away, slightly embarrassed, "Err. Yes. They do."

"Yes, Brian, you did a lovely job."

"What are you talking about woman?" snapped Mr Urmenthine, "Can't you see that the boy has no interest in flowers?"

"Err. No," agreed Brian half-heartedly.

"Ooh, but he does, Herbie."

"...or you..." added Mr Urmenthine maliciously.

"Yes, but you did a lovely job, Brian," continued Mrs Urmenthine, completely oblivious to her husband's insults.

"She's as deaf as a post Brian, ignore her. She's also batty," he said, shaking his head. "I mean, as if you would be interested in the flowers?" he laughed as if he really did find the notion ridiculous.

"Err. Quite," was the best that Brian could manage.

"Now come on Hilda, we are leaving this place," said Mr Urmenthine shaking his legs slightly to encourage his beloved to shift herself. He probably should not have. That kind of thing could cause her to break a hip or something. *More's the pity that it doesn't,* Mr Urmenthine may have thought. "Come on Hilda, my legs are getting tired. Let's go home and get naked."

"Oh, OK Herbert," agreed Mrs Urmenthine.

"See Brian?" he said as they both pushed past Brian as he stood up, "She hasn't got a clue. Probably thought I was talking about doing the crossword or something."

"Did you say crossword, Herbert?"

"Yes, that's right dear, I want you to give me a blow job when we get home."

"OK dear, but we'll have to buy the paper on the way home since it didn't come this morning."

"It wasn't the only one," he lamented, "honestly why do I bother?" he said as they both disappeared out of God's sanctuary for the socially inept.

"Lovely flower arrangement this morning," said Mrs Fobwell as she hurried past Brian on her way out. Brian stood staring at the door.

As all the parishioners now went about their normal business and returned to their homes safe in the knowledge that the ironing that they were about to embark upon could, in no way, be described as sinful, Brian stood and tended to the flowers that he had so beautifully arranged that very morning.

"Why do I bother trying to hide it?" said Brian to any flower that would listen. "I like flower arranging. I'm a security guard that enjoys flower arranging. What is wrong with that?" he said tendering to a flower before he caught himself. "More importantly, what is wrong with me?"

He wandered across the floor to another set of flowers, "I mean it's not like I'm gay or anything is it?"

He moved to another set. "OK, so I watch Will and Grace on TV, usually over a bottle of wine, but you know, who doesn't? Right?"

At this point the vicar returned and it seemed to Brian that he looked slightly flushed. Tanya followed shortly afterwards wiping her mouth with the back of her red chorister sleeve.

Brian didn't seem to notice. "Ah, hello vicar," he said.

"Oh, hello Brian," said the vicar, slightly embarrassed, "Erm. I didn't expect anyone to still be around."

"Hello, Mr Grangle," said Tanya, spitting out a hair or something.

"Hello, Tanya, how are you?"

"Pretty good, apparently," said Tanya as she made for the exit.

Chapter Twelve

Thursday, a reason to celebrate

Denton's eyes opened. It was 7:19. *Yes,* thought Denton, *for once I have beaten the alarm clock. Just for once I am not going to have to listen to that god awful…*

Beep beep beep beep.

Bollocks.

Denton crawled out of bed like a car crash victim escaping from an overturned vehicle. "Oww. Oh God, another day, another hangover."

Cautiously, he put on the dressing gown and moved towards the door. On opening it he met Randall who was also moving very cautiously.

"Morning," whispered Denton.

"Morning," whispered Randall.

Shortly afterwards, the sound of two lethargic showers could be heard emanating very quietly from both bathrooms. On this particular morning, Denton was not in any mood to have a rant at his shower for its unpredictable behaviour. On this morning, Denton could not care less if turning the tap by precisely the same amount that he had done so on the day before produced a flow of water which did not have the same temperature as it had on the previous day. He was not interested that the water was barely tepid. Tepid was fine. Anything above freezing and below boiling was perfect for a man in as much pain as Denton; a man who was showering in the same way that you might expect an octogenarian with a bad hip to negotiate a shower. Slowly, Denton turned off the taps and got out of the shower. He went back into the bedroom. He could hear that Randall's shower was still going. Slowly, he got dressed and left his room. He could hear that Randall's shower was still going.

"Randall?" shouted Denton. "You nearly ready?"

"…"

Denton waited but no response came from Randall. "Oh well," he said to himself, "I'll see you later then."

It would be much later. Randall was fast asleep, standing up in his shower.

And it was today that Denton became his own worst nightmare: another one of the saunterers in the City. Slowly he ambled into work on the one day where he was very much glad to be living life in the slow lane. He would also have happily allowed anyone to execute him with a magnum for his inexcusable dawdling.

In work, it was much the same. Denton sat quietly at his desk trying at the very least to be inconspicuous and, at best, to be invisible. As a result, he was sat with a pad under his right hand, with a pen resting between his fingers, while his left hand supported and partially obscured the top of his head. Yes, today was definitely a day to pretend like you did not exist. It was certainly not a day when you wanted to hear someone say…

"Denton. Urgent deal on at the moment. We have a completion on today and we need you to help. You up to speed on Project Flimflam?"

Denton removed his hand and looked up.

"You alright there, Denton?" came the soft Irish tones of Devlin Hawkes, one of the partners in the unit. "You look awful. Are you coming down with something?"

"Er. No, well maybe," said a very uncomfortable Denton.

"OK, well I need you to go to see Colin, he'll give you all the info that you need."

Brilliant, completion, thought Denton. Now, 'completion' is a terrible word at the best of times, let alone when you're hung over. 'Completion' is the part of the deal where, after both parties have agreed that they want to go ahead with the deal and after their solicitors have agreed that the documents achieve what the parties want them to achieve, 'completion' is the part where the documents get signed by all the people who need to sign them and the deal is done.

Sounds simple, yeah? And yet, no. Completion is the most frustrating thing you'll ever have to do and if you never have to do it, then well done. It is a very slow and meandering beast. The reason why it is so slow is manifold. First, you have to get all the interested parties in one venue at the same time. This, in itself, is no mean feat. Secondly, once you have trapped the respective clients in different rooms, and even after you have told them that they are not leaving until they have signed, you will still encounter problems on account of the fact that this is usually the part where the clients start to get a little edgy. It's like a form of cabin fever. You keep several people trapped in a room together who have money at stake in seeing a deal go through, and suddenly they're panicking about everything. The problem is of course, the longer you leave them alone, the more focused their minds become on the reason why they are being held captive. They start thinking about the documents that they had previously given their consent to. They ask to take another look at them before they will sign them. Then, if they start to read the documents, they start to spot things that they might have previously missed or glossed over. Letting your client actually read the document they are about to sign, before they sign them, is a real school boy error.

"Are you absolutely certain that this document does what we want it to?", they will typically say, *"I'm not sure that it does, perhaps we could just change this little bit?"* *"No, we really don't need to,"* you will advise them. *"Yes, that's as maybe, but I'd feel slightly happier if you would do,"* they'll say. Now, I think here the problem is that clients do not appreciate just how many hours it has taken the lawyers to agree the wording on clauses, how many telephone conversations have been had, which

have been along the lines of "*Now, my client would rather the 'may' in the third line of clause fourteen be changed to 'should' and the 'will' in clause 7 be diluted by adding 'use reasonable endeavours,*" to which the response may have been, "*well I appreciate that, but my client cannot accept the change from 'may' to 'should' without adding 'if appropriate' and we will only accept 'best endeavours' from your client in respect of clause 7*". That kind of conversation can go on for days and days, and so to have those negotiations take place and be resolved in moments is not as simple as it may appear, primarily because every time a single word is changed every lawyer around the table will try to come up with some highly convoluted example of how the clause might now be used to disadvantage his client in a way that it could not have done before.

Third problem then becomes the issue of waiting. Waiting occurs because the solicitors then all have to go back and type out all these bloody amendments that they have just made. This usually leads straight into the fourth problem which is that one of the signatories, and I'm sorry, but it's always a female, will start to complain. "*This is taking a jolly long time. Could we not speed it up a bit?*" To make matters worse, the complaining is usually done to a trainee, which is akin to saying to Ted Ramsbottom, the eponymous Local Councillor of Ramsbottom Town Council, "*You couldn't just speak to the Prime Minister about changing a few of those more burdensome laws, could you? Thanks awfully.*"

You'd like us to speed up a bit? Oh God, sorry. Yes, of course, right away. How rude of us to take this long. In our defence, we were all getting so giddy rushing around making needless amendments at your behest and generally trying to sort this deal out for you that we clean forgot about how important it was that you attend your bridge session tonight. I tell you what, I'll just round up the others, which won't be hard since they're just sat in the next room, smoking fags, having a laugh and generally not doing much other than sitting on their hands, and I'll tell them to stop messing around and get the job done. Is that OK? I mean, personally, I can understand your frustration, I mean you're just sat here, with nothing more to look forward to other than walking away at the end with £10,000,000 simply for being a sleeping shareholder on account of your husband buying shares for you in this company, whilst my colleagues and I, who have been working until the small hours each and every day for the past week, why we get to go home, have four hours sleep and then go back to work. Ooh, I know, it's totally selfish on our part, in fact, it's inexcusable. And you're right, as the trainee, in many ways, I am the one that is completely responsible for this hold up. Please excuse me, I just got so wrapped up in listening to you constantly whinge, whine, sigh and generally pull faces whilst persistently looking at your watch, that I really just did not want this magical time to end.

Thankfully for the firm and for his job, Denton didn't tend to say these things out loud.

He hauled himself up from his chair, grabbed a biro and a pad of note paper and headed in the general direction of Colin Hooley's office, walking slowly in a bid to stand a greater chance of not walking into inanimate objects. In his head, he was constantly berating the fact that the office was generally spinning more than he would otherwise prefer.

He walked into Colin's room without warning. Fortunately, Denton was not paying enough attention to notice either Colin's look of complete despair or the fact that he stuffed a leaflet on impotence into his desk drawer as soon as Denton wandered in.

Colin looks a little pink in the cheeks, thought Denton, *I wonder if he was out on the razzle last night as well?*

"Ah, good morning Denton," said Colin, who suddenly frowned, "Are you feeling alright? You look a little white."

"Er. Yes. Although I think I might be coming down with flu or something."

"Well, Denton, you know, there's a lot of it around at the moment, you should be careful," said Colin in a genuine and serious voice, and then he lowered his voice and pointed upwards as if 'they' were listening. "It's the air conditioning. Bad thing, spreads lots of germs. Plays havoc with your immune system."

"Yes...." agreed Denton, but only for something to say. "Anyway, I'm here about Project Flimflam - Devlin sent me."

"Ah, yes. Project Flimflam. That is completing today. Interesting deal, although there's no point boring you with the details now, Denton."

"No," said Denton outwardly whilst thinking, *But you'll expect me to know the damned thing inside out by the time the Bible needs doing.*

"Essentially, Denton, we'll need you to prepare the Companies House forms today. Here is a copy of the various board meetings, if you could do this by 12 so that I could have a look at them first, that would be great."

"Yep, no problems," said Denton.

"Oh. Also, you'll need to work with Delia...er...Lounge-Rat is it? You should probably e-mail her to set up a meeting room or something."

"Yep, no problems," lied Denton. *Christ, why her again? Why always her?* thought Denton, although he had to admit it that it did beat working with Dom. It was also quite funny to hear Colin say her name wrong and so it was perhaps ill-advised though understandable that he should respond to Colin's next question in the terms in which he did.

"It is pronounced Lounge-Rat, isn't it?" asked Colin.

"Well, I'm not sure," said Denton vindictively, "although I don't think that I have heard it said any other way."

"OK," said Colin, "Well, I'll leave you to arrange a meeting...."

Denton started to move to the door with a wicked smile on his face.

"Oh, hang on a minute," said Colin. "I need to speak to her myself anyway so we might as well ring her now."

Colin pressed the speaker phone button on his telephone and dialled Delia's number.

"Hello, Finance department...." came the response.

"Hello, can I speak to Delia Lounge-Rat please?"

"..." You could almost feel the heat from her face even from Colin's office and you could certainly imagine her little face fuming. *This is great.* thought Denton. *What a great way to cure a hang over.*

"This is Delia Lonnn-je-rayyyyyy speaking," she said over-exaggerating the French origin of her name.

And whilst Denton found this hysterical in his head, Colin hardly seemed to even notice the point that Delia was making. In fact, it was possible that he was hardly even listening.

"Ah, Delia, hello, it's Colin Hooley here, I have Denton Voyle with me as well, we're phoning about Project Flimflam."

"Ah yes, I've just sent Denton an e-mail about setting up a meeting. I've booked a room through reception already. I thought it would be a good idea to go through what needed to be done on the deal, what documents needed signing and how best to utilise Denton's time and my own in order to facilitate the process."

Oh God, thought Denton. *Why does she have to be so bloody efficient? It just isn't normal.*

"Very good Delia," said Colin, "That's excellent, although Denton won't have read that e-mail yet - he's been in with me. Now I just wanted to run a few points past you on where we are with the banking documents."

Resentment poured out of Denton. Actually, it was more the hangover that he was currently sweating out, but the point was the same. This was too akin to a red Ragboy to a bull. Things became worse when Delia then proceeded to spend the next five minutes droning on about the bleeding banking documents. It was perhaps politically incorrect to do so but given the enormity of Denton's hangover he could not resist the temptation to perch on the corner of Colin's desk and mess with one of his stress balls, much to Colin's obvious annoyance.

"Well, thank you Delia for such a comprehensive explanation," said an exasperated Colin. He pressed the hands free button again, disconnecting Delia.

And so Denton found himself in a meeting room with Delia, inexplicably holding a cup of coffee that he had absolutely no recollection of making.

"Well," said a disgruntled Delia as she moved a few papers around, "you could perhaps have offered to make me one."

"Sorry," said Denton sincerely. *I don't even remember making one for myself,* he thought.

And so for the rest of the day, Denton and Delia sat in their usual tiny meeting room, arranging papers to be signed and generally not doing much to progress the matter despite their best efforts to that effect.

"Looks like this could be a long one." said Denton. "Do you know if the clients have arrived yet?"

"Don't think so," replied Delia.

Denton glanced at his watch. It was 4.17pm. Stage one had not even been accomplished yet and so there could be no way that anything would be completed until at least 9pm.

"Did you have any plans for tonight then?" asked Denton, running out of things to do and say.

"No, not really," replied Delia. "I suppose you had a long night of drinking planned though."

There was venom in that reply, Denton was sure of it. "Well, yes. If we get out on time, you are more than welcome to join us."

"No thank you," replied Delia, as cold as ever. "I don't drink during the week," she said as if she may continue, "and neither should you."

Denton wondered why Delia was acting in such an odd fashion. Naturally, he was kind of paranoid. After all, at the end of their last incarceration together they had been getting on quite well and Denton wondered what had happened. Since then they had not spoken at all and he had not even seen Delia around. He was also more than a little edgy because he was acutely aware of the fact that Delia had grown friendly with one of the secretaries in her department whom Denton believed to be one of the secretaries he had found in his bedroom that time. He wondered if they had been gossiping about him. He hadn't exactly been at his most generous when she had finally left his bedroom and he had not spoken to her since (and he was not really that aware of ever speaking to her before either). Perhaps this was the reason for Delia's new, reinforced, cold treatment of him. But then why should he care what she thought?

Desperately, he tried to think of something to say but at this stage the hamster had well and truly fallen off its wheel. Probably with a miniature bottle of JD in its tiny little paw.

"So…." he began without really knowing how he would finish his sentence, "……are you going to the corporate weekend away? I know it's coming around soon."

"Yes."

"Yeah, me too."

Why God, why? As if the hangover was not punishment enough…. thought Denton looking forlornly at the ceiling. If everyone knows God is omnipresent then why do they always look up?

"Weekends away", Denton had told Billy only the other night, "are when an entire unit goes away for the weekend to some remote location. There is an urban myth that these locations are places like Barcelona, Paris and Madrid. In reality, they are held in such conference heavyweight towns as Bury St Edmonds, Peterborough or Melton Mowbray."

They were in Fluid bar at the time, another dimly lit bar, sat on two marshmallow seats. Fluid is a pretty ordinary bar but the unique selling point is that it has loads of old arcade games in it.

"OK," said Billy, only half listening as they played two player 'Pac-man', whilst sat at opposite ends of a small table that had a small screen built into it.

"It is sold as a 'team building exercise' but in actual fact, it's just an excuse for partners to leave their wives for a weekend, get absolutely shit-faced and then letch over all the fit (and not so fit so long as there is sufficient cleavage on show) female trainees in the hope that all the money and power will be enough to get them into bed."

"And does it work?" said Billy, noticeably miffed at the fact that he had just been eaten by a yellow blob.

"Yeah, sometimes," said Denton. "Some of the female trainees get convinced that it will enhance their prospects of being taken on at qualification if they lay a partner or two, even though most of them are married."

"And does it?"

"Bollocks," said Denton, as his little man got eaten by the blue blob he had just walked into. "Yeah, mostly. On the whole, partners respond well to blackmail."

"Oh."

"Annoyingly, these trainees tend to be the ones that have fucked up the most," he said, knocking back an Asahi while scrabbling in his pockets for another 20p. "I mean every trainee has a fuck up story but some of these ladies really take the biscuit."

With his search for more coinage ending in futility, he looked hopefully at Billy. Billy tutted but duly obliged, rummaging around in his pockets for silver pence pieces. On finding enough, the game began again.

"There are some great fuck up stories though. One guy was working as a trainee in the DRG."

"The what?"

"DRG. Dispute Resolution Group. Dispute resolution is the PC term for litigation these days. Clients don't like the word litigation. It upsets them. Litigation is long, laborious and highly expensive. Depending on the severity, some litigation can take between two to six years. If points are appealable, that bad boy can keep going for a decade. That's why solicitors use the term DR. DR implies that the matter might be resolved a different way. Perhaps through arbitration, mediation or even early settlement."

"Oh."

"So anyway, one guy was working in DRG. His job, which was quite boring to be fair, was to compile bundles of all the documents that the firm would seek to rely upon in proving their case. Some of these bundles contained original documents. Hey!" shouted Denton in delight, "I just got a cherry!"

"Good for you." said Billy.

"Anyway, we're talking about a lot of documents and hence a lot of binders containing them. After a hard day of compiling, this guy had finished the job but since there was not enough room on the table, he put the binders on the floor. Damn it," cursed Denton. "My hand slipped and that thing just ate me."

"Oooh. Nasty."

"Next morning, he comes into work, sits down, switches on his computer, makes himself a coffee, then realises that something is wrong. No binders. After twenty seconds of panicking, it slowly dawns on him that maybe the cleaners have thrown them away."

"So what does he do?" asked Billy.

"What could he do except take a headlong dive into the industrial sized refuse bins."

"What, in his suit?"

Denton nodded.

"God, that's awful. Did he find them?"

"Yeah, but no one thanked him for it."

"Why, it wasn't his fault,"

"No. No, they didn't thank him because he stank. And he didn't thank himself either since he'd just ruined a £300 suit."

"Was this you?" ventured Billy.

"No!" sneered Denton. "Another example. A girl, this time working in Construction. Again, litigation is involved, only this time, the people that have brought the claim have gone very quiet to the extent that the solicitor in charge thinks that they are neglecting this claim and not working on it. The partner in charge reckons the silence is due to the fact that there is no case to answer. He asks the trainee to fax a form to the Court, which would basically ask the court to end the proceedings on the basis of his client having no case to answer. This is not a risky tactic but in order to maximise his chances he did not want to put the other side on notice of what he was doing and therefore just wanted to fax it to the Court."

"Right."

"In these circumstances, it is generally not a good idea to fax your form through to other side in the mistaken belief that the number you have written down is the Court's fax number and not theirs."

"Is that what she did?"

"Yep."

"Oops."

"Yeah. I don't think that the partner in charge took it all that well. It's times like that a girl should have seriously consider getting under his desk and getting her hands dirty."

"Did she?"

"Probably. Damn it. Lost again. Fancy a game of Space Invaders?"

By the time that it got to 3 am, Denton and Delia had reached the point where they were beginning to think that they had been forgotten altogether, sat as they were in that tiny meeting room. Even when Devlin Hawkes opened the door, his look of almost surprise did not do much to inspire them into believing that they were an integral part of this deal.

"Thought that you guys might appreciate some champagne." said Devlin.

"Have we completed then?" ventured Denton.

"I'm afraid not," said Devlin, "but we have decided to break out the champagne early although no one seems to want any just yet."

Devlin deposited a tray of twelve full glasses of champagne in the room and promptly left. After five glasses had been consumed, Denton and Delia seemed a lot more relaxed about the whole idea of 'working' (in its loosest sense) at such a ridiculous hour.

"I'm sorry, but sometimes you are so stuck up," said a tie-less and generally more dishevelled Denton who was slouching in his chair.

Luckily for him, Delia took the insult well.

"I know. Sometimes I am, I know. But I just get so frustrated when things do not go my way or if things are not done how I want. I get quite stroppy," said an equally dishevelled Delia, whose usually pristine tied up hair was hanging out in places. On noticing this, she pulled her hair bobble out and her long hair was released. She attempted to re-adjust it and put it back up again, but Denton stopped her, grabbing her hand.

"Leave it," he said. "It looks good down."

At first, Delia looked slightly startled by Denton's reaction but then her eyes betrayed her. It seemed to Denton that she actually quite liked it when he was masterful.

"Thank you." she said. "I will."

Denton, for the first time, felt very relaxed in front of Delia. In fact, he almost liked her. Maybe it was just curiosity. Who was Delia Lounge-rat?

"It was very funny what happened to you earlier in the day," ventured Denton. This was certainly a brave move and would test whether Delia felt the same as Denton.

"What do you mean?" she asked.

"Well, when Colin mispronounced your name."

There was a slightly awkward moment of silence which was shattered when Delia burst out laughing, which caused Denton to laugh too, though mainly out of sheer surprise that she had not taken offence.

"I know! No one can pronounce my name and I find it really annoying!" she smiled.

"Well, you're telling me, with a name like Denton Voyle? I get all sorts of variations."

"Well, I can imagine, although mine tends to be the mispronunciation that gets to me the most. What's the funniest variation that you've had then?"

"Oh, I dunno, I get all sorts. I've had Dennis, Benton, Benson, Brendan, Bruno - which was probably the weirdest - then I've had Boyle, Royle, Foyle."

Delia chuckled, "Boil!"

Denton smiled, "Annoying isn't it? What annoying variations do you get?"

"Well, nothing that good. But I used to get called Rat at University, which annoyed me. You know, as in the whole Lounge-Rat thing - I get that a lot."

"Rat," chuckled Denton. "I like that..." he grinned.

Delia pulled a face of mock horror and started to slap Denton in a playful way, "Well, you had better not start calling me that on a regular basis!"

The door opened which caused Denton and Delia to sit up straight in the hope that it would not be apparent that they were now slightly intoxicated. Devlin Hawkes was at the door again.

"We've completed. You're free to go," said Devlin, who had suddenly taken on the mantle of a jailer. It was 5.20 in the morning.

"We should do this again sometime," smiled Denton as he looked at Delia who could do nothing but burst out laughing.

"Maybe not," she said, although she might later admit that in many ways she had enjoyed the night. She would not admit, however, to anyone, that Denton Voyle was the last thing that she thought about before she fell sound asleep that morning.

Chapter Thirteen

"Denton."

"Nope."

"Denton."

"Seriously, Randall, no."

"Denton, it's the phone. It's your mum. I think that she just wants to know that you are still alive or something," said Randall from outside the door.

Denton reluctantly sat up in bed and looked at the door. His head pounded as he did so, caused by all nine pints of blood rushing past his ears at tremendous speeds, screaming "Stop, stop! I want to get off!"

"Well, just tell her that I'm not. Tell her that is the reason that I cannot come to the phone right now."

"I don't think that is going to appease her much, Denton."

"Well then would you kindly inform her that it is Sunday and I am not moving until Sunday plays fair and just goes away."

From outside the room, Randall looked confused.

He was not the only one. Colin was also slightly confused. As he sat there in his big double bed wearing his brushed cotton PJ's, he accompanied his wife in holding up the duvet as they both peered underneath in confusion, staring at the same inanimate object that Colin was once so proud of. Embarrassed, he looked away whilst his wife had another going at prodding it, like a snake charmer encouraging the beast to wake up by poking it with a stick.

"Nope. It is definitely not playing today, dear," said Colin. "Perhaps we could just talk instead."

His wife was obviously not satisfied (*'and not for the first time'* she might say) by this response.

"Oh come on, Colin, can't you try a little harder?" she said, unable to hide her frustration.

Colin now looked totally uncomfortable and thoroughly embarrassed at the whole situation. "Well, you know I'm under a lot of pressure at work," said Colin as his wife continued to wiggle her hand under the cover in frustration and certainly without much tenderness at all. From the concentration on her face, she was obviously taking this business very seriously.

"Yes, Colin, but I *need* this," she begged.

Colin seemed oblivious. "I mean, my application for partnership is due for review soon."

"Yes dear, now come on!"

"...and Mr Muftny is likely to take his business elsewhere..."

"Concentrate Colin…"

"…for that big titted bitch, God I would love to strangle her until she chokes…"

A look of surprise suddenly spread across his wife's face. "Ooh, I think that it is working Colin. Look!" she said pointing.

Distracted, Colin dropped the grimace from his face and had a quick peek, which had the effect of scaring the turtle (who had begun to show a little interest in what was going on) back into its shell.

Collectively, they both sighed. "Oh well," said Mrs Hooley, "Have lost interest myself now." She slammed her hands onto the sheets in frustration and squeezed the covers with tight fists.

Colin stood up and put his dressing gown on. "Cup of tea, dear?" He walked to the window. "Oh look, dear. I think the new pool boy has arrived."

As Colin left the room, Mrs Hooley got up and peered out of the window. She stared at the twenty year old whilst he removed his T-shirt. His rugged body exposed, he grappled with the net to skim leaves from their swimming pool. As he did so, Mrs Hooley's eyes glazed over as she watched the gentle waves, forming from the entry of his net into the waters, lapping softly at the edges of the pool. The sun glistened and reflected onto his bronzed body. Absent-mindedly, she stroked the top of her leg through her silk negligee.

Chapter Fourteen

Friday, at last and not before time

"Meeting clients is always very interesting," Denton would tell people, "Quite often this is someone that you have spoken to over the phone or have sent e-mails to, so you might already know a little about them before you meet them in the flesh. It is always a surprise though to see how they look in real life and whether this marries up to the image that you had in your head. Of course, the answer is always that it doesn't. The woman who had the sexy, husky voice over the phone always turns out to be a chain smoking, buck-toothed pig. The bloke who sounded like the kind of guy who would be a real laugh if you were out drinking with him inevitably turns out to look like he's on day release from the mental institute for the criminally badly dressed. And there are the people who work for the council who always, always, always wear really cheap suits with horrible print ties. Or the blokes who work in construction who always look like caricatures of themselves."

"But then as a trainee, you don't always get exposure to a client. If it's a particularly big deal or a new deal, you might not even know who the key players are. This is why when you meet them for the first time, it's usually a good idea to remember what they are called. It's this part that I don't seem to be able to get my head around."

Denton found himself stood in the kitchen stirring sugar into a cup of coffee, or at least something designed to have the taste and texture of coffee but which inevitably didn't. He wasn't entirely convinced that it wasn't still Sunday and he was either dreaming or was actually in work on completely the wrong day. Anyone who came into the kitchen at that point would no doubt have been slightly concerned by the strange behaviour of the trainee that they saw there, who seemed lost and generally confused by everything around him.

He returned to his desk, delighted by the fact that he had a new e-mail waiting for him. This feeling soon passed though when he realised that it was in fact new mail from Colin. Denton couldn't altogether rule out the possibility that he tutted out loud on realising this. Reluctantly, he got up from his desk again and wandered down the corridor to see what the big man wanted. When he got there, he discovered that Colin was missing, although probably not presumed dead. Denton turned to Gladys, but she wasn't there. Instead another secretary was sat in her place.

"Is Colin around?"

"Yes, he's just popped into meeting room one. One of his clients has turned up unexpectedly wanting some advice."

"Oh right. Where's Gladys?" asked Denton.

"Oh, she's on holiday for the next two weeks. I'm just covering for her. I'm Amber."

"Oh, hi Amber, I'm Denton."

"Hi. Did you want to see Colin then?"

"Yeah, he told me to come see him. Would you tell him that I did?"

"Certainly, yes. Now hang on, let me find a pen so that I can write that down."

Denton rolled his eyes and only half hoped that she hadn't seen him. He could just tell that this simple task was going to take her a lot longer than it probably should have.

"The thing about secretaries is, there are three types," Denton would often say. "The first type is usually always miserable. This may be because they have issues with their boyfriend, their lover or their husband. It may be because they don't feel that they are paid enough. For whatever reason it is, everything they do is greeted with the kind of reaction that demonstrates they consider that asking them to actually do some work is a totally unreasonable request for you to make. Every time you approach them, you are creating an unacceptable interruption to their busy social life. These type of secretaries are recognisable by their permanent scowl, which is evident even when they're not scowling, by embittered angst driven wrinkles carved into their foreheads like scars borne from conflicts of war. Only approach these secretaries with work when you are both a) desperate and b) not particularly attached to your testicles or the idea of having children."

"The second type of secretary smiles a lot and acts as if nothing is too much trouble. Beware of this kind of secretary. They are just lulling you into a false sense of security. The fact that they are so keen should be a warning sign. Usually keenness is a very shallow façade behind which lurks ineptitude, incompetence and, more generally, a complete lack of ability. Every time you give them work you must do so in the knowledge that it will be too much trouble for them and they will get it completely wrong."

"The third kind are like gold dust. They will do your work for you. They are excellent at their job but they also know that the competition is extremely sparse. If you push these secretaries too far they will never do your work for you again. You must treat them gently and, where possible, buy them flowers regularly. If your wife gets jealous, that's fine, you can always find another wife - but you will never find another secretary like this one."

Denton chose not to think about which category Amber fell into, but since he was not inclined to buy her flowers, he thought that that was quite indicative.

"Bear with me a minute," said Amber, scrabbling around. "Can't find a pen that works. So. Right. Here's one. Right. What is your name again?" she said, predictably poking her tongue slightly out of her mouth as she battled with the complexity of it all.

"Denton. Denton Voyle." said Denton as politely as possible in the circumstances as he bit his lip to stop himself saying. "You might remember that name from the name that I told you I was called not more than twenty seconds ago."

"Right. Denton. Is that D....E....N....T....E....N?" she asked.

Denton started to correct her then realised that he was hungover, he had been stood up now for more than five minutes and all the blood rushing around past his ears was a good indicator that he should return to his desk and sit down as soon as possible.

"N....Yes. Yes it is. Denton. Spelt Denten. That's right. Well done."

Amber smiled, as if she was actually pleased with herself.

"OK, which department are you from?"

No. It was no good. He was struggling to maintain his composure. "This one. I'm from this one. I sit at the end of the corridor. This one."

She looked at him blankly.

He sighed loudly, but it was no good. "Corporate Finance," he said wearily.

"Thank you," she said. "Corporate Finance." No doubt she wrote corperete finance.

"Oh," said Amber, slightly startled. "Denten Voyle, Corperete Finance." She looked at him and back at the pad. There was a pause that was just slightly too short for Denton to say, "Is there a problem?" but just slightly too long for him not to say anything at all. It was as if the hamster had fallen off his wheel and was struggling to clamber back on.

"I've got your name and department written down here too," she said as if she was secretly thinking, *How can that be?* She looked at Denton again and then back at the pad. "Oh, it's next to another message. Colin says can you meet him in meeting room one. He has a client in there."

A thousand questions passed through Denton's mind, all in disbelief, ranging from such questions as *but surely you wrote that message down - why did you not think of it when I said my name?* right through to *How has the process of 'natural selection' not eradicated people like you yet?* He didn't say any of them out loud. Neither did he grab her scrawny neck and start shaking until her large hoop earrings dropped off.

Exasperated, Denton could only just manage, "Thank you," before wandering off.

"You're welcome, Denten," smiled Amber.

Denton grabbed a pad and a pen as he walked past a stationery cupboard and meandered down to meeting room one, stopping on the way to make sure that his tie was straight and looked more or less like he hadn't put it on whilst completely hungover and in the dark. Of course, he had, but he did not want his tie to give him away, although in fairness the rest of him probably did anyway.

He knocked at the door before entering but obviously not hard enough.

"Well, Colin, it's no great loss. I hear the man was completely crooked."

"Really?"

"Oh yes. Word has it he's dealing with some very dodgy people. Very dodgy. Take Gunt, for example." Colin's client was about forty and sporting the world's least convincing ginger beard. It was terrible. It was patchy, sparse and to be honest, it had more in common with the aftermath of a bush fire than a beard.

"It still bothers me though. I mean, we really should have spotted that typo. Mr Muftny was not impressed that the deal did not go through," said Colin.

"Muftny will get over it," said Bushbeard. "As I said, it's no great loss. The law will spot his dodgy dealings sure enough and you wouldn't want to be associated with that, would you?"

Colin blushed and looked away.

Can they not see me? thought Denton. He gently coughed and when that did not work, he wandered straight up to the table.

"Oh, hello Denton. Thanks for coming down." He turned to Bushbeard, who did not get up. "This is my trainee, Denton Voyle."

Denton extended his hand.

"Oh, what happened to the blonde girl. She was very nice," said Bushbeard, not accepting Denton's hand, even though it was just hanging there, with nothing better to do.

"I know," said Colin ruefully, "but they all rotate seats every so often." Denton still had his arm extended.

"Pity. She was tasty."

By now Denton's arm was seriously starting to ache and he was beginning to wonder whether he had completely misunderstood the practice of shaking hands.

But then the moment of truth - Bushbeard extended a grubby fat ginger freckled hand. "Denton this is…."

Now, everyone knows or at least everyone should know that shaking hands is one of the most common ways that people judge other people. Denton thought. *If you have a limp hand shake, soggy handshake, or the kind of handshake that it so firm it brings tears to people's eyes, then they will always associate you with that. It is, therefore, imperative, absolutely imperative, that you get the handshake right first time, no messing.*

Denton obliged by placing his hand in to Bushbeard's and squeezed firmly but not too firmly, shaking lightly but not so lightly that he looked like a nonce, and not too wildly that he looked like he was trying to remove the guy's arm in one single movement. *Excellent,* thought Denton. *A perfect handshake.*

"Pleased to meet you," said Bushbeard.

What? thought Denton, *What was his name? Damn it! Did I miss that part again? Every time!*

"Denton, the reason that I've asked you into this meeting is because I want you to take an attendance note."

Denton smiled, sat down and duly opened his Pukka note pad.

Damn it! thought Denton again. *Attendance notes really suck. You have to sit there listening to two people witter on, in no particularly logical way bouncing from one topic to the next, then coming back to something they had said earlier before hinting at something they may say in the future but never do. And at the end of it, you have to go back to your desk to make a coherent note out of the whole sorry affair.*

"OK, so from the discussions that we have had so far, I understand that you want to acquire a Scottish salmon distribution company," said Colin.

How hard would it have been for Colin to have mentioned the client's name there?, thought Denton. *Now every time that he speaks I'm going to have to either put a big question mark next to it or just refer to him as capital B. Either of which is going to look embarrassing when I have to type this thing up. Damn it, Denton, pay attention! You're going to miss all of this if you do not concentrate.*

"…found a great company that might be ripe for a take over. I've got some great ideas for how I can build up the business. There's always a market for salmon, it's just a question of contacts and marketing angles."

Great, well I missed the start of that bit. I can't exactly ask him to repeat that bit now can I? thought Denton.

"…you want this to be a business acquisition or a share acquisition?" asked Colin

"The difference being?" asked B/?

"Well, in a share acquisition, what you are buying is the entire share capital of the company. In effect, you will own the company, lock, stock and barrel. You will get everything, warts and all. If you make a business purchase, you can decide which bits you wish to acquire and which bits you want to leave behind. For example, you might acquire the depot, plant and machinery, but not the lorries or other assets. Basically, you can pick and choose what you want to take and what you don't, within reason."

"Oh, OK, I understand. No, I want to acquire everything. I've already spoken to Mr Mackenzie about purchasing everything. He is the single shareholder of the company. There are three directors and he is the chairman."

"OK, what is his full name?"

"Spurt Mackenzie. S…P…U…R…T," said B/?, as if that were an actual name.

"Spurt. Is that short for anything?"

"What? Oh, yes. Malcolm."

Malcolm? thought Denton. *How the hell is Spurt short for Malcolm?*

"OK, so how much does Spurt want for his company?" asked Colin.

"£500,000."

OK, Denton, get the details, get the details. he thought. *Don't drift off, whatever you do. Concentrate. Don't think about women. Or Delia,* thought Denton as he frantically scrawled down the words coming out of their respective mouths. *I wonder if Delia is in today. She looked quite fit the other day, with her long flowing hair let loose, cascading over her slender shoulders, her bright blue eyes sparkling, her full lips glistening… I wonder how neat her bush is?*

"Does Spurt have any employees?"

"Yep, several. They're mostly packers and drivers though. I have a list here." B/? passed a piece of paper over to Colin.

"OK, any issues with them?"

"Yeah, one. A driver called Fuz Shurschakle."

Oh God! thought Denton, *how am I meant to spell that?* He made his best effort to spell it phonetically. Fuzz Sure Shack El.

Colin looked downed the list, "I don't see a Fuz Shurschakle here."

"No, well you wouldn't. His real name is Geoffrey Tiddleton. The problem with Geoffrey is that he seems to think that he is still living in the seventies. Afro-Caribbean lad. He's twenty seven, has a massive afro and wears shirts with collars big enough to poke your eye out."

"OK, so what is the issue?"

"Well, he's the only black guy there and has been getting a lot of stick from the other guys, which has led to some punch ups."

"That's awful. On account of his colour?" asked Colin with a note of concern.

"No, his football team. He supports Rangers and the other guys support Celtic."

"Right," said Colin, almost despairingly

"They call him things like Rangers scum, etc., you know, the usual, and this has led to some heated situations. In order to sort out the problem, Spurt tried to keep Fuz away from the other lads by making him work night shifts whilst the others worked day shifts."

"OK…"

"Yeah, but now, Fuz has brought a race discrimination claim on the basis that in making him work the night shift, Spurt's treating him less favourably on account of his colour."

"Right. How much is he claiming?"

"Dunno for sure but think it's something like £20,000."

"Oh, right," said Colin. "That seems a lot for a one off incident."

"Yeah, well, he's had some dodgy advice from some high street firm. You know the type. They big up their clients to make them think they're going to win a fortune from the Tribunal lottery, then they try to settle minutes before they have to go into a hearing and so avoid exposing their own inadequacies."

"Right," said Colin, knowingly. "OK, anything else?"

"No, well yes. One of the packers injured themselves whilst working at the depot. Dropped a whole load of packed salmon crates on her foot. I have the accident report right here."

He passed a piece of paper to Hooley who then passed it to Denton. It read "Name: Maisy Dean. Date 03/03/02. Description: When loading crates on to lorry, one end slipped out of my oily hands, hit me on the foot. Really hurt, cut right foot causing big gash. Left foot swelled up. And I swore a lot." Denton tried not to laugh.

"So what about property. Are you getting any in the deal?"

"Yes, there's a depot where the fish is packed, etc., and then passed on."

"OK, any issues there that you know of?"

"No, although I think someone is claiming that there's asbestos in it or something. But there probably isn't. Although, I'm not going to spend much time there if I can possibly help it, just in case."

"Have you had it checked out by anyone?"

"No. There doesn't seem to be much point. I mean there's no point wasting good money on bad, is there?"

"Well. We'll come back to that when I've had a chance to look through all the documents," said Colin, as diplomatically as he could under the circumstances.

Frantically, Denton tried to write everything down verbatim. It didn't work. Every fifteen minutes or so he drifted off. Suddenly, he would return to reality, thinking, *Oh God! I'm supposed to be writing this down.* He could not rule out the possibility that from time to time he may have said this out loud.

"OK, well I think that I have pretty much got everything that I need to be getting on with. We'll go speak to Mr Mackenzie's solicitors and get some info. When are you hoping to complete by?"

"Four weeks if possible," said B/?

"Yeah, that should be do-able. Anyway, Basil, pleasure to see you as always, we'll speak again soon." Both men stood up. "Denton would you mind showing Mr Loughton out? Denton. You can stop writing now. Denton. What are you scribbling?"

*****

In another part of London, Badger found himself in a strange room, sat in a chair that he didn't recognise, which formed part of a circle of seats that he hadn't seen before, which in turn were occupied by a whole load of unfamiliar faces. If he didn't know better, he would swear that he was drunk. At the head of the circle, if there is such a thing, sat a little middle-aged man, sporting a shoddy, uneven black moustache, a white short-sleeved shirt with accompanying standard council issue print tie and terrible steel rimmed glasses that appeared so misshapen that it seemed to Badger that a toddler had sat on them repeatedly for a bit of a laugh.

"Right," he said. "Thank you all for attending the 227th [East Finchley and region] Narcoleptics Together meeting. As you all know, my name is Sam Buckfast, co-chairman of the group. The other co-chairman is Dave Gettis, to my left."

To his left was another short man, who was slouched in his chair, head bent back over the edge with his mouth wide open, emitting strange and terrifying sounds as if some orthodontic spectre was performing dentistry on him.

"As you can see, Dave is 'power-saving' at the moment." And as he said 'power-saving' he did the bunny rabbit ears thing with his fingers which everyone knows everyone hates and yet people still do it regardless. It was "really annoying".

"Today's minutes takers will be Cheryl, Anna and Stuart. As you can see,

Stuart is also in "power-save mode", but he will be ok in a moment. Hopefully between them, they will be able to take the minutes of the entire meeting."

Sam held up a single piece of A4 paper, which Badger found he already had in his hand.

"Now, has everyone received a copy of last meeting's minutes?"

Those that were still conscious seemed to nod.

"Right then. Before we start, a big hello to Winston who is joining us for the first time today. Welcome Winston."

"Welcome Winston," they all said. Well all with the exception of those already asleep and the man who fell straight off his chair, flat on his face at that precise moment. "Can someone help Jonathan up please?"

"Winston, since you're new here..."

"Wahey!" interrupted Stuart for no apparent reason as he regained consciousness. No one found this to be particularly odd except Badger, who stared at him with a look of abject horror. His big goggly eyes even bigger them normal. He pushed the bridge of his glasses as an automatic reaction to disguise his terror.

"...perhaps you could tell us a bit about yourself?"

"Well..." the whole thing was very distressing for Badger. "I've recently been diagnosed with the condition by my doctor. Or rather he suspects I have it. I had not really noticed anything was wrong myself, I mean I put my falling asleep..."

"Tut tut tut," interrupted Sam. "We don't like the expression 'falling asleep' here or elsewhere. It paints a negative picture of our situation. We prefer to think of it as "power-saving"." Again with the bunny ears. Why?

"...right...no, my mistake. I put my "power-saving" down to a serious lack of exercise, lack of a well-balanced diet and excessive consumption of alcohol." Someone audibly gasped at this last point, which put Badger right off.

"We don't encourage drinking here, Mr Thurlgood," added Sam and then promptly fell off his chair. Since the meeting was chairman-less no one thought to prompt someone else to pick Sam up.

Badger blinked, briefly tugged at his little ear and pushed the bridge of his glasses once more until they had nowhere to go. He looked around the room, as if to ask, "Shall I carry on?". Since no one looked as if they would rather he didn't, he did. "Anyway, it was my flatmate Billy who suggested that I should go to see a doctor about it, so I did. He recommended that I come here, so I did. Personally, I don't think that I do have narcolepsy but the doctor said..." and with that he passed out.

*****

It had reached the stage of the day where Denton, having finished dictating his attendance note, and all the other work that needed to be done, had nothing to do but wait for one secretary to begrudgingly start typing. It seemed odd to Denton that the secretaries had a tray marked 'non-urgent' work, if all that meant was 'no way am I doing this' work. Anyway, it wasn't Denton's problem. He had no authority to make the secretaries do his work. He couldn't tell a qualified solicitor that his work was not being done or risk being indelibly branded a grass by the secretarial sorority. What could he do except flick elastic bands at the wall and try to catch them on the top of his head? Anyway, it was nearly five o'clock, which could mean only one thing. Drinkies.

A new e-mail popped up on his screen. It was from Randall and read simply, "Bored. Have just choked on a Kit Kat Chunky. Should I put this in the accident book? Think throat is too dry, when do we go for drinks?"

"Now?" replied Denton.

A brief pause ensued until. "Tempted. Give it fifteen minutes then we'll go. Want to get absolutely lashed."

"Any particular reason?" ventured Denton.

"Not really. Strange request, but can I bring Delia?"

Denton paused. Looked up. Paused. Typed, "yeah, do" but then deleted it. Somehow, it sounded too enthusiastic. Then typed "yeah, why not?". Still too enthusiastic. Paused. Looked up again and then finally settled upon. "Why?"

There was a bigger pause. Then: "Yeah, I know. Sounds odd. Well, have had quite a good day with her. She made me laugh at one point. She said something really funny. I think that it was intentional. Am not sure but will give benefit of the doubt. In any event, I think that it might be interesting to see her drunk."

Denton paused. Thought. Paused. Thought again. "Well, ok," he replied. Suitably vague enough, he thought. Also ensured that the responsibility for her was on Randall. He smiled. He was looking forward to the evening even more than usual, although he was unsure quite why.

Fifteen minutes later, Denton had his coat on. His computer was shut down, or at least shut down enough for him to leave the building without feeling guilty, and he was in the lift heading for the level marked 'freedom', also known as 'ground'. As the lift doors opened, he saw Randall waiting for him, beside an attractive girl whom he thought he had misidentified until it became clear that it was Delia.

"Hi guys," said Denton as he walked up to them. "Are you both ready?"

They both nodded. Denton walked off and they followed.

"Night, Brian," said Denton.

"Night, Brian, have a good weekend," said Randall, as they walked past the security desk.

"Night guys," said Brian, who was stood next to his security desk, too close to the flowers for it to be accidental.

"OK, this is the plan," said Denton as he and Randall rushed through the busy streets filled with commuters desperate to leave their misery behind them for another week. In ridiculously high heeled shoes, Delia struggled to keep up, "we'll start off in the pub around the corner and then we will move on. We are only stopping for one. I repeat, we are only stopping for one. I am not having a repeat of the unfortunate incident that happened the other Tuesday. I am not getting bogged down talking to other solicitors on a Friday night. I do that enough during the week. Does everyone understand that?"

"Yes," said Randall. *Every time...* he thought.

"Er. Yeah." said a slightly confused and disorientated Delia. *What am I doing here?*, she thought of her brave new world.

"Then we're moving onto Smithfields, where we shall be meeting Badger and Billy. We're then going onto Dust and then Match up the road from there. If we get absolutely twatted then I won't rule out Turnmills, but only if absolutely necessary. Is everyone on board?"

"Erm, when are we going to eat? And where are we going?" ventured Delia. This was enough for Denton and Randall to stop in their tracks. They looked at each other and then laughed.

"We don't plan where we're eating!" said Randall. "It just happens at the point when we really need to eat."

"Oh," said Delia, vaguely trying to think of a plausible excuse to escape from an adventure that she was not sure she was adequately prepared for.

All three walked into the bar. "My round," said Denton as he and Randall strode up to the bar with Delia in tow. "Two bottles of Asahi and..." Denton stopped and looked at Delia.

"Erm, Bombay sapphire and slimline tonic please," said Delia, as if it were a real drink.

Denton looked confused. "Did you get that?" he asked the bar man, who was looking at Delia with an equally confused look on his face. He looked back at Denton, shrugged and carried on.

"Right, drink up quickly," said Denton as he distributed the drinks. "I do not want any talking to anyone else other than us. There can be no meandering, no slowing down and certainly not, under any circumstances, any talk of a 'quick second round' - make no mistake, this will lead to you becoming embroiled in a discussion with another solicitor from our firm and there will be no escape. Mark my words."

"I agree," said Randall.

"Erm, understood," said a very nervous Delia, who had not quite appreciated that drinking could be such a military procedure. She picked up her drink from the bar and sniffed it suspiciously. It was a little pinker than she had been expecting. She looked at it and then at the bar man, who had been looking optimistically at her for some moments. When her eyes caught his, he looked away, almost in shame and returned to drying some beer glasses.

Quickly, Denton and Randall downed their drinks. "Right, we're leaving," they said and promptly left the pub. Delia looked momentarily confused and a tad shocked when Denton re-entered, grabbed her arm and pulled her out with him.

Smiths is one of those bars that every one tells you is really trendy. One of those places that everyone who has been out drinking in Smithfields will say, *"Oh, you must go out drinking in Smiths, it is just so cool."* And it is probably because so many people tell you that it is cool that you think, "*Well, it must be.*" The trouble is that when you're there it's really hard to figure out what all the fuss is about. Smiths is unique in as much as it does not serve regular beers apart from Guinness. It serves organic beer (whatever that is) in bottles and Czechagothumpian beers on tap. Both of which taste awful. The place is pretty massive, set across four floors with various VIP sections (Apparently. Although Denton had not seen anyone that recognisable in there). The trouble is that the ground floor has the feel of a gutted abattoir. Probably on account of the fact that it is. There are about four big leather sofas in one corner, which are always taken, probably even when the bar is closed. Then there are several wooden upmarket picnic tables, which were pretty much always taken as well, although God only knew why - they got quite painful to sit on after a while. After all that, there was not much in the way of standing space, even though the majority of people seemed to be standing and since the bar was at the back of the room, it meant that you were constantly moving in order to allow people to get past you. But, for whatever reason, Denton and Randall kept going back. It seemed that only after two pints of Pravostamenprust, or whatever it was called, and a lot of elbows in the ribs later, would they remember just how bad the place actually was.

"So," said Denton as someone elbowed him in the ribs as they walked by, "how are you finding things, Delia?"

"What you mean work?" said Delia as she tried desperately hard to push herself into a wall so that no one could get behind her.

"Yeah," said Denton as someone knocked into Randall as he went to take a slurp from his pint causing his glass to hit his teeth and the contents to hit his shirt. Randall scowled.

"Not too bad. I enjoy the work, I guess, although it sometimes bugs me when people ask me how to fix the photocopier."

"Yeah," said Randall, as someone tapped his kidneys causing immense pain for a second. "I get that too. Do people think that we took a course on it at law school?"

"I know what you mean," said Denton, as someone tripped up over his heel sending their drink into the person in front of them. "I mean, I am beginning to wonder if there *was* a class on photocopying but I missed it on account of being in the session on proof-reading."

"Yeah," said Delia, her eyes lighting up. "I get a lot of proof reading. I don't mind it though because it really bugs me when I see letters going out with typing errors or documents with the wrong type facing."

"Really? I hate proof reading," said Denton as two toffs walked into each other behind him, clashing drinks and exchanging empty threats of vengeance *"You buffoon! Watch your step before you go ploughing into people! You made me spill my Pimms!" "I say, who are you calling the buffoon, sir? You clearly strode into me at full steam without checking the way was clear. For this, I am now wearing your cucumber. Please remove it before I put one on you." "Oh yeah? Why don't you just push off?" "Oh really? Well you, sir, are a cad and your mother never went to prep-school!"*. Denton slurped on his pint some more. "Especially if it's a letter that a secretary has just typed up for you. Shouldn't the secretaries be proof reading?"

"Well, not really," said Delia. "I mean the secretaries did not write the letters and in most cases won't know enough to correct it anyway."

"Some will," said Randall as someone knocked into him again causing him to spill even more drink. He was now wearing more beer than he had actually consumed. "Can we go now?" he said, shaking his hand to flick excess beer off. He made a feeble attempt to brush more beer off his shirt and glared accusingly at anyone who happened to walk past.

"Yeah, ok," said Denton, as someone else tripped over his foot, fell into a group of people and got lanced straight through the spleen by an upturned chair leg. Or something like that. "Let's go to Dust on Clerkenwell Road."

Now, Dust on the other hand was a great venue. Not much to sell it from the outside but the inside had character. It was difficult to explain why though. Perhaps it was the arrangement of the furniture. Maybe it was the abundance of beaten up leather sofas and foot high wooden tables that said this was a place of comfort. Maybe it was the long bar and chilled tunes that said that this was a stress free environment. Maybe it was the sofas and soft lighting outside the toilets that said this was a place where the rules were all wrong.

"Now," said Denton, working his way through a pint of Grolsch as he sank into a sofa. "There are four types of secretary."

"Are you going to be derogatory about secretaries?" asked Delia.

Denton flinched involuntarily. The level of alcohol that he had consumed was such that he was quite happy to let Delia in on some of the views that he held about the world around him and was more than a little irked by her display of pre-emptive disapproval of those opinions.

"Why not?" asked Randall.

"Because my secretary is a very nice lady."

"Right. But she's not your secretary is she. I mean, does she do work for you?" asked Denton.

"Well, no," said Delia. "She happens to be a very busy lady."

"Doing what?" asked Randall.

"Well. Other people's work, I guess. I do not know. I never asked her."

"So why do you not ask her to do your work?" asked Denton.

"Well, she told me on day one that trainees are expected to be self-sufficient. We should not need a secretary."

"But isn't that a bit short sighted?" asked Denton. "If you were really self sufficient then you would not need a secretary right?"

"Well, yes."

"So, if you did not need a secretary through your training and you managed entirely without one, you would probably qualify being able to do the job without a secretary. The more people qualified not needing a secretary, the less a secretary is needed and hence gets the push."

"Well," said Delia, "I do not agree with that. I mean I'll still need a secretary when I qualify."

"Aha!" said Randall. "But that is the second trap, isn't it. If you do need a secretary on qualification, you won't know how to use one. You won't know how to dictate properly, and so when you're rushed, you'll resort to typing stuff out yourself because you'll have trained yourself to think it's quicker."

"I don't think that that is true," said Delia.

"Have you dictated anything yet Delia?" asked Randall.

"Well. No."

"Are you a quick typist?"

"Yes."

"Point proved." said Randall.

"Oh."

"Anyway," said Denton. "There are four types of secretary. There's the fit kind that you'd really like to sleep with, so who cares if she's any good or not?"

Delia couldn't help but show her disapproval at this comment which Denton noticed with a small amount of curiosity.

"Well, perhaps you wouldn't classify them in the same way Delia," acknowledged Denton. Delia didn't respond. "Then there's the annoying permanently grumpy type that is pretty much useless and doesn't give a rat's ass what work you have since you're a trainee and you're meant to be "self-sufficient". There is the good intentioned secretary who tries really hard but just gets it wrong all the time."

Delia was not convinced by this analysis but since she was already quite a few Bombay Sapphires down, her powers of resisting the conversation were subdued.

"And then, there is the type that is just superb, does their job well and knows exactly what you want them to do."

"Ah," said Randall shaking his head lamentably. "A rare breed."

"There is one in corporate," said Denton. "She is great but she is hardly ever available because everyone wants her. I always get stuck with someone like Colin's stand-in secretary, Amber, instead."

"What's she like?" asked Delia.

"Useless. Utterly useless. She thinks she is being helpful but is actually just slowing you down. You give her something to do, you tell her its urgent, you go out half an hour later and find that she hasn't done it because she is too busy. Either that or she denies any knowledge of ever receiving it in the first place. You casually mention that you are a bit cold in your room and you find out that she has ordered you a new window, a heater and thermal underwear. This would be fine but the whole time you're thinking "You could have done my tape in the time that it has taken you to do this!". And she keeps forgetting my name. You know I don't like it when people forget my name. Then there was the time I dictated a letter and I spelt out exactly where it was meant to be going. When I get it back the name of the town reads 'Karlmarlven'. It was meant to say Carmarthen. I wouldn't mind but I spelt it out, I fucking spelt it out!"

By this stage Denton's cheeks had turned a little pinker than they were before he had begun speaking.

"Oh," said Randall, examining his empty pint glass. "Shall we move on?"

Match is the kind of bar that you really have to concentrate in when you are there. It is quite dimly lit to the point where you wonder whether you should just bite the bullet and give a pound to the barman to put in the meter. It is well furnished. Well, it looks as if it might be, if you could actually see what it was you were sitting on. The real trick, though, comes in not falling down the stairs when you try to get to the bar. Most of it is on one level, but then the bar itself is set slightly lower in what might have been a bear pit at some stage. The greater skill is required in reaching the toilets which are up a sharper incline and around a bend. After all the effort involved in reaching the floor that the toilets are on you are often left too exhausted to really care which is the gents and which is not. Even when you're inside, you are still left wondering whether you are in the right place or whether there is another door to go through. When you have had a few pints, you really do not need that kind of mental challenge.

"OK," said Delia, "I need to eat otherwise I am going to be sick."

"What?" said Denton.

"Eating is cheating," suggested Randall.

"No, seriously, you guys, I need something now and then I need to go dancing."

"What do you feel like eating?" asked Denton

"I dunno," said Delia, feeling very light headed.

"Kebab?" ventured Randall.

"Yeah, yeah, I just fancy that..." said Delia in a manner serious enough to suggest that she was not kidding.

Denton looked at Randall and smirked.

"Yeah. You're drunk." said Denton

"No I am not," said Delia defensively, making a point of sitting up straight, as if that was the litmus test.

"Well, you just passed the drunk exam. People only eat kebab when they are drunk. If you fancy a kebab it means that you are drunk. Never fails." said Randall.

"OK, I'll go and order some food," said Denton. He got up from their table and slowly edged his way down into the bear pit, successfully managing to stay on his feet, more or less.

Twenty minutes later two big platters of food arrived. It was too dark for Delia to make out exactly what there was.

"What's this?", she asked.

"This is the ideal Friday meal," said Randall.

Denton picked up a skewer and began to lead Delia around the plate whilst Randall dived in.

"OK, first we have barbecue ribs, next up, oriental wrapped things, spicy chicken gougons, err, dunno what they are, sweet chilli sauce, spicy plum sauce and an as yet undetermined sauce."

Randall picked up something slippery between his fingers, and not convinced that it would make the distance, he lunged in to make sure his head was underneath it when it fell.

"What's that?" asked Delia.

"Ah," smiled Denton. "The *piece de resistance* - squid."

"Urgh," said Delia.

"It's nice," said Randall chewing...and chewing...and chewing some more, until finally he gave up chewing and just swallowed the damned thing.

"I think that I will skip food," said Delia. "Can we move straight to the dancing?"

Now the Itchy guide to London, every serious drinker's bible on the subject, claims that Turnmills 'is like your oldest mate from school'. Denton did not know when the good people at Itchy had met his friend Joe, but he was amazed that they had accurately described him as a club. Joe had a hygiene problem, he smelt - smelt bad, he had athlete's foot, weeping acne and you never wanted to touch anything that he had come into contact with. That was Turnmills, or at least, its clientele.

Delia seemed to be enjoying herself though.

"This is great," she could be heard to say as she minced around on an empty dance floor. Or at least she would have been heard to say if the music had not been so deafening. Denton and Randall stood leaning against the bar, unable to communicate on account of the fact that their ribs were vibrating and their ears were bleeding.

No way am I drunk enough to dance yet, thought Denton as he nodded in time to the music.

Me neither, thought Randall.

Randall gestured another drink to Denton. Denton stuck two thumbs up. Randall pointed in the direction of Delia. Denton shook his head. He pretended to dance then held one finger up thereby indicating that he needed more drink before he could dance. Randall shook his head, his message had clearly been lost in translation. He pointed to Delia, made an hour glass figure shape with his hands and pretended to drink. Denton threw back his head in recognition and shrugged. Then he looked at the manner in which Delia was dancing wildly, thrashing her arms about, one of which was still attached to a handbag with a vice like grip. Denton looked back at Randall, shook his head, pretended to drink then wriggled his body and cross his eyes as if leg less. Randall nodded.

He duly bought two drinks at the bar. Delia had clearly had enough.

Chapter Fifteen

Denton sighed. Deliberately. He looked around the living room for something, anything, to occupy his attention. There was nothing to do. Randall had cleaned the entire flat. It was spotless.

Activity hogger, thought Denton resentfully.

He tapped his fingers on the sofa cushion and sighed again.

Ironing? he thought with a flicker of excitement. *Mmm,* he thought with a tad more realism. *Nah, that would take effort. Besides, don't want to spoil the afternoon by doing that now. Maybe later.*

He looked around the room again. He turned the TV on and flicked through the channels. *Mmm. Religious discussion programme, repeat of Grange Hill, Sunday Worship, something political, porn. Porn?!! Oh. No, its not. Just some programme on channel 5 about life guards or something.*

He turned the TV off.

I should have stayed in bed, he thought, banging his hands on the settee then tapping his fingers on the cushions. *Damn you, body for making me get up!*

Randall walked into the room, still wearing his dressing gown. He flumped down onto the other sofa. "Where's the remote?" he asked. Denton handed it to him. He flicked through all the channels, briefly pausing on channel five, before turning it off.

Randall sighed.

Denton sighed.

Randall coughed, then sighed again.

Randall stood up. "Do you mind if I use the washing machine?" he asked.

"No, not at all," said Denton. *Damn. Why didn't I think of that?,* he thought, *Activity hogger.*

Randall drifted off into the kitchen.

Denton sat, sighed and banged his arms down on the sofa again. It didn't help. He was still bored. His head throbbed. Mainly on account of the arm banging. He got up. He sat back down again. Then he got up and went into his bedroom. He came back with a book. He opened it to page one. Briefly he read the first two lines, then he closed the book and put it by his side. Reading just made his head hurt. He banged his hands down again. He caught the edge of the book and yelped. Quickly, he checked his hand to see if he had a life threatening paper cut that may need urgent medical attention necessitating an afternoon spent sat in the hospital waiting room. It didn't.

Damn, he thought.

"Oh balls!" shouted Randall from the kitchen.

"What?" exclaimed Denton as he got up to investigate.

"I think that I broke the washing machine."

"Damn it, Randall, how did you do that?"

"Well, I don't know," said a forlorn Randall, scratching his head as he stood next to the once perfectly reliable machine. "All I did was press the 'on' button."

"And then what happened?"

"Well, nothing. It started fine and then gave out a big choke and stopped."

Denton stood shaking his head at Randall and partially wished that Billy was there to witness the event, recollecting a conversation the pair of them had once had.

"The thing about Randall is," Denton had said over a nice bottle of Sol in a bar on Clerkenwell Road, "he has this really annoying knack of breaking any machinery that he comes into contact with."

"That's ridiculous," said Billy, grappling with the leather sofa he was sat in, in a desperate bid not to become another statistic in a long line of people sucked into the back of comfy leather sofas never to be seen again. "How can he possibly break every machine that he comes into contact with?"

"No, seriously he does," said Denton, sat at the other end of the sofa, wishing Billy would stop fidgeting. He was beginning to get sea sick from all the movement. "He claims that he is more statically charged than ordinary people, which is why he affects machinery the way that he does."

"I'm not convinced. Examples please," said Billy, demonstrably unconvinced.

"Well, at work, his telephone always breaks down."

"Yeah, well, so does mine in most of the places that I work. It's probably just a rubbish phone."

"No, this phone thinks that it is a fax machine. Every time that Randall goes to use it, he gets this funny noise. In fact, I think that someone actually believed that it was a fax machine. For a week, people kept trying to send faxes to him. He had to go to the doctors with earache from the noise."

"It's just the phone."

"No, it's not, he has been through five."

"Oh."

"Then there was his new mobile phone," continued Denton, "it was one of those ones with picture messaging, etc. None of the special features that it was supposed to have worked. Also, you couldn't hear him when he spoke."

"Right."

"And the reason why he bought that phone was because he could never get a signal on his previous phone. It did not matter where he was, you could never hold an entire conversation with him without it cutting out. In fact you were lucky to get a single sentence out."

"I see."

"Then there was his car, which would only start first time on Fridays and religious holidays. His digital watch went backwards from time to time and sometimes his laptop couldn't be switched off. This is not a man to have around if you are in any way attached to the technology that you own."

It was for this reason that Denton was in no small way surprised that Randall had broken the washing machine. In fact, Denton was only surprised that it had taken him this long to do it.

With the excitement now over, Denton returned to the living room, sighed and sat back down on the sofa. He turned on the TV again, briefly flicked through all the channels, before turning it off with contempt. How he loathed Sundays.

*****

In another part of London village, Colin Hooley was having one of those days. His wife was out in the garden, sun-bathing of all things, wearing the skimpiest outfit that he had seen her in for years.

"Will you not be cold?" asked Colin.

"No dear, I'm fine," she said visibly shivering. "Besides, we really don't take enough advantage of the swimming pool."

"But, it's freezing today," said Colin, understandably confused.

"Yes, dear." said Mrs Hooley, as she stretched out her long, shapely, tanned legs on the reclining chair. "Pass me the sun tan lotion."

"I really don't think you've got much chance of getting sun burnt today dear," said Colin, stood in the patio door way, safe from the elements.

Mrs Hooley turned on her chair and glared at him. As she turned, Colin thought for the briefest of moments that her ample bosom might fall of her practically see-through white bikini top.

"Forget it," she snapped as she leaned over to reach it herself, almost toppling out of the chair (and her top) as she did so.

For a woman of thirty eight years, she had not lost her figure. Colin might even have been aroused by the sight of his wife sunning herself as she caressed her flat stomach with lotion, had it not been for the fact that at that precise moment he was pretty much barged out of the way by a pool net and tubing.

"'Scuse me," said the pool boy as he followed the net and the tube past Colin, "I can't get past."

"Sorry," said Colin, momentarily forgetting he was stood in his own house where he had the right to stand where he bloomin' well liked.

The pool cleaner wandered up to the side of the pool and took his jumper off. He lifted up a net from the floor and began to slowly skim the leaves from the surface of the pool. It did not seem to bother him that Mrs Hooley was staring from the reclining chair next to him whilst she absent-mindedly rubbed more lotion into her inner thigh and across her chest.

"Oh well, I'll leave you to it then, dear," said Colin as he went back inside, scratching his itching neck underneath the brace. It was more than likely that Mrs Hooley did not hear him.

Colin wandered back through the house. He went upstairs and passed his son's bedroom door. From within came the painful sound of a badly played guitar. Colin stopped and returned to his son's door. He hesitated then knocked loudly. The guitar playing ceased but there was no reply. Colin knocked again. From within he could make out a noise which sounded like 'whuh?', which was probably supposed to be 'what?'.

"Son - can I come in?"

"Whuh fur?"

"Well - to chat."

"Whuh fur?"

"Well. I feel like I have been so busy just lately that I haven't been around for you very much." Whether it was his house or not, Colin was beginning to feel slightly embarrassed by the fact that he was opening his heart up to a door.

There was a pause, which only served to amplify Colin's embarrassment. Nervously he fidgeted with his collar. "You huhn't ever."

Colin stopped. He was right. He hadn't. Kids could be so cruel. Why couldn't they just accept it as read that the reason you worked so hard was a sign that you loved them so much and wanted to provide for them. Colin opened the door and was suddenly hit by an invisible wall of stench - probably comprised of sweat, cheap deodorant and God only knew what else. It made Colin's eyes sting as he wandered in. The room was almost entirely black. The curtains were drawn. Whilst waiting for his eyes to adjust, and to stop watering, Colin could barely make out the shape of a gangly, awkward looking youth with long, greasy blonde hair. For a brief moment, Colin thought that he was in the wrong house.

Since when did little Frank have long hair? he thought. Perhaps it had been a long time after all.

Cautiously, Colin edged up to the bed and tentatively sat next to his son, who was holding the neck of his guitar and staring solemnly at the floor.

"Have you put new posters up?" asked Colin, most likely for something to say. With a slight sense of horror he looked at the hideous looking posters that adorned his son's walls, trying desperately not to think about how much blue tack was, even as they sat there, slowly seeping grease into the magnolia emulsion underneath, permanently staining his property.

"No," his son grunted. "Been up ages."

"Oh," he said, "it's just that it's very dark in here, isn't it?"

"No."

"Son, I just wanted to say sorry for the fact that I have not been around lately."

Frank shrugged. " 'S alright. Don't care."

Undaunted, Colin continued. "It's just that I've been worked really hard lately in the office."

"..."

"I'm hoping to get promoted."

"..."

"Would you like to see Daddy get promoted?"

"..."

"So, you're playing the guitar now then?" said Colin, hoping that a change of subject might ease the atmosphere.

"Yuh."

"Are you any good?"

"S'pose."

"Right," said Colin. "I used to have a guitar when I was 13 too."

Suddenly his son erupted into life and looked up at his father. He stared him straight in the eye, which took Colin aback, especially on account of the abundance of acne that had burst forth onto his son's face. His eyes were wild and his hair was translucent on account of the grease.

"I am not thirteen anymore," he bellowed. "It was my fourteenth birthday last weekend! And you were not here!"

Shit, thought Colin. *I forgot!*

"You bought me this guitar. You bought me this guitar, right here!" he said shaking the guitar wildly. "I'm in a band now! Do you even care?!"

"Well, of course I do," said Colin meekly, but it was no use, his son had already stormed past him, slamming the door on the way out. Colin's heart sank. He briefly looked around the room, trying not to look too closely for fear of what he might see. *When did he grow up so quickly?* thought Colin. *Why did he have to stop being ten years old, enjoying his lego? He was a lot easier to keep happy then.* Colin sighed, got up and left the room. After he had left, he closed the door, as if the room had stopped being part of the house that Colin owned. As if, without his knowledge, it had become annexed and sold to a stranger who he did not know and who he did not feel it was his place to disturb.

Part Two

Chapter Sixteen

You know, sometimes it's like you suddenly wake up. You're there and you're acting like you're the big fish. Then you suddenly realise that all you are doing with life is going round and round, never really achieving anything, never really making any kind of difference, just going around and around and around, endlessly.

And it's during times like this that you really have to think about who you are. Yeah, sure, you could think about changing. You could think about doing something different, but can you really just put the brakes on at this stage and become someone else? Can you really just stop and change?

And suddenly, when you make this realisation, you find that you are not just going round and round like you were before but now you have the thought in your head that this isn't what you were meant to do with your existence. Now you're in hot water because the thought that is swimming around in your mind just goes to highlight the pointlessness of your current existence. And when you realise this, you suddenly feel like you're drowning.

"Yeah - what you looking at Buddy? You looking at me? Yeah? Take some kind of joy in witnessing my misery? You never seen anyone depressed before or something? Well, I'll show you - oh yeah - I'll give you a real show to enjoy."

And then it hits you. Like a brick. If you don't enjoy it. If you can't see a way out. If this is all you'll ever do - with no satisfaction guaranteed - then what is the point? What is the point of any of it? Why bother? And it's then that you realise that you will never enjoy this life - so its best you just leave - to get out - to pack your bag and buy that one way trip - to take the train to Suicide-Ville - to just leave that goddamn fish tank...

"Tapman, your fish just jumped out of its tank again," said Denton in a matter of fact tone, his nose touching the recently vacated fish tank.

"Shit, you're right," said Randall stood next to him. "It really is suicidal."

"Oh no..." came the voice of Billy from the toilet.

Having completely cleaned and tidied their flat and done far more ironing than was strictly necessary, Randall and Denton had decided to visit Billy's pad for a spot of entertainment. They found themselves stood in a living room that looked like it had been lifted straight from the pages of an IKEA catalogue, staring at a fish tank.

"Told you that it would," said Denton, as Billy came rushing into the living room, desperately pulling his trousers up from around his ankles.

"Oh, Jesus...Happy!...stop flapping around for just a minute," squealed Billy as he cupped his hands and walked back to the tank quickly.

"That's better," he said. "You just be still for just a moment."

"Tapman…" said Denton, just before biting into an apple and returning to his seat on the leather sofa or the Kipchim as the good people at IKEA had named it.

"Not now, Denton, I'm concentrating…"

"Fine," said Denton, picking up a newspaper from the Swedish coffee table (referred to as Blim for reasons known only to the good people of Sweden) in front of him. "But I just thought you should now you dropped your fish on that rug just there." Otherwise known as an Olmjunck.

"Damn it, Happy!" said Billy, as he swirled around and attempted to scoop up the little flapper again.

"Why does he do it?" enquired Randall, both puzzled and amazed, as he moved from the Olmjunck and sat on the Kipchim.

"Dunno, maybe it just has a deep rooted appreciation for its ultimate insignificance in the world," he said putting his feet up on the Blim.

"Come here, Happy," said Billy, oblivious to them.

Randall became distracted from the conversation, drawn instead to the complete ineptitude now displayed by Billy.

"Well, either that or the fact that it just doesn't want to be the pet of a loser like Tapman." said Denton.

"Get in, go on," said Billy trying to force the fish into its tank.

"Yeah, you're probably right," admitted Randall.

"Still, can't be easy on Billy, having a fish with a death wish," said Denton.

"Yeah."

"I think it has affected him mentally," said Denton lowering his voice as he watched Billy angling his hand trying to force the reluctant fish into the water.

"You think?"

After successfully accomplishing the task, Billy turned on the two reprobates sat on his sofa, who were both now staring at the disenchanted goldfish in the tank on the sideboard.

"Right, which one of you spilt cranberry juice on my Olmjunck? And Denton get your feet off my Blim when you're sat on my Kipchim!"

Denton turned to Randall. "See what I mean?" he whispered.

"I think you're right," he whispered back. "Completely lost it - what's he on about?"

"And more to the point, did you guys remove his lid?" said Billy, undaunted by the whispering.

"Nooooo…" they said in unison, looking away from Billy's accusatory glare.

Denton looked back. Billy was still glaring. The look made him seem quite terrifying.

"Well, yeah ok, it was us…" Denton admitted, "…but seriously Billy, who calls a suicidal fish, Happy?"

"More to the point, who buys a suicidal fish?" added Randall to which Denton could only nod his approval whilst finishing off his apple.

"Look, I didn't know that he was suicidal when I bought him, did I? Besides, he's not suicidal - he's just curious."

"Yeah, curious to see how long he can live outside of water," said Randall.

Billy glared at Randall.

"It's so odd though," he commented. "He always gets a bit…"

"Jumpy," interrupted Randall. Billy ignored him.

"…distressed at this time, pretty much, every Sunday. I don't understand it. It's just so weird how he gets this way. Maybe he gets distressed because he knows that I am going back to work tomorrow."

Denton and Randall looked at each other. Maybe it had all become too much for Billy. Denton tried to be positive and act as a distraction while Randall desperately searched the Yellow Pages for a psychiatrist specialising in people with unhealthy relationships with pets.

"Look, I know you probably both think I'm a bit crazy…" said Billy.

They didn't disagree.

"…and maybe it is just me, but I swear he becomes more agitated on Sunday afternoon than at any other time of the week. Maybe there's something about it he just doesn't like…"

They both continued to stare blankly at him.

"Ok fine, it's just me."

"Actually," said Denton. "I have a lot of sympathy for your fish…" he stood up and wandered over to the now secure fish, who swam with what appeared to be a forlorn look about his face. "I feel exactly the same way every Sunday myself. I mean Sunday afternoons really are a miserable time, aren't they? When I sit and try to work out what the point of Sunday is, it makes me feel a bit jumpy too."

He stared deep into the tank, almost mesmerised by the little fellow swimming around and around. "By now, the miracle of Friday afternoon is nothing but a distant memory. The Nirvana of Friday night is just a blur. The sacred temple of Utopian Saturday now lies in ruin with nothing but the rubble of a grotty hangover to serve as a painful reminder. And amongst the empty Alka Selzter wrappers, half spilt, half drunk pints of water and the lingering taste of rotten meat that someone called kebab, what salty dregs of your weekend remain?"

Denton turned back to look at Randall and Billy, and then looked back at the forlorn and miserable Happy.

"Nothing but disappointment. Nothing but the prospect of swimming around in a circle for another week. Nothing but the realisation that you're a fish trapped in an unfulfilling bowl seeing the same people, doing the same things, living the same tedious existence over and over again. My friends, welcome to the remainder of the weekend, Fish Sunday."

Chapter Seventeen

Easter

From a battered cigarette packet, he pinched an end between two greasy, stained fingers and pulled a cigarette to his cracked lips. He paused, looked up and down the length of her, as she sat on the chair in front of his desk and smirked with approval as he lit up.

As he slowly blew smoke in her direction, his lips parted and from an ill cut moustache he muttered, "You don't mind if I smoke, do you Easter?"

Would it matter if I did? she thought, trying to hide her obvious disgust.

"Not at all, Mr Macey, after all it's your office."

Macey look around with a misplaced sense of satisfaction. He smiled and it was enough to make Easter ill as he revealed two rows of deformed and discoloured teeth. "Yes. Yes, it is, isn't it?"

Easter looked away and concentrated instead on the rest of the room - the false brown wooden panelling that covered the entirety of the walls. The scattering of what appeared to be certificates hammered unevenly into the plasterboard, though God only knew what they were awarded for. Services to chauvinism? The pictures of Macey in various ill-fitting brown suits, with thick, unruly hair unnaturally parted, shaking hands with local figures in poses that suggested both parties were more important than they actually were. And then next to the window bedecked in yellow, age coloured, net curtains, there was not one, but two calendars of young topless models in various suggestive poses. Not the image of a Lake District environment that Easter had in mind when she decided to move here.

Easter coughed as more smoke was blown in her direction. Macey ignored her from behind his aged mahogany 1970's prefab desk. He continued to stare at her. To save herself from her continued discomfort at the thought of Macey having thoughts of a sexual nature about her, she looked at the carpet and concentrated on the stained and bare threaded plaid beneath her feet and prayed that this 'important meeting' would not take too long. He fidgeted on his chair. God only knew what he was fidgeting with.

"You know, Easter, I didn't get to the position of editor without having a lot of talent. Do you know what that talent is?" he asked through a semi-permanent, sleazy smirk.

"No," said Easter paying lip service to his question.

"Spotting talent."

What? thought Easter.

"You Easter...are talent," he said blatantly staring at her legs, past her short grey skirt. "Real talent," moving up to her white shirt, through which he felt sure he could make out the outline of a lacy white bra. "Real talent," he said distantly.

Disgusted, Easter coughed again. *Why did I ever leave London for this?* she wondered.

"But the point is," said Macey, quickly brought back to reality, "that you are not producing that talent at the moment, Easter. You're hiding your quality, aren't you?" He smiled again, which caused the filth ridden dentures to make another appearance. Easter felt sure it would only be a matter of seconds before she was actually sick.

"And if you want to stay here, writing for this paper, then you are going to have to get it out. You are going to have to show me your talent. I want to see your quality." He moved one hand slowly though his dark, greased back, ear length hair and adjusted his thick set spectacles. Leaning back in his chair, he played with his hideous patchwork tie.

Feeling uneasy, Easter re-crossed her legs and immediately wished that she had not. Distracted, Macey's eyes followed, perhaps he was hoping for a quick flash of her white pants. *Why didn't I wear tights today?* she thought.

Easter's unease was beginning to increase. She felt decidedly uncomfortable and not in control of the situation at all. She prayed that he would remain on his side of the table. Suddenly, she wondered whether she could get out of the office. Irrational thought piled on top of irrational thought - had he locked the door? Would she be within her rights to get up and leave right now? Should she scream, even though he hadn't really done anything just yet? Could he really just get away with sitting there and threatening her? Had he actually threatened her or was it all in her mind? Somehow, the idea that it was just in her head suddenly gave her a crumb of comfort. Say something - anything - show him you're not intimidated.

"Erm," she began. "Mr Macey, are you disciplining me?"

His eyes lit up. "No, Easter. I'm not *disciplining* you." He took a drag on his cigarette and his eyes visibly glazed over. "I'm not disciplining you. I just need to see more from you if you are going to continue to work here."

His eyes moved from her crotch to meet her eyes. She did not know whether to look away or not.

Don't show him you're scared, Easter. Don't show him that you're petrified, she thought.

"You've definitely got it Easter. You could be a great journalist. You've got great potential. You just need to show me if you're going to progress. I need to see your qualities. I need to see them. Do you understand what I am saying?"

His eyes moved down to her chest again. Easter felt as if she had visibly flinched. She was disgusted, but too frightened to do anything about it. *So what was he saying? She had to flash him to keep her job? Did she have to sleep with him? Was that it?*

She stood up abruptly. "I understand," she said and walked towards the door praying that it wasn't locked. It wasn't and he didn't say anything as she walked away. She moved down the corridor to another room that contained two desks, facing each other, each with a computer on top. The walls were a faded pumpkin mash and the carpet had the distinct look of creosote about it. At one desk sat a guy, aged somewhere between thirty to thirty five. In the corner sat a large completely fake rubber plant - its leaves were old and battered.

"Urgh," said Easter. "Horrid."

"How was your 'chat'?" said the guy, chewing on a pencil.

"What an insipid little weasel," she said, picking up her handbag from her desk, secretly immensely relieved to have escaped without being violated. "Horrid. I feel, urgh, like a need a shower."

The guy grinned.

"I've got a great power shower," smiled the guy, winking at her.

"Don't you start, Malcolm," she said, shooting him a look of disgust.

"Oh, don't let him get to you," said Malcolm. "It's just a bit of fun. What's wrong with you? Stop being so sensitive."

"That is very easy for you to say, Malcolm, you don't have to put up with it - the sexist pig."

"Hey - you're his prized journalist. He doesn't go home and have a wank thinking about me, does he?"

Easter stopped packing her handbag and shot him a look of complete contempt, but his comment had the desired effect and she shuddered.

"That really is not very funny, Malcolm. This is the twenty first century. I should not have to put up with crap like this." She pulled her hair band out and readjusted her blonde bobbed hair.

Malcolm leant back and smiled, admiring the view as her chest heaved with the strain of it all. Her shirt pulled and gaped revealing soft, unblemished, peach skin.

"What are you doing tonight?" he asked.

"The dishes," she replied curtly.

"Really? Sounds dull - how 'bout doing me instead?"

Easter stopped again. She was tempted to pick up her monitor and throw it at him.

"Where do you people get off?" she said, slightly raising her voice. She put her coat on and stormed off leaving Malcolm chuckling. No doubt he would soon get up and scamper into Macey's room recounting the conversation leading, no doubt, to the time where he had got very, very lucky with her. *He certainly was lucky*, thought Easter, *If I had had my wits about me more I would have done him for indecent assault. Bastard. Should not have got so drunk. Shouldn't have let him grope me. But I was new - I didn't know this town. Uh, you idiot! I didn't want to seem like a square but I really did just want a friend. You stupid girl. Disgusting little man. Disgusting little dick.* She shuddered again as she briefly remembered her awkward, rough, stupid experience with the seedy Malcolm. She only put up with him now because of the pair he certainly was the lesser of two weasels.

She stepped out of the door, onto the street and nervously lit a cigarette. She sucked away and briefly looked at the end to make sure it was lit properly before continuing to walk down the high street.

Look what they have driven me to do! I hate smoking. I only do it to help relieve the stress. God, I could murder a drink right now.

She walked up to the bus stop and waited. Nervously, she looked behind her while she stood. It had not been unknown for Macey to slowly drive past in his BMW and offer her a lift. She could not cope with that tonight. Not after her day. She needed a drink. She pulled away at a cigarette. Opposite her, the lights of Quincey's bar burned bright. The neon sign flickered on and off mesmerising her.

"No," she found herself saying. "No drink. No drink. No drink. It's been seven months now. No drink. Come on. Be strong. Don't give in. Don't give in. Not for them. Not for those bastards."

She smiled as a little old lady and a shopping basket quietly wheeled themselves into the shelter next to her.

Why do I do it? she thought. *Why do I stay?* But it was a pointless question, she knew the answer. *Because I want to be a successful journalist and this is the only place that will have me. Oh, but do I have to put up with this shit every day to get there?*

She inhaled another lungful of smoke.

If only I could get that really big story. The big story to get me noticed. The big story to get me out of here.

She stubbed out the cigarette as the bus turned up.

Safe at last, she thought as she embarked and watched the tempting lights of Quinceys retreat as the bus moved away.

Chapter Eighteen

The Corporate Weekend Away

There are certain people that you meet in this life that seem to serve no other purpose than to really bug you. What makes the situation worse is the fact that often these people seem to be completely oblivious to just how annoying they actually are. It is these people that really bring the world down and all those around them. It is these people that cause suicide, manic depression and despair in their co-workers. It is these people that you try to avoid as much as possible. It is these people that you do not want to spend a second with, let alone an entire weekend. It is these people that, if you want to avoid an hysterical episode bordering on breakdown, you really should not, under any circumstances, end up trapped with in a Peugeot 205 en route to a corporate weekend away in Scarborough.

Why me? thought Denton.

Why me? thought Delia.

Why me? thought Randall.

"..." thought the vacuous Bonnie Cecilia Belcher.

Bonnie Belcher was another trainee working in the corporate department. By anyone's standards she was actually quite fit. Five foot something, she had a great tan, a great waist, great tits and great bleached blonde hair. Her eyes sparkled and her teeth were perfectly straight. What more could any man want? Well, a personality would have helped. An inkling, just a hint, just the smallest sign that she had any kind of clue about the world that she had somehow managed to infiltrate, would have been a bonus. Bonnie was the kind of girl who could get lost following the plot of a shampoo bottle. The kind of girl who found the TV remote control too complicated, "the Sun" too intellectual and thought the theory of man evolving from apes applied only to the working class - which was ironic since if any scientist wanted to find the missing link between man and beast, she was right there. Or maybe the link between beast and amoeba.

It was with a certain sense of despair that Denton had agreed, at Devlin Hawkes request, that he drive Bonnie to the off site event. Even though Denton had been asked three weeks ago, he still cursed the fact that he had admitted he would be going to get his car from his parent's house that weekend in order to drive up. Gladly, he offered Randall a lift. Gladly, he offered Delia a lift. Begrudgingly, through clenched teeth and tight fists, he had offered Bonnie a lift.

Two days later, Bonnie had asked him if she still needed to get train tickets to Scarborough.

"Well, you could do, but I thought that I was giving you a lift, Bonnie."

"Yes, I know but I didn't know if you still were."

"Well. Yes. I only asked you two days ago."

"OK, but do I need train tickets back?"

"No. I told you. I'll give you a lift there and back."

"OK. So should I not get train tickets then?"

It was at this point that Denton picked up the nearest stapler and took out both her stupid rabbit eyes before skewering a propelling pencil straight through one cheek and out the other side, harpooning her tongue along the way just before he picked up his monitor and smashed it down over her brainless head, thus ending her wasted life and saving all that oxygen for people who might actually put it to good use.

Or at least, he did every time he recounted that story to anyone who would listen.

Bonnie was the girl who, on first meeting Denton had had a conversation with him pretty much along the following lines:

"Hello, I'm Bonnie Belcher."

"Oh hello, I'm Denton."

"Hi. How are you? What seat have you just done?"

"Commercial Insurance."

"Oh, OK. Did you enjoy that…erm…what was your name?"

"Denton."

"…Denton. Did you enjoy that?"

"Yeah, I did, it was good fun."

"Good. Have you lived in London for long …erm…" she said looking lost.

"Denton," he prompted.

"…Denton…have you lived here long?"

"Yeah, for a while now. You?"

"No. I'm from Manchester. Do you know London? Erm, I know you." Her face crinkled in a distinctly unpleasant and pained way as she said it.

"Sorry?"

"I know you. I know your name but you haven't said it."

"What?" Denton was utterly confused, mostly since this was the oddest conversation of his adult life and probably the oddest of his childhood too.

"Your name. I know it but you haven't told me?"

"Yes I did. It's Denton - Denton Voyle - Denton, Denton," he said exasperated.

"Yes. That's right," said Bonnie, as if asking him his name was part of some kind of test.

Four times, thought Denton. *Four times she had forgotten my name in one conversation not lasting more than five minutes. Four times. Where did they find people like this to employ? Why did I bother studying at University if they were going to let in brainless melons like this? I would not have minded but she was stood in the doorway of my office at the time and it was written on the door. Even a cursory glance would have given her a good hint at what my name was. Four times. Denton Denton Denton Denton!*

Delia wasn't best pleased either. Delia loathed girls like Bonnie with a passion. It was women like Bonnie that gave hard working girls like Delia a bad name. Delia prided herself on the fact that she had worked hard, very hard, to get to where she was. She hadn't slept with anyone to do it. Hadn't flirted with anyone either. Hadn't once had recourse to get her tits out. She did it on brainpower and business sense alone. And what happened? She got stuck in the back seat of a car with Bonnie 'Blue-eyed Big Breasts Bang ya Bollocks on my Backside' Belcher.

No one said a word during the journey for fear that Bonnie might try to join in. No one wanted to have to explain to Scarborough police why there was a dead girl on the backseat who had been beaten to death by three corporate away pack A4 lever arch folders and a six bar packet of Kit-Kat Chunky.

All of them were extremely tired. Well, Delia, Denton and Randall certainly were since they had had to get up at 4.30 that morning in order to be in Scarborough before the 10.30 start of the conference. Goodness only knew whether Bonnie could even recognise the feeling of being tired, let alone suffer from it.

Thank God for the radio, thought Denton. *Thank God we're only thirty minutes away from Scarborough.*

It was really unfortunate that Denton's car did not share Denton's eagerness to get to Scarborough as quickly as possible. At first, it was easy for Denton and Randall to ignore the funny noises that the car was making. It was not quite as easy to ignore the juddering. It was nigh on impossible to ignore the fact that the engine had cut out and the car was free wheeling down the road.

Great, thought Denton as he pulled over.

"I don't believe this!" said Randall.

"What's wrong with it?" asked Delia.

"I dunno," said Denton. "It felt a bit funny a while back - kept juddering as if it was about to stall, but then it was fine."

Denton turned the engine over but nothing happened.

"Well, we're not going anywhere." They all sat in silence for a moment thinking. Well, with the exception of Bonnie, who maintained the same glazed look that she had had since they left.

"I'll just phone up one of the secretaries and ask them to ring ahead for us to let everyone know that we will be late," said Randall. He pulled his mobile phone out of his pocket and quickly phoned work.

"OK - thanks Gladys. Much appreciated," said Randall as he finished telling Gladys what had happened, having asked her to let Devlin Hawkes know that in all likelihood they would not be there for some time.

"Cheers Randall," said Denton.

"Mmm," said Randall, scratching his head. "How much petrol have you got left?"

Denton squinted as he looked underneath his steering wheel at the petrol gauge. "No, I don't think that it's petrol - says here that we have got just under a quarter of a tank left. Having said that, this is such an old car, the gauge might have got stuck."

Whilst Denton and Randall considered the petrol situation, Bonnie suddenly leapt into life. "Should I telephone my supervisor to tell him that we have broken down?"

My God, she has an annoying voice, thought Denton. And probably Randall too. Delia also.

Everyone ignored her. Delia even leaned forward to make sure that it was clear she was concentrating on what Randall was saying.

"Well, there's a pub just there," said Randall, ignoring Bonnie. "Perhaps we could go and ask inside to see where the nearest petrol station is. If we eliminate lack of petrol as a problem then we'll know it's something else wrong with the car before we phone the AA."

"Maybe I should phone my supervisor to tell him," said Bonnie.

"No, you're right Randall," said Denton, equally ignoring her. "I'd forgotten that the first thing the AA usually ask is, have you got any petrol in the car? It's like the motoring version of the IT helpline - *have you tried turning it off and back on again?*"

"I'll just telephone my supervisor quickly then should I?" asked Bonnie.

Denton turned around. The situation was difficult enough without having to put up with Bonnie's stupidity as well. "Why do you want to telephone your supervisor?"

"To let him know that I'll be late."

"But Randall just did that. We can't keep telephoning people - what good will that do?"

"Oh, is that who Randall was talking to?"

It was at this point that Denton could quite happily have turned to Randall and said, "Look - let's just kill her. Nobody need know. We could just bury the body under the hedge over there and pretend like we never picked her up at all. We could just say that she must have gotten confused about what day it was, thought it was the weekend and just went off somewhere. People would believe us and, in any event, no one would notice the difference."

It was because he knew that Randall would probably agree that he did not say anything.

"Maybe Bonnie and I should go to the pub and find out where the nearest garage is," said Delia, realising that Denton might happily punch Bonnie at any moment.

"Good idea," said Denton.

"OK," said Bonnie. "Maybe I should just telephone my supervisor whilst we're over there."

Bonnie and Delia left the car.

"Seriously, Randall, what is the matter with that girl?" said Denton as he watched Delia and Bonnie walk up the road a short distance to the pub. Not that 'walking' really described what Bonnie was doing, it was more like a totter, as if she may fall over at any moment.

"I don't know. Although I'm getting closer by the second to ripping my own arm off and beating her to death with the soggy end."

Denton stopped and looked at Randall, with a slightly disturbed look on his face. Randall looked backed at him. "Well, I am!" he said, adamant yet slightly embarrassed at the same time.

Shortly afterwards, Delia and Bonnie returned carrying a small petrol can and a funnel.

"The guy at the pub sold this to us," said Delia as she handed the can to Denton.

Denton funnelled the petrol into the tank. Everyone piled back in to the car.

"Ooh," said Delia. "I forgot to mention, the guy at the pub asked for the empty can and funnel back when we'd used it."

"Well, we'll just drive around and drop it off," said Denton ambitiously. A bit too ambitiously. The car refused to start.

"Do you think that we should have gotten more petrol?" asked Bonnie.

Randall put two fingers under his chin and pretended to blow his brains out.

"Can I borrow that when you've finished with it?" asked Denton as he looked at Randall.

"OK," said Delia. "Well that didn't work. We'd better go and take the stuff back to the guy at the pub while you ring the AA?"

"OK," said Randall.

"OK," said Denton.

There was a pause. No one moved. Denton and Randall turned around. Delia was sat with her hand on the car door handle as if she was about to get out but her eyes were closed and she was breathing out very slowly.

"OK," she finally said, "I'm ready. Come on Bonnie!" she barked as she got out.

Denton pulled his phone out of his pocket as Delia and Bonnie walked/tottered away. At one point, Bonnie went over slightly on her ankle, much to Denton and Randall's obvious amusement.

"Where's the number for the AA?" said Denton rummaging around in the side pocket of his car door. "Oh, here it is." He quickly dialled the number.

"Hello, welcome to the AA…"

"Hello, I'm a member and I've broken down…"

"If you would like to hear about joining the AA, please press 1," said a pre-recorded voice.

Oh… thought Denton, *answer phone thing.*

"If you would like to renew your membership, please press 2 now…"

Nope… thought Denton.

"If you would like to hear about promotions that the AA presently have then please press 3..."

Not really...

"If you would like to hear how the AA started and how it continues to grow then please press 4 now..."

Quickly... thought Denton.

"Is it not ringing?" asked Randall.

"No, it's one of those 'please press one' thingys" said Denton.

"Oh," said Randall, "I hate those."

"I know. Maybe we should get one for work. If you would like legal advice, please press one - if you would like to complain about the size of a bill then please press 2 - if you would to hear a trainee with a sexy voice speaking, then please hold and have a tissue handy..."

"If you would like to hear about why the AA is so great and why it is better to join the AA than, say the RAC or those jokers at Green Flag, press 5 now..."

Come on... thought Denton.

"For all other non-essential calls, including complaints/over charging/motor insurance and breakdowns please hold...."

About time... thought Denton.

"Hello..."

"Hello, I'm a member and I've broken down..."

"...and thank you for holding..."

Damn it! thought Denton. A cacophony of noise struck Denton's ears and it took him a while to figure out that this was supposed to be Beethoven's fifth, presumably being performed by a guinea pig using a twig on a rubber band, backed by a group of water voles sucking grass through a comb.

"Hello, AA. How may I help you?"

"..." Denton hesitated.

"Hello?" asked the voice.

"Are you a real person?" asked Denton hesitantly.

There was another pause.

"Yes."

"Thank God for that. Right - I'm a member and I've broken down."

"OK. Can I just take some details down first."

"Yes."

"OK. What is your first name?"

"Denton."

"Sorry?"

"Denton."

"No no, your first name, Mr Denton."

"No," said Denton, a little hurt, "Denton *is* my first name."

"Oh," said the baffled voice as if she might add *are you sure?* "How do you spell that?"

"D...e...n...t...o...n. Denton."

"Oh, OK. And your surname?"

"Voyle."

"What?"

"Voyle."

"Sorry…"

"Voyle - V…o…y…l…e. Voyle."

"Right," said the voice, as if beginning to think that this was some sort of hoax. "And where do you live."

He told her.

"OK. And what is your membership number?"

"But…" protested Denton, already thinking that this process was taking more than a little too long. "Have you not got enough information inputted already to make my name just pop up on your screen?"

There was another pause.

"Yes - but we need to check your number to see if you are who you say you are, Mr Denton," she said hastily trying to justify her actions.

"But why would I lie?"

"Weelllll…some people do, and we can't be too careful," she said, implausibly.

"OK, OK," said Denton. "But why didn't you ask me for my number first then ask me to confirm a few details?"

There was a further pause.

"Yes…well," said the voice in a very school ma'amish manner, "sometimes we do it that way and sometimes this way."

Denton looked at Randall aghast and whispered, "I think that I'm talking to Bonnie's sister."

"So Mr Denton…"

"Voyle."

"What?"

"My name is Voyle - I told you that a second ago. Is your surname Belcher by any chance?"

"No, it's not Mr Denton. What seems to be the problem?"

"Oh, for pity's sake - I've broken down!"

"OK - where exactly are you?"

"Right - good - progress - I'm on the A64, heading north-east to Scarborough. I've broken down near a village called West Heslerton."

"Mmm. Can you spell that?"

"Yes, 'West'…well, as in not East…and 'Heslerton', spelt H…e…s…l…e…r…t…o…n."

"Right…" there was another pause. "Mmm. Nope - it's not coming up on my screen."

"Well, I'm not lying…" said Denton.

"I'm not saying that you are, Mr Denton, I'm just saying that it is not coming up on my map - perhaps you're misspelling it."

"I…I can't be!" said an incredulous Denton. "I've broken down next to a road sign that says in big black letters WEST HESLERTON. West Heslerton. West Heslerton. West Heslerton!"

He turned to Randall, "Where is she losing me?"

"..." Another long pause. "I don't think that I like your tone, Mr Denton."

"Well, you know what, I don't like yours! I've been on the phone for ten minutes now and all we have established is that you're a cretin. Forget it. We'll walk the rest of the way. The exercise will do us good. Gooddaymiss."

Fuming, Denton threw the mobile onto the back seat.

"So..." said Randall, after waiting a moment or two until he thought it would be safe to speak. "Now what?"

Denton turned to look at him. "I dunno," he said shrugging his shoulders.

Bonnie and Delia returned to the car and got in. Delia did not look like she was enjoying herself. Bonnie did not look like she had a clue where she was.

"So," said Delia talking slightly faster than usual. "Are the AA on the way yet? Are they here? Have they been? Are we going now, are we? Are we going? Can we go? Mmm?"

Denton and Randall were exhausted on her behalf by the effort.

"Not quite," they both said in unison.

Now, they say God moves in mysterious ways. But Denton thought that this was just bollocks. God did not move in mysterious ways at all, he was just a grumpy old man with a cruel sense of humour. When Denton tried the car again, it started first time.

"Should I phone my supervisor to tell him?" asked Bonnie.

"NO!" they all screamed.

As always seems to be the case with these things, the hotel that someone, somewhere, had chosen, turned out to be truly terrible. In fact, it seemed to Denton that the very construction of the building was some sort of miracle in itself. It must surely have been that the whole place had been designed by a manic depressive, financed as a final act of defiance by a banker perhaps on his last day, having been dismissed for gross misconduct, and built by a team of alcoholic builders. Nothing worked. Nothing looked like it would work. Nothing matched and nothing looked clean. To make matters worse, all the rooms were shared. This was fine for Denton and Randall. Not so good for Delia...

"Oh, I do not believe it!" said a visibly shaken Delia. "I'm sharing a room with Bonnie!"

Randall managed to stifle a smirk.

"How can this be?" asked Delia. "Did I do something wrong in a previous life?"

Bonnie by this stage had trotted off. No doubt to make sure that her supervisor knew where she was.

"Delia, don't worry. It'll be fine," said Denton.

Ten minutes later he had changed his mind.

"Now, I don't believe this!" he said dropping his bag in disbelief as he stood looking at his and Randall's room. It was located in what looked to have once been a military dorm. All the facilities were shared. The room was so narrow that Randall and Denton could not pass each other to get to the sink at the window. The lock didn't work properly. The window wouldn't close. The room had bunk beds and nothing else. No wardrobe. No mirror. Nowhere to make little cups of tea and coffee. Nothing. Prison cells were more spacious and well equipped.

"I need to get drunk," said Randall. "Fast."

"Seconded," said Denton.

"My round all night," said Delia, terrified to even venture the extra distance to see what her own shared room would look like.

The advantage of a weekend away is that typically the drinks are free all weekend. Partners are not known for their generosity. But then, typically, the partners are quite happy to take advantage of the trainees that typically drink all the typical drinks. What better way to get ahead with a partner than to give a partner head.

"Typical," said Delia. "Just look at Bonnie. She's all over that crowd of partners."

"Yeah, I know." said Denton. "She'll probably get a job on qualification quicker than we will."

"She'd better not," said Delia with a passion in her eyes that Denton had not seen before. "Otherwise that will just be game over for me. Game over."

Denton, Randall and Delia stood in a circle in one corner of the bar just watching the partners ogle Bonnie. So were the rest of the male solicitors. In fact, about the only person who didn't was Colin, who seemed to be just stood on his own, knocking back vodka shots.

"Hooley's not holding back now, is he?" said Denton.

"Well, the word is that Colin's putting in for partnership," said Delia.

"Oh right. Is he likely to get it?"

"Not really," said Delia, "Not after he lost his only big client to a rival firm this week. The partners are spitting feathers."

"Oh," said Denton. "Oh, hang on. Yeah, I think I was there when he did it."

"Yeah, well it's pretty much certain he won't get partnership this year, if at all."

It was now night time, well past five in any event, and having not finished a delectable meal of mechanically reconstituted chicken and Chernobyl affected carrots and potatoes, the group decided to hit the bar. Unfortunately, the bar wasn't really ready. There was one bar man, who seemed to get confused by any order, no matter how simple, and straightforward it may seem to everyone else. *'One pint of bitter, please. No. One. One! No, that's two glasses. Still two. Yeah, no, beer. Bitter. No. No, not that one. No, no! Can you hear me? Hello? OK, no, vodka's fine.'*

The bar itself was terrible. It featured damp affected, once-white-wallpaper, dim lighting and deep red, paisley patterned carpet containing all manner of stains, as standard.

There was giggling from one side of it as a slice of lemon got placed on Bonnie's exposed cleavage whilst she lent back, held up by a partner, whilst another one took the lemon slice off her with his mouth. As you would expect, the partners cheered as one of their colleagues got lucky. Pretty much every male was nearby, perhaps hoping for a turn. Only Colin refrained, stood as he was, in the corner, by himself, in his own little world.

"Urgh. That's disgusting," said Delia.

"You're just jealous," said Denton. "But with good reason. Bonnie does give female trainees a very bad name."

"I just don't get it," said Randall. "She's so dumb. How come they don't just want to kill her like we did?"

Denton and Delia looked at Randall and then looked back at Bonnie who was now having salt licked from her cleavage.

"Oh. Right. The massive tits," said Randall. "Yeah, I guess I can see why now."

"Urgh. I really do despise her for living up to dirty old men's fantasies," said Delia. "I can't promise that I won't garrotte her on the way back."

"Fair enough," said Denton. "But just don't get blood on the seat, will you?"

"Done," said Delia.

"Right," said Denton clapping his hands together. "I've had enough of this. Who fancies coming back to our room to help me drink the bottle of vodka that I brought with me."

"Did you?" asked Randall. "I brought a bottle of vodka too."

"OK, well in that case, we have two bottles to get through. You coming Delia?"

As they marched away, a glace cherry popped up in the air having emanated from Bonnie's belly button, followed by a massive cheer.

"Yeah, OK," said Delia, distracted by what was happening in front of her. "I definitely need to get drunk before I can go back to my room tonight."

"Right," said Denton back in their room. "Drinking games. Randall - choose one."

"OK, erm, the celebrity name game thing."

"What's that?" said Delia.

"Oh, Delia - you've led a sheltered life," said Randall shaking his head. "What happens is one person starts by saying the name of a famous celebrity. The next person in the circle then has to say a different celebrity's name, only this name has to start with the letter of the previous celebrity's surname. So, if Denton says 'Donald Trump', you have to name a celebrity who's name starts with a 'T'."

"Like, 'Trevor MacDonald'?" asked Delia.

"Exactly. Now, if someone says a celebrity who has the same first letter in both Christian and surname, the direction is reversed."

"Like, Bridget Bardot?" asked Delia.

"Yes, very good," snapped Randall, almost agitated by her enthusiasm though more likely annoyed by the constant interruptions.

"Easy," remarked Delia.

"Well, it's not that easy," retorted Randall. "You have to drink the entire time that you think. You won't find it that easy later on. You have to be a hardened drinker and have a good recollection of names, like me, in order to do well. Oh, yes - this is no walk in the park. There is no picnic here. Only the best survive. Only the tough will prosper," he said with a knowing nod.

Two hours and one and a quarter bottle of vodka later, Randall was spread eagled, unconscious on the floor.

"OK…" slurred Denton. "Terry…Thomas. HA! Reverse direction. 'S your go again." He said, his head nodding like an upturned cup on a stick.

Delia frowned. "But it was anyway?!" she scrunched her face up, presumably because she was concentrating and not, for the love of God, because she thought it was attractive. "Terence Trent D'arby." She finally volunteered.

"Nope - we've had that one."

"Thomas the Tank engine."

"Nope. Had it. And I'm still not sure you can have it anyway."

"Thom Yorke."

"Had it."

By this stage, the game consisted solely of Denton and Delia who, thanks to Randall's selfish occupation of the carpet, were confined to a tiny area of the room next to Denton's bed. To save room, they were sat opposite each other, cross legged with knees touching, the remaining bottle of vodka in between them. Denton was not sure if he would ever be able to get up but he really did not seem to care.

"Terry Scott."

"Done it."

"Tracey Island."

"What?"

"Erm, Thierry Henry."

"Had him."

"Really?" giggled Delia.

"What? Oh…very good. Name another."

"Ermm…"

"Drink while you think!" chastised Denton.

"Oh, I don't know!" she said between sips, "Mr Tickle."

A devilish grin spread across Denton's face. "Are you ticklish?"

"Nooo…" said Delia, playfully, at which point Denton wrestled her to the bed.

"Get off! No! Stop it!" she giggled, as she wriggled around, her hair falling out from its slide as she did so.

"No way," said Denton. "This is the most fun that I've had all day -

watching you squirm!"

"Oh yeah?" said Delia, as she grabbed Denton's sides and tickled him back.

Now they were both squirming around the bed until Denton realised that his face was right in front of Delia's. As he stared into her sparkling big blue eyes, it dawned on him slowly that he wasn't tickling anymore. Neither was Delia struggling. She lay perfectly still *staring back into his eyes.* No one said anything and it felt like it was taking an age but Denton didn't feel uncomfortable and he sensed that Delia wasn't either. He wondered in a drunken stupor what was going on in those eyes. They sparkled at him. He could not remember them ever doing that before. It was as if it was the first time that he had ever seen them and he dared not look away just in case he never saw anything so beautiful ever again.

Silently, they lay. Slowly Denton realised he was close enough to Delia to feel her heart pounding through his own ribs. Her pulse rate seemed to be just as wild as his own, and he wondered where it would take them if he simply nestled further and indulged in those soft glistening lips…

But he didn't. His mind suddenly caught up with his heart. Curiosity had gotten the better of him. Cats - those poor pioneers - had taught valuable lessons on what would happen next. It wasn't for him.

The look of warmth and intrigue that seemed to be trying to escape from Delia's eyes, was suddenly lost as Denton's expression snapped back into a more serious look. Denton felt a slight twinge of loss as he saw it disappear back into those two deep blue pools as if it might never be seen again.

"Well. That's enough excitement for me," said Denton, his tone almost cold. "Time for my bedtime I think."

Delia briefly looked confused and upset as her alcohol induced mind tried to fathom out what had just happened.

"Yes, you're right. I should get back," she said, noticeably deflated.

She got up and paused briefly. She looked back at Denton and, on seeing his resolute expression, let her head drop. She left quietly without saying a word, slowing only to step over the spread-eagled Randall. The door closed heavily, as if it may never open again.

Denton sat alone on his bed. In his drunkenness, he struggled to rationalise any of the feelings he was now experiencing but since one of them was extreme tiredness, he decided to ignore all of them in favour of sleep.

Night soon ended as a new day began. Everyone accepted that this was the case when the sun rose, except for the moon, who just sat there stubbornly refusing to budge. After all these years you would have thought he might have worked that out but the permanent look of confusion on his face suggested otherwise.

"God, I feel hungover…," said Denton, as he crawled onto the floor from the bottom bunk. Light cascaded unwelcomingly through the paper thin curtains in their room. Denton spoke with his eyes closed.

"Me too," said Randall, whose voice, oddly enough, sounded as if it were above Denton.

Denton opened his eyes in confusion. He looked around. There was no spread-eagled Randall to be seen. He looked up. Sure enough, there was a hand protruding from the top bunk, which Denton assumed to be Randall's, mainly because he had no reason to doubt it.

"How did you get up there?" said Denton, looking up at the top bunk.

There was a pause and much shuffling, as if Randall were asking himself the same question.

"I have absolutely no idea," he finally conceded.

"You going to breakfast?"

"No way. It's going to take me the best part of the morning just to figure out how to get off this thing again."

"Fair enough," said Denton. "I'm going to go and get a shower. I smell like Gandhi's flip flop."

"Too much information," groaned Randall, covering his eyes with his forearm.

Denton left the room with a towel and wandered slowly down the corridor, into the communal shower area. He hoped to God that he did not have the misfortune to see any of his superiors naked. There are some people that it really does help to imagine have Action Man private parts.

What was that about last night? thought Denton as he stepped into the shower, which for whatever reason, had the effect of triggering memories from last night and forcing them to the forefront of his mind.

Did I nearly kiss Delia Lounge Rat? Did I want to kiss her? Did I instigate it? Prissy Missy Lounge Rat? What was I thinking?

Denton's thoughts were interrupted as he realised that some other people had entered the shower room.

"…seriously?" said someone who sounded a lot like Devlin Hawkes.

"Yes. All night apparently," said someone else who sounded a lot like another partner, Campbell Oliver.

"That cannot be true. He must be lying. You know what Dave is like - prone to exaggeration…"

Dave? thought Denton. *Who is Dave? What are they talking about?*

"Ordinarily, Dev, I would tend to agree with you. But seriously - she was all over him. His story is certainly consistent with what I saw."

It slowly dawned on Denton that he might know what they were talking about.

"Oh come on, Campbell - she was drunk! She was all over everyone. Even you at one point."

It then dawned on Denton that he knew exactly what they were talking about.

There was a pause. Perhaps Campbell was blushing and working out how to explain himself. Equally, perhaps he was just secretly reliving a moment he had had with her.

"I know," he said eventually, as if about to confess all, "she whispered in my ear that I could suck an olive out of her belly button if I wanted to."

"Did you?" asked an excited Devlin Hawkes, as if he were a teenager.

"No way!" Campbell retorted. "Shirley would have killed me!"

There was another brief pause.

"…I was tempted though," resumed Campbell. "Did you see how small and pert her arse was in that skirt?"

"Oh God, yeah!" said Devlin.

Water started as one of them got into a shower cubicle. The volume of their conversation intensified as they countered the effect of the running water.

"So where did it happen?" asked Devlin. "Wasn't he sharing with Alistair Bramble from Tax?"

Sounds of trickling water emanated from another shower cubicle.

"Yes. So they could hardly get any action there. She took him back to her room instead the filthy minx. When Dave questioned whether her room mate would mind, she just winked and said that the room mate was a definite 'Lezza' and would probably enjoy watching them."

"Nice! Who was the room mate?"

"What? Oh, I don't know. Some dull trainee. She did tell Dave her name but Dave couldn't remember it. I can't recall myself who it was. Wasn't anyone on our 'fitties' list."

"Oh right. So was the room mate there when they got back?"

"No. But Dave wasn't messing about. I think she said the room mate was a bit of a prude so Dave was a bit worried about getting caught so he tried to keep it as brief as possible…"

They both laughed.

"Yeah - bet that's what he tells all the women. Sorry, love - didn't wanna get caught!"

They chortled again.

Dave, Dave - who is Dave? thought Denton. Then he realised. *No - surely not - surely it wasn't David O'Dwyer, one of the most senior partners in Corporate?!*

"Yeah. Although he did say that after a while he settled into it. I mean it was just a quick one. She was up for all sorts of stuff. The kind of stuff that your mother, and probably even your father, would not approve of. Told him that she liked foursomes with men and women filling every available hole."

"Dirty slut!" commented Devlin. "A proper little whore - well done to the Graduate Recruitment team for getting her in, I say!"

"Quite. Dave reckons he took her up the arse, but I don't think he did. I've seen her this morning and she doesn't seem to be limping much."

"Yeah, well maybe that says more about Dave's performance than it does her!"

The inane guffawing started again.

I do not fucking believe it! thought Denton.

"So what is Dave going to do? Surely he's not thinking about seeing her again?"

"Well, he reckons that it is not going to happen again and that it was just a one off departure from the straight and narrow. He doesn't want his wife to know."

"Fair play to him, but don't think for a moment that this is a one off. O'Dwyer is notorious amongst the equity partners for buffing trainees. Don't you remember that girl in '92? The trainee that had to leave after six weeks?"

"No?" said Campbell. "Oh, hang on - yes. Yes, I do. The one who tried to top herself by jumping off the building."

"That's right. That was one of O'Dwyer's. She was lovely and very beautiful. She was, what, twenty three? Big Dave had her pregnant within six weeks of her starting her training contract. When he refused to leave his wife, she tried to kill herself. Think they compromised her out of the business in the end. Last I heard that she's working as a night manager for Tesco now."

"Do you know, I never knew that? I often wondered where she went - she was lovely!"

"Yeah."

"Hasn't Dave got kids himself anyway?"

"Yeah, two. Little Bobby is five. Matilda is seven. She's a real angel - real bonny looking. Just like her mum."

The sound of running water stopped from each cubicle.

"So this trainee - is she any good? Maybe she won't get taken on, on qualification."

"She's useless. Utter rubbish. Every appraisal that she has had has been atrocious. But they can't get rid of her now, can they? She'll just bring a sex discrimination claim - we don't want that in all the papers - would ruin the firm's profile."

"True."

"Think they'll just stick her in Pensions or something. Somewhere she can look pretty and hopefully not do too much damage."

Denton heard a door close and suddenly the voices were gone. He was alone, freezing in his shower cubicle.

"Well that is just bloody fantastic!" said Delia, moments after Denton had recounted his story. "I just knew something like this would happen - I just bloody knew it!"

"I know," said Denton. "It's disgraceful. I heard someone else talking about it too."

The conversation died. Suddenly Denton had the feeling that there was an uncomfortable silence.

"So..." he began without really knowing where he was headed. "How are you feeling today?"

"Yeah, fine," said Delia awkwardly. "A bit hung over, I suppose. Well, OK, a lot hung over. Don't really remember much, you?"

"No. No. My memory's a bit patchy. A vodka induced blank," he lied.

As Denton stood there recounting his story, he could not work out whether he had been desperate to tell Delia because they shared the common bond of despising Bonnie Belcher, or whether it was because that after recent events he was actually beginning to like her. He hoped that it was the former. The latter just felt too odd to deal with and the very mention of it brought his hang over symptoms out in more force.

"What time is it?" asked Delia.

Denton looked down at his watch and as he looked back up he caught the briefest of glimpses at those two beautiful eyes.

"Erm, nearly eleven I think."

"Doesn't our team-building exercise start soon?" she asked.

The buzz word in all these weekend away events is usually 'team-building'. The people that organise these things seem to be under the illusion that what is missing in every unit is the appreciation of being a team. It is blindingly obvious that these people, whether internal or external, really do not have any kind of understanding of what solicitors actually do. Neither do they seem to understand that the core skills that are utilised in a department like Corporate are different, sometimes fundamentally different, from the skills that you need to work in Property or Employment or Tax. In any event, in large corporate firms, the importance of being in a team is already recognised by the people that work there. As a result, the people that work together on a day to day basis will either already be a 'team', or they won't, and no amount of 'trust exercises' will change that.

But that is not to say that trust exercises do not afford unique opportunities.

Denton, Delia and Randall found themselves in a team of seven people stood out in a field on a fresh summer's day, next to one end of a picnic table. The others were Colin Hooley, a female partner called Loraine, a senior solicitor called Olivia, and Bonnie.

Colin had not been very impressed to learn that Bonnie had slept with one of his colleagues. In fact, it was rumoured that Colin was 'disappointed' with Bonnie. It was said that Colin had attained the level that he had in the firm on account of the success of his 'disappointed' chats that he would have with individuals. Denton had never actually witnessed one as yet, but apparently they were incredibly nerve-wracking and always brought the individual down by a peg or two. Denton still found that hard to believe, given how placid Colin was and how easy a walkover he appeared to be. When Denton had mentioned this to another solicitor, he had been told that he was grossly underestimating Colin, which was apparently part of the ploy - a false sense of security. It seemed more likely than not that Colin was brewing up a 'disappointed' chat right now.

Equally, Loraine could not honestly say that she was impressed either since she had worked very hard to battle through daily sexist comments to get to partnership level. Olivia, who had once been told, 'you'll never go far in this firm unless you start wearing more low cut tops and some revealing underwear once in a while,' was also less than chuffed that Bonnie's antics had sent a couple of the partners her way expecting the same behaviour.

If Bonnie had to pick a team of people to participate in a team-building exercise with then this was quite possibly the worst group of people that she could have picked.

The exercise that they had to do was simple enough. One member of the team stood on the picnic table with their back to the group. The group would be expected to stand next to the table and link arms, thus supporting the victim as they fell back. They call it the 'exercise in trust' designed to help people rely on their team members.

If Bonnie had a brain, which was in severe doubt, then she might have been feeling slightly uneasy about the idea of flinging herself backwards off the table. She wasn't.

If Bonnie really, really put her mind to it, she might have ensured that some sort of witness was present to make sure the group did the exercise properly. She didn't.

And if Bonnie really was not just a brainless bleached blonde vacuous slut then she might have at least checked to see if the group was even linking arms before she fell. She hadn't.

More importantly, it wasn't.

"Begin," called the co-ordinator. At surrounding tables, the same event was occurring with the noticeable exception that in those groups, there was a lot of cheering and celebrating, not just the empty sound of a dull thud.

In fairness though, whilst it might have seemed like a mean thing to do, it was probable that Bonnie did not even feel any pain as she fell straight though the unlinked arms to the floor.

How unfortunate though that the group had picked the one and only table that had concrete underneath it, where every other had grass.

The group wandered off, leaving Bonnie to consider why she was on the ground alone. She had not broken any bones, which in many ways was a pity.

In every one else's minds, the exercise in trust had been a complete waste of time. For Denton, it was a revelation.

An exercise to gain people's trust.

Chapter Nineteen

Life begins, begins to end, at Thirty

Denton winced. His head was resting firmly between his hands, his palms exerting pressure onto his inflamed temples. *It hurts, it hurts,* he winced inwardly like a seven year old child. With a hangover.

When he slowly looked up, he found himself at work, perched on his chair. His computer was already switched on, logged in and brimming with far too much enthusiasm. *Mmmmm,* the fan in his PCU purred. *Mmmmm, I'm just so excited to be here - to serve you today. What can I do? How can I help? I can work out the most complex of sums - the most intricate of calculations - the most tantalising of formulae. And I can do it all in an instant. Mmmmm. Mmmmm. Or I can just display these simple pixels rearranged simply on the screen to form letters. That's good too. Mmmmm.*

Denton had no idea how he had gotten there. He didn't even remember getting to work. He tried to, but he kept getting the same response from his brain. *What? No. Go away. No, I don't know where you are. I've got a hangover. I'm not working today - need to stay lying down. No, you can't come in and try to work it out for yourself, I need to keep the lights off. Need dark. No! Shut up. Go and get me a drink of orange or something. Owww. Poor me.*

It was the Monday following the corporate weekend away. Denton was only aware of this information on account of the fact that Outlook 2000 was displaying the calendar for him. Since he had no reason to suspect that it would lie to him, he had no qualms in accepting the information as fact.

A new e-mail flashed up on Denton's screen entitled *Birthday cakes in the usual place!* The exclamation mark presumably had been added to inject that certain sense of fun and excitement that would be all too painfully missing if it were not there. It was from Amber. She was still working there because, for some inexplicable reason, she had been offered a permanent position. Maybe Daddy was someone important.

Brilliant, thought Denton. *One of the secretaries is having a birthday, which can only mean one thing: namely, that they'll all take a long boozy lunch; and, spend the whole afternoon directing a barrage of abuse at any fee-earner who gets within spitting distance of their desk.*

Denton was slouching deep into his chair, surreptitiously (though some might say blatantly) using the back of it as a head rest. Lazily, he moved the mouse cursor over the e-mail and clicked twice as slowly and lethargically as he could to cause it to open up.

"Today is my birthday," began the e-mail. *"I have baked a cake,"* Tight-wad,

thought Denton *"and have placed it in the usual place,"* i.e. within easy reach of all the secretaries and furthest away from Martha, the fat secretary in the corner that no one spoke to *"so please help yourself"* i.e. fuck off partners, you should be buying me gifts, not the other way around, you capitalist pigs. *"A few of us"* (Pissheads) *"are going out for drinks after work tonight and it would be great to see some friendly faces there too"* i.e. again, not applicable to the partners unless you're paying *"to help me celebrate my thirtieth birthday,"* during the course of which I will end up sobbing in the toilet for no logical reason other than the fact that now I'm in my thirties, I've lost my nice arse and my neck is sagging.

"Well, at least that gives me something to do this evening," said Denton to absolutely no-one.

He watched as Amber walked past his office and placed her homemade cake on the table next to his office. From his vantage point, he could just see Martha's small (on account of her being far away) fat face looking forlornly at temptation. Even from here, he could see the tiny cogs whirring in the vacuous chamber that housed her food chooser, trying desperately hard to figure out a way to manoeuvre her lumbering mass, without seeming too keen, towards the chocolate delight in front of her. The chocolate desire that called her name softly in the air conditioned, bacteria saturated, breeze. Unfortunately, before the cogs had had chance to complete a single revolution, her legs had already concluded *ahh, fuck it* and were already well on the way to the table carrying their heavy burden with them.

Cake sounds good, thought Denton, although his stomach had other ideas. "Or maybe not," he said, suppressing the urge to vomit. "Later, perhaps." Though on reflection, that was probably wishful thinking, given the fact that Martha had arrived on the scene.

The telephone rang. Denton thought this highly unlucky on his part. It never usually rang. He answered it, but only to make the ringing stop.

"Hello? Denton Voyle?" he croaked, the last part not intentionally meant to be a question but in his present state, quite fitting, since he was not altogether convinced he had guessed his own name correctly.

"Hi," said a chirpy young go-getter voice. "Is that Denton Voyle?"

Denton paused. He recalled that he had just confirmed his own name so he replied "Yes!" in an agitated fashion. He wondered what the caller would have said had he thought it through a bit more and replied, "No."

"Hi, it's Loretta here. Loretta Kingsley?" she said, stating her own name as a question. The question mark either signified a short cut to avoid asking the question *do you remember me* or else she too was having trouble remembering.

"Hello?" asked Denton, confused by everything and anything. He pondered whether he could get away with putting the phone down altogether.

"I'm working on Project Sunflower Oil?"

Well, you either are or you aren't, love. Come on pull yourself together! thought Denton.

"I'm from Needles Solicitors?" she volunteered.

I dunno - check your letterhead if you're not sure, it normally says on there.

"Ah, Loretta. How are you?" said Denton wincing as he recalled that this was the annoyingly over-keen girl working in the Corporate department on the other side of the deal. Denton also seemed to remember that apart from being incredibly annoying she was also not very good. Needles was a small firm that he had never heard of. It seemed that this was her first deal, which to her was probably a big deal but to Denton's firm was so insignificant that they had entrusted Denton to do the entire deal by himself, with minimal supervision.

"I'm fine, Denton but you sound awful - are you coming down with a cold?"

"Yeah, something like that," said Denton. "How can I help you?"

"Well, I'm just wondering if you have had chance to consider my latest amendments to the draft BPA - the Business Purchase Agreement?" *I know what a BPA is!* thought Denton, a little more agitated. Today, was really not the best day for Loretta to start patronising him.

As explained previously, the Business Purchase Agreement or Share Purchase Agreement is the key document in any corporate transaction. That's the part that tells you what should happen and what everyone has to do to make it happen. Sometimes BPA's or SPA's can be voluminous tomes extending over many hundreds of pages. Quite often the size of the deal is reflected in the size of the BPA/SPA. A three hundred page BPA/SPA signifies a mega deal. A leviathon. A huge, mammoth, cutting edge, state of the art, mother fucker of a deal.

A fourteen page BPA on the other hand…

"Yes, I have had a chance to take a look at it," lied Denton. "Can I just confirm that I'm singing from the same hymn sheet?" he asked, adopting his most polished Corporate twaddle speak.

"Sorry?" asked Loretta.

Virgin, thought Denton.

"Can I just confirm I'm looking at the same draft as you?" he sighed with deliberate *Don't waste my time* petulance.

"Of course," she said, noticeably taken aback. "I'm looking at version 18 point 2."

"Ridiculous," muttered Denton.

"Sorry?"

"Here it is," he said, as if repeating his original comments.

"Right then," said Loretta. Denton could hear her fidgeting in her chair, as if she might say at any moment, "and are we sitting comfortably? Then I'll begin…"

Once upon a time, in a land far far away…

Loretta commenced, taking Denton through each and every change. Of course, Denton had not read her amendments. He had lost interest on or around version 5 point 17, so he did not even know what changes had been made anyway. 'Helpfully', Loretta had underlined her changes from her previous draft in red but since Denton did not know what the previous eighty odd versions had said anyway, it did not help him. He thought that Loretta would have noticed that he was not playing anymore when he had stopped marking up the document with suggested changes and additions, but apparently not. She simply made amendments to the amendments that she had already made.

To make matters worse, Loretta sounded like a loose window on an intercity train. Her mouth flapped open and closed in the wind causing all these hideous screeching noises to come out and no one did anything about it. This was not assisting Denton to recover from his hangover. By the time she had reached clause 10.1 of 32, Denton had decided enough was enough, especially considering he hadn't even said anything yet.

"Loretta!" he said interrupting her, "I hear you loud and clear. I agree with the principle of your proposals but not the detail. Yes, we need to get our ducks in a row, and yes we need to establish a synergy, but the fact of the matter is, we're just not travelling from the same port. We want to be going to the same destination, sure, because that's where the party's at - but our tickets are for two different trains. We need to strip this thing down, concentrate on the middle ground, the common goal, and take the commercial view. This plane needs wings, yes - but does it need the baggage? We've got to streamline in order to maximise and we need to be aiming to put this thing to bed before it goes off the rails. OK? Look, leave this one with me. Let me think it through, consider the angles and then touch base with you next week? OK? By then, hopefully - though I make no promises - we'll have something watertight that we can really cast off with. Capiche?"

There was silence.

"Yeah. Sure," said Loretta, demonstrably lost. "Yeah, my thoughts exactly. Let's do that and we'll, erm, put this to bed," she said, regaining her composure and enthusiasm, as if she knew what it meant.

"Ok, then, byeeee," said Denton, replacing the hand set. "Who's says I'm not getting the hang of this? Grade A perfect Corporate Twaddle there, Denton. Well done."

If Denton was wearing a pair of braces, he would have tweaked those bad boys right out and let them slap his nipples with a satisfying tingle of pain. A broad smile wrenched across his face only to be instantly replaced with a wince as his hangover reminded him that it was still there. He grimaced.

Honestly, he thought. *All this for the sale of a fish and chip shop in Vauxhall.*

*****

Brian sat at his desk.

Idly, he tapped away with a biro against the mock marble work surface. His head was sitting firmly in his right hand. His glum expression mirrored the gloominess of his fake marble surroundings. His eyes flicked from the tiny TV monitor on his right, hidden between his desk and the raised lip of the shelf above it, to the lift doors which sat inactive to his left. Occasionally, he rolled his eyes to get the circulation back in his eye lids. *Welcome!* said the sign in front of his desk in bold, proud letters; a sentiment that was ill-befitting of its environment.

Good god, I'm bored, thought Brian. *I mean, I'm not just bored - I'm booorrrrreeeddd.*

He lifted his head from his hands - stretched - cricked his neck from left to right. Looked left. Looked right. Then returned to his former position. Exercise break over.

I just long for a bit of excitement. Anything. Something! Just give me something to do that I might enjoy! A hold-up! A shoot-up! A flower arranging contest! Anything.

He flinched as he recollected his own thought.

Damn it! I'm thinking about flowers again! Why? Why!

He glanced over at the poorly arranged lilies at the far end of the shelf.

Right. That's it! he declared in his head. Hopefully. *No more flowers. No more. It's not right for a man to be so obsessed with flowers. Or wrapping paper. Or ribbons. Or kimonos. Not right at all. I'm a security guard for goodness sake!*

A lift door opened and a young man walked out, straight past him, towards the doors.

"Good afternoon, Brian," said the man as he walked past.

"Good afternoon, sir," said Brian, sitting to attention. *Nice trousers. Good cut.*

Brian's head returned to his hands.

Now, where was I? Oh yes, hold ups. Hang on? Why would anyone hold up a firm of solicitors?

*****

By the time that lunch became a viable option, Denton was feeling almost refreshed. Of course, he wasn't refreshed and he was not anywhere near it, but he didn't have a tangible longing for his own death anymore, so that had to be a good thing.

An e-mail bounced on to his screen and his computer sang to herald its arrival.

It was from Randall.

It simply read *Lunch?*

"Yeah, if you want. When? And also where? And I suppose, what?" Denton replied.

"Now. Downstairs. Doesn't matter. Just heard something that will make you laugh."

"OK..." typed Denton, intrigued.

Denton stood, grabbed his jacket and headed for the lift. Once inside it, he pressed the button marked '*temporary release*'.

When the lift reached the ground and the doors opened, Denton discovered Randall was stood almost with his nose pressed to the door to the lift, such was his excitement. A big grin had spread across his face.

"I've got some information!" he said.

"Yes, but what are we going to eat?" said Denton, thinking with his stomach. "I need food to cure this wretched hangover!"

"Doesn't matter," said Randall. "You won't be as interested in food when you hear what I have to say!"

They both hurried out of the building and into the throng of people who were also struggling with the effort of selecting an eatery in the middle of the financial district.

"What?" asked Denton. "And where are going for lunch?" he added in case Randall had forgotten the importance of the point.

"Hang on. Will tell you in a mo once we're a safe distance from the office. Spitalfields Market for lunch?"

"OK. But it's a bit of a trek though, isn't it?"

"Yeah, but it's worth it, isn't it?"

Spitalfields market is fantastic. It's akin to a giant aircraft hangar, which, amongst other things, contains every type of eatery you could possibly ask for. Each one has it own kiosk area where you can purchase all kinds of lavish and exotic foods from across the globe and then suffer the ignominy of trying to consume the blessed things from shallow plastic containers using disposable cutlery prone to bending in every direction other than the one you would prefer it to go in.

"So, what is it?" asked Denton, his excitement certainly containable but in the absence of being able to cut through his mussel and Hoegaarden square pie, there seemed nothing better to ask.

They were sat at a rickety, steel-effect plastic table, perched on equally rickety, steel-effect plastic chairs. Randall briefly ignored his portion of chop suey.

"Well, you remember that Bonnie shagged that partner."

"Vaguely," joked Denton.

"Yeah, well, our whole department is talking about it. I mean not openly, but there are certainly lots of whisperings going on."

"Really?"

"Oh yeah, but there's more to it than you've heard."

"Like what?"

"There was more than one partner that got laid by her that night!"

"No way!" said Denton, his mind racing. "Who was the other?"

"I have no idea, but the guy in the office next to me said that he had heard it was one of the Corporate partners. A well placed Corporate partner too, and that they are planning to continue seeing each other.

"Really?"

"However, there's another bit that you are really going to love."

"What?"

"Seriously, you are not going to like this."

"What?!"

"She has been offered a job on qualification in Corporate!"

Denton's heart fell into his stomach.

"You must be fucking joking!"

"Nope."

"Seriously, do not mess with me."

"I'm not. The offer has been formally made and she has been told to not to tell anyone about it."

"But she's shit!"

"Exactly. But apparently, there is a major client who has told the firm that if they continue to retain her, he will put two million pounds worth of fees our way."

Denton could feel the muscles in his jaw slacken.

"How come?"

"Well, apparently the managing director of this Company is desperate to bed her and thinks that this is the only way he will do it."

"Hang on. How do you know all this?"

"I told you, the guy in the office next door told me."

"Yes, but how does he know?"

"Well, he would not say for sure about the second Corporate partner thing, but in relation to the client thing he was at the pub one night on a works social and happened to be stood talking to this managing director. He said the guy just would not shut up about Bonnie and spent the entire evening moving back and forth between lusting over her and talking to his mates about how perfect she was."

"Shit me!" exclaimed Denton.

"Well, exactly," said Randall, as if that were the appropriate response.

"Well, that just fucking confirms the theory that I had. There is no fucking justice in this job, Randall, none at all. I mean, what is the point of even trying when some stupid fucking blonde can beat you just by wearing a low cut fucking top." Denton could feel his own blood pressure increasing.

"I know. Ridiculous, isn't it? Utterly ridiculous."

Although he was sure it was normally exquisite, Denton gnawed without appreciation at his pie, swallowing whenever it seemed appropriate. He sighed loudly.

"I mean, it's not even as if I particularly want the job, but there is something galling about the fact that it is not even on offer because some stupid bimbo beat me to it!"

"I know," said Randall. "I agree with you."

Denton glanced at his watch. "Is that the time? Look, I have to get back to the office, for all the use it will do me. I have a very important business purchase agreement to review."

At 3pm, Denton's doze was rudely disturbed as an explosion of howling, stumbling and the all pervading scent of perfume and extra strong mints (feebly concealing the alcohol fumes they were laced with) stormed the building. The secretaries had decided to return. No good could come of this.

*****

"Sorry, we're late Devlin," shouted one of them, which was followed by a giggle and then an outbreak of over-emphasised shushing.

Denton could see Devlin dictating in his office. He scowled at them as they stumbled past his window. Clearly he was not amused. He forced a smile at one of them.

"There we go," muttered Denton. "End of the working day. The secretaries have been drinking. Fuck all's going to get done now."

Gradually, the secretaries became more comfortable in their own environment. They began to chat amongst themselves. Then, not quite as gradually, they became a little too comfortable in their own environment to the point of almost becoming unaware of it, and started shouting and heckling. As Denton tried in vain to concentrate on the document in front of him, he suddenly realised that the noise was so loud he had been reading the same line over and over again for about fifteen minutes. He looked up towards the other offices and realised that he was not the only fee-earner who seemed to be struggling. Nearly every office door was now firmly shut. The secretaries, however, carried on, unabated.

As an act of kindness towards them, or perhaps, an act of mercy towards the fee-earners, the head of Corporate finally relented at 3.30pm and allowed all the secretaries to go home early. Denton presumed that he realised that this did not mean they would go home but instead meant they would go down the pub. Certainly, it was to be hoped that he understood that by releasing them early from the office, he was inflicting them on anyone stupid enough to be out drinking tonight.

Denton watched them as they turned off their computers and left the building for the night. He envied them. *Lucky bastards. Why should they get extra drinking time?* Of course, had he thought it through, he would have realised that it was a good thing that they were leaving now, before Brian was given the unenviable task of physically removing all of them from the building for their less than appropriate behaviour.

"Bye, Darling!" shouted one towards Devlin Hawkes. "The drinks are on you tonight, big guy!" whooped another, which was followed by an almighty cackle from the rest of the crones.

Stumbling and struggling to focus, they all made some attempt at trying to shut down their computers before lunging for their associated bags and jackets piled in the middle of the room as they unintentionally weaved their way towards the lift like a pack of mutton high on sheep-dip.

Denton returned to concentrating on understanding the finer legal points of the document in front of him and reflecting upon their usage in this transaction. And for 'understanding' read 'glossing over' and for 'reflecting upon' read 'dreaming about' and for 'their usage in this transaction' read 'drinking beer'.

Suddenly, Randall's head appeared at the frame of Denton's door. Denton squeaked in a manner not becoming of a man approaching twenty four. Even though the head appeared at a height consistent with it being attached to the rest of Randall's body, Denton's mind had already concluded that Randall, having just sent an e-mail, could not be anywhere other than at his desk, and therefore the appearance of his head could only have been an oversight by the rest of Randall's body.

"Alright!" said Randall, with far too much enthusiasm, even for four thirty on a Monday.

"Hi, Randall," said Denton. "What are you doing here?"

"Just got some documents to deliver to your floor so I thought I would pop by."

The rest of Randall's body now entered the room, which caused the information processing department in Denton's brain to feel a tad ridiculous at its previous conclusion that Randall's head could somehow separate and float off from the rest of his body. With a certain amount of egg on their face, they reluctantly cancelled the planned research programme into whether they could do the same with Denton's body. Sensing that there would be much gnashing of teeth on the realisation that they had not found the ultimate cure to hangovers, several brain cells decided that the embarrassment was too much and that the constant barrage of alcohol was perhaps affecting them after all. Certainly, this was one of the biggest *faux-pas*'s since the time the message had been sent around, which read *Previous reaction: 'Beer tastes like Dad's smelly socks' amended to 'Beer still tastes bad but worth it'.*

"Are you coming out to the pub tonight?" asked Denton.

"Nah. Can't - have got loads of work on at the moment. Think it will be a late one."

"OK," said Denton.

"Are you?" enquired Randall.

"Yeah, well all the secretaries have gone to the pub and so I thought I'd join them."

"My God, you're brave!" responded Randall. Without warning, he undid a cuff and whipped his sleeve up. "Look at this scar. Got that from a trip out drinking with secretaries."

Denton eyed the angry red scar on Randall's arm.

"Did you get so drunk you fell over or something?"

"No - that was from one secretary trying to claw my shirt off!"

Denton suddenly wondered whether this was such a good idea. Then he remembered that pubs sell alcohol and so everything once again seemed right with the idea.

At five o'clock he shut down his computer and left the building, heading for the 'Old Swan and Dustpan', which although no secretary had confirmed that this was their destination, Denton instinctively knew that it would be. He remained confident that the principle *Find the nearest, cheapest, ugliest and most run down pub in Central London and you'll find them* would stand him in good stead.

Having reached the door, Denton walked in with a tangible sense of trepidation at the sight that would face him as he entered. Even though it was likely to be a packed venue, he just knew that the location of the secretaries would immediately become painfully obvious.

As expected the place was packed and yet Denton instantly knew where they were.

"DENTON!" came the shriek.

"WOO-HOO!" they screamed.

"OI! SEXY BUM!" hollered one of the more desperate ones.

Great! thought Denton, solemnly noticing the complete lack of other fee-earners stood with them. They were stood just away from the bar in a massive huddle. Many of them seemed to have changed outfits from earlier in the day. Aside from the noise, Denton could easily have spotted them, even if they had been silent, blinded as he was by the ensemble of silver sparkling tops that confronted him. It was like going drinking with a disco ball.

"Come on, Darling! Get your kit off for the laydeez!" one cried.

Timidly, he approached. *Maybe I should just have one then go home,* he thought as he neared the pack. *Is losing my trousers really worth it for a pint of lager?*

They had collected around a solitary table. An assortment of drinks and empties had already accumulated.

He smiled, noticing the abundance of tall glasses filled almost entirely with sparkling straws, sticks, cherries, fruit, plastic stars, sparklers, trees, armoured personnel carriers, lost luggage and several types of endangered species. *Is there even enough room for the alcohol?* he mused.

"Everyone ok for drinks?" he ventured, praying that the answer would be 'yes'.

The trouble with secretaries is, when they get drunk, they suddenly lose it. They lose their self-restraint. They lose their inhibitions. They lose their dignity. They lose the ability to speak. And walk. They lose their handbags. And, usually, by the end of the night, one of them will have lost their knickers.

Denton approached the bar and, for one of the first times in his life as a fully fledged alcohol consumer, Denton prayed for a slow service time.

"What can I get you?" asked a barman, appearing from no-where.

"Erm," said Denton, slightly taken aback. "Surely, someone else was waiting before me?"

"Nope. Not many stopping now that crowd has arrived," he said, nodding towards Elton John's dance troupe.

"Really? What about that guy?" asked Denton.

The barman hesitated before looking, unaccustomed to such a display of chivalry from a patron.

"Er, no. Listen, it's your turn. Do you want a drink or not?"

"Go on then," complained Denton. "Five bottles of Michelob please."

"Oh shit," said the barman. "Don't tell me they've moved onto the beers after cocktails. I've just had the toilets redecorated."

"They haven't. These are for me."

Denton clasped four bottles between the fingers of his left hand and raised the other to his mouth with his right hand, before moving away and returning to the Starlight Express wannabes.

What, at first, had appeared to Denton to be an incoherent mess of jumbled sounds and utterances followed by inane giggles and horrific cackling, soon became an intelligible and altogether informed discussion of modern life with every swig of beer that Denton took. Having initially dismissed the prospect of remaining out for the duration, Denton soon re-evaluated his position when he took into account certain key facts:

1. Every secretary had now consumed a sufficient amount of alcohol to believe that he was actually attractive;
2. Every secretary was giving him the eye or, less subtly, copping a feel whenever the opportunity arose;
3. Every secretary was buying him a new drink the moment he finished the old one;
4. Every secretary was likely to be after sex with him, whether they were married or not;
5. He could outrun all of them.

On the basis of this, he was happy to proceed.

Pretty soon, Amber ventured over.

"Happy birthday!" said Denton, hugging her, having reached the point of drinking where physical contact with strangers was not only acceptable, but also obligatory.

"Yeah!" said Amber as she began needlessly dancing. "It's ma birthday! It's ma birthday," to a tune that Denton did not dare admit he didn't know for fear of upsetting her.

"So can I mention the age?" asked Denton, although as soon as he said it, he wished he hadn't. For an instant, he thought he saw her well up.

"Of course! Why not?" she said slightly too defensively, which had the effect of giving her away.

"Well…" Denton began and then, having briefly thought about it, stopped.

"No, it's fine. I mean, some people get nervous about thirty. They don't like it. They wonder what it means to be thirty. Have they done enough with their lives. Have they achieved enough?" she chugged nervously on her 'screaming orgasm' cocktail. "And I have no doubts I have. I mean, I haven't travelled, I didn't go to university or anything but I have had so many other kinds of worthwhile experiences. The University of Life, my man! That's where I have been - that's what I have achieved! In my own way, on my own terms!"

Suddenly Denton was struck with how introspective and thoughtful Amber could be, which seemed astonishing considering she couldn't easily spell his name.

"Well," he said not knowing how to respond. "That's great!"

"Yes," she said, definitively. "It is. I am happy. I am happy with my life and where it is going. I have achieved. I mean, not in my career. Not there. But then, who is happy with that? Who actually enjoys their job? No one! Just a means to an end, isn't it? You work to live, don't you? You work to live. I enjoy my personal life. I have achieved there. OK, so I don't have a boyfriend, and I am available…" Denton became uncomfortable. "…but that is not a sign of success anyway. I have great friends! Great friends. Like you guys! Like you,

Denten."

'Denten' was suddenly flattered at the new best friend that he had acquired. So flattered and chuffed that he couldn't not help lifting his eyeline up to check for the familiar safe glow of the green neon exit sign, just in case he needed it. *There it is, twelve o'clock, dead ahead.*

"Completely achieved!" continued Amber. "Completely. I could not want for anything. And, you know, I'm where I should be for thirty, Denten, I'm where I should be. Here. This is it. This is the spot that I *wanted* to be in when I was thirty, right here."

Next to the bar in the Old Swan and Dustpan?! he thought.

"Well," said Denton slowly, realising that Amber had run out of steam and was now looking at him for some sort of acclamation, "that's great!"

"Isn't it?" she said. "Now, if you'll excuse me. I need to go to the toilet." And with that she hurried off leaving Denton stood alone holding his drinks wondering if there was any chance he could possibly avoid being thirty.

*****

By the time that he had reached the point where he could no longer remember a) how many bottles of Michelob he had drunk; b) who had bought drinks for him; and, c) the names of half of the secretaries still left, he was beginning to wonder if he should continue to stay out. He was also seriously doubting whether he could still outrun any secretary that tried it on.

It was not without a certain feeling of concern that he watched Gladys approach him. Gladys, all fifty something years of her, drifted aimlessly towards him. Her eyes were fixed on his - the only thing about her which seemed to retain any sense of purpose. She was a short, plump lady who wore a semi-permanent smile. Nothing seemed to phase her. She moved throughout life with a noticeable spring in her step and warmth in her eyes. Perhaps once, in her youth, she had been an attractive lady but now, in her later years, she was forever doomed to suffer the compliment/insult that she was a 'handsome' woman.

"Hello!" she blurted. Unfortunately, whilst her eyes remained static, transfixed on Denton, the rest of her body seemed to sway around them. It was as if her eyes were some fixed point from which the rest of her body rotated. In fact, it was as if her eyes were the anchor, sat firmly at the bottom of the ocean, whilst the rest of her bobbed along on the waves.

"You alright?" asked Denton.

"Yes - though I fear I may be drunk!" she hiccupped, stumbling slightly over Denton's foot, which had not moved at all during the time that she had been standing there.

"You don't say?"

She smiled.

"I like you, Daniel."

"Actually, it's…" But even at this stage of the night, Denton knew it was pointless. "That's very kind of you."

"You're not like other trainees that Mr Hoo-oo-leeiggghhh has had," she said, her back and neck straightening, as if she were trying to make a serious point.

"Yeah?"

"Yes! And I have worked for Mr Hoo-ooo-oo-l-l-leeyyy for a ve-ry lo-ong time!"

"Yeah?" said Denton, not really knowing how to respond, and since all his brain cells were currently occupied trying to maintain his balance and generally ensuring that his legs stayed underneath him for long enough to get him to a taxi, there were no remaining mental resources available to try to construct meaningful responses in return.

"Fifteen years!" she exclaimed. "That's - well - isn't it? A long time!" she mumbled, almost incoherently.

"Yeah!" agreed Denton - swigging on a now empty bottle.

"Sa - oh - eh - Daniel! You've no drink! Well we can't have that! I shall buy you another! What are you drinking?"

Denton held out his empty bottle to show her the label, moving slightly with an almost imperceptible stagger. Well, at least from his point of view.

"Fifteen years!" said Gladys, as if she had forgotten the offer that she had just made.

Denton continued to have his arm extended.

"And do you know what I discovered during that time?"

"Yeah?" asked Denton, presumably on account of the fact that somewhere in his mind, the lone brain cell assigned to replies and responses figured that it kind of worked as an answer to pretty much everything.

"Mr Hhoooleeey has a secret!"

"Yeah?" asked Denton, suddenly more sober and confident that the response worked as a response.

"Shush!!" said Gladys, looking around surreptitiously and almost collapsing in the process.

She stopped. Her gaze fell to the floor and she frowned as if her brain were coping with some complex equation to process. Nothing was said for a good few seconds.

"Shush!" she said, as if suddenly realising that she should be keeping Denton quiet. She looked around again, this time grabbing on to Denton as a support.

"You cannot tell!" she said solemnly.

"I won't!" lied Denton, practically sober now.

"Well…" began Gladys, slowly. "He keeps it in his room. In the top drawer. Sss always locked you see."

Gladys looked up at Denton, as if looking for some sort of response. When none came, she ventured.

"You not notice that?"

"No," responded Denton.

"Yes! He does!" affirmed Gladys.

There was a pause again and her eyes returned to gazing lifelessly at the ground.

"Gladys!" prompted Denton.

"What?" asked Gladys.

"What is it?"

"What is what?" asked Gladys, as if genuinely confused. Her brow furrowed in a manner unbefitting of her face.

"What is Mr Hooley's secret?"

She gasped audibly.

"You *know* about that?"

Denton gazed at her, momentarily considering whether it was him. His head was beginning to hurt and he was seriously reconsidering whether it was worth pursuing this line of argument.

"Yes!"

"Oh," said Gladys, almost deflated. "I thought I was the only one. Well, then," she shrugged.

Even for a pissed person, Denton was struggling to find this funny.

"Gladys!" he said.

"Yes?" asked Gladys.

"You just told me he has one!"

"I did?"

"Yes!"

"Well then."

"Well what?"

"Well what is it then?" asked Gladys.

"I don't know, you didn't tell me!"

"I don't know either!" said Gladys, at which point Denton concluded that the alcohol had not only pickled her brain but had placed it in a jar labelled *eat me, I'm done.*

"So how do you know he has a secret?" asked Denton, trying hard to encourage his brain to apply as much logic as possible to the current conversation.

"Ah!" said Gladys, "well then. He keeps his top drawer locked and sometimes I hear him talking about bombs!"

"Bombs?"

"Yes!" she said. "I think that he may be a dirty agent or something, I mean Hooollleeeyyy isn't an English name, is it?"

"But he doesn't look the type," said Denton, momentarily remembering that they were talking about Colin 'the Crowbar' Hooley here, and not some secret agent wearing a tuxedo and a bad wig.

"Ah yes! But then maybe that is why he is one! Maybe he's a spy because he does not look like one at all!" she looked at Denton sincerely, as if she really meant what she was saying.

"Perhaps," said Denton, indulging her.

"He could be a terrorist!"

Despite the fact that Denton's brain was completely beyond rational thought, the notion that a terrorist would work at a law firm and keep a bomb in his desk drawer struck Denton as completely at odds with any kind of logical deduction.

"Mmm. Maybe!" said Denton, humouring her.

"Sometimes, I listen closely to what he says so that I can keep a note of his conversations, but he never mentions the bomb when I'm writing. Only when I'm not really listening."

"Mmm," said Denton. *Odd that.*

"All makes sense though. Just last week, he said that he has something to destroy the firm with."

"Right!" said Denton. "Would you look at the time, Gladys?" he said. Unfortunately, she couldn't.

"Why? What 'sssss it?"

"Time to go home, I think!" he said.

"But - you still have no beer! 'Ssss empty!" she said pointing to the empty bottle in his still outstretched arm.

"Well," said Denton. "It will still be empty tomorrow."

He placed the bottle down and sauntered off. As he walked past the toilets, a girl entered and he caught a view of Amber, mascara streaks down her cheeks, sobbing into the mirror.

Thirtieth birthday parties. Always the same, he thought as he exited the building.

Chapter Twenty

A bad day in the office

Denton stood very still with his eyes closed.

I'm not opening them, he thought, defiantly. *I refuse to accept that today is another working day and that I am, once again, stood making another cup of coffee.*

He continued to stand.

I wonder how long I can stand here until someone notices that I am missing. God, I need my bed. Maybe I'm asleep. Maybe this is a dream. Maybe I will open my eyes and find that it is actually Saturday morning after all and that I am not stood at work in front of the boiling water dispenser holding a mug containing one spoonful coffee, two sachets sugar and a dribble of milk.

Cautiously, he slowly opened one eye and peered around to discover that he was, in fact, stood in front of one white hot water dispenser holding one white mug containing what appeared to be one spoonful coffee two sachet sugar and, uh, yep, one dribble of milk.

God damn it, he concluded.

"What are you doing, Denten?"

Denton jumped and turned around.

"Jesus, Amber, you scared the life out of me there."

"Sorry, you just looked very spaced out."

"Well, you know, I just had the Monday blues for a minute."

Amber frowned. "Denten, it's Wednesday."

"Oh," said Denton. "Well. You know. I've obviously got it bad," he said, slightly looking away out of embarrassment.

"Well, you're not the only one. Have you seen Colin this morning? He's in a very bad way. He's banging about the place. Keeps scratching at his neck brace…"

"Has he STILL got that thing on? That happened months ago!" said Denton.

"Yeah, apparently the doctor told him to keep it on as a precaution, although between you and me, me and the girls think he's just milking it for a bit of attention at home…"

"Attention at home? Why?"

"Well, we don't reckon that he is getting much at the moment. Us secretaries are very perceptive…"

Denton stifled a chuckle.

"We may not know much, but we know when you lot have been getting some and when you haven't," she said, those deep chestnut eyes peering into his soul.

Denton hoped to God that he was not blushing. *For God's sake, do not let your face give you away, Denton. Quick. Change the subject.*

"So - is that why he's been in a bad mood lately? Why is he in a bad mood, why?" said Denton folding his arms and generally looking very defensive. Amber continued to look at him in a manner that was far too analytical for his liking.

The frown dissipated and she continued to speak, as if she was reserving her position on Denton. "Well, he was supposed to find out today if his application for partnership has been successful. From the look on his face and the way that he has been acting, us girls don't reckon that he's got it."

"Oh," said Denton. "Right. Well, I'll try to stay out of his way then. Don't want to bug him if he's having a bad day."

Colin Hooley was not the only one having a bad day.

"Oh, God, no!" said Billy, wearing a big red apron that clashed with his ginger hair and freckles, and a badge that said, "Hi. My name is Billy. How can I help you today?"

He was stood in a store room just off from the shop itself, speaking into a telephone attached to the wall. "I still cannot believe that it is true." Any colour that he did have in those pasty cheeks had now drained away into his apron and he wondered whether he might be sick right there and then.

"But I don't understand, how can this have happened?" he said, looking forlornly around for a stool or something to rest on.

"No, I know. No - I am sure that you did do everything that you could to help. I mean - it's just such a shock isn't it? Are you shocked? He really wasn't that old. It's just so unexpected."

There was a pause while Billy listened.

"No. No, I know but you just don't expect it do you? I mean for one so young, it's still such a shock." There was a pause. Billy twiddled with the cord in that manner which everyone hates since all it does is cause the damned thing to get knotted.

"No. No. I know, it must have been awful for you being there when it happened. I'm sure that there wasn't anything that you could have done," he said as a supervisor (his status denoted by a bigger apron and a bright red baseball cap) walked by, briefly tapping him supportively on the back. Billy nodded his appreciation.

"No, everyone at work has been great." The cord was now so knotted that the next bugger to pick the phone up would probably end up pulling the whole thing off the wall at the same time.

"No. No, I'm not working there - that was last week."

After a brief pause, he continued.

"No. No, it's a supermarket this week…yeah, cheese counter…yeah, not the counter I wanted but, hey…mmm, what? No couldn't get that one. Not after the incident with that girl and the smoked salmon…yeah I know it wasn't my fault. No. No. Broken leg I think…yes, they did get the baked bean can out…erm, surgery I think. Anyway, listen. Thanks for telling them at work. I don't think I could have done it myself. It's just all too much. Have only now been able to return your call."

He sniffed.

"Has anyone been to check him out? Do they know how he died?"

Another pause.

"A heart attack, you say!" said Billy, shocked. "Really? That's a little unusual isn't it? Self-induced? What do you mean?"

The other person on the end of the phone began to explain.

"OK. But they're not sure. Will they need to carry out an autopsy? Because I can give permission if they need it."

He paused, expectantly.

"Oh right. Oh, it's not standard practice. I see. But still. A heart attack? He was so young." Billy shook his head in disbelief.

"Did you find him?" he asked with concern.

"Floating upside down? God, that's awful. Are you alright?"

"Well, yes. No. I can imagine that it was a shock."

Billy dragged a stool across, which was within reach, and perched upon it.

"Dispose of the body? Well, I'm not sure. No. Well. It's all too much to think about. I mean, I did think about it briefly before I phoned you. I think that he would have wanted to have been buried - you know, have a decent funeral. He wouldn't want to have been cremated."

There was another pause and Billy began to get agitated.

"No. No, I realise that it is an expense but it's important to consider his wishes."

"Yes, I realise that I don't have the money."

"No, I know he didn't leave anything behind."

"Yes, I know that would be a whole lot quicker but it is not what he would have wanted. Well. Well, if you'll let me finish, I just think that it would be a little disrespectful. No. No, don't you dare. No, Badger! No. I do not want you to flush him down the toilet. He was my fish, Badger!"

Billy slammed the phone down and looked around him with an incredulous expression.

"My God!" he said, enraged and out of breath. "Some people!"

*****

"Some people!" echoed staff nurse Mitchell as she was bustled out of the way by a team of news reporters. For a second she stopped, deliberately brushed herself down, scowled at the offending reporter and moved on. Easter smiled at her nervously in a manner which she hoped conveyed 'sorry!'.

"Watch where you are going!" she said, turning to Malcolm.

"Whatever!" said Malcolm.

They were wandering around the entrance to the new children's wing of the local hospital. There was activity everywhere. Newsmen were stood in front of their camera's rehearsing their own addresses to the nation. As she walked past, Easter eagerly listened in.

"Today, is the official opening of the new children's ward at the…shit, what is this place called again?…"

"…part of a new initiative that will also see three…pedo…pedio?…podo…can I not just say doctors?"

"…and it's all thanks to the money of one man, local millionaire Montague Gunt…is that right?…Gunt?"

"…who has recently retired and decided to put something back into this, his hometown community…"

"What are we doing here?" said Malcolm.

"This is a big story, Malcolm," snapped Easter. "If you don't want to be here, just go back to the office."

"Hey, with the top you're wearing today, I'm not leaving your side for one moment! I have a bet by Macey that by the end of the day, that wraparound will have come completely apart, and I want to be around to see it."

Easter felt as if she was blushing as she pulled her top together. Several cameramen eyed her up as she walked past which lead to angry comments of *'Steve, darling, can we keep the camera on me, please?'*, and *'John, that's not the opening we came to see'* from their newsmen and women.'

"Shut the fuck up, Malcolm!" she barked in self-defence.

"Jesus, Easter," said Malcolm. "I'm just having a laugh with you. God, you are so far up your own backside."

"Look. Forget it. I'm nervous. I just…I want to concentrate on what I'm doing and I don't need you acting like a dick."

"What's the big deal anyway. It's just a stupid children's ward. Big deal. So what?"

"It's not the children's ward that I'm interested in, you idiot," said Easter. "It's the man who funded it. Gunt. I've met him before and there is something about him. Something not quite right. Something…" Easter drifted off. Malcolm was just stood staring at her. "Oh, I don't know."

"When did you meet him?"

"At his party. You remember, Malcolm?" she said in an accusatory tone.

Malcolm blushed. "Look, I said sorry for that once, didn't I? I can't keep apologising now, can I?"

"Anyway. It was at that party that I saw him and spoke to him briefly. There was just something about the guy. Something that intrigued me - he didn't quite seem how I thought he would."

"Really? Why - he wasn't eyeing you up was he?!"

Easter scowled at him. "No. Not all men are dirty little shits like you." She looked away, towards the temporary platform that had been erected for the ceremony. All around it were banners emblazoned with the Gunt Empire logo.

"There was something about him that just didn't seem right. Something in his eyes. A desperation, almost. Something is going on and there is a story here, I know it! A big story."

"Hey, Easter," said Malcolm, his bruised pride recovering, "the only big story around here lives in my trousers." He chuckled to himself.

Easter scowled again and sneered, "yeah, Malcolm, unfortunately, we both know that's not true now, don't we?"

Malcolm's smile quickly evaporated. Easter ignored him and carried on walking. In front of her was Gunt, looking as awkward and melancholy as usual. Surrounding him were various characters, perhaps bodyguards, perhaps just fellow executives. Who knew? Cautiously, Easter approached, hoping to catch his eye and just a glint of recognition. Gunt was the key to her leaving this godforsaken place. She knew he was. She just needed to eke that story out of him so that she could leave this place behind her and make something of herself. But before she could get near her salvation, the way was blocked by eighteen stone of pure, unadulterated, dumb ass bouncer.

"Sorry, love, you can't come this way," said the drone, not looking directly at her.

"But," she began to protest, the agony of her frustration seeping out into her words and causing her voice to strain under the pressure of it all, "I'm a reporter!"

"Then stand behind the line like everyone else," he said.

"But. But I know Mr Gunt!" she protested again.

"Really?" said the bodyguard, his voice dripping with sarcasm. "Because it seems to me that if you knew Mr Gunt you would already be talking to him."

Oh great! she thought, *I get the one bodyguard/bouncer on the planet with enough brain cells to know what sarcasm is. Just perfect!*

"Look, I…" she said, beginning to lose all hope of ever catching her story.

From nowhere, the briefest, slightest hint of salvation returned to her with the smallest crack of open arms imaginable.

"Excuse me," said a warm, kind voice, "I don't know who you are, but would you kindly step aside so that I can talk to this young lady."

Confused, the bouncer turned slightly to see Mr Gunt directing him to move. It was too much for his tiny brain to take, and he simply stood agog at the direction he had just been given.

"You do speak English, I take it? I mean, we have been able to spend enough on security to get someone who has a basic understanding of the language."

The guard, still visibly confused by the whole thing, gave the merest indication of a grimace, and moved aside to reveal Mr Gunt to Easter.

"My dear child, how lovely to see you," he said.

"Hello, Mr Gunt," said Easter, slightly embarrassed that he remembered her.

"Montague, please," he pleaded.

"Montague," she corrected. "I was afraid you would not remember me."

"My dear, of course I do! It is nice to see a friendly face on a day like today."

She smiled. "I wondered if I could get a word with you for the paper?"

"Why, yes, of course," he said shortly before another man appeared and whispered in Gunt's ear.

By now Malcolm had caught up with Easter, having pushed past the disgraced bouncer.

"Where did you get to?" said Easter accusingly.

"I'm not as well placed as you are to get around men!" he said, gesturing at her bosom.

She scowled. The Whisperer finished and Mr Gunt returned to Easter.

"Dear child, please forgive me. I have just been summonsed away. I would dearly like to speak to you further. I hope you will forgive the apparent presumption, but would you be free to accompany me to supper sometime this week?"

"Of course!" replied Easter, almost giddy. "When?"

"Do you have a card?" asked Gunt.

"Yes, here," she said scrabbling around in her handbag.

"I will arrange for my PA to telephone you with a date. Until then…" he said, before moving on.

"I thought he was retired," said Malcolm.

"He is!" said Easter. "But a man like that still needs a PA."

"I wouldn't mind a PA," said Malcolm. "Maybe one day you'll be mine," he added, almost predictably.

In your wet dreams, she thought.

*****

"What? No. No, it's not good," said Colin speaking into his phone. "I didn't get it. No. Well, no, they didn't give a reason. There's no need to shout, dear," he said awkwardly adjusting his neck brace and glancing up. His office door was open and it was quite obvious that Gladys was ear-wigging.

"Hmm? What's that?" said Colin distracted. "No. No, you can't appeal. No. No, it doesn't work like that. No. No, I don't think that it would help if you spoke to them. What? No. No, I don't think it would make any difference if I resigned to go somewhere else."

A distant look flashed across his face. *Although there may be something that might help me.* He leaned forward in his chair and delicately stroked at his desk drawer.

Distracted, he glanced up again and saw that Gladys was shuffling papers at the printer, walking past his office and generally not doing any work at all.

"I really can't talk now. I'll explain when I get home. No, I'll be home on time. What? No. No. I'm not going out for drinks after work. Well, there's nothing to celebrate is there? What? What do you mean 'maybe if I work late they'll reconsider'? No, I told you." He fidgeted with his neck brace.

"What? No, I am listening. Blooming neck's itchy. No, I'm not supposed to take it off. No, that's not what the doctor said dear. No. No. No, he didn't. He used the word 'precaution'. He did. Well, the neck is a delicate thing, dear."

Colin glanced up again. Gladys was definitely listening. Was she noting this conversation down? What was she writing?

"What?" said Colin, distracted again. "No, dear, I'll be coming home on time. Out? What do you mean out? Where are you going? A friend? Which friend? Who? Who's Sylvia? Well, I've never heard you talk about her. Where are you going? Oh. Oh, so you're not going out. Oh, so I'm going out. So, where am I going? What do you mean I can't come home? It's my home! She's shy? What? Oh, Ok! OK! But when can I come back? After 8? 10.30! What do you mean you'll have finished by then? Finished what? Oh. Bridge. You'll have finished your bridge game by then. Doesn't Bridge need four of you? Not the way that you do it. Oh, Ok. Well, where's Frank going to be? At a friends. Oh, alright then. Listen, I'll try but....hello? Are you still there? Hello...."

He put the phone down. "Must have got disconnected," he said.

There was a knock at the door.

"Oh hello, Denton. What can I do for you?"

"I promised that I would get this legal research memo to you by noon on Wednesday," said Denton.

"Oh right, yep. Well, leave that with me then."

Denton placed the memo on his desk and began to leave. Colin had a thought.

"Oh, Denton."

"Yeah," said Denton turning at the door.

"Do you fancy going out for a few beers tonight?"

"Sorry?" said Denton. He must have misheard.

"Are you around for a few quick drinks after work?"

"Erm," hesitated Denton. "On a school night, Colin?" he said, virtuously. He presumed this was some sort of test.

"Why not? Nothing too raucous, I promise. See if anyone else is interested. Drinks on me."

Free drinks! Well why didn't you say so before, Crowbar.

"Yeah, sure, why not?"

"Why not?!" said Randall in an e-mail on the subject. "Because he's your boss. Which means that he will talk about work. Which means that you'll have to remain relatively sober. Which defeats the whole point of drinking. What's the point of going at all?"

"Did you not read the part about free beer?" asked Denton in reply.

There was a pause.

"Yes, I read the part about free beer, but why is he asking us out for free drinks? I'll tell you why. Qualification. He'll no doubt talk about qualification. 'Where do you want to qualify?' he'll ask. And then if you even give the slightest hint about it and that it's in his department, then bang, he'll hold you to it - bang - he'll have you. You watch. Banged to rights. On qualification. Bang. You'll have been earmarked. Bang. Earmarked. And no one likes earmarking."

Denton frowned. He paused before replying and re-read Randall's ramblings again.

"Have you been drinking?" he asked in his e-mail.

There was another pause - slightly longer than before.

"Well. Yeah. I had a couple at lunch time. Is it that obvious?"

"Kinda. Anyway, there's nothing sinister in the invitation," replied Denton.

"Well, I don't like it. It stinks. The whole plan stinks. Although, as there's free beer on offer, I'm prepared to overlook this on the sole condition that I can bring Delia with me and use her as a human shield in the very likely event that the conversation moves on to qualification talk. Which it will. Inevitably. Qualification. Mark my words."

Denton paused.

"OK, but seriously - how many constitutes your 'couple' at lunchtime? I'll meet you downstairs at 5.30pm," he replied.

At 5.27pm Denton and Colin took the elevator down, pressing the button marked *'See you again real soon'*. Delia and Randall were already waiting for them.

"Colin," said Denton introducing the two of them, "obviously you have met Delia before but have you met Randall Leaver?"

"Erm," said Colin studying Randall's face, "no, I don't think that I have."

"Pleased to meet you," said Randall, more than a little narked. "I was actually on the Corporate weekend away with you."

"Nope," said Colin studying harder, "still doesn't ring any bells. Are you in Corporate then?"

"No. I'm in Finance, but I did Corporate a couple of seats ago and was asked to come on the trip."

"Oh - that's right," said Colin. "Now I remember you - I thought you looked familiar."

Yeah, thought a cynical Randall, *it was probably the lack of tits that made you forget.*

"Delia, weren't you at the Corporate weekend away as well?" asked Colin.

"Yes."

"But you're in finance too - why were you there?"

"Because I'm female," she said, deadpan. When Colin responded with stony silence, she laughed awkwardly. Nervously, she messed with the flowers on the security guard's desk.

"So," said Denton, sensing the awkwardness of the situation. "Shall we get the drinks in then?"

They all nodded and grunted in agreement.

"See you later, Brian," said Delia.

"Goodnight, Brian," said Colin.

"Night, Brian," said Denton.

"The pub around the corner, Brian," said Randall.

"OK, I'll be there later," said Brian, trying hard not to make it obvious that he was annoyed the flowers had been rearranged without his explicit say so.

As they left the building, Delia found herself walking with Colin, whilst Denton walked with Randall. Delia was not quite sure how this had happened and suspected that this was deliberately planned.

"Is Brian coming out with us later then?" asked Denton.

"Yeah, I got chatting to him after lunch - he seems like a really nice guy and we never go drinking with him."

"Do you think that that may have something to do with the fact that we don't have an ounce in common with him?" asked a disgruntled Denton.

"Yeah, well - we'll see," said Randall.

"Randall, the postman seems like a nice guy. The guy who runs the chip shop seems like a nice guy. The landlord at the Frog and Nettle seems like a nice guy but we don't ask any of them to come drinking with us, do we?" said Denton, needlessly emphasising his point.

"Ah, well that's not entirely true now, is it?" corrected Randall. "I mean, two weeks ago, you asked the Landlord at the Frog and Nettle to join us for a drink during last orders since you thought that he would delay 'drinking up' time if we did."

"OK, well, bad example, my mistake."

"Yeah. And whilst you didn't ask him for a drink, you did ask the guy in the chip shop if you could marry his daughter, which I think would have gone down a lot better if you had offered him a drink first…"

"Well…" said Denton, struggling to think of an end to the sentence.

"Or if you'd noticed that she was only fourteen…"

"Yeah, well, Juliet was 14 and that didn't stop Romeo."

"We've discussed this before, Denton, Juliet was a fictitious character in a Shakespeare play, and her dad did not run a fine emporium of all things potato-y…"

"Yeah, well, she doesn't look fourteen."

"But she has told you twice that she is, and it still hasn't stopped you."

"Well. Maybe she's just shy."

"Yeah. Whatever. Get in the pub."

"Oh, is this where we're going?" asked Denton as they stepped through a wooden door into a smoky nether world infused with an eclectic mix of pea green carpets, mock chandeliers, eighties soft rock and one armed bandits.

"What's wrong with the Cabbaged Eagle?" asked Randall. "It's a quality establishment."

"But…" whispered Denton surreptitiously as they approached Delia and Colin at the wooden bar, "if you stand still for too long you end up stuck to the carpet."

"All adds to the charm, Denton. All adds to the charm."

"And they only serve Carling."

"Oh shit, I forgot that bit."

"What would you like to drink?" asked Colin. "Would you like, erm," he turned to the oversized bar 'lady' stood behind the bar, "What beers do you have on tap, please?"

"Carling, love…"

"And…" said Colin expectedly.

"Carling Premier."

"Oh, right," said Colin, adjusting his neck brace, "diverse. Well, erm, two pints of Carling then guys?" he asked.

Denton looked at the bar 'lady', and was suddenly filled with fear. Even the one armed bandits in the corner suddenly looked fierce. He felt extremely traumatised by the whole situation and was increasingly of the opinion that the toothless old man sat slowly decomposing on the wooden stool next to him was looking at him in a menacing way which would only spell trouble if he did not say yes with a smile.

"Yes," he said and then, feeling as if he had missed something, promptly added the smile.

"Oooh. Yes, please," said Randall. He always had to go one better.

Watching the bar lady serve was like slowly driving past a car crash. It felt wrong, but you instinctively had to do it anyway. She was the kind of woman that probably got kicked out of weight watchers for being outside their target audience. She wore a faded light blue polo shirt, which clung to her in all the places that it really should not have. Her greasy once blonde hair was pulled back above her head to form a ponytail held together with a faded pink bobble, which gave her face a slightly puzzled look. Her face itself was formless, the fat distorting and concealing the bone that undoubtedly lay beneath - somewhere. However, the intriguing part of her was that she had very well groomed and manicured nails. It looked as if she had spent both a fortune and a great deal of time and energy in sorting out those nails. Why? Why bother, love? Did she honestly think that men sat there and said to each other, *'check out the nails on that!'* Alternatively, why spend all that time and energy on one part of her when the rest was crying out for urgent attention. Would you buy a brown Austin Allegro just to spend a grand on the alloys?

The fat from her arms sagged as she pulled away at the pump, and as she did so she stared at Denton, gently stroking the long slender tool in her hand, with the merest hint of a kiss and a tongue poking out of her warty mouth.

"AAIGH!" screamed Denton, before he realised that he was doing it out loud. Everyone looked at him, even the old man. Well, no, actually the old man just rolled one eye around in his general direction.

"Erm," winced Denton, "shall we go and find somewhere to sit?"

"Sure," said Colin. "I'll get these in."

"I can bring these over, if you like," said the bar monster in a voice hoarser than Denton's.

But you'll never get through the opening in the bar!

Denton quickly looked at Randall to see if he had said that out loud. Randall's lack of reaction suggested that he hadn't. He wasn't convinced, so he looked back at the old man. He hadn't moved either, although his eye had returned back to its normal position. Thinking about it - he hadn't moved since they had come in.

What is he? A fossil? thought Denton.

"Thank you very much," said Colin. "Much appreciated."

They all sat around a small table in the corner - shoulders squished together.

"What did you order?" Denton asked Delia, who was sitting virtually on his lap.

"Erm, Chardonnay spritzer."

"Oh," said Denton. He looked across with bemusement to Randall who looked equally confused and shrugged, shaking his head. "Right. Sounds nice."

"Maybe we should pull two tables together," said Colin, who objected to having Randall's elbow lodged in his fifth rib down.

"Yeah," said Randall, "I thought of that but the tables are bolted to the floor and none of them are big enough to seat four properly."

"Hmmm," said Colin pulling slightly at the table. He looked up. "Well, in that case, why don't we stand at the bar instead?"

"AAIGH," yelped Denton. Everyone looked at him. "I mean, good idea. The bar. Good idea."

The four of them stood by the bar. Delia stood inspecting her glass, convinced that there were lipstick marks on it. Randall stood next to her contemplating whether anyone had actually checked to see if Carling really was entirely, or at least partially, constituted of hamster piss. Colin stood next to them, trying to figure out why his wife had spent so much on sexy underwear lately if she was not prepared to wear it for him. Denton stood in front of the bar beast from another world, fearing for his own life as she stood cleaning the wood in front of him. *How long exactly does it take to clean that one particular section of the bar?* he thought.

"Well, this is nice," said Colin, shaking himself from his own morbid thoughts.

Everyone looked up, smiled at him and then returned to what they were doing before.

"More drinks?" suggested Colin to which everyone raised a glass to the bar woman.

Eventually, Billy and Badger turned up, much to Denton's obvious delight.

"Denton, Denton," said Billy. "You can stop hugging me now."

"OK," said Denton, wiping a tear from his eye.

"I got your text. Where is the…AAIGH!" said Billy as he turned to the bar. The bar monster was smiling at him. "Oh, I see," he said as he recovered.

Colin looked across towards the commotion.

"Billy Yeovil, Winston Thurlgood, may I introduce you to my boss, Colin Hooley."

"Pleased to meet you," said Colin shaking both their hands.

"Would you like a drink, guys?"

They both nodded and looked fearfully at the bar 'maid'. She poured them two pints of Carling and smiled at Denton, who shuddered involuntarily. Billy and Badger took their drinks and went to Delia and Randall's end of the bar.

Denton could just about make out Billy say, "fuck me, that was scary."

Denton looked across and saw Delia being introduced to them both. Something unnerved Denton about this. There was something not right about it. Introducing Randall to his friends had never been an issue. Randall had always seemed to Denton to be like a University friend anyway. They had met on day one of their training contract induction course, which was practically a university session in itself. The only difference was that they were being put up in a flash hotel to attend to some hideously expensive and ultimately pointless course. Being in the lap of luxury whilst still feeling like a student were two feelings that Denton had struggled to reconcile. That training course had caused him to feel as if he were being paid for three weeks to be a student again, which of itself was an odd feeling.

But, as a result, it did not seem inappropriate for Denton to introduce Randall. After all, Denton felt as if he had always been one of them anyway. But Delia? That didn't seem right at all, and Denton could not for the life of him begin to rationalise why it was wrong. Was she Randall's colleague or his? Was she a friend? Was she more? Bearing in mind eight weeks prior she had been a total stranger to him, perhaps it was the elevation in her status that Denton could not come to terms with. He knocked back the rest of his pint and was brought out of his introspective drifting as he looked back at the bar to see Widow Twankie's ugly sister right in front of him. He could not be sure that the start it had given him had not been noticed.

"Another pint, please." he whimpered.

*****

Alcohol, of course, has many uses. Temporarily, it can operate as a stimulant. Long term, it's more of a depressant. The less talked about uses include: muscle relaxant; pain reliever; mind eraser; and, time inverter. At the extreme end is, of course, the fact that it enhances the perspective of beauty. This has its limits though, and even Denton, in the drunken stupor he now found himself, could not possibly drink enough to convince himself that spending a night with the black sheep of the Frankenstein household currently residing behind the bar sounded, in any way, like an attractive proposal. Although, it would have been an experience. Of course, the psychiatric treatment that would inevitably follow made it a prohibitively costly one.

It was way past Colin's bedtime.

"So…" he bumbled to Denton, "where do you want to qualify?"

"Lawyer…want to be a lawyer…" said Denton.

"Oh," said Colin, desperately trying to focus on the Denton sat next to him, of which there now appeared to be two and maybe even four. "Yes, yes. But. Which depart-a-mint?"

Denton looked confused and his head wobbled like a belly dancer, slightly off balance.

"Well, I…I dunno. I mean, I'm so young. I want to be a partner…"

Colin suddenly looked very tearful.

"Me too…"

Denton slapped Colin on the back. Perhaps a bit harder than he had intended.

"You will, big guy. You will. You will. Will you?" he frowned again and rubbed Colin's back, mainly because he couldn't remember where his arm was before it was there.

"I will. I will - my wife is having an affair…" said Colin. He stared at Denton, looking for a flicker of recognition.

"She is?"

"I didn't make partner…"

"I know…is she?"

"Yes. Well. She might be. I don't know. Do you know? I don't know."

"No. I don't know. She might be…" volunteered Denton, on the basis that he thought it might be helpful.

"Women."

"Yes. Women," nodded Denton, perhaps too energetically.

"Women," said Colin, looking forlornly for the answer at the bottom of his pint glass.

"Yep. Women." Without warning, Denton turned in his chair. "Hey, Randall!" he shouted looking across to Randall, who was sat around a table with Billy, Brian, Delia and an unconscious Badger-shaped-lump. "Women!"

"I hear you," said Randall, raising his glass.

"You know," said Colin, "it's all that fucking bitch's fault…"

"Your wife?"

"What? No! That fucking big titted bitch that stole my client, Mr Muff…Mr Muf…Mr Muf-ner-tit-tee…Mr Muf-n-ty…you know."

"Hooley…can I call you Hooley?…Hooley, baby. Women. You know. Women," said Denton, putting an unsolicited hand on Colin's shoulder before burping with such force that his whole body shook.

"Yeah. Yeah, I know. Bitch. Muftny did not forgive me for the fuck up on his dairy deal."

"Well," said Denton finishing his pint, "they say that cheese is a safe investment these days."

"Moon cheese!" said Colin.

"That's right, Hooley," said Denton, turning once again on his bar stool. "Hey Randall!" he shouted.

"Yeah?" came the reply.

"Moon cheese!"

"I hear you," said Randall, raising his glass.

"I have a love-r-ly house, you know," said Colin.

"Yeah," said Denton, returning to look at Colin.

"Big garden. Swimming pool. Lovely, it is."

"Great."

"And a lovely cottage in the Lake District. Beautiful thing."

"Really?"

"Oh yes. Beautiful. Go there for the summer. Lovely. Very relaxing. Same village as Gunt, you know."

"Right," said Denton, slowly losing the will to leave.

"Oh," said Colin, looking down into an empty glass, just about to drink from it. "S'Empty!"

Denton examined his and, on holding it upside down, concluded much the same thing.

"Me too!!"

"Oh yeah? More drinks?"

Denton turned on his stool and promptly fell off. Vaguely embarrassed, he said, "Just a minute. Bear with me," as he attempted to re-mount.

"Hey, Randall!" he shouted again after successfully regaining his former elevated position.

"Yeah?"

"More drinks for you and the lovely ladies?"

"I hear you," said Randall, raising his glass.

Chapter Twenty One

An advertiser's dream

You have to have this.

Your life will be incomplete unless you get it.

Everyone else has it. You just have to have it too. It will change your life. You need it.

What is life about these days, if not the pursuit of meaningless acquisitions? The purpose of modern day life is not to survive or to develop, but to consume. If there were three ages of man, then this epoch must surely be our end. The sad decline of man.

When you look around you at the people that form this city, this country, this world, there seem to be very few who want to aspire to achieve greatness.

The people that we look up to; the people that we aspire to be like; the people that drive us, are not great thinkers. They are not academics that have developed a new theory on some ancient problem. They are not great scientists. They are not inspirational artists. They are pop-stars, footballers, actors, actresses, and more worryingly, they are just every day slobs that, having nothing better to do, volunteer to parade themselves around in houses containing concealed cameras. These are the people that we aspire to be like, not for the talent that they may have, which might range from a modicum through minimal to non-existent, but for the one thing that they have that we don't.

And what is this factor? What is this element of their life that is missing in ours? What is it that they have that we need? If the populous were to collectively think this question through, I would imagine that they would all jump to the wrong conclusion. They are all likely to say *God, I wish I had their money!* But this is wrong. This is not what people want at all. What people want is the seemingly inexhaustible ability to consume.

Society, in any age, displays the same characteristics. It is always geared towards holding one particular facet of life up as being the thing to achieve. Those who achieve are recognised. Now that society has worked out a sustainable (or at least on the face of it sustainable) method of ensuring that we all, pretty much, have shelter, and don't go hungry, life is just one big waste of time until its over. In order to ensure that you don't feel as though you're existing in one big waste of time, you need to have an end goal. You need to have something to achieve.

In days gone by, society was geared towards recognising great thinkers and doers as being worthy to receive the accolade of *having made it.* Therefore, the pursuit of scholarly activities was recognised as being remarkable, and those that achieved that recognition were held in high regard. Yes, money came with it, but it wasn't the *money* that people admired, it was the achievement that earned the money. Newton, Pasteur, Da Vinci were all great men, but I challenge anyone to remember the value of the assets they left behind for others.

And this gearing towards recognising talented individuals who worked hard in order to achieve is easy to understand. People like Beethoven, Bernini and Michelangelo were all great men who worked tirelessly for their art, but they still died. They did not live any longer than those around them simply because of their fame. They probably didn't even enjoy themselves more than those around them simply because of their greatness, and yet society places them on a pedestal as being notable individuals who did well. What exactly was it that made their lives more remarkable than others, if not the fact that they did something that society considered important?

But the gearing in this society is slightly harder to understand. The people that adorn our cheap glossy magazines are, by and large, cheap glossy people who have nothing in common with these great men. Society no longer recognises hard work. It does not appreciate men of valour and courage. Our heroes are drunks, wife beaters and slappers who get their tits out whenever possible. The people that our society recognises and, more worryingly, aspires to be like, quite often, couldn't work a hard day's slog if their plastic appendages depended on it. Our idols are the ones who made it without trying. They achieved the goal of 'consumability' without lifting a finger. They are transitory, they are meaningless, they are shallow. Their endurance in our memory is as brittle as their hair-dos and as sustainable as their collagen filled lips.

No longer does society recognise men of science. No one seems to recognise great thinkers anymore. Where are the doers? Where are the achievers? What place in society is there for philosophers, academics and mathematicians? What coveted prize is there for brilliance? Where is the driver for genius?

We are in danger of becoming a morose society where free thinkers are neither encouraged nor welcome.

In light of this, what are the ambitions of youth? A career is no longer something to aspire to. A career is something that you become burdened with when you don't find yourself, accidentally or otherwise, on the pages of a tabloid. A career is a disaster not a reason to be cheerful. Our society doesn't recognise hard work as being remarkable. It regards it as unfortunate. Hard work is an inhibition on our ability to consume. Hard work interferes with the time we have to consume. Our fake plastic friends do not suffer from this inhibition. They are seemingly free in all the ways that we are not. Their ability to consume supersedes the need to follow the timetables imposed by others. Nine to five is the timetable of their consumption. And we admire our fake plastic friends for it. We admire them because they can consume in ways that we can only dream of. Our society wants to be like this. Our youth wants to emulate it. Our goal in life is to have this 'consumability'. We want it because society teaches us that we need it.

And where has this need taken us? Where has the incurable epidemic of shiny silver items brought us? Our society is meaningless. Our lives are meaningless. Our world is slowing down. It's brain is getting mushy. Our society is fattening up. It is concentrating on the goal of doing little and achieving nothing. Our cheap nasty plastic imports have become our lives. Our minds are cluttered with crap that we don't have any use for. Technology is no longer our saviour, it is our cancer. It has weakened us and made us useless. We can't grow food. We can't hunt. We can't find shelter. We can't survive without the cheap, nasty, shiny, silver objects that have drained our resources and made us miserable.

Our society is wrong. Our life is wrong. Our life teaches us that we *need* more. Anything, everything. We need gloss, we need gossip, we need plastic, we need shininess, we need products! We need the easy way. We need convenience. We need quick fixes. We need garbage. We need more.

But we don't.

We no longer live in a society that needs. We have enough. What we need to do is challenge our definition of *need.* We need to re-evaluate our perception of *need* and align it with a more realistic image of the world.

So what do I *need*? What do I do with *this* life in *this* world with my *only* chance? What do I occupy my life trying to achieve? If I reject the plastic ambition of those around me, what do I do with my time? What do I do on Fish Sundays? What do I do with my life? What do I do to make myself feel fulfilled and happy?

Chapter Twenty Two

Everyone's bad day in the office

As Denton lay there he really could not decide whether it was actually day times themselves that filled him with dread, and not the prospect of work at all. Perhaps he had some, as yet, undefined illness, which explained why he felt so awful first thing in the morning. Perhaps the excessive amounts of alcohol consumption and the tedious, unfulfilling waste of time that they called work, were actually just convenient smokescreens masking the fact that he was actually ill. Perhaps it was like a low grade form of Vampirism. OK, so sun light didn't actually burn his skin to the point of ignition but it did cause him to shudder sporadically and feel a distinct and dreadful sense of malaise. Perhaps he should not go to work at all, but spend his time productively in a darkened room wrapped in his duvet writing a paper entitled 'Sunshine: God's daily method of shitting on your head' and submit it to *the Lancet*. Perhaps they would publish it with a suitable photograph of a pigeon, with a halo, on the cover.

And why not? This discovery would save the NHS and businesses millions. No longer would people simply go to their doctor when they felt a bit down since their doctor would simply say, "Don't worry love, it's Voyle's disease - we've all got it - what do you want me to do about it? I'm at work and you don't see me complaining do you? So why don't you get off your fucking hairy backside and do some actual fucking work rather than pestering me for fucking sick notes all the fucking time." No one would ever need to take anti-depressants ever again. Either that or we would all be on them. In any event, life would be great.

And the fame? Denton need never work again. People would stop him in the street and say "I know you. You're Denton Voyle, aren't you? You changed my life! You put a name to my condition - I am forever indebted to you. Here, please take my wallet and the keys to my car. And here, my wife, she has lovely breasts, doesn't she? Please drop your trousers so that she can show you her gratitude too."

Beep beep beep.

He must have pressed the snooze button and fallen asleep again.

"You're only jealous," he mumbled to the alarm clock as he stumbled out of bed. "You only woke me because no one sucks your cock."

The alarm clock chose to ignore him and rise above his filthy comments.

Denton stepped into shower and the usual, awful sense of foreboding crept across him *Why am I doing this job?* thought Denton as the water hit his face. *I hate it. I do not enjoy the work. I do not enjoy spending time with the people. I can't stand this for the rest of my natural life. Why, why am I doing it? What is there for me in a career as a solicitor? Late nights, hours of paper pushing, miserable, penny pinching clients and for what? So some fat partner can cream off the money we bring in, live it up in a big house with a doting wife while he bangs some twenty year old trainee?* Energetically he scratched away the suds from his hair. *What is the point? So that one day I become the fat partner?*

Silently he wandered back into his bedroom, dressed and walked into work with an equally quiet Randall.

"I didn't sleep much last night," yawned Randall. "Magnum," he mumbled as some idiot knocked into him at Moorgate station.

"Why not?" queried Denton as he stepped over a drunken tramp clutching at a copy of the Big Issue, extending it out in his paralytic way to any one who would notice him. No one did. No one noticed the important people let alone those society classified as the 'dregs of humanity'.

"Been thinking about qualification."

"But I thought that someone from finance had already told you that the job was yours if you wanted it."

"Yeah - they did - but that's just it. It dawned on me last night what I am doing. I mean qualification is not that far away for us and do I really want to spend the next twenty five years handling banking documents?"

Denton did not say anything. He would have probably disagreed but for the fact that he thought Randall had a point. The idea of committing twenty five years to law did seem a trifle off-putting.

They continued walking to work, completely miserable as they stepped over more of the homeless. As is usually the case in summer, it began to rain heavily for no apparent reason. Whilst those around them quickly hid away under their micro-umbrellas, Denton and Randall were pelted from above but they continued unfazed by it, like men who have accepted their fate. Or maybe they were more like men who were determined to go against the system and take on the world, including the elements, and not let any man or any thing stand in their way.

Or maybe it was just because that, even between them, they did not actually own an umbrella.

*****

In another part of town, Billy solemnly found a fish net and, having delayed the matter for forty eight hours, reluctantly accepted the fact that it was time to say goodbye. Gently, he scooped up Happy and neatly placed him in the Tupperware container, filled with broken ices cubes, that had only this morning been known as Badger's lunch box. He placed the lid firmly shut and slowly took the container to the fridge. Having hidden the box behind the pickles and wholegrain mustard, he then returned to the empty fishbowl and took it to the toilet to empty the water for the last time.

*****

Up and across town from there, Badger was sat snoring. Most people find any one who snores to be really quite irritating, but not many found it quite so annoying as Mr Lupsman. Perhaps it was because the snoring was accompanied by an inordinate amount of dribbling. Perhaps it was the fact that Badger was asleep bolt upright in a chair, arms folded with his head leaning to one side with his inch thick glasses hanging off one ear. Perhaps it was this that Mr Lupsman found to be so irritating.

Or perhaps it was because he was paying the guy fifteen pounds per hour for the privilege of, at present, watching him sleep, when he had thought he was paying him to be a security guard.

Or perhaps it was because Badger was not only sound asleep, but also bound up in electrical tape in a security kiosk at Mr Lupsman's computer components warehouse where Mr Lupsman was once the proud owner of a fully functioning warehouse shutter door, which appeared to be missing, or at least, a very large part of it was.

"Give him the hose," hissed Mr Lupsman to some more of his workers.

The two men stood on either side of him twisted the nozzle of the hoses they were holding, causing water to gush out at speed, which slowed down only as it hit a screaming, and soon after, blubbering Badger.

*****

With a start, Colin awoke. A film of cold sweat had formed across his face. It was dawn, and he had no idea where he was, although through his blurred vision he was able to work out that he had been sleeping in the back of his people carrier. He fumbled around for his glasses. Finding them under a discarded empty crisp packet, he put them on. His vision focused and the awful reality of why he was there hit him like a brick in the gonads. His heart sank as if it was falling through the leather upholstered seats and he clasped his mouth as if he might vomit again at any minute.

He remembered that he had left the house immediately after he had seen it.

He had fled straight down the stairs as fast as his legs could carry him, as if his body could have torn from his thighs and carried him away without them if they did not keep up. He had paused only to vomit in the flower bed outside the porch before jumping into the vehicle and speeding off.

As he drove, he had kept reliving it. Over and over again. Every second of it. He had driven, not knowing where he was going, or what he was doing. His neck had ached from the violent vomiting and he had pulled at his collar. His neck still hurt now. His heart had been beating to the point where he thought he could taste blood. His breathing was so heavy that his lungs felt as if they were collapsing. His breath had tasted vile. His limbs were numb and his head had felt light, as if it was an effort just to keep his body on the ground. He had felt as if he could see himself from outside the vehicle. The tears that had formed in his eyes made the lights of the cars in front blur and drift into each other. The tears that ran down his face had burnt like acid.

*****

"...I mean can you believe it?" asked Delia. "She just had no sense of occasion at all. Where did she think she was? A lap dancing club? Carrying on the way she did - did she not know where she was?"

Olivia nodded. "I know - its disgusting. It really is. I must have been stood at the far end of the room from you. The utter seediness of the venue did not help either. Seriously, it was disgusting. She should be sacked. No doubt about it."

Olivia and Delia were stood in one of the small kitchens on their floor making a cup of tea whilst comparing their respective notes on *'Bonnie-gate'*.

"What makes it worse though is the fact that the partners all bought into it. Not one of them seemed to think it was inappropriate. It was disgusting - the manner in which they were egging her on," said Delia.

"Worse still, one of them tried it on with her afterwards," said Olivia.

"Noooooo!" said Delia.

The pair hushed as Campbell Oliver walked into the kitchen.

"Have either of you seen Bonnie?" he asked, frowning.

In unison, they shook their heads. "OK, well if you do, please tell her to come and see me immediately."

At that moment a clip-clopping noise, not too dissimilar from the one that a horse might make, could be heard emanating from down the corridor adjoining the kitchen. Bonnie then emerged, wearing a short tan skirt, white blouse and tan jacket. Delia winced involuntarily as she noticed Bonnie's blouse was too small and gaped noticeably open around her breasts, allowing Campbell a good view of her oversized cleavage and lacy white Wonder bra. As soon as Bonnie clocked that Campbell was there, she arched her back so that her chest flung out in front of her almost causing her shirt to rip open there and then. Delia almost shook her head in disbelief as she noticed Campbell fall headlong into the not very subtle trap. His eyes were already in that gap trying to unbutton that shirt and cop a feel. With his eye-line firmly fixed, he muttered, "Bonnie, a word in my office, please," whilst almost dribbling.

They both scuttled off.

"Finally," said Olivia. "Someone is going to say something to her about her behaviour."

"How do you know?" asked Delia.

"I've been in this department for three years now. That was Campbell's best, *'I am not amused'* voice."

*****

For Colin, it had been a normal day like any other. The partners in the Corporate department had been ignoring him, mutterings of *'as if it wasn't bad enough with the recession without losing Muftny'* and *'everyone likes a challenge but making money without your clients is too much'*. He had heard them, clearly enough, but he had ignored them all. Muftny or no Muftny, life went on, and he had much to be thankful for without this. Or so he thought.

He got home around nine, nine thirty. Nothing unusual about that.

Partnership or no partnership, he still worked long hours. He entered the house, nothing unusual about that. Music was pounding out from upstairs. Nothing unusual about that. All the lights were out downstairs. Nothing unusual about that.

*****

Delia returned to her work station in the corridor. If she were to lean far enough to the left, she would have been able to see into Campbell's room. But not today. His blinds were drawn and the door was firmly shut. About half an hour later, Bonnie emerged and tottered down the corridor in Delia's general direction. The urge was too much for Delia to hold it in.

"What did Campbell say?" asked Delia as Bonnie wandered past her desk.

"Oh, not a lot."

"Really?" exclaimed Delia, unable to hide her disappointment.

"Yeah, there is a new deal on and he wants me to help out."

Delia's eyes narrowed. "Oh, really? Which one?"

"Oh, I don't know. They all sound the same to me. Erm, something about an electricity supplier buying another electricity supplier or something. I don't know. Sounds like a waste of time to me. I mean, why don't they just make more electricity rather than buy another company?"

*****

Colin shuddered as he recollected how nothing had seemed out of place or unusual. Even as he had walked up the stairs, nothing seemed out of the ordinary. The giggling from their bedroom, he presumed, indicated she was watching TV. The clothes strewn across the stairs must have been his teenage son's. *Honestly,* he thought, *why can't the boy clean up after himself?* It had only been as he reached the top of the stairs when he heard the dialogue. It was the dialogue that made him feel so ill. The awful dialogue.

*****

"But. But," stuttered Delia.

"Not very interesting is it?" said Bonnie. "Anyway, to be honest, I wasn't really listening."

"But," Delia continued. "That is a massive deal!" she exclaimed. "There is going to be loads of work in that. It's ground breaking stuff!"

"Yeah," said Bonnie. "I know. It does mean that my social life is going to be affected. Although I am sure I can get away with doing very little work, but, yeah, I suppose it will look good on my CV."

"But. But. How did you get this work?" asked Delia, now incredulous.

"Well, Cambie said I had impressed him. He said he had noticed me and wanted me involved."

Cambie? thought Delia with disdain.

"He said all of the partners had been impressed with me. Most noticeable trainee apparently."

At this point, Delia turned back to her monitor, ripped it out from the wall socket and pulled it down, right down, over Bonnie's stupid giggly little vacuous head, electrocuting those stupid fucking freakish tits.

Well, at least she did in her own mind. In reality her eyes simply glazed over and her nose twitched. Since this was how Bonnie usually ended conversations herself, she thought nothing of it, and returned to her own workstation as if nothing had happened.

*****

"Oh that's right - yes. Show me you big hunk - show me what you have for mommy. Show me that big fucking fuck machine of a present. Yes. Oh yes, I like presents. Let me hold it. Yes, yes, in the mouth. Mmm."

Colin reached the top of the stairs almost in autopilot, completely numbed by what he was hearing. The bedroom door was ajar. It was open enough for him to see his wife, slowly standing, wearing the stockings, high heeled shoes, red G-string and lacy bra that he had found in their wardrobe only the other day. The one he had quizzed her about. The things that she would not wear for him. Her wavy black hair was messy, and her bright red lipstick was smudged everywhere. She leaned forward slightly and placed either hand on a dresser admiring herself in the mirror. Colin wanted to look away, but he could not - he was utterly transfixed by the events unfolding before him.

Behind his wife emerged the pool boy wearing nothing but a huge smile and an even bigger erection. Colin felt like he was a trespasser in his own home. He should not be seeing this, and he wanted to run into that room, grab that kid by the throat and strangle the pair of them there and then, but he couldn't. His arms were jelly and his legs were lead. He could hear his own heart beat pounding through his chest, and the blood rushing through his ears.

The boy - he was a boy! - leant forward and groaned as he pushed himself into Colin's wife's buttocks. With one hand he reached around and cupped one of her large breasts. She gasped and groaned all in one. "Ohhhhh, big boy. Oh God, you fill me up. Oh, I've never been so full. Oh, oh, I could just come right now. Oh yes. Oh squeeze my titties, take me however you want, oh yes! Oh, I feel so dirty!"

Tears ran down Colin's face. They burned. He could not reach to wipe them away. He could not remember his own name. He did not know if this was his house. He did not make a sound. He did not want them to hear him.

"Oh. Oh, I'm so wet."

He was an intruder in his own home…

"Oh. Oh, I'm gonna come. Come on big boy, give it to me - punish me."

…and his own marriage.

Suddenly something in Colin reacted, and he turned on his heels and ran. He heard her shriek in pleasure just before he vomited into the bushes outside the front door.

Eventually, after driving for an hour or two, he pulled up in a lay-by off some country road. He guessed that he had fallen asleep around three, although his sleep was disturbed. As he sat there, he felt as if he were in mourning for someone. Perhaps mourning for the twenty three years that he had wasted. A life of wrong choices that he couldn't change. An emptiness that he could not fill.

He sat up and climbed into the driver's seat. Worryingly he had absolutely no idea where he was.

*****

When Delia had finished imagining all the grizzly ways in which she could cause Bonnie to suffer at her hands, she sat lifelessly slouched in her chair, looking at her computer, as if someone had just ripped her spinal cord out in one go.

"What is the point?" she mumbled.

*****

"You're absolutely right Randall," smiled Austin Monks, "what is the point?"

Austin was one of the youngest partners in the firm. A salaried partner at thirty and equity at thirty two, he held the record for quickest to partnership. He had seven Top One Hundred clients under his belt, and was known as the proverbial rainmaker in the banking industry. If a company wanted a deal done in a particular way, then more often not they would phone Austin to ask him to do it.

"It is over complicating things to do it this way but you know as well as I do there is a lot of Companies Act red tape slowing us down."

Austin sat on the corner of Randall's desk, Randall being about the only trainee across the firm to have his own office. Casually, Austin bounced a blue tennis ball in his right hand. Being only five foot six his legs did not quite reach the floor and Randall had a legitimate concern that if the ball ricocheted off the floor at just the wrong angle, causing him to overreach, then Austin would impale himself on the corporate golf umbrella that he had perched somewhat precariously in the umbrella stand next to Randall's desk. With more than a passing interest, Randall wondered whether death in these circumstances amounted to corporate manslaughter, and whether any blame would lie at his own door.

Austin caught the ball and looked at Randall.

"So, Randall, tell me, how do we do it? What's the answer? Show me the way through."

Austin really was a sad little ginger twat.

*****

Billy wiped a tear from his eye as he heard the keys jangling in the front door. He wandered into the kitchen to compose himself and heard the door slam shut. He was about to call out when he stopped. A look of confusion spread across his face.

What on earth is that noise? he thought.

He couldn't place it at first. It was akin to the sound that you might hear if you were squishing whole plum tomatoes in a bowl or if someone was throwing freshly used teabags against a wall. Billy would have been mildly afraid if he was not so intrigued. He briefly recalled something about cats in similar scenarios and the kind of treatment that they suffered upon investigation, but quickly dismissed the thought before the full implications of the truth of that old adage were allowed to register.

Billy wandered into the living room to find a drenched Badger standing in the door way, his arms outstretched like a scarecrow just after the monsoon had passed. Badger looked as if he did not have a clue what to do next in order to remedy his situation.

For a moment nothing was said. It was obvious that Badger was surprised to see Billy at home. Billy simply stared at Badger. Badger stared at Billy.

Eventually, Billy ventured, "Alright?"

"No. Just got the sack."

"Why?"

"Usual."

"Oh," said Billy. "Can I get you anything?"

"Cup of tea?" suggested Badger.

"Anything else?" asked Billy as Badger continued to drip all over his pine flooring. "Digestive biscuit with the chocolate on top?"

"No thanks," said Badger politely, staring down at the floor in embarrassment. "It's too absorbent to hold."

*****

"You two really are disgusting," said Easter as she sat at her desk. Malcolm was sat at his desk with a bowl of cold tomato soup, that had formerly been hers but that she did not, under any circumstances, now wish to reclaim. Macey was stood behind Malcolm, his hands on the shoulders of his favourite lap dog.

"Look at it grow!" said Macey, staring at the object in the soup which was expanding at a rate of knots. Malcolm giggled in a childish fashion like a fourteen year old on a playground. "It really is absorbent, isn't it Easter? Look at how it swells up - don't they fill right up?" He stroked at his moustache as he said it. His eyes lit up and soon his eyes were off the soup, and on Easter's chest.

Easter ignored him and looked away. Stupidly, she had left a new tampon in the communal bathroom and they had gotten hold of it over lunch time.

"Disgusting," she said again with contempt in her voice.

"Well, if you will leave it in the bathroom," said Macey. "You obviously wanted us to find it. So it's your fault. Pretty disgusting that you would leave it lying around. Pretty disgusting that you would let us know about your condition. Idea put me right off my lunch - didn't it you, Malcolm? Disgusting, yourself. Maybe we should buy some dirty mags and leave them in there too. Right, Malcolm?"

"Yeah - she'd like that though," said Malcolm giggling again.

Macey's eyes glazed over. "Really?" he mumbled and stared intently at the tight fitting top that Easter was wearing. He mumbled something else and shuffled off into his office breathing awkwardly like a pot bellied pig jogging into his pen to play in his own filth.

Easter grabbed her bag. "I'm going out."

"Where?" said Malcolm. "Oh come on, we were just mucking about. God - can't you take a joke?"

"Jokes are funny, Malcolm," she retorted. "That was not. Anyway, I'm due somewhere else. I'm covering that gerbil story, aren't I? You know - the local school where the gerbil ran away and came back again."

"Sounds like fun."

"Yeah - it might be. My angle is, what on earth possessed it to come back to a shit hole like this when it had the chance to be free?"

She walked off.

"And stop looking at my arse!" she shouted back.

"Erm - Sorry!" he said in surprise.

As soon as she was out of the door, she lit another cigarette. Her blood was up and she wanted to cry.

"Disgusting, slimy, oily…" she said as she walked down the road, "…insignificant little toads."

She pulled her mobile phone from her handbag and dialled the number of her best friend. After a lot of swearing and almost constant talking from her, her friend offered some friendly advice: "The answer is simple. Do not wear revealing clothes."

"But why shouldn't I?" she protested down the phone, "why should I not wear what I want to wear? I should not have to deal with this kind of behaviour anymore. No woman should."

"Easter - you're not in London now darling - you're in some pokey little village in the middle of nowhere. Things are different. People are different in rural communities. After all, most of these people are related to each other!"

"Oh come on, Lesley - it's not like that. That's just a myth. This is a good place. These are good people - on the whole. I'm just working with a pair of twats. You know what Malcolm said to me, after the incident, when I told him that I did not want a relationship? *'Dirty sluts like you deserve what you get - you walk around with your tits out then wonder why people are always copping a feel.'*"

"Ergh - that's disgusting," said Lesley. "Look just ignore them. He's just a bitter little pervert who has probably never even had intercourse before. But you have to look after yourself Easter - don't get yourself into situations that you cannot handle. If he has that attitude then the chances are that your boss does too. Don't make yourself an easy target for these wankers."

"No!" said Easter defiantly. "I will not change. Looking good gives me confidence. I need that to handle the situation. I am not overly tarty and I do not lead these men on - I look smart and well dressed. Women all over the country wear these clothes and they do not suffer in the same way that I do. I'm not backing down for these little pricks."

"But I worry about you, Easter. Be careful."

"I know. Me too."

Easter finished her cigarette, and having tossed it on the floor, she took a certain amount of pleasure in stamping on it as hard as she possibly could.

"Maybe the gerbil had a point to prove as well," she said in the direction of a rather bemused old lady at the bus stop, who in the confusion, felt it only right and proper to nod in agreement.

*****

"I'm sorry, Denton, but that really is not good enough," said Devlin Hawkes, who was stood in the doorway to Denton's office. "You spent three days on this, and this alone, because you had a point to prove?" His soft Irish lilt certainly helped but did not altogether disguise the fact that he was well and truly pissed off.

"The thing is Devlin," said Denton, trying to justify himself, "I was told that the index was wrong so I just wanted to prove that I could do it?"

"Prove you could do it? Delia Longuerait was specifically assigned to help you. Do you know how expensive resource trainees are? Do you think you can justify your time by saying that you were trying to prove yourself? Prove yourself? There was nothing to prove! Delia rearranged the index and I approved it - there was nothing for you to prove - it had been done!"

"Well, I did not actually know that it had been done, Devlin."

Devlin cringed noticeably at the informal use of his name and carried on as if Denton had not spoken. "Then you rearranged it, showed it to a different partner on a day I had off and sent it straight to the client."

"Well, I thought that I was doing the right thing."

"You thought that you were doing the right thing? We now have a disgruntled client who thinks that we do not know our arse from our elbow. Even if we do, it's clear that the arse and the elbow are not talking to each other."

Hideous thought, mused Denton at perhaps entirely the wrong time.

"Denton - are you listening? This is very serious. We've lost enough clients recently and I do not want to lose another - especially one that we just billed £35,000 to. The client is now asking for a complete breakdown of the bill to see if there are any other areas that we have charged them for duplicated time on. I do not need this Denton. I do not need this."

"Well, I…"

"Denton. Let me be clear, you are speaking to an elbow that does not have a communication problem."

"Then maybe you should speak to the arse who sent off the bill without checking it properly," retorted Denton instantly.

Whilst Denton originally thought that sticking to the same analogy would show that he was listening, the effect was not quite as he had hoped. As Devlin correctly and quite rightly pointed out, he could not be both the arse and the elbow at one and the same time.

There were many words that Devlin then used that Denton had to keep a mental note of to look up later. For example, 'belligerent' was a word that he was not particularly *au fait* with although he did not doubt that it did not have a favourable meaning. It then took twenty minutes to find an on-line anatomical dictionary to discover the meanings of some of the other words that Devlin had used, most of which Denton thought were a little harsh.

Devlin had exited the room fuming, leaving Denton more than a little red-faced. This was the side of the job that he hated the most - the responsibility for tasks that were mind-numbingly dull. Yes, he could understand that he would get a bollocking if he were to advise a company that if they bought the business of another company and decided that they did not fancy taking all the employees with them, that this would not be a problem and, no, he didn't know what TUPE was either, but figured it was something to do with construction. He could accept a telling off if he advised a company that it didn't matter how long it took them to register an interest against the property of another company, and that there was no difference between registered and unregistered creditors. He could take those on the chin. But being held accountable for losing a 'platinum' client because you didn't spot someone else was billing your time when it duplicated someone else's when: a) all along you had been told *'bill all your time', 'bill all your time';* and b) no one had run the proposed bill past you anyway, was just a little hard to deal with.

Worse still there was a definite inverse correlation between the tasks (and responsibility for them) delegated to individuals from partner to trainee compared to the extensiveness of the instructions. Any task that landed on a trainee desk invariably had one post note on it with the prescriptive instructions, *'sort this out, Denton'.* Not helpful when one quarter of the instruction is your own name.

Denton looked dazed. Devlin's stinging attack had left him numb. *Why do I bother?* he repeated in his head. He shuffled a few papers around and then looked blankly out of the window. Suddenly, he felt like he did not recognise anything around him and began to seriously doubt whether he would even turn up tomorrow.

"The trouble is," said Randall later as they exited the lift having pressed the button marked *'you'll be back'* and wandered to the nearest pub, "it is not as if I could say that this is a job with no prospects."

"I know," said Denton, clutching a piece of white paper.

"I mean, it has got excellent prospects. There is an entire road marked out for you with an accompanying map entitled, *'How to get to the top.'*"

"Yeah," said Denton, still clutching at a white piece of paper.

"The trouble is though - even from my lowly position, I can see the people at the top, and to be honest, the view that they have does not seem to be that great."

"I know," said Denton, "most of them seem bloody miserable. OK, so they get well paid, but is it worth it? Is the stress and constant pressure worth it?"

"And when you look at the partners, how many of them appear as if they have happy family lives waiting for them at the end of the day?"

"Not many," said Denton, now awkwardly clutching at the piece of white paper.

"It really has been a shit day," said Randall.

"Why?" asked Denton. "What happened to you?"

"Well, you know Austin Monks, the top partner in finance?"

"Yeah, the little ginger one. Looks like a ferret."

"That's right. Well he came into my room today with a legal conundrum and asked me what I thought."

"Yeah. Let me guess, he completely bollocked you when you didn't know. All the same, bloody partners, think they rule the bloody world."

"No, actually, it wasn't like that. I knew the answer. And when I told him he fell off my table."

"Wow. OK. But then he completely bollocked you for making him fall off the table - right?"

"No. He heaped a load of praise on me and told everyone."

Denton stood momentarily amid the waves of people crashing past them desperately trying to get the 18.06 train to Weekend-Ville.

"You're kinda losing me here. When do we get to the part where you get a complete bollocking?"

"There is no bollocking, Denton. That is the point. This is a job that I can do. I know I am at the lower end of the spectrum but getting praise from a top partner should feel good, shouldn't it? But, it didn't."

"I wouldn't know. I have absolutely no experience to compare it to. How did it feel?"

"Well, transitory."

"Transitory?"

"Yeah, as if, ok now I'm the big fish, but pretty soon, I wouldn't be. Transitory."

"Right."

"And the thing is, as well, being good at this job doesn't make me feel anything. It doesn't make me feel good about myself. I don't feel like I'm contributing to society in any real sense. I just feel, well, transitory."

"Right," said Denton, as if he was missing something that he really should have being getting.

"I mean, I suddenly felt like a lab rat running down these mazes only to find a piece of cheese at the exit and thinking, *'is that it? Is this it for missing the pit falls, dodging the electrocuted wire, and rope swinging over the crocodiles while they snap their predatory jaws - a bit of cheese?'*"

Denton stopped a second time and felt the wave of commuters crash into him again, the odd one splashing out onto the rocks of Evening Standard salesmen.

Suddenly, everything clicked into place.

"I know exactly what you mean," said Denton. "Well, apart from the crocodile pit thing. But, yeah, you're right. What is it for? The long nights, the disrespect, the mind-numbing paper pushing. A big car? A nice house? Two and a bit children?"

"I don't know," said Randall, introspectively. "And, what's more, from the moment that I thought that, I could not do anymore work. I just sat there at my desk, staring at the bits of paper on it. They meant nothing to me."

"Yeah. I had something similar happen," said Denton. "Complete de-motivation."

"But what do we do now?" asked Randall. "How can I go back to work on Monday? What if my de-motivation has set up camp permanently?"

"Randall," said Denton putting a sympathetic arm around him as the throngs of people surged past them, most failing to withhold their obvious annoyance at a two man clothes line in their way, "we're young, and whilst that's about the only thing that we have got, it is the only thing that we need to give us freedom."

Randall, slightly uncomfortable with Denton's tactility, looked at Denton with a scowl.

"What on earth are you on about?"

Denton smiled and shook his head, "I've no idea, but I thought it sounded good. Can we drink now?" And with those words of wisdom ringing in his ears, Randall walked into the Old Monk and Sidecar with Denton.

As they pushed past the suits stood in packs of two or three, no doubt exchanging mind-numbingly boring tales about the week's successes with work and pretty trainees, Denton turned to Randall.

"Normal rules apply Randall."

"I know," said Randall shaking his head.

"One drink and we're out," said Denton, obviously concentrating more on reaching the bar than listening to Randall.

Every time! thought Randall.

They moved up to the bar where Denton promptly ordered two drinks, still clutching at a piece of paper.

Finally curiosity got the better of Randall, "What is that piece of paper that you're holding?" he asked, chugging away at the life affirming pint of Stella in his hand. "Cheers," he motioned to Denton and the barman.

"Cheers," said Denton receiving his change. "Did you not get this?" he said in between slurping.

"No. I don't think so. What is it?"

"It's an e-mail from Cynthia - you remember her? She was the lady we spoke to at the estate agency when we got our flat - face like a gerbil? She says that since our flat has three bedrooms, the landlady have decided to put someone else in with us."

"Hang on," said Randall. "Our flat has three bedrooms?" He frowned. "Where?"

"You know. That room we keep boxes in."

"The box-room?" asked Randall, although it was not instantly apparent why he thought re-arranging the order of words would bring clarification.

"Yeah."

"But it's tiny! Surely you couldn't even get a bed in there."

"M'dunno," said Denton. "Anyway, that's what they want to do. Who are we to argue?"

"True," acknowledged Randall. "But who?"

"Doesn't say," said Denton studying the text. "I only just got it now and to be honest the implications of it didn't really register."

"She can't do that! Can she?" asked Randall.

"Dunno," said Denton. "Says here that because we rented on a 'room only' basis she can."

"Really?" said Randall, now wishing that he had paid more attention before signing the lease. He also wished he had attended more property lectures at University.

"Dunno, but all I can say is, she had better be blonde, busty and have a tendency to do all the household chores wearing only her bra and a G-string."

Randall frowned, "I thought that all women did that anyway."

*****

Somewhere in the firm, a storm was brewing. An image of neatly plaited hair and hidden features was whirling around logging off computers, throwing paper from the printer into envelopes and hurling them into post trays as it made it's way for the exit.

*****

"OK, Randall. Now listen very careful," said Denton as he stood in front of Randall, grabbing both shoulders, staring into his eyes with a very serious look on his face. "I need the toilet," he said, shaking Randall slightly every time he uttered a word, perhaps to emphasise the seriousness of the situation. "Now, I have finished my pint. I calculate that you have one eighth left. I am going to the toilet now. I am going to be leaving you momentarily. Do not, I repeat, do not, let anyone buy you a drink. Understand?"

Randall frowned and thought about the question, briefly looking up as he did so. He looked back at Denton.

"Yes."

"Right," said Denton and promptly vanished.

Thirty two seconds later, he re-emerged from the mass of people near the toilet door.

"That was quick," said Randall.

"Oh yes," said Denton proudly, "no mucking about for me."

"Clearly," replied Randall.

"Right," he said looking at the empty pint glass in Randall's left hand. "Let's go....NO!" he suddenly exclaimed in horror as he looked at Randall's right hand. "You have another pint in your hand!!"

"I know," said Randall, matter of fact.

"But. But?" said Denton in utter disbelief. "How did that happen?"

"Dom bought it for me," said Randall, as if this was perfectly acceptable.

"Dom Peasgood?! But. But. Randall - what did I tell you!?!" said Denton, still noticeably flabbergasted.

"I'm sorry," said Randall. He knew he had done wrong. "I couldn't help it. I was weak. Dom came up to me and started talking. I asked him if he wanted a drink as an attempt to leave the conversation but he offered to buy me one instead."

"But. But." Denton flashed around wildly, "Where is he now?"

Randall nodded his head forward. "He's at the bar getting you one."

"But. But."

"When he brought this one back, I thought that I could get rid of him again by telling him I was with you, and it was my turn to get you a drink but he insisted he get you a drink too."

"But. But."

"We probably could have gotten away but you've been flapping for so long that he's coming back now. Look there he is."

"Oh, fuck!" exclaimed Denton and he turned on his heels. "Oh fuck. Oh f....fank you, Dom" said Denton momentarily adopting a mockney voice that Dick Van Dyke would have been proud of, "that's love-er-ly."

Dom just stared. Denton smiled nervously and took the drink off him. With the distinct lack of space in the pub, Denton half thought about simply turning his back on Dom to speak to Randall and exclude Dom totally but thought that this would probably be a bit too obvious, even for a half-wit like Dom Peasgood.

Awkwardly, Denton turned around and backed up so that he was stood next to Randall with the two of them looking at the half-baked Dom.

Dom didn't say anything.

"Well, thanks Dom," said Denton. *I cannot believe this is happening,* he thought.

"Cheers, Dom," said Randall slurping his drink. He winced. "Oooh. What beer is this, Dom?"

"My favourite," said Dom. "Fosters. Great, isn't it? Don't like any of that other stuff. Too wheat-y. Not good for my bowel."

Randall and Denton both stared at Dom in disbelief. Its not very often that you meet the man that is keeping the good people at Fosters in business.

Denton winced inwardly, *After all my weeks of careful planning and training,* he thought, *and the boy still doesn't learn. You never, ever stay for a second drink. If you stay for a second drink in the pub on a Friday night after work then you stay there all night stood talking to bloody boring people you do not want to be with. This is social death. This is misery. Goodbye Nirvana Friday. You were wasted and we know it.*

By now Randall was just looking at his feet. Denton on the other hand was studying Dom's face. He had not noticed before that it was almost featureless. He had two little piggy colourless eyes. No real jaw to speak of. Or cheek bones. In fact, his face was more like a badly cut potato, with a non-descript mop of brown/black hair piled on top, and cut awkwardly. His lips were pursed and slightly fat, standing out in stark contrast to his pasty skin. He had the look of a man who was slightly overweight without being portly. And he stood there with nothing to say and every opportunity to say it.

Randall looked up and smiled.

"Did you see the football?" asked Dom, slurping noisily on his beer.

"No," said Randall.

"No," said Denton.

"Oh," he slurped again. "Have you got anything planned for the weekend?"

"No," said Randall.

"No," said Denton.

"Oh," said Dom, slurping once more. "Have you had your appraisal?"

"No," said Randall.

"Yes," said Denton.

Dom stopped and turned his head towards Denton. "Was it any good?"

Why didn't I pick no? thought Denton. "Alright," he said out loud.

"Oh," said Dom, with another slurp. "Have you been on holiday yet this year?"

Oh God, thought Denton, *how much longer can this go on for?*

Suddenly a hurricane entered the building throwing most people out of the way of the door, hurling them into the wall. A space opened up as the hurricane flew in, threw her handbag down by Randall and Denton's feet, before storming off to the bar.

"You will not believe the day that I have had," it said as it flew past. "Tanqueray and slim line - no lime," it could be heard to say from the bar.

Like a rabbit caught in headlights, the barman stood looking confused. Was it the fact that a violent weather condition had just entered his premises and he wasn't sure whether the insurance policy covered this kind of disaster, or was it because he had no idea what she had just ordered. Who could tell?

"That's GIN!" screamed the elements. "Mother's ruin. Give me Gin - anything. Any kind. I'll even take Gordon's!"

"Seriously," said Delia as she wandered over to them, "I do not know why I bother I really don't. Why am I working so hard when sluttish little bimbos are getting ahead of me!?!"

Everyone acted as if Dom wasn't there. Equally, Dom looked as if he hoped that Delia couldn't see him.

"I presume that you are talking about Bonnie," ventured Randall bravely.

"Of course! Who else?" said Delia, knocking her drink back. "Who's this?" she sneered, looking at Dom.

"Dom Peasgood," said Randall.

"Does he?" she said. Denton chuckled.

"Dom Peasgood," Dom Peasgood needlessly repeated. He nervously held out his hand. Delia shook it.

"Oh yeah," she said. "I've met you before. You're in Commercial at the moment aren't you? Yeah. Just saw the head of your department over by the bar."

"Really?" said Dom, looking anxiously at the bar. "Well, if you'll excuse me, I should really go and talk to him."

And with that, the human blight that is Dom Peasgood wandered off in search of fame and fortune.

"Did you really see him at the bar?" asked Randall.

"Of course not," said Delia. "But there is no way that I am going to stand here talking to Dom bloody Peasgood. Do you know how boring he is?"

Denton laughed. "Delia Lounge-Rat, I do believe you are becoming one of us."

Delia would previously have objected to the blatant mispronunciation of her name, but she didn't. She just smiled.

"So how has Bonnie upset you today?" asked Randall.

"How hasn't she?" retorted Delia.

"Look, don't worry about it," said Denton. "She'll get caught out eventually. It's galling, I know but people will see through her, I'm sure."

"Oh yeah? So how come she's working on Project Methane?"

"Methane," chuckled Randall, at perhaps the most inappropriate time.

Delia ignored him. "That little bitch! I did all the preliminary research for that! Now I'm not even involved. I'm telling you, I'm really disillusioned with this. I do not know why I bother. I bet she is going to get kept on and I won't! What is the point of all this?"

"Mmm. You haven't heard then?" ventured Denton.

"Heard what?" sneered Delia.

Denton looked at Randall. He did not want to be the one to tell Delia. Randall cowered slightly before speaking.

"Well, I've heard that she has already been offered a job in Corporate and has accepted it."

They both looked at Delia. Her nostrils were flaring. All she needed was a red timer counting down on her chest and she could have been in a Bond movie.

Perhaps at the most inopportune (or opportune, depending on whether you were Randall or not) moment, the head of Tax, already starting to look a bit ropey, wandered over and made straight for Randall.

"Ah!" he said, trying desperately hard to make it look like he wasn't trying desperately hard to focus. "Randall! I've just been speaking to Austin Monks. Great things. Randall. Great Things! I've been hearing. Randall. I've been hearing." And with that, he put an unwelcome arm around Randall.

Could everyone just leave my shoulder alone?! thought Randall.

Randall's new best friend pointed to the ceiling.

"The limit, Randall, the limit."

Randall presumed he was actually using the ceiling as a metaphor for the sky, and that Randall was actually supposed to be imagining he could see through the ceiling to the aforementioned sky. From the smell on Randall's new friend's breath, it was probable that the Head of Tax could already see through the ceiling.

"Oh God!" said Denton to Delia. "I knew that this would happen. We're trapped now. Trapped. Let's get another drink in."

Randall was led away - never to be seen again - ensnared in a net of empty promises to be placed in a cage of relentless work and misery.

Denton and Delia consoled each other at the bar. Another round followed. As Denton had rightly predicted, this was not the last. Another one came and went. Then Dom wandered back over. He made subtle hints, about wanting Denton to buy him a drink in return for the one he had bought Denton earlier, such as *'did you enjoy that pint I bought you earlier'*, *'goodness, I'm thirsty'*, and *'do you believe in the concept of what goes around, comes around?'*. It was only fair. In fact, it was the only way to get rid of him. Denton couldn't buy Dom one without buying himself one - it would just look tight. It was dark outside - there was no point going anywhere else now. So Denton bought another. Delia collapsed somewhere, muttering something about strangling Bonnie. Randall returned.

"Where have you been?" slurred Denton.

"I…I...only just made it out alive," said Randall, with mud across his face, his shirt in tatters.

"Well," said Denton, struggling to concentrate on what Randall was saying, his head spinning with Stella. "What happened?"

"Well, one partner spoke to me. Then another. Then another. Then one said *'work for me'*. And another said, *'no he's working for me'*. Then another said *'back off, he's mine'*." Randall gulped down the beer placed before him.

"Then what?"

"Then a punch up kicked off. Then the successful partner, having beaten up all the others, pushed me into a cage and took me off to a hidden jungle location, where I was beaten and given nothing but Powers of Attorney to complete."

"God," said Denton, slurping on his beer. "That's awful."

"I know. Then one day, I escaped and, having nothing but a paperclip, a pin, a piece of cardboard and a bit of thread, I constructed a primitive compass and navigated my way back to the pub."

"Well," said Denton. "You're here now."

"Yeah."

And then, before either of them really noticed, Colin was stood next to them.

"I'm so sorry about all of this," said Colin, his arms draped around both of them.

"'S fine," slurred Denton. "He's back now."

"Yeah," mumbled Randall. "No problem. Can just get a new shirt."

"No," said Colin, shaking his head. "Really. I am. Didn't want this to happen at all. I had no idea about you. It's just awful."

Denton frowned. "Colin - what are you talking about?"

"Yeah," said Randall. "What are you talking about?"

"Well, you know," said Colin. "The fact that I'm moving in with you. Cynthia rang you, didn't she? I'm so sorry. I had no idea. I was just looking for a room to rent. I had no idea it would be with you. I tried to find another place but there was nothing so convenient. I feel so bad!"

And with that he stumbled off to the bar.

The effects of their excessive alcohol consumption suddenly wore off and their heads quickly turned to face each other. They both looked back at Colin as he wandered off and then frowned.

"What does Colin mean, he's being moved in with us?" barked Denton.

They watched as Colin yelped and fell straight over the unconscious Delia.

*****

It was Monday morning. Randall and Denton were stood in the office of Cynthia, still wearing the same frown they had done since Friday.

"It was made very clear to you at the onset that this could happen," said a sour faced Cynthia Limpton, as if their presence had just interrupted her daily eleven o'clock ritual of sucking a lemon.

"How?" asked Denton.

"When?" asked Randall.

Both had their arms folded tighter than a female trainee's legs in the managing partner's office.

"It was all detailed to you on a previous occasion," said Cynthia providing more explanation by using synonyms of exactly the same words she had used before.

"But this is an outrage," protested Randall.

"You can't do this!" protested Denton.

"I'm sorry you take that view," said Cynthia in her least apologetic voice. "Your landlady has been very generous to you. She continues to be very generous towards you. You should be grateful to her," she said.

"But…" protested Randall.

"You are aware that you are in a three bedroom flat. You are aware that there are only two of you. You are aware that there is one bedroom that stands empty."

"But…" protested Denton.

"But," protested Randall. "Colin Hooley is not a random person. We know him! He is a senior solicitor at our firm who, more importantly, has about 20 years on us. This can't be right."

"Can't you find someone our age?" said Denton. "Someone we don't know - preferably blonde and busty?"

"Yeah," said Randall, echoing the sentiment.

"No," said Cynthia flatly.

"But can't you see the awkwardness of the situation for us?" asked Randall.

"No," said Cynthia.

"But he's so much older than us," said Denton. "It's embarrassing."

"Your embarrassment is no concern of mine, Mr Voyle, and neither is it a concern for your landlady. She owns this property and can place whoever she wants in it."

"But."

"Look, I'm sorry Mr Leaver and Mr Voyle, but if you look at the terms of your lease you'll see that it does not distinguish between the people that you may or may not be expected to live with now does it?"

"But," they both protested in unison, both aware of how pathetic they sounded.

"No, once again, I'm sorry but the simple fact of the matter is that your landlady owns this property. She dictates who lives there. There is no more discussion to be had."

"Oh really?" said Randall defiantly. "Well, we'll just see about that."

"You mark our words," said Denton tapping the table with an irate finger. "The landlady may control you but she does not control us. She will not get away with this. We'll take the matter higher, and we will not stop until we reach the top."

"Yeah," said Randall.

"Colin Hooley will not be moving in with us!" he said firmly.

Cynthia gave a rye smile.

*****

"Hi Roomies!" said a partially embarrassed Colin, a suitcase in each hand as he stood in their doorway.

"Hi, Colin." said Denton, still fuming.

"Damn it!" said Randall, stood next to Denton. He stamped his foot.

"I've just got a couple more things in the people carrier. Will be back in a mo. Put the kettle on, Denton, there's a good chap. Oh, this is going to be so much fun!"

Denton turned his head and looked at Randall. "This could only happen on a Sunday!"

Chapter Twenty Three

The incredible awkwardness of being

Denton opened his left eye and closed it again. It was still the same.

He opened his right eye and closed it again. It was still the same.

To be sure, he opened both eyes. He held them open for two, maybe three, seconds and then closed them tightly, scrunching his face up like a fat person's dog. The image was still the same.

No! he screamed in his head. *It's true. It's true. This is really happening! Arrghhhhhh.*

In front of him sat a rather bemused Colin, nervously holding a mug of coffee. He was perched on the edge of the sofa, as if it would be inappropriate and presumptuous of him to look any less ill at ease.

"Is he alright?" he asked Randall of the twitching, blinking, Denton. They were both sat on the adjacent sofa.

Randall turned to Denton. Denton's face twitched as if in the preamble to a gurning contest. He turned back to Colin.

"Yeah, don't worry about it. It's normal. He's just challenging his own perception of reality. Happens all the time. Especially on Sundays. Can I get you some more coffee?"

"No!" said Colin frantically waving his hand above the mug, as people do when they desperately try to impress upon someone that they have already been more than generous. Unfortunately, Colin's attempt at good manners looked the same as most peoples attempts to attract attention to a small fire. In fact, his flamboyant arm movement suggested more that his arm was on fire rather than anything else.

"Fair enough," said Randall, choosing to ignore DJ Colin's inexplicable momentary outbreak of scratching. "Do you need anymore help with your stuff, Colin?" asked Randall.

"No, no! I'm fine," said Colin, awkwardly twisting his head around in the neck brace to look at the three suitcases sat next to the front door.

He's milking it a bit with that neck brace now, thought Randall as he said "Is there no more to come in?"

"No, no. That's it. I didn't really know what else to bring apart from some clothes and a few personal items."

"No, well…" said Randall, desperately trying to think of a way to link the current topic into a subject matter that would form the basis of a semi-decent discussion, "...quite," he said, conceding defeat.

"I can't imagine that you guys have that much stuff here either do you? I was told that the flat was fully furnished by your landlady."

"Well, yes, that's true," said Randall, as Denton continued to twitch next to him, occasionally muttering *damn it* in a semi-audible tone, "although you would be surprised at the level of junk that you can collect."

"Yes, I can imagine," said Colin.

They looked at each other and smiled politely. Colin slurped on his coffee, presumably in order to detract from the deafening silence that had now descended.

"Feel, free to move in to your room whenever you are ready," volunteered Randall, trying to figure out why Colin continued to remain so noticeably unsettled. "Is there anyone you need to phone? The phone is just there." He pointed to the phone on the coffee table in front of Colin. Despite the fact it was blindingly obvious where the phone was, Colin acknowledged Randall's comment by looking at the phone in front of him just to confirm that he knew where it was.

"Thank you. Oh just like the one at work," he noted with some enthusiasm. He looked away from the phone and got up. "Well, I had better start unpacking then."

"OK," said Randall.

"What are you guys doing about food tonight? Do you take turns to cook?"

"Erm..." said Randall, wondering how to break the news to Colin that on the rare nights that they did find themselves in the flat sober enough to cook, they would, more often than not, use the aforementioned and now successfully located telephone in order to dial out for curry or the like. "Well, I wouldn't describe it as a formal system, but yes we have been known to cook for each other."

"OK, well since it's my first night here, I'm more than happy to do the cooking."

"Great," said Randall.

Colin wandered off into the kitchen. Since he remained seated for the duration of Colin's excursion to the kitchen netherworld, Randall could only assume that the audible gasp which emanated from the kitchen was on account of Colin discovering that not only did Randall and Denton cook on an irregular basis, they also washed up on an equally irregular basis. Colin's face was almost ashen when he returned, one hand clasping his mouth and nose, the other holding the wall as a support.

"On reflection, maybe we could eat out?" he mumbled when he had found the strength to do so.

"OK, that would be great," said Randall turning to Denton, who was at least now blinking with a smile on his face.

"Anywhere you guys fancy going? I hear that the Old Duck and Shovel do a great Sunday lunch platter. It's just up the road from here. They are one of the few pubs in the City that still serve real ale!"

Denton visibly shuddered.

"Actually Colin, we tend to go to the Living Room on a Sunday if we fancy a bite to eat - they do fantastic food."

"Mmm, well, when in Rome I guess…" he said scratching his collar.

Being part of a chain of pubs is usually the first sign that the place you are about to enter will lack any sense of character. Ideally, you should never consider entering one unless there is no way that it can be avoided, but even then you should know that if you get caught in there by anyone that you even vaguely respect, you need to have a bloody good excuse to hand. Something along the lines of *'there are these six guys holding my Mum and Dad hostage and they say if I don't drink here they'll set the house on fire'.*

However, the Living Room in Farringdon displays none of the usual trappings associated with the usual soulless chain drinkeries. For a start there is a revolving piano. Then there is a guaranteed decent selection of tunes that are entertaining without being invasive. The food is always superb and the range of beers is very commendable. Finally, there is the guaranteed array of over-dressed women flaunting their ample wares. Why would anyone want to drink anywhere else?

At first, Randall and Denton were collectively concerned that the presence of Colin at the same table as them would completely shatter the low level of self-respect that they so desperately clung to.

Of course, when they realised that he just kept buying all the rounds, their concerns quickly ebbed away.

"Damn it, I'm in serious danger of a Yeoman!" smiled Randall as he shuffled off his chair, realising too late that Colin would not have any idea what he meant by that. The three of them were sat around a small table near the back of the dining area. "Back in a mo!" he said, probably for Denton's benefit (and reassurance) as he jumped up and headed for the urinals.

Denton looked up at Colin, who could not contain his confusion at Randall's reference, and realised that he needed a topic of conversation quickly. In a group of three, silence could be easily hidden and blamed on someone else. When there were just two of you, there could be no place to hide.

Having had three pints to induce himself, Denton was feeling a lot more conducive to discussion with the old Hooley, and a thought entered his head.

"I was talking to your secretary the other day."

"Gladys?" asked Colin, although for reasons only known to himself since everyone knew that Colin's secretary was called Gladys.

"Yes," said Denton. "She was absolutely hammered!"

"Yes, she does that occasionally," said Colin, knocking back his pint. "She's a lovely lady though. I'd be lost without her."

"Yeah, she seems nice enough, but I think she's losing her marbles a bit."

Colin frowned and looked at Denton.

"What makes you say that?"

Denton chuckled to himself. "Well, you're going to laugh but she was asking me if I knew that you keep a bomb in your desk drawer?" He would have continued to chuckle if it weren't for the fact that Colin did not react quite as dismissively as he might have hoped.

"She said what?" said Colin, fidgeting nervously with his neck brace.

"I know!" said Denton, trying to laugh the conversation off, "A bomb! Can you believe that?"

"No," said Colin, "I cannot believe that she would have told someone that." His eyes glazed over momentarily, causing Denton to feel uneasy at the situation. *Hurry back from the loo, Randall!* He thought.

"I know! She's crazy!"

Colin smiled nervously and looked away as he drank the last of his pint.

"More drinks?"

Without response, he got up and walked over to the bar.

Well, God, you got me. There's me thinking that life could not get any worse just for you to sit there and say 'Oh yeah? Wanna bet?'. Thank you very much for the gift of Colin. The mind-numbingly dull and odd, little straw that broke this camel's back. My God, my life needs to change.

Chapter Twenty Four

A Happy funeral

"I didn't even know you could get pet cemeteries," muttered Randall.

"Shush!" said Delia with an over zealous flapping finger movement.

All seven of them were dressed in suitably sombre attire whilst stood, against a backdrop of decayed gravestones and overgrown tombs, around a small hole in the ground. A lone bell rang out from the small church beside them.

"How long has this fish been dead for now!?" whispered Randall to Denton.

"M'dunno - two weeks? Three?"

"Dragging this out a bit, isn't he?"

"Well, apparently it's hard to get a spot in the graveyard. You have to wait a while for a space to free up."

Randall turned and looked at Denton. "Is that true?"

"No! How the hell would I know why we've had to wait?!" said Denton raising his voice slightly.

"Shush!" said Delia again, having taken on the maternal role that the situation necessitated.

Understandably, many of those stood around that miniature grave felt more than just the slightest amount of embarrassment. This was not so much due to the fact that they were sending off a fish, although that did contribute to it, it was more to do with the fact that since the hole was no bigger than a matchbox, the "circle" that they had formed around it was a little cosy to say the least. On reflection, the fact that they were almost touching noses tended to undermine the reverence of the occasion.

"Brian," whispered Randall. "You're standing on my foot!"

"Sorry!" whispered Brian. "It's these Japanese sandals - the base is so heavy, I can't feel a thing through them."

"Shush!" snapped Delia.

"Sorry," they both mumbled.

Brian fidgeted slightly in order to readjust his standing.

"Ow!" howled Colin. "That was my rib you just hit with your elbow!"

"Sorry!" said Brian.

Annoyed and uncomfortable, Colin tried to raise an arm to scratch at his neck beneath the collar. The action only served to cause everyone else to fidget in order to readjust their own positions. After a while the fidgeting ceased and the forced sombre mood descended once more. Each person stared down at the tiny box just visible at the base of the hole. Tears formed in Billy's eye and fell to the ground.

"Brian," whispered Randall.

"Yes?"

"Your foot. It's still there!"

"Oh, sorry," said Brian as another fidget broke out.

Delia looked accusingly at Brian once more. She put a comforting arm around Billy.

"It was a lovely service that the vicar gave," said Delia.

"Yes, very moving," said Denton, brushing his eye as if a piece of grit had gotten into it.

"I like the headstone," said Colin, as if subconsciously he felt that it was the right time to drive the conversation towards focusing on the positives. Or perhaps he really did just like the headstone. "*A tragic waste of an enquiring mind…*"

"Yeah, we couldn't get one that said '*Try jumping out of this then*'", said Randall.

Delia glared at him whilst Denton tried hard to suppress a smirk.

"Sorry," said Randall, catching Delia's glare and nearly losing an eye.

Undeterred, Colin tried to resurrect the line of conversation he was trying to bring previously, which no one had been listening too anyway, ".., no it's very clever as a lasting effigy of the little fellow. You know, all this reminds me of a book that I read recently about fish. Fascinating they are. Fascinating. Did you know that fish sleep with their eyes open?" He looked into the eyes of those around him with that desperation that he so often had, as if just hoping that someone, anyone, would be interested in what he had to say. No one was. He chortled to himself as if just remembering something amusing. A couple of people looked at him.

"It also reminds me of that joke about the fish with one eye. Did you hear that one?" again he looked desperately into their eyes. Only Brian was looking directly at him with a look of confusion. Colin felt a little daunted by the fact that someone was actually actively listening to him. The pressure was almost unbearable. Nervously, he pulled on the sleeves of his tweed jacket. "What do you call a fish with one eye?"

He paused for dramatic effect. Several more people looked up at him now and the pressure definitely was now unbearable.

"FSH!" he blurted out with no timing whatsoever. He chortled nervously, and then thought about what he had just said. "No wait. Wait. No, that's wrong. No, it's wh…what," he said stumbling over his own words through his own embarrassment. "What is a fish with no eye, er, eyes called?" Again he paused though God only knew why. "FSH!". Again, he chortled nervously in a way that almost made everyone in the circle want to pat him on the back to reassure him that everything would be ok.

"FSH!"

But no one did. There was only stony silence. Delia glared at him.

"Sorry, Billy. Perhaps a little insensitive of me to say that," he said staring down at his own feet, partly out of embarrassment, mainly because there wasn't room to look anywhere else.

As if to relieve the tension, or perhaps as a consequence of the light meal he had wolfed down before leaving the house, Denton inadvertently belched.

A look of horror descended across Delia's face - mainly because she had been in the firing line of the burping. She waved a hand frantically in front of her face.

"Oh, Denton!" she cried. "Did you have sardines for lunch?!"

Denton nodded, and then felt the uncontrollable need to justify himself in light of the looks everyone else was giving him.

"Well, I was hungry and it was all we had in!"

"Little inappropriate, wasn't it?" ventured Randall.

"Sorry," said Denton.

Billy's bottom lip quivered slightly, "I loved that fish," he whispered. "It was the only thing that felt like it had any permanence in my life."

Delia and Denton, who were both stood next to Billy, each put a comforting arm around him. From across the circle, Colin felt it appropriate that he gently ruffle Billy's hair.

The group fell silent and looked down once more at the grave of the recently passed on.

"Erm, Brian," came the whispering voice of Randall. "I don't want to sound like I'm being a pain, but seriously, it's still there. You're crushing my little toe!"

"Sorry," said Brian, fidgeting again.

"Let's go to the pub," said Billy, "I've said goodbye now."

The circle slowly moved away, and as it did so, the pressure that had kept Badger upright dissipated, causing him to fall in a heap on the ground.

"Should we take Badger with us?" asked Colin as the rest of the group moved off.

"Nah," said Denton. "We'll get him on the way back."

They walked out of the graveyard and wandered towards the nearest pub.

"Shall we go here?" asked Denton.

"Yeah, why not," said Colin. "*The Plough and Half Tulips* - sounds nice."

They wandered in. The pub was practically deserted with the exception of the odd local scattered untidily about the place.

"So, who's buying?" asked Randall. The group looked at Randall before turning their gaze to Colin.

"That will be me then," said Colin, taking the hint.

The rest followed Denton into the back of the bar where they found an empty snug to sit in. Colin soon arrived holding a tray of drinks - though not soon enough for some peoples liking.

"Oh, God, I definitely feel like I need this," complained Delia as she gulped away at her 'alcopop'.

"How come?" asked Brian.

Delia frowned, as if it seemed obvious to her why she would need a drink at this particular time on this particular day.

"Brian!" she retorted, "it's 4pm on a Sunday afternoon! My weekend is now officially over! I have nothing to look forward to but work tomorrow. Don't you feel like you need a drink when you reach this point on a Sunday?"

Denton smiled and looked at Randall.

"And to think, she used to be such a nice and well adjusted girl until she met us."

Randall smiled at Denton and looked across to Delia. He raised his glass to her.

"Welcome to the world, Delia. It's a dark cold place where beer is your only relief from the misery of it all."

"Amen," said Denton raising a glass. "To the misery of Fish Sunday."

"Fish Sunday!" they toasted.

"Why Fish Sunday?" whispered Colin to Randall. Brian looked at them, equally confused.

"I'll tell you some other time," said Randall. Colin remained confused but appeased. Brian lent towards Colin.

"Why Fish Sunday?" he whispered.

"He didn't say," whispered Colin. "I think it must be because we buried the fish today."

"Of course," whispered Brian. "That makes sense."

"God!" said Delia, oblivious to their conversation. "Wouldn't it be great if we could all just get away from this? Wouldn't it be just perfect if we could escape the misery of working life and just do whatever we really wanted to?!"

Colin chuckled to himself.

"Delia, dear girl, you have only been working for five minutes. You can't be more than, what, twenty three, twenty four?"

Delia blushed. "I'm actually just twenty two."

"My apologies, twenty two. Whatever your age, the point is that you haven't lived yet. You haven't experienced work for long enough yet. Yes, it might be depressing now and it might involve a lot of hard work from you, but in time it will get better - and easier. You'll see when you're a partner in ten years time. And anyway you shouldn't talk about alcohol like that. None of you should - it is not the answer to the issues you perceive you have."

"OK - who brought the Dad along?" asked Randall, trying to lighten the mood a little.

It didn't work, they just talked over him.

"But Colin, what happens if you look around yourself, at those above you who have worked for longer, and you realise that actually they seem just as miserable as you. What then? It doesn't seem to me to get any easier," added Denton.

Badger nodded.

"I've certainly found that the pursuit of a career is one of the most daunting and frustrating ventures of my existence so far," he said. Delia visibly flinched.

"Where did you come from? We left you at the cemetery!" she said, noticeably concerned.

Badger looked a little hurt. "I came too and saw you entering this pub. I followed you in."

"Oh," said Delia, a little coldly. It dawned on Denton that she had not spoken to Badger much before. In fact, she probably had not heard him speak much before either. Perhaps she had grown to consider him as an appendage or an accessory that the group simply transported from venue to venue. She certainly looked at him now as if her own handbag had just added its own contribution to the debate.

"I'm certainly struggling with life," added Billy with a mournful note to his voice. "All I looked forward to was seeing Happy, and now that's been taken away from me."

"But it will get better," said Colin, undeterred by the overriding pessimism of the group. "Life gets better and your job is not your life. It's just a job!"

"Yes, but that's not true Colin," added Denton. "A job is your life, whether you want it to be or not. You spend more than half your waking life at work. Monday to Friday - sometimes weekends - 8.30 until whenever they let you out of the door - constantly doing work. And then you go home and worry about the work you were doing during the week! You're never away from work!"

"Well..." said Colin struggling to find an answer - especially considering the rest of the group seemed now to be staring at him as if he were the fountain of all knowledge.

"You can't argue with that, Colin. Work is an integral part of everyone's life - especially professionals."

"Yes, but..."

"No, there's no 'yes but', it's there. All the time. And if you don't enjoy it and it simply makes you miserable, what then?"

"Well, you should try not to let it dominate your life..."

"We do - hence the alcohol."

"Well, I really don't think alcohol is the key - you need to re-evaluate your chosen career path if it really is that demoralising to you. After all, you only get one chance at life and you need to take it with both hands..."

Here speaks the man who just found his wife in bed with a man half his age, having spent the entirety of his life dedicated to providing for his own home life... thought Denton, but also thought it prudent not to raise that point with the group.

"But how do we address it?" asked Randall. "Being a professional naturally entails a lot of hard work to a cause or project that we don't necessarily agree with or have an interest in."

"I wouldn't go that far!" objected Colin.

"But it does!" added Delia. "We've already seen how pointless an exercise this career malarkey can be. You work hard and you watch others succeed simply on the size of their bosom?! How fair is that?"

"Or..." added Randall, "you find that you can do the job well but that you don't get any satisfaction from it at all."

"Or..." added Denton, "you find that you have trained your entire life working towards a point, a precise moment, where you qualify as a professional only to find out that the entire process has been a lie right from the start. There is no moment of satisfaction. This process isn't like climbing a hill, where you can stand and admire the view. There is no point at which someone will slap you on the back and say 'well done'. All there is, is a point where some twat in a loud suit comes up to you and says, 'Great! Welcome to the party - now go tidy this floor, it's a mess.' Is that really what I worked hard for six years to achieve? Is it?"

Colin looked visibly distraught - as if he had done ten rounds with a professional boxer. He looked as if he wanted to surrender and give them whatever they were after, but he couldn't because he didn't know what they wanted in the first place.

Denton felt almost relieved that everyone seemed to feel the same way as him about working life. Then the relief soon passed as he realised that it wasn't just him that was ploughing on regardless. They were all miserable. Something had to be done.

"Anyone fancy a game of dominos?" asked Brian.

Chapter Twenty Five

Swirling, twirling, turn after turn in circles of delight, gently nudging and bumping into each other playfully, row after row, column after column in a sea of sparkling light. Full of life, bubbly, moving without a care in the world, they danced and danced in front of her eyes. She smiled and succumbed to them, entertained by their charms, they giggled and fizzed gently upon her tongue.

A broader smile spread across her face as she became intoxicated by the simplicity of it all. Lightly, they swirled, without concern and without inhibition. They did not care what the world around them thought. They had no ulterior motive. No agenda. No desire to take advantage of her. Their only goal, their only reason for existence in the first place was to entertain and relax her.

She sighed and set down her glass.

Why can't everything be as fulfilling as drinking fine champagne?

Easter's shoulders had now relaxed and she felt more at ease with the high brow environment that she had somehow infiltrated. No raised eyebrows caused her embarrassment anymore. Quickly, she indulged in another sip. Briefly, there was a sense of guilt, a feeling that she had worked too hard to succumb to the temptations of alcohol again. But these soon passed. This kind of hospitality was too good to turn down.

She looked around, as inconspicuously as possible and with a certain sense of dissipating disbelief. Not fifteen minutes earlier, she had arrived at the luxurious *Châteaux Cheroux* restaurant, well known in these parts to be the eating place of the rich and famous, who had found themselves somewhat adrift from the sights and sounds of Mayfair. It was well known amongst the self determined higher echelon of society, cementing its place by being outside the budget of the humble ordinary man. After a moment of too much consternation over whether she should even have tried to find her table without her host, which itself had followed her own internal conflict over whether it was even a good idea to be here at all, Easter had found the courage to approach the *maitre d'* in order to enquire what on earth it was she should be doing right now, having entered such a beautiful and sumptuous palace of fine cuisine without the man who would act as guarantor for any drinks she felt she had to consume whilst she waited for him. She also sincerely hoped that this man would not be suggesting they 'go Dutch' at the end of the night.

Much to her delight, and she hoped, not too obvious relief, she had been greeted warmly by the *maitre d'*, who had promptly seated her at her table with the finest bottle of Bollinger on the wine list, and a message from her host. Whilst the cork popped, Easter nervously read the exquisitely hand written note, which apologised profusely for the 'inexcusable delay' that had caused his absence and offered the hope that the gift would be a 'sufficient enough incentive' to remain whilst he made his way there.

A moment's hesitation had crossed Easter's mind as she sat there with the tall fluted glass. For months, years it had seemed, she had fought the desire to drink. Should she not continue to resist? Was she now able to drink sociably without feeling that need? Was she ready for this?

Only one way to find out… she thought.

It was with a greater moment of concern that she had realised she was also wearing the best dress she owned, which whilst being very expensive and designer, was also very revealing. It did cross her mind, on several occasions, whether that would prove to be a big mistake. Concern like that certainly made it a whole lot easier to continue drinking.

*****

"I think you've made a mistake," said Denton. It was perhaps the most unhelpful comment he could have made.

"I tend to agree with you," said Colin, trying to keep his annoyance both at the situation and Denton's unwelcome counsel, at bay.

"Oh. And again."

"Yes, I think you're right," said Colin.

It was dark, and rain swept down on the car bonnet causing a rattle to reverberate around them. They had pulled up at a set of traffic lights somewhere in the confused system of one way streets and dead ends that was Manchester city centre.

"I can still see it though," said Denton, unable to disguise his mild sense of frustration. "It's right there!"

He pointed past Colin's still crooked nose and precautionary neck brace to a flood lit building.

"Yes, I'm well aware of that," Colin snapped.

"It's just so infuriating that we do not seem to be getting any closer to it!" said Denton, almost apologetically.

"Yes, that had also not passed me by, Denton," said Colin as he went down another one way street.

"There, there, there!" said Denton as he pointed at the building that they had driven past again for what must have been the twentieth time.

"I see it," said Colin calmly - the kind of calmness that a psychopath has shortly before garrotting his next victim.

Denton sighed loudly in a manner that caused Colin to believe he still had his teenage son in the car.

"So unfair!" snorted Denton.

"I know, but there was no turning to go down there," explained Colin.

Denton sat with a map in his lap, which had become redundant as soon as they realised that it did not work. In fact, they sincerely doubted that any map could do justice to just how hideously and horribly complicated Manchester city centre is to negotiate. All too briefly, they had given up on the idea of asking directions after one man, having spoken non-stop for fifteen minutes with a barrage of instructions, continued to insist that they were only two roads away from where they needed to be, but in order to get there they needed to head back to the motorway and start again.

"There! There! Right there!" screamed Denton again as they shot past the road they needed, heading in the wrong direction.

"I know," said Colin, again calmly, "but it is a one way street and we can't enter from that side."

Colin had now reached the stage where he would quite happily have paid any exorbitant price to ditch the car and hire a helicopter, since he figured, and perhaps quite rightly, that a chopper was the only way they would ever reach their destination.

It was probably due to the fact that Colin could hear a helicopter and had been able to for at least the last thirty minutes that he had had this idea. What he did not know though was that the helicopter was circling the city above, deliberately following their car which had been circling non-stop for the last hour and which had been driving around in a figure of eight, in various directions, for the last fifteen minutes. The occupants of the helicopter were either concerned that the car contained terrorists of some description, or were just amused by the whole sorry affair.

What am I doing here? thought Denton. *How did I get stuck in this hell hole?* Suddenly he was reminded of how the morning had begun.

"Denton - are you alright?" Colin had asked having found Denton slumped at his desk.

"What?" said Denton, waking with a start. "Yes, of course I am, why do you ask?"

"Oh, nothing," said Colin, mildly annoyed. "It's just your novel appearance. I can't say that I've seen many people this morning with hair like a bird's nest and paper stuck to their face."

Denton glanced with annoyance at the memo attached to his face by drool.

"It's important," said Denton. "I wanted to make sure I didn't lose it."

"Are you sure, Denton?" asked Colin. "Because if I didn't know better I would suspect that you were asleep at your desk."

"No, not at all."

"So why are you unable to open your eyes?"

"I can. I just choose not to," retorted Denton. "Anyway, was there anything in particular you wanted?"

Colin sighed. Denton wondered why he continued this kind of ridiculous façade each morning. He knew that Colin knew for a fact he had a hangover - after all, Colin had provided the finance for it. What did he expect him to look like? For three hours during the preceding night, Denton had had to listen to Colin's semi-constant whining about his wife's adultery. To his credit though, he had made the conversation more interesting by going into lurid detail about what his wife had been up to. What made this conversation even more farcical was the fact that Colin had seen Denton bumbling around not one hour earlier at the flat as Denton walked into a series of static objects complaining bitterly that they had been moved in the night. Why then did he continue this routine at work? Was he making a point?

"Denton, I wondered if you would assist me with a completion."

"Oh, for the love of God," muttered Denton under his breath. "Sure," he said out loud. "Which meeting room do you want me to set up in?"

"None of them. It's in Manchester."

"Where?"

"Manchester. It's in the north somewhere. Your first job is research."

"Ok, what?"

"Find out where on earth Manchester is. I think it's somewhere north of Watford."

"North of Watford! You mean Scotland?" said Denton in mock confusion.

"Not quite."

"You mean there's something north of Watford that isn't Scotland?" said Denton in mock disgust.

"I know, I was confused as well," said Colin so genuinely that Denton was only half certain he was joking.

*****

"My darling! A pleasure to see you. You look divine!" said Gunt with that air of plausible genuineness that only great men can pull off.

"Oh, hello, Mr Gunt," said Easter trying to stand whilst realising the futility of the attempt. The champagne bottle was empty, and she had lost the instructions on how to move her legs.

"Please," said Mr Gunt waving an arm dismissively, "we're at dinner together. There really is no need for such formality." He stood behind his chair as the waiter moved his seat in behind him, easing the process of sitting. Easter admired how elegantly he was able to sit down. When the waiter then tried to assist her in the same manner she had almost ended up on the floor, though in fairness this may have had something to do with the alcohol. "I must again apologise for my tardiness. Something cropped up that needed my urgent attention."

"It's no problem," said Easter, "really. The champagne certainly helped entertain me in your absence!"

Mr Gunt smiled. "I'm glad. Now tell me, how have you been since we last spoke?"

Despite the alcohol, Easter felt slightly uncomfortable with the situation. Here she was dining with a man she had spoken to maybe three or four times, who was currently as warm and genuine as a long lost friend. No wonder this man was so powerful. Any man who could be so genuinely charming had to go far.

"Oh, you know," she said, slightly intimidated, "I can't complain."

"Are you enjoying your stay in the Lakes?" he asked whilst perusing the wine list.

"Erm, yes, on the whole. The scenery is really breath-taking. A far cry from London."

"Definitely!" he agreed. The waiter re-appeared. "Now would you care for some wine?"

No, Easter, you wouldn't. Say no! said some part of her brain.

She looked at her empty glass.

"Well, if you're offering…"

Mr Gunt turned to the waiter.

"Number 62 please."

The waiter nodded and disappeared again.

"And your accommodation? How are you finding that?" asked Mr Gunt.

How much longer will this small talk go on for? thought Easter. *Remember why you're here. Don't get so drunk that you don't remember why you're here! The story! The big story!*

"Yes, it's lovely thank you. It's just on the outskirts of the village. It's small but it's cosy. Very different to your lovely house."

Mr Gunt smiled coyly, as if slightly embarrassed.

"Well, you know, sometimes I wonder whether I should just sell up and move into something more modest myself. A large house like that, well, sometimes it's quite foreboding when you're catering for one."

He turned away as the waiter appeared again, but not before Easter had had time to spot a look of sorrow on his face.

*****

Denton looked across at Colin. *What on earth is his secret? What does he keep in his desk drawer? What is the 'bomb' that Gladys was so serious about?*

Denton stared at the man in the neck brace, with the bent nose. He looked so ordinary. He looked so normal. He looked so fucking dull. Could there really be something sinister about him? Something interesting? Something that a life of tedious paper pushing had done to him to make him flip and begin mindless acts of terrorism. *Well,* thought Denton, *it's always the quiet ones, isn't it?*

"Is everything ok, Denton?" asked Colin.

"Of course," said Denton, quickly returning to reality.

"It's just you're staring intently at me, and to be honest, it's beginning to scare me."

Denton suddenly realised that he was in fact simply staring.

"Sorry," said Denton. "Just thinking."

This comment did little to appease Colin's distress.

Seriously though, thought Denton, *what the hell is he up to? What is the bomb? What is the bomb? Maybe I should just come out and ask him. After all, we are in a car. Where is he going to go?*

Denton opened his mouth to speak. There was a rush of nervous activity in his brain. Apparently someone hadn't been watching his thought processes carefully enough. This was probably due to some brain cell having become of a victim of last nights binge.

What are you doing? You're about to ask an underground terrorist, out loud, whether he's a serial murderer? What the hell are you going to do if he says yes? Just say 'oh right, that's interesting.' Worse still, what if he doesn't admit it? You are none the wiser but he knows you're on to him. You're going to wake up tomorrow dead! Or worse!

"Everything alright, Denton?" asked Colin.

"Yes!" yelped Denton. "Why do you ask?"

"Well, you're sweating profusely."

Shit! Shit! He knows! He knows you know! That neck brace! It's probably not a neck brace at all! It's probably a mind reading device given to him by the CIA. My God, of course! The broken nose! It wasn't a biking accident - he got it on some secret underground mission stealing secrets from the Americans to sell to the Russians and betraying them both to the Middle East. Suddenly it all makes sense. Oh god! If he can read my thoughts he's going to pull my brain out of my head with a coat hanger and pickle it in vinegar so that the Feds can't discover he's the informant. My God, I need a drink. The minute we get back to the office, I'm breaking that desk open with a crowbar to find out what evidence he's got in there then I'm ratting him out to the cops for a big pay off. Or something like that.

Denton felt sick. He looked out the window. The office was still right there, and they were still no closer.

*****

Easter absent-mindedly swirled her glass of Sancerre. Her head was beginning to spin slightly. In the past she could have easily finished the bottle and started on the next with no ill-effects. Apparently, she was out of practise. She hoped it wasn't beginning to show. She also hoped that she wasn't about to fall out of her top. Why did her only good outfit have to be so revealing? Much to her surprise though, Mr Gunt didn't seem to have noticed.

Remember the story!

"So tell me more about yourself. I know nothing about you, except what I read in the papers..."

"Oh?" said Gunt, with a look of intrigue on his face. "And what do you read in the papers?" His tone was almost accusatory, though still soft enough for Easter to feel comfortable in his company.

"Well, the usual. You know."

"No, I don't. I don't read newspaper stories about myself. But I would be very interested to know your opinion of me, having read them."

"Well," said Easter, feeling slightly uneasy. "I wouldn't say I've formed an opinion, as such. I mean, I work in the media so I know that whatever is written is about five percent truth and ninety five percent bullshit. But I have read a lot about you. Your success during the sixties and seventies. How you started out with nothing and became a self made man, almost overnight. The speculation in the press about how you did it. You know that stuff?"

"And what do you make of that speculation in the press?"

"Well, I think it just smacks of jealousy. Many great businessmen have done the same thing. It happens all the time. The press think there's something else to it, but I sincerely doubt there is. After all, look at all your charity work. Your donations to hospitals, for example. The discounted service that your restaurants provide to hospitals, and the like, is commendable. It always has been. The press think there must be a story, but I doubt there is." *Though I really hope there is.*

Gunt laughed. In her slightly drunken state, Easter's inhibited intuition tried to analyse that laugh. Was it sinister? Was it with malice? Not really. If anything, there was tinge of regret in it, perhaps. Or. Or. *Oh, who cares. Bring on the Sancerre!*

*****

"Denton, you've gone very quiet - are you sure you're alright?"

"Positive!" said Denton, as un-positively as humanly possible.

Typical! thought Colin *He's gone quiet because he's feeling sick. Probably the hangover. And the fact we're travelling around in huge circles. Trainees today. Wasn't like this in my day.*

"I'm starting to get dizzy from all this driving," said Colin. "I'm sure you are too. There's a hotel over there. We'll pull over. I'm desperate to use the facilities, if you know what I mean." He laughed. It wasn't really sinister but it sounded that way in Denton's head.

I know what you mean! You're going to take me to a hotel room and shoot me in the head, aren't you, you Jackal!

They pulled up in the car park of a Jury's Inn hotel.

"You coming in?" asked Colin.

Denton nodded and followed him in. The building was fairly drab and dull. Well, what did you expect? It is Manchester after all.

"Won't be a mo," said Colin, disappearing into the toilet. As he walked off, Denton noticed that he dropped something. Intrigued he ventured over and picked it up. It was Colin's wallet. Denton froze.

Oh God! he thought, *his secret papers! His true identity! The mystery uncovered!*

In fact, it was none of these things. It was just a wallet containing several important looking credit cards, a tube season ticket and, at least, four hundred pounds in fifty and twenty pound notes.

How dull, thought Denton despondently.

Colin soon returned. Not soon enough though. It was clear he had betrayed the brotherhood and washed his hands.

What manner of man are you? mused Denton. *No wonder your wife left you if you act like this. Come on! Live a little. Take a risk now and again.*

"You dropped this," said Denton handing over the wallet.

Colin looked at the wallet, briefly checked inside (*thanks a lot!* thought Denton, *that's trust for you)* and looked back at Denton agog.

"Denton," said Colin. "Thank you very much for returning this to me. I'd be absolutely sunk if someone had spotted this before you!"

"Not at all," said Denton, a little peeved that Colin had had to check the right amount was there.

"No seriously Denton, I'm very impressed. Honesty is an undervalued virtue these days."

Sensing a long, and ultimately, pointless speech was about to commence, Denton interrupted.

"Really, Colin, it was nothing. I just saw it lying there so I picked it up when I realised you'd dropped it and…" *(being relieved it did not identify you as a terrorist…)* "I was happy to look after it for you until you came back."

"No, really Denton, I am impressed. There's a lot of money in here. Believe me, I've encountered solicitors before who would steal your chair and desk the minute your back was turned. Returning this means a lot. Trust is very important and something I cherish greatly, which is ironic given my current position. A man without morals is a man without meaning. Remember that, Denton."

They left the hotel and returned to the pursuit of finding the office at the end of the rainbow.

As he got into the car, Denton felt himself blushing. Oddly, he felt almost embarrassed that he had considered breaking into Colin's desk. But, that said, what Colin had said made him all the more intrigued. *A man without morals is a man without meaning. Bit rich coming from a guy with a bomb in his desk drawer. What the hell is in that desk!?*

*****

"Would you like to sample the wine, Madam?"

Three times now the waiter had asked that question. Three times. Manners are all very well and good but if the answer is always the same, what on earth was the point of asking?

"No thank you, please, let the gentleman try it."

By now, Easter was beginning to believe she was so slumped in her chair that she was almost horizontal. She dreaded to think how drunk she must appear to Mr Gunt. She also shuddered to think how her dress appeared. She had the sinking feeling that her tits were trying to escape and were currently clambering up and over her top looking for the exit. As subtly as possible she pulled up the front of her dress.

And yet, Gunt didn't seem to notice. Not once had she caught him staring at her. When he asked her to dinner, she assumed that he wanted to perve on her for an hour or two. Not that she minded if she got her story - so long as perving was the only thing on the menu.

So what had he invited her out for? He hadn't told her anything. And yet, Easter had the strangest feeling that there was something he wanted to say. Something he had to get off his chest, maybe? What was it? What could it be?

She watched as he sampled the wine. The waiter poured the smallest amount and retreated. Gunt picked up the glass, swirled it three times and then took a long, deep sniff. He nodded and the waiter poured. What was he hiding? What caused the sorrow in those eyes? Was it the drink?

Ah, who cares? Here's more Sancerre. The answer to all our problems.

"Cheers," said Easter, raising her glass to Gunt.

"My thoughts precisely," said Gunt, raising his own.

Chapter Twenty Six

Freudian slips

It's surprising how much simpler life is when you're completely wasted. Suddenly, all those hopes and dreams are reduced exponentially the drunker you become. By the end of the night you have two, maybe three. You hope that somewhere in your mind is a coherent memory of: 1) how to get home; and, 2) how to identify home once you're stood in front of it. Your only dream is sleeping in your own bed (as opposed to the gutter that you currently find yourself in).

Simple.

Simple had been the byword of the entire night. Keep things simple. The venue for drinks was simple. Freud's bar. Classic. Elegant. Hard to find and easy to miss. A complete no nonsense bar. You go in, you order a cocktail, you watch the barman blend together something exotic, classy and simple involving a lot of alcohol, a little mixer and plenty of foliage. You hand over your money. You sit either in one of the three seating areas available, or more likely, you stand. And you like it.

Simple.

So simple in fact that one might wonder whether the owner or creator dwelt so much on the idea of opening a cocktail bar that served great cocktails that he omitted to add certain other factors to his idea. Seating for a start seemed to have been overlooked. Ditto for inside toilets. Most crucially, prominence. The damned thing is so hard to find on Shaftsbury Avenue that you can be stood outside the blessed place staring at the sign, and even then there is still a good chance you'll completely miss it.

You might, therefore, be thinking that the owner or creator had shot himself in the foot and that since the place was so difficult to find that no one would ever experience those moments of cocktail delight. Not so. The place is permanently packed, which begged the question of how on earth the people in there found it in the first place. It also begged the question of whether, in actual fact, it wasn't that these people had found the venue time after time, but had simply never managed to find their way back out again. Perhaps those people were concerned, and rightly so, that if they were to give up and leave, the prospect of never being able to find their way back was just too much to stomach.

As Denton looked around, he could certainly understand why these people never wanted to leave. What he couldn't fathom out though was, if these people had been here since the dawn of man and would remain for eternity, why didn't the bastards give up their seats more often?

It was the start of the night and, as so often happens, the life altering moments that were about to occur hadn't happened yet. Pity really. It would have saved everybody a lot of time, effort and money if they had.

Around Denton were Randall, Delia, Colin, Brian and Billy. Badger was also lurking about somewhere too, though no one was quite sure where. The six of them were huddled up near the bar, partly out of choice to guarantee a 'quicker' (irritating bunny rabbit ear thing) service, partly out of necessity. As so often happens at any kind of drinking establishment, the longer you stay in one place, the smaller your personal space becomes. At the start of the evening there had been enough room for them to stand in a decent sized circle, now they found that they were stood in three 'circles'. Again with the bunny rabbit ears, but in this case justified - technically, you can't have a circle with two people. Though if you're being pedantic, is it ever possible to create a circle with people? After all, even if there's six of you, that's surely a hexagon isn't it?

"I can't honestly say I've ever heard that before," said Randall knocking back a cocktail of bright purple fluids with a twig of something or other sticking out. "Nope. I have never heard someone refer to a group of people as being in a hexagon. It's usually a circle or a pair. Nothing else."

"I suppose it just strikes me as being odd," said Colin, drinking a concoction that seemed to be more leaf than drink.

"Yes, well I can see why it would!" said Randall, hoping that his sarcasm was not quite as obvious as he had initially intended. Desperately, he looked around to see if there was any way he could join into Denton's conversation with Delia, but it was no good. He was well and truly pinned in against Delia's freakishly long back. He would even have opted for the chance to join Billy's conversation with Brian.

"Your drink Brian..." ventured Billy, a look of confusion on his face.

"Yeah?" asked Brian.

"Well," said Billy, trying to find the words. "It's just. Well, it's more plant than drink, isn't it?"

"Do you think?" said Brian, examining his glass.

"Yes," said Billy, his look of confusion intensifying. "I mean, if I didn't know any better I would say that it wasn't a drink at all that you were holding, but the small vase of brightly coloured flowers that, until recently, was sat on that ledge over there."

Brian looked away sheepishly. "Nah..." he said, without conviction. Billy frowned, unconvinced.

Denton looked towards the conversation that Billy and Brian were having, then turned back to his own conversation with Delia. He hoped it was not too obvious that he was finding the situation difficult. Almost awkward. Delia and Denton had not really been alone together since the Corporate weekend. Worse still, Denton could not stop admiring how great Delia looked. Her top was unusually skimpy, and for perhaps the first time ever, she was wearing a very short skirt. *What had happened to frumpy old Delia?* he wondered. *Those legs look fantastic!*

"Am I boring you?" asked Delia, candidly.

"Sorry?" said Denton, turning back to look at her.

"Well, it just seems as if you would rather be elsewhere…"

"Not at all!" said Denton, also without conviction. He polished off his cocktail, which left him with a mouthful of mint and God knows what other foliage between his teeth. Not wishing to appear uncouth, he simply swallowed, instantly regretting the decision.

"Are you alright?" asked Delia with a look of concern.

"Mmm hmm," mumbled Denton, a tear rolling down his cheek.

"But you're crying!" pointed out Delia, perhaps trying to be helpful.

"No," choked Denton, "still fine. Would you like another drink?"

"Erm," she looked at her almost full cocktail. "Well, no, not really."

"Go on," said Denton, "be a devil!"

"Oh, ok then," she said succumbing.

Denton grabbed Randall by the shoulder and yanked him out of the conversation he was having with Colin, much to his obvious surprise and delight.

"We're going to the bar!" said Denton. Randall was powerless to disagree, mainly because he was, by now, already at the bar.

"Everything alright?" asked Randall, needlessly. Clearly, something was up.

"Yep, it's all good," said Denton. "Just wanted a bit of male company for a while."

"OK," said Randall hesitating. "There's a problem with Delia then."

"No!" lied Denton. He paused. "Tell me this though. Do you think Delia looks different tonight?"

Randall looked back at Delia who was reapplying makeup in a little compact.

"Erm, well, I dunno. Are you thinking of anything in particular?"

Denton looked at Delia and back at Randall.

"I know we have only known her a short time…"

Randall looked at Denton with a slight look of disgust.

"…not in the biblical sense, Randall!"

Randall looked relieved.

"…but can you ever recall seeing Delia wearing make up?"

"Well..." said Randall considering the point.

"Or wearing a short skirt?"

"Erm…"

"Or looking like the missing fourth member of Atomic Kitten??"

Randall frowned. "I thought there were four members of Atomic Kitten."

"Is there?" asked Denton. "I thought there were two blondes and the ginger one."

"Nah, they're all ginger aren't they?"

They both stopped to consider the point. The counting of digits was involved.

"Anyway, it doesn't matter, you're missing the point. Don't you think that Delia looks, well, unusually sexy?"

Randall's jaw almost hit the floor. *Where did that comment come from?* He thought.

"Denton, are you saying that you think Delia is…sexy?!" asked Randall, slightly shocked.

"No I'm saying, don't you think it's a bit odd that she's dressing up sexier?"

"No, not at all," said Randall. "Maybe she just feels more confident around us - or maybe just with herself. Now stop thinking and start ordering."

It was Denton's turn.

"Hi, can I get sex on the beach…"

Randall sniggered.

"And I think we know who with!" quipped Randall. Denton's cheeks flamed up.

"…three times."

"Easy tiger!" joked Randall. Denton blushed further.

"…erm, a screaming orgasm…"

"Do you think she'll be that good?" said Randall, almost crying.

"…and a BMW…"

Randall started to open his mouth, but Denton got there first.

"Yes, Randall, I appreciate that's a 'black man's willy', and yes, she probably will be wishing for one too."

Randall looked embarrassed that he was so transparent.

The barman looked at the pair of them, openly tutting before muttering *'bloody students!'* under his breath.

"Look, Randall, I don't fancy Delia!" protested Denton.

"I never said you did!" said Randall.

"Well, you insinuated it, and its not true, I don't fancy her. Not at all," said Denton protesting too much.

"I believe you," said Randall. "Now let's hand out these drinks - our guests have no plants to consume."

Randall helped Denton back to the group with the drinks.

Denton passed a drink to Delia. Randall moved past her, nudging her shoulder as he did so. As she stretched out an arm to claim her drink the strap of her top fell, revealing that she was wearing a red slip underneath. Denton, following the movement of her arm caught the briefest glimpse of Delia's breast before she was able to re-arrange herself. He felt himself blushing again.

"Nice slip," he commented, perhaps hoping to alleviate the situation. Delia looked at him and blushed as well, not knowing what to make of the comment.

"Thanks," she said ambiguously. She sipped at her drink. Denton sipped at his.

Well this is awkward, he concluded.

Thankfully, for all concerned, Randall emerged in between them.

"I'm just off to the loo. Where is it?" he asked.

"Ah. The toilet. Yeah, it's outside."

"What?" asked Randall, hoping he'd misheard.

"Yeah, it's outside. You have to go back out the door, over a path, and it's in front of you. Stinks a bit, so prepare yourself."

Randall gulped.

"Great," he said, before disappearing.

In the time it took for him to re-emerge, Denton and Delia had had the most strained conversation that anyone could ever have about the state of modern toiletry. It was obvious that both had forced the conversation to continue past breaking point, simply to avoid having to find another topic of conversation. It was also clear that neither of them had much idea how a toilet actually worked aside from the fact that it was invented by a guy called Crapper. They concluded that it made sense that a man with a vested interest in ensuring his waste was properly disposed of, would be the one responsible for perfecting the system.

"I've just been to the toilet. There were two people stood at the urinals and since the only free one was the one in the middle, I applied the usual rules and used the vacant cubicle."

"What have you done?" asked Denton sensing there was a problem coming.

"Well, I've learnt three things. One, someone in this room has eaten something that didn't agree with them. Two, the flush doesn't work. Three, mobile phones don't float, even in liquid of a high density."

"Oh Randall!" scalded Denton, like the boy's mother.

"Please tell me you didn't fish it out!" said Delia, about to gag.

"I thought about it briefly," said Randall. "But I didn't know where to begin so I've left it there."

"Look on the bright side though," said Denton. "Your phone was rubbish, after all - now you've got the ideal excuse to sort yourself out with one that actually works."

"Yeah, maybe," said Randall, a little miffed by his own misfortune. "But knowing my luck with technology, it will only break down as soon as I get hold of it."

Delia moved to change the subject in light of her difficult conversation with Denton, and Randall's obvious depression at his technological inabilities.

"How is life working out with Colin?" she said nodding in the direction of Colin who was stood with Billy and Brian, frowning at the vase in Brian's hand.

Denton looked at Randall.

"Awful," they both said in unison.

"Come on now, it can't be all that bad!", she said.

"But it is!" cried Randall. "It's like living with your Dad. And not just any old Dad, but a Dad who's really disapproving of everything you do. It's awful!"

"Really? How so?" asked Delia.

"Well, it's not so much what he says…" said Denton, "…more what he implies..."

"Yeah, like whenever you go for a drink after work, he will sort of look at you as if to say *'should you really be doing that on a school night?'*. It's really off putting."

"And he's very critical of our cleaning habits."

"What, like personal hygiene?" asked Delia.

"No," said Denton, "more like how clean the flat is, that type of thing. He's always hoovering. We're thinking of buying him a pinny."

Delia giggled.

Denton stared at Colin. *Who is this man that has managed to infiltrate my life?* thought Denton, *is he really a terrorist? Does he really have a bomb in his desk drawer?? What the hell am I doing drinking with him? What else was I supposed to do? I couldn't exactly say to Randall 'I can't go drinking with Colin, he might end up blowing up the bar if he doesn't get the drink he wants'.*

Delia interrupted his train of thought. "My turn to buy drinks, methinks."

Billy brushed past Colin and into Denton and Randall.

"You alright, Billy?" asked Denton.

Billy's eyes had lost the ability to function as a team. The left one was currently looking over Randall's shoulder. The right one was just staring at the left one, no doubt trying to figure out what it was looking at.

"Fine," mumbled Billy incoherently. "I've just been to the toilet. It's outside you know!"

"We know," said Denton, feeling almost sober in comparison.

"Anyway, where's Brian? I thought he was here. I was talking to him, wasn't I?"

Denton and Randall looked around. Brian was stood talking to Colin. He now appeared to have a vase in each hand. Colin was scratching his head.

"He's with Colin," said Randall pointing behind Billy. Billy's right eye followed the direction of Randall's finger. The left eye was clearly still tired from earlier on. It remained motionless. *I'll catch up with you later. Let me know if you see anything interesting,* it may have said.

"Oh yeah," said Billy. "Brian's a nice guy. Likes flowers though, doesn't he?! Did you know that the Cape floral kingdom is the smallest floral kingdom of all the floral kingdoms? I didn't. Did you?"

There was no answer to that.

It was probably around two in the morning when they stumbled out of Freud's. Everyone had had a little too much to drink, including Colin. His frazzled hair appearing even more unkempt than usual. Billy's eyes still refused to obey orders, and Brian was coy, having managed to smuggle two pot plants and a rose bud out without being caught.

"Home!" shouted Randall.

They all agreed. "Home!" came the response. Yet no one moved. After a short while, Denton raised a valid point.

"Where is home?"

"North!" cried Randall.

They all agreed. "North!" they cheered. Still no one moved. After a short while, Denton raised a further valid point.

"Which way is that?"

They all looked to Randall. He reflected on the point.

"I have no idea," he conceded.

"Well, I need to go for a pee otherwise I'll just explode!" exclaimed Billy.

Denton's mouth engaged without consultation with his brain.

"Well, if you're gonna explode, you wanna speak to Colin about that!"

Colin glared at Denton. Even in a drunken stupor, Denton registered his cheeks flushing. Thankfully, Billy distracted everyone before anyone else could ask questions.

"Look we have to go home now. I know the way, follow me!"

Such had been his enthusiasm to leave that he had not stopped to check he had all of his possessions with him. Co-ordination, for example. The left leg tripped up over the right one. Presumably, the left leg had been following the lead of the left eye and the right leg likewise. From their lowly position, they had not appreciated that the left and right eyes were looking in completely different directions. Billy hit the ground.

He was followed by Randall.

Who brought down Denton.

Who caused Brian to fall.

Whose left leg, Delia avoided. She failed to spot the right leg though. This caused her own limbs to catch Colin's hair. The weight, having been shifted, affected his balance and caused him to topple over.

Denton winced from the gutter he now found himself in. In his drunken stupor, a moment of clarity descended upon him. His mind cleared just long enough for him to hear the words and understand their true meaning.

"What are you doing? What's going on?"

Badger had woken up and left the bar, to be confronted with the image of all his drinking buddies in a heap on the floor.

"You've been hanging around me for too long," were his wise words on the subject.

Chapter Twenty Seven

God moves in mysterious ways, but then so do squirrels

Denton found himself sat in front of Colin's desk. Colin was wearing a flowery tie and a stern expression, neither of which suited him.

Denton knew why he was there and yet he still felt incredibly awkward. He was almost fearful of what Colin was about to say. In fact, the fear was to such an extent that he had almost forgotten about the painful hangover that was now sat somewhere at the back of his head.

"Denton, thank you for coming to see me…" began Colin, looking down at what might have been a pre-written script. The words caused Denton to stir uneasily in his seat as if he were a naughty school child in front of the headmaster.

"…I think that you know now that I have received some complaints about the quality of your work, and well, your general attitude to this Firm and this profession."

The oxygen in Denton's lungs began to burn. He felt sick.

"In particular, your recent work has been criticised by several partners. You are not pulling your weight, and it is not on."

Denton was almost scared of Colin. Well, as scared as one could be of a man with two yellow/bluish tinted eyelids, a neck brace and a confirmed broken nose.

"Denton, this is not easy for me to say but it has been noted that you are working well within your comfort zone at the moment. Other trainees in the department seem to be excelling. Take Bonnie Belcher for example…"

Since everyone else has, I'll give that a miss, thought Denton.

"…she is doing exceptionally well, and is putting in a real effort. Just the other day I heard Campbell Oliver telling other partners in the department that he was really impressed with what she could do. In fact, I even heard him say that she could do things that his wife couldn't do. And that really surprised me, since she's a fourteen year qualified senior Corporate solicitor at one of the other major practices around here!"

Even though Denton could see how Colin could have arrived at that explanation of the conversation he had overheard, he was still amazed that Colin would have retained that explanation as being the most plausible of all the conclusions that he could have come to.

"I hear that it's because of how flexible she is," said Denton, unable to resist.

"Yes, that's right!" said Colin. "That's exactly what Campbell said! See,

Denton, that kind of flexibility gets you noticed. You need to be getting noticed in the department. You need to let other people in the department know that you are available and ready to assist them! Just like Bonnie!"

Oh, good God, what an awful thought, reflected Denton.

There was a pause as Colin let his comments sink in for a moment. Colin interpreted the look of horror and disgust on Denton's face as recognition of the ways in which he had let himself down.

"Denton, as I say, I'm sorry that it has to be me that has to have this chat with you. As your supervisor and, lately, flat mate, this is not easy for me to do, and I hope you appreciate that."

Denton tried to contain his frustration at the injustice of it all.

"I do, Colin."

"The debacle over the bible of documents cannot happen again. Devlin is absolutely spitting feathers about it! You really cannot afford to make enemies of the partners. You need to engage these people. You need to get them on side, otherwise you're going to find yourself outside of this firm looking in. Bonnie won't be in that position. She has made a lasting impression on Campbell, I can tell you. In fact, she has made a lasting impression on all the partners."

Denton tried to hide the brewing rage inside him.

"OK, so she did herself no favours at the Corporate weekend away by flaunting herself in the rather vulgar manner that she did, but I really think that most people are over that now, and have seen it in the light of her attempts to get her personality over."

That word should have been 'leg', Colin.

"She has made a genuine attempt, and whilst her understanding of the law is sometimes suspect, she has come on in leaps and bounds…"

And on most of the partners, in most of the offices in this department, probably with the aid of leather and whips.

"…to the extent that nearly all the senior fee-earners and partners want her in their team."

And in their laps.

"Look, Denton, I know that the idea of, well, to be blunt, sucking up, is something that may be abhorrent to you, but Bonnie manages it and I think you should to. Please try to suck up a bit, like Bonnie."

Denton could not prevent a look of disgust spreading across his face.

"Denton, I can tell from the look in your face that this is a lot for you to take on board, but seriously, please consider your options carefully. As a friendly word of advice, why don't you lay off the booze for a while. Start being more pro-active at work and take things more seriously. This is your career at the end of the day. Don't throw it all away."

Denton gulped down the anger that was now threatening to escape from the jail of his clenched jaw.

Like an angel at the gates of Hades, Gladys appeared and interrupted their conversation.

"Mr Hooley, I'm very sorry to interrupt you."

"What is it, Gladys?"

"You are needed urgently in room 17. There is a problem on Project Olive, and Devlin is asking for you to go down immediately."

"OK, thanks Gladys." Colin turned back to Denton as Gladys disappeared again, playing her miniature harp as her little wings carried her to heaven. "Denton, wait here will you? I will be back in a moment."

Colin rose and left the office, leaving Denton silently fuming.

Denton shook his head violently, just to let off a bit of steam.

Be more like Bonnie fuck face Belcher, my arse!!! Fucking whore.

He felt slightly better but not much.

Fucking big titted freaking bitch face!! he thought, trying to vent his frustration using some sort of Tourette's Syndrome cleansing technique.

He looked over at Colin's desk. The top drawer was open.

Who the fuck does he think he is? Giving me this lecture. He's not exactly a paragon of virtue himself is he, after his little attack on that client. Seems to have forgotten about that with all his talk of keeping bombs. Little shit can't even make partnership or stop his cheating bitch face yummy mummy from fucking around with the pool boy.

Denton stopped and re-evaluated momentarily the image that had just been processed through his eyes and displayed in his head. Colin's top desk drawer was open.

The secret!

Denton could feel his breath getting heavier and faster.

The secret is in that drawer!

His heart rate started to quicken.

I could expose the little shit. I could find out his secret. The bomb!

His legs felt like lead, and initially seemed to resist his instructions, but before he was fully conscious of what he was doing, he found himself stood up and hovering towards the drawer.

What am I doing? What am I doing?!?! I'm in enough trouble as it is without this!

He stood over the drawer.

He's coming back! He's going to come back and catch me! I live with him! He's going to kill me! How do I explain why I'm standing here!?

He looked up at the door, Gladys was gone. No one was around.

What about trust? What about the things Colin said about trust!! A man without morals is a man without meaning!

He placed his hands into the drawer.

This is wrong. This is so wrong, he thought as he quickly sifted through the contents. *I'm going to get caught. I'm going to get caught.* Anxiously, he looked at the drawer, then the door, then the drawer during which his head felt light, his heart was thumping and his eyesight was so affected that everything took on the perception of being ten times smaller than it had been a second before. Denton was definitely outside his comfort zone right about now.

Trust! What about trust?!

He shifted some papers to reveal three leaflets, all with the same title.

"Living with impotence?!" said Denton, suddenly realising that he was speaking out loud.

He quickly brushed past these and came to something else. He saw a project name that meant nothing to him. *Project Maybury.* There was a name there that he recognised. Someone famous. He continued to sift until something caught his eye. At first, he almost dismissed it out of hand, but then something about it attracted his attention. Suddenly, he realised what he held in his hand.

"Well, well," said Denton, slightly calmer, "so Gladys was right after all. He does keep a bomb in his desk drawer."

Carefully, he placed everything back as he had found it, and pushed the desk drawer to its original position. Without a word, he returned to his seat, and with his heart beating so loud that he was convinced it was lodged in his throat, he tried to look as casual as he could for a man that had *guilt* written all over him.

Guilt. Guilt, guilt. Guilt guilt guilt. GUILT.

That was wrong. That was so wrong. That desk has my fingerprints all over it! he thought with more than a hint of complete paranoia. *Trust, where is the trust now? That was so wrong.* The words repeated and repeated in his mind, rolling over and over each other. *Trust.* What had he done. *Guilt.* Suddenly he caught himself and the knowledge that he now had. *I cannot believe what I have just seen.*

"I must tell someone," he mumbled, almost deliriously. *Trust.* That word flashed through his mind again quickly followed by another: *Guilt.* He could feel himself blushing.

Trust. Guilt.

He recoiled from what he had just done and what he had just learnt. He wanted to leave the room. He wanted to run away.

Trust, he thought, the word biting into him like venom from the jaws of a snake. *I've just bitten into a very big apple, and I really shouldn't have.*

Guilt

He sighed out loud as he concluded his own dilemma.

I can't tell anyone about this. If I tell anyone then Colin will know it was me who went through his drawers. What does that say about me? About trust?

Denton stood. Waiting for Colin to return was not an option now. It would be impossible to look him in the eye right now. He needed some time. He quietly returned to his desk where he spent the remainder of the working day silently trying to assimilate the information he had just acquired. He spent much of this time reflecting on his actions. *It is not right that I should know this,* he found himself thinking at various times.

An e-mail popped up on Denton's screen, and although the tone that accompanied it was pitched at exactly the same, annoying, level that it had always been, Denton jumped in his seat. *You have new mail - would you like to read it now?*

Denton silently panicked. He could feel his heartbeat increasing. *It's from the senior partner. I know it is - I'm going to be sacked!*

Frantically, he opened it. It was from Randall.

"You still coming out tonight?" it said.

A sense of temporary relief spread through Denton. He remembered that he had organised a lads night out tonight with Randall, Brian, Badger and Billy in Clapham.

"Yes - why wouldn't I?" asked Denton, with just a little bit too much of a hint of paranoia.

"Easy tiger," came the response. "What time do you want to leave?"

Denton glanced at his watch. It was 4.30pm. *Fuck it,* he thought, *I'm going to get the sack anyway.*

"I'm going now. Care to join me?"

"What! Are you crazy? It's 4.30pm!"

"Nope. I'm going - you coming?"

There was a pause.

"OK - my supervising partner is out of the office anyway. OK, I'll come."

It did not take them long to reach Clapham. The tube was unnaturally empty, reflective of the fact that the ordinary people of the city were still chained to their desks begging for the key. They descended into the sewer system of the underground at Moorgate - one of the darkest and dankest entrances to the Tube. Rifling past the dawdling tourists stood still on the right hand side of the descending escalator they marched down the moving steps running towards the south platform for the Northern Line.

"If there's one thing I can't stand…and it's commonly accepted that there isn't," said Denton, as he marched along the ceramic tiled corridor, "it's people who stand still on the escalators on the Tube."

"I agree," said Randall.

"I mean, what are they doing? Taking in the view? Why are they stood still?! There is nothing more annoying than getting stuck behind one of those jokers - even if it's just for a second - and then arriving at your platform just to see the train doors closing."

"I hear you," said Randall, appreciating that it was going to be one of *those* nights.

"God, it's annoying - and I don't care if there's another train just on its way - not more than four minutes away - that's four minutes of drinking time that I won't get back! That's four minutes of freedom that wasn't given to me for some joker to take away by standing still for absolutely no God damned reason!!"

"Absolutely!" agreed Randall, appreciating also that agreement would be the easiest and least painful way of getting through the night.

They jumped on the first train to arrive and were almost confused by the fact that there were seats available.

Soon they passed through Bank, crossed the river, past London Bridge, Borough, Elephant and Castle, Kennington, Oval, Stockwell before arriving at Clapham North.

"Just think," said Denton as they arrived. "We just passed under some of the most historic and interesting parts of London there."

"I know," said Randall.

"Ah, there's nothing like sight-seeing, London style."

They ascended from the grit and grime of the underground and reached the barrier. They each inserted their tube ticket, and rather sportingly, the machine released the lock and allowed them to pass through into the bright world that existed outside the sub-terrain.

"Have a nice day," it didn't say, being a Londoner at heart. Instead its doors slammed shut squeezing the life out of the poor bugger behind.

Denton and Randall briefly basked in the sunshine before diving across the road into *Arch 635*. A classic bar on Lendel Terrace, it didn't suffer from the chair bar invasion that had recently descended on poor, unsuspecting Clapham.

"Quick Randall, get the beers in, I think I'm dying of thirst."

"No probs," said Randall. "Happy to help." He approached the barman, who seemed noticeably confused by two suits approaching him whilst it was still light. With a hint of suspicion, he checked his watch, and briefly shook his wrist to make sure it was still working.

"What can I get you, lads?" he asked.

"Erm, two pints of Stella, please."

"No problem," he said picking up two pint glasses before flicking them over his head into his waiting hands.

Twat, thought Denton. *We want a drink not a sideshow.*

"Good day?" asked Randall.

Denton gulped down two thirds of his pint before answering.

"God, I needed that!"

"I take it you've had better days then?" said Randall.

"Sorry, yeah, today has been a bit of a shitter. I can't remember the first part, but the second half was awful."

"Yeah - I saw Colin today."

Denton's heart started pounding again.

"Oh yeah?" he said, trying to appear calm.

"Yeah - he seemed to be in a foul mood. Looked very annoyed about something. When I asked about it, he just said he'd tell me later."

Denton's heart leapt into his mouth.

"Did he say what it was?"

"Nah."

Denton gulped down more of his pint. The bubbles stung his throat but he didn't care.

"I think it could have been me," he said, trying not to let the guilt show through on to his face. He felt as if his forehead had become transparent and Randall could see all of his innermost thoughts.

"I heard about this today!" said Randall. "The whole thing with the bible - something about the client paying twice or something?"

"Oh, it's a complete mountain out of a mole hill," said Denton, trying to play down the situation. "And anyway, how was I supposed to know that whoever prepared the bill didn't also examine the contents of it? Was it really for me to make sure it was ok?"

"No, you're right. If they're going to treat you as if you're at the bottom of the pile - below the cleaner - they can't then put you at the top when they feel like it."

"I know. I mean, I still feel guilty, don't get me wrong, but what the hell kind of environment do we work in where the partner hides behind the trainee?"

"Tell me about it. Even before your incident, I've been increasingly aware of the scapegoat mentality people have with trainees. If it goes wrong - blame the trainee. It's perfect - I've even seen people get magnanimous about it and it makes me sick. *'It's my fault entirely - I didn't spot the fuck up that the trainee made. If you want to blame anyone, blame me - I should not have trusted the trainee to be able to do the work as much as I did.'* Oh fuck off!"

"Yeah, I know," said Denton finishing off his drink. "Let me buy you another one."

Randall glanced down at his drink. It was almost full though that did not stop him from nodding anyway.

"Still, Colin did look very angry," said Randall.

Denton's heart pounded again. *The bomb. Colin knows I know about the bomb.*

"Ah, he'll get over it," said Denton, trying not to look guilty.

"Yeah. What was it like though being bollocked by Colin?" asked Randall.

Denton wandered over to the bar. "Two pints of Stella please," he said to the barman. "Surreal," he said turning back to Randall.

"I can only imagine," said Randall.

"Come on, let's drink these, then meet the others in Bierodrome."

"OK. Is Brian coming out tonight?"

"Yeah, think so. He hoped to anyway."

"He's a nice guy, isn't he?" said Randall.

"Yeah, but bit odd around flowers, don't you think."

"What do you mean?" asked Randall.

"Well, I dunno, he just acts in a way that's odd. He always goes on that he doesn't like flowers, right? But then whenever you're with him and he's next to you, it's as if he is constantly trying to demonstrate to you that he isn't interested in the flowers."

"Yeah, you're right," said Randall. "Do you think he's gay?"

Denton flinched. "Bit of mental jump in that thought process, wasn't there?"

"Well, he is very camp. And he likes flowers. And he wears weird clothes. Like those Japanese sandals? What were they about?"

"Yeah. Maybe. Come on, drink up. I'm thinking about my Belgian beer," said Denton, lying.

Bombs, bombs, bombs.

Chapter Twenty Eight

Seminars - The lost art of Teaching

Denton frowned.

A reminder had just appeared on his screen.

It simply read *12.30: Seminar by Pensions, Employment and Tax Strategies.*

Denton stared at the reminder. The reminder stared at Denton. Having considering the matter for a moment, Denton realised that this was one stare out competition he was bound to lose and so he returned to the urgent work that he had to attend to.

I'm sure I can miss this one training session, thought Denton. *After all - this is chargeable work and the client has given me a very tight deadline.*

To most, this would seem to be a highly logical pattern of thought for one so hungover. Clear, concise and fee-earner driven, Denton thought that this was a plan with no flaws. Ignore training - it's internal - concentrate on the client since he pays your wages. Flawless.

Not so, apparently.

"Denton," said Devlin leaning into Denton's room, hanging on to the doorframe. These days, he did not even maintain eye contact with Denton. He just stared at the floor with a disappointed tone in his voice. "Are you not ready for the training session?"

"Erm," said Denton, hoping the masses of paperwork around him might give away the reason why Denton was not leaping up to attend. "Well, I have this urgent work to do. I thought I could miss it."

"Ah now, away with ya," said Devlin, in a way that only Irish people can get away with. "I'm not having that. Come on. We could all say we're too busy. Come on."

"But..." stammered Denton, figuring that this must be some sort of test. "I have a 4pm deadline."

"Sure, well, you should have planned for that earlier on. Come on now, it can't be that important, you're just the trainee. Let's be having you for the training."

"But...but..." said Denton, struggling to think of further excuses, having seen his best reason for non-attendance shot down in flames.

"Denton!" said Devlin. "I don't want a repeat of the unpleasantness. Would you not just come on?!"

Denton bowed his head like a naughty schoolboy, and dutifully followed

Devlin.

Stupid me for thinking the client was more important, he screamed in his head - along with a ream of other abuse.

And why is training more important than the client? Because training has a one hundred thousand pound budget, and if not enough people turn up it means that this money is not being well spent, and if it's not being well spent, then it won't be allocated the following year and the training partner will have a not insignificant amount of egg on his face.

Having been frog-marched into the seminar, Denton sat. The room contained somewhere between ten and twelve rows of seats. Despite the fact that the front two rows contained perfectly good seats, naturally everyone had filled from the back. This had the effect of making the room appear as if a small nuclear detonation had occurred, with the small reading stand at the front being ground zero.

From there, a small screen was lowered by a technician and a projector was placed in between the chairs on the third row. The screen displayed the foreboding message *no input signal detected.* A second technician soon appeared followed by a third. Soon, a fourth was loitering by the door, and Denton noticed it was now twelve fifteen.

Brilliant, he thought.

Just outside the door to the room, Denton could see three nervous solicitors peering in - the main attraction to follow the technician warm-up act. Eventually, after some cussing, a picture appeared on the screen. The title of the seminar appeared, and suddenly Denton realised that he had been right to try to avoid this talk at all costs.

Pensions, Employment and Tax Strategies: PETS - the kind of animal you want to have around the Firm!

Great, thought Denton, *It's going to be one of those kind of lectures - the kind where every second sentence is supposed to be witty.*

From somewhere near the doorway, Devlin appeared again. His timing coincided with the arrival of Delia, who entered the room just as Devlin was walking to the stand at the front of the room. Delia looked embarrassed, which must surely have been a look reflective of her own position in actually being at the seminar at all. The doors to the room were closed and presumably locked.

Delia moved into the room and sat next to Denton. She looked relieved to see a friendly face. There was no sign of Randall. *Lucky bastard,* thought Denton.

"Hello, everyone - thanks for giving up your time this lunchtime. We really appreciate it."

I bet you do, thought Denton, *you're the training partner.*

"I'd just like to thank David Sudgwell, Marcus Dickinson and Rufus Greenall for giving up their time to speak to you today. I'll hand over now to David."

Onto the 'stage' bounded a middle-aged man with not much of his original ginger hair remaining, and a toothy forced grin on his face. He made big arm gestures as he strode which only served to make him look insincere.

Balding and ginger, thought Denton. *I wonder if hair loss in those circumstances is a good thing or not?*

"Hello, Devlin, and hello, Corporate!" he said, as if he had just walked onto the stage at Wembley holding a guitar.

There was silence followed by a small groan - presumably it was someone's lame attempt at 'hello' in return. *This isn't Butlins, mate,* thought Denton.

"It's great to be here!"

You are referred to the previous comment.

"Right then," said the ginger man, his confidence noticeably starting to wane, which only served to demonstrate that his smile was a big con in the first place.

"Well I can tell from the looks on your faces that you're all delighted to be here too!"

Stony silence again. Nervously, he tugged at his collar.

"Erm, and who wouldn't be delighted to attend this discussion? I mean - PETS?!" he placed his hands on his hips and made another feeble big gesture. "Who in their right minds gives a talk about PETS? During a lunch time seminar?" He made an audible exhalation of breath and snorted uncomfortably. This was followed by an audible gulp.

"Well - I can tell you that these are the kind of PETS that you will want to have around the firm!" He pointed lamely at the screen, trying to draw the listeners' attention both to the comment he had made, and the title of the seminar.

Oh my God, thought Denton, *he's going to choke. This is almost too painful to bare.*

"Well," he gulped. "I'm here to tell you about what we do. Why you need us and why PETS in the Corporate department are a good idea." Briefly, he pointed again at the title, snorted, and then seemed to realise that the whole pointing thing really was a bad idea.

Oh for God's sake - let the lame link go and just get on with it! thought Denton.

"Well then. What do we do? Well, as you'll all know PETS is the pensions, employment and tax strategies department..."

A completely needless introduction, thought Denton, *we know exactly who you are and what you do. You're all always sniffing about for work on our floor. And why is it that these cretins that give talks always begin with some lame ass joke which no one - ever - is going to laugh at? You're giving a talk to lawyers about the law - even we think it's terribly boring and we practice it!*

"And as Devlin's already said, my name is David Sudgwell..."

So why are you telling us again?

"...and I'm from the pensions department..."

Well, that much is obvious...

"And today I'm going to spend five or ten minutes..."

Can I get that in writing?

"...briefly, going through some hot topics in the pensions world at the moment..."

Oh good - I can't wait.

"…but before I do - and I know you're all desperate to hear about those issues, I'd like to introduce you first to Marcus Dickinson, who will be giving you a quick chat on share valuations in a private company context. Marcus, if you would…"

A tall, gaunt fellow emerged into the room. His hairline was receding rapidly, and this had the effect of making his forehead appear much larger than it actually was. In fact, it led Denton to the troubling conclusion that he could, in all likelihood, read Denton's mind. The word 'bomb' flashed in front of Denton's mind, and he felt nauseous.

"Hello, as David has just said, my name is Marcus Dickinson…"

So why are you telling us again? thought Denton, wondering if these people just had a script which they simply refused to deviate from, no matter what had already been said, and how much subsequent repetition would be involved.

"...and I'm here to talk to you today about the valuation of shares held by individuals in private companies…"

We know! We know! He already told us that! Why would he lie?! We already know all of this! screamed Denton in his head. He glanced at his watch. It was now 12.30 and they had not even begun. He shuffled uncomfortably in his chair. *Oh, get on with it, for the love of God!!!!*

"I can already see from the look of fear in your faces that this is not a subject close to your hearts," he said, which would have been quite a good line had it not been blindingly obvious that his monotone delivery betrayed the fact that he was simply repeating this statement from some memorised script, "but it is important nevertheless for you to consider when advising individuals on share sales…"

Take me away from all this. Please, let it just end.

"A common mistake made in share valuations, is to overlook the fact that the role of specialist tax advice on the calculation and distribution of shares, particularly minority share holdings, in companies is essential. All too often, we see that people look at the individual valuation of a single share and not the global valuation of a share packet. In this way, people quite easily fall into the trap of believing that x number of shares will be worth x multiplied by the value of the individual share if the total price value of the packet were divided by x."

What? What? What the fuck are you talking about?

"And so, I would encourage you all to be mindful of this trap. Do not fall in to it yourself. If you are involved with the calculation of shareholdings, be mindful that a minority share holder's shares may be less per share than that of a majority shareholder in the same company."

Kill me, someone kill me.

"I would also urge you all, once more, to be mindful of the need to obtain specialist tax advice on this point alone."

Oh God, that monotone voice! It's driving me mad!

"Permit me now to run through some figures with you using empirical evidence obtained recently during a number of interrelated share transfers…"

Do they really let you speak to clients with that voice? Oh, for the love of God, why don't they serve beer at these things? It would make the whole thing a lot less painful.

Denton continued to peer down at his watch and was very concerned that time, conversely, did not appear to be advancing at all and yet it was already 12.55pm and the lecture did not seem at all near ending.

Finally, the tax guy concluded, much in the same way that he had begun.

"…and so, if you do encounter any issues involving the valuation of shares held by individuals in private companies, then please do not hesitate to contact me, Marcus Dickinson. I will now hand over to Rufus Greenall, who will be discussing current employment issues. Rufus…"

Right, thought Denton, *there is absolutely no need for this guy to introduce himself or his topic - the last guy did it already. I don't know the guy but I already know he is called Rufus, Rufus Greenall, and he's going to be talking to us about employment issues. He does not need to hammer this point home anymore than it already has been.*

"Thank you Marcus, my name is Rufus, Rufus Greenall and I'm going to be talking to you about the latest employment issues…."

Unbelievable, thought Denton.

Rufus, Rufus Greenall, appeared to be mid to late thirties and looked fairly dishevelled. From the fast pace in which he was talking he was either under prepared or desperately needed the toilet.

"OK - brief run through of current employment law issues. You'll see in the packs in front of you that the case summaries have already been provided, so I don't intend to go into any more detail than that…"

So, in many ways, it would be completely pointless for you to continue talking if we already know what you're going to say. Come on now, Rufus, wrap the thing up, there's a good fellow, don't waste any more of my time.

"…but for the sake of completeness, I will just take you through the cases briefly…"

Bastard…

Denton was suddenly conscious of the fact that even though he could see people talking at him, all he could hear was three words going over and over in his mind.

Trust, Guilt, Bombs.

He was then conscious of the fact that he had been thinking the same thing for days and days now, and it did not matter how much alcohol he consumed, the issue was not going away.

Project Maybury. Bombs. Guilt, guilt, guilt.

Oh my God, he thought, *I'm going mad. I'm going completely mad. I need to do something about this. I need something to change. Something has to change.*

Delia suddenly distracted him. Apparently, she wasn't listening either.

"What you thinking?" she wrote on his notepad.

"Nothing," he responded back. "I'm just trying not to fall asleep."

She looked at him and frowned.

"Seriously. You had a look of horror on your face. What is wrong?"

"Really, nothing," he wrote.

"Come on," she wrote, "Don't be shy Denton." He looked up and saw her winking at him.

"Everything is fine honestly - I just need a drink."

"God, I know how you feel!" she responded.

Suddenly, David Sudgwell appeared again. Well, not suddenly at all really, it had taken him the best part of one hour and a half to do so. He then proceeded to drone on about some obscure aspect of pension law before concluding.

"Well, that's our presentation on PETS. As I hope you will agree - they truly are one animal that you need around the office..." he looked longingly for anyone to even chortle, no matter how briefly. No one did.

Tosser, thought Denton.

Devlin put the guy out of his misery by commencing the applause. "Thank you guys, that was...entertaining and informative..."

You're kidding, right?

"I don't know about you, but I certainly feel like I know a lot more about PETS than I did before. Cheers guys for giving up your time."

The three stooges smiled smugly. Goodness only knew what they had to be smug about. Perhaps somewhere inside their tiny minds they were thinking *'we rocked'*.

"I'm sure when you return to your desks, you will be able to use this new found knowledge you've just acquired."

This has taught me nothing. Absolutely nothing. I've listened to a cretin witter generally, a spod speak on one highly specialised point of law in minutia and a lazy arsed lawyer speak rapidly on everything I could ever need to know about employment law (but was too afraid to ask. Mainly because he might then waste more time in telling me the answer). What a ridiculous waste of time. What am I now supposed to do with this 'knowledge' I have acquired? Absolutely nothing. Ridiculous.

The audience began to chomp on the bit. They could smell the end was near. Eagerly people began gathering together pens, papers, coats and generally fidgeting in a way that said, *Can we go now please sir?*

"That concludes part one of our talk..." said Devlin, sadistically letting the words hang in the air until they had fully sunk in.

Part one? thought Denton. There was a general mumble of discontent.

"We will now have a short, unscheduled, presentation on the new money laundering regulations that are due to come in. As I'm sure you will have noticed from the press, the new regulations have already attracted a lot of attention, particularly with the recent conviction of a solicitor for his involvement in unwittingly assisting in a money laundering scam."

Denton's daydreaming ceased. He was certainly listening now.

"I cannot stress enough how important it will be for everyone to be vigilant. This is something that could affect all of us. We must remove the idea from our minds that incidents of solicitor involvement in money laundering are limited to suspicious men asking solicitors to look after bundles of notes in bin-liners. As the law becomes complex in this area, so do would-be money launderers become more devious and deceptive. You may be involved in a transaction which appears legitimate on the face of it, and yet behind it is the potential for serious money laundering. It will not be long before this occurs, and a Firm as large as ours is implicated. It may already have happened, and we just didn't realise. I cannot stress enough how easily it could happen, and how vigilant we must become."

Denton felt a little uncomfortable with this statement. He looked around the room. He could see from the looks on peoples faces that they were wondering if they had already assisted in money laundering.

"So what should you be looking out for? Well, to give you more information on that I will now hand over to our top tax partner, Gavin Gifford. Gavin…"

A fat, short and balding tax partner appeared from nowhere. It was likely he had been stood there for the entire duration of the talk. Denton glanced around. Everyone seemed to have the same look of surprise that he did. This was to be expected. No one tended to notice tax lawyers at the best of times. Certainly, no one ever admitted to knowing one.

With his work completed, Devlin left the room, leaving behind him a huddle of terrified lawyers, including one trainee who was day-dreaming of bombs and his increased knowledge of their application.

*****

After a brief fag break, Devlin returned. The room was silent. There was a general look of shock at the implications of what they had just heard. Fines. Imprisonment. *Try being a partner!* thought Devlin. The consequences of an unwitting involvement in money laundering had not been lost on them. The publicity would be bad enough, but imprisonment as a result? That just did not bear thinking about.

"Thank you, Gavin," he said. "I'm sure we'll all spend time reflecting on what you have just said. And, finally, thank you," he said turning to the audience to point like he was holding imaginary six-shooters, "for attending today."

There was a squeak of chairs followed by a stampede for the door. Most people made it out alive, Denton being one of them.

Delia caught up with Denton as they returned to their respective offices.

"You feeling alright now?" she asked.

"Yeah, I'm fine. More importantly though," he said changing the subject, "how are you feeling?"

"Me, I'm fine. Why do you ask?" she said frowning.

"Well, what with Bonnie's 'news'."

"What, that she's now 'officially' knocking off Campbell Oliver?"

"Is that official then?" asked Denton.

"Apparently," said Delia. "I heard that they are no longer covering up, but then query when they ever were covering it up?"

"Yeah, and also query whether she is covering up the fact that I know of two other partners who are regularly getting their end into her?"

"Denton! You're so crude!" said Delia, smacking him on the arm, playfully.

"So what news were you referring to?"

"Well, you know, the fact that she has now accepted the one and only qualification job in Corporate that, really, should not have even have been offered yet."

"I didn't know she had accepted the position."

"Yeah, didn't you hear? Randall told me this morning that she has officially accepted."

Delia's face dropped.

"When you told me before I convinced myself it was a wind-up. Certainly it did not hammer home. This is so annoying. I was told that I should not even get my hopes up for a job in Corporate because there would not be any available."

"Yeah, well that's right. There aren't any. Bonnie got it."

Delia's distraught expression turned to one of anger and despair.

"That little bitch!" she said venomously, and with that she stormed off.

"OK, then," Denton said to no one, "I'll see you later!"

He stared at the image of the fast departing Delia, and then looked back at his feet.

I don't think she's best pleased with that news.

He wandered back to his desk. *Right,* he thought. *It's nearly 2pm now and the client wants this thing done by four. OK, no need to panic. I can do that.*

He entered his security code back in to his computer to remove the screensaver, and continued where he had left off in trying to find company searches for all the companies that the client was considering. A figure appeared at the door. It was Campbell.

"How are you getting on with those searches, Denton?" he asked.

"Yeah, fine, Campbell," he said. "I should get them done in time for the deadline."

"Great. Once you've finished can you get them over to Bonnie - she'll need some time to review them before discussing them with the client."

Denton tried to hide his frown. "But…do you not want me to deliver this information to the client?" He felt a little forlorn, and struggled to keep it from his voice. A voice that sounded like it had been borrowed from a teenager. And a spotty, wimpy one with steel rimmed glasses, at that.

"Nope - the client has specifically asked for Bonnie, so don't dawdle in getting that information to her."

"Fine," said Denton, trying to hide his disgust. *I bet the big titted freak has been asked specifically to deliver the information. Probably so some twat of a company director can dribble all over her while she does so.*

"Everything ok, Denton? You look like you're in pain…" asked Campbell.

"No, I'm fine."

"OK, listen, is it going to take much longer? Bonnie really does need some time to go over this stuff, and the meeting's at 4pm. Speed reading isn't her strong point."

Is there anything of a vaguely legal nature that is?

"I'm going as fast as I can. I have to look up the names of each company, and then try to find out if they're connected. It's taking a while to do it," said Denton.

"Oh Ok, but there is a quicker way you can do that, you know."

"How?" asked Denton.

"Just search against the director's name instead."

"You can do that?"

"Yeah, easy."

Denton's eyes glazed over again. The words *bomb* and *trust* resurfaced for reasons only he appreciated.

"Thanks Campbell, you've just given me an idea."

"No problem," said Campbell. "Remember - Bonnie needs that information as soon as possible."

Denton quickly disposed of the task given to him, then set about his own task. *If I can search against the names of directors, then I can make the link,* he thought. *I can find out about the other companies. That's the way in!*

Excitedly, he typed away, trying to find the information he was after, but two hours later, he conceded defeat.

"Not one! Not one of those searches was any good. Damn it! I can't find the link. I can't find the link between that person and the bomb!!" he muttered, just as Randall entered the room.

"What?" asked Randall, awaking Denton from his daydream.

"Oh, Randall, hi - didn't see you there." His sense of guilt returned.

"Who are you talking to?"

"What? Oh, no one."

"What are you talking about?" said Randall, unappeased.

"Nothing."

"Oh," said Randall, not convinced. "Anyway, just wondered if you fancied coming out for a drink."

"Was John Paul II a goalkeeper?" said Denton.

"Erm…" said Randall, unsure, "well on the basis that I have never known you to turn down a drink, I suppose he must have been."

Denton wasn't really listening. They soon left work with Denton distracted all night by the link. His brain nagged him constantly. *Find the link, find your way out.*

Chapter Twenty Nine

An exercise in trust

It was dark. Denton moved to find the light switch. His mind was telling him that he was in an office but he could not be sure. It seemed too dark to tell. His mind was also telling him that this was Colin's office. He wondered how he knew this. It was far too dark to tell. Somewhere else in his mind was concern. What was he doing in Colin's office in pitch black? The office should have been lit, even at night. His mind told him to ignore the questions and move on.

"Hello Denton," said a voice.

Denton turned. In front of him stood Colin. He was lit by a single spot light. Something wasn't right though. Was it the fact that even though Denton's brain was telling him that he was looking at Colin, it did not seem like Colin at all? In fact, it looked a lot more like, well, Michael Burke.

"What are you doing here, Colin?" asked Denton.

"What are you doing here, Denton?" asked Michael/Colin. "Why have you come here? What are you looking for? Your clothes perhaps?"

Denton looked down and noticed in horror that he was totally naked. He gasped. He could have sworn he was fully dressed moments ago. He felt embarrassed and ashamed and desperately tried to cover himself up with his hands.

"I know what you found!" said Colin, appearing to ignore Denton's nakedness. "I know you know. I'm not mad. I just want to know what you're going to do about it!"

"What do you mean?" asked Denton.

"Well, Denton - how are you going to use this information - are you going to save us?"

"Save you?" queried Denton.

"Yes. Are you going to save our lives, Denton?"

Denton looked confused, and felt even more confused and embarrassed when he realised that Colin had transformed into his old Home Economics teacher. He felt even more awkward when he realised she was wearing nothing but a pinny.

"Mrs Maybury!" said Denton. "What are you doing here?"

"Just making sure you're taking care of yourself dear. Now..." she said walking towards him. "Will you let me sort you out or would you rather this young lady did it?" She pointed to another person who had just appeared next to

Denton. Denton turned with a start to see Delia in a skimpy negligee lying on the ground next to him. Before he could say anything, Delia began to wander over to him and started to force his hands away from their current protective position.

"Don't be shy, Denton…" she said winking.

Denton woke suddenly with a start. His face was clammy and hot. Naturally, his head pounded and his mouth felt dry. Instinctively, his hand reached down for a glass of water to quench his thirst. Naturally, there was no glass there since, as always, he had forgotten to fill one before he stumbled into bed. His heart was pounding as the thoughts in his mind began to dissipate.

Oh God, thought Denton, *what am I going to do?* He winced as he realised that it was 4.30 am on a Saturday morning.

*****

By Saturday afternoon, Denton was in Bierodrome on Clapham High Street drinking one of the mind boggling array of Belgian ales. With him were the usual suspects all supping away on similar beverages. All of them were chatting to each other, with the notable exception of Randall who was engrossed in the new mobile phone he had purchased that day. Every so often a tuneless noise emanated from the device as Randall scanned through the new phone ring tones in an effort to presumably determine which tone would be the least irritating to those within ear shot of the blessed thing going off.

"Ooh," squeaked Randall like a little girl with her first pony, "it has the Knightrider theme tune."

Denton's dream had been replaying in his mind for the whole duration of the morning. He struggled to look at either Colin or Delia. He felt too embarrassed and ashamed. He had to keep reminding himself that they hadn't actually seen his winky. Still, he couldn't escape the fact that he felt a certain sense of foreboding about the afternoon. He also couldn't get his plan out of his head. There was a semi-constant thought going over and over in his mind: *Save them, save them!*

Oh don't be so melodramatic! he thought, trying to pull himself together.

Still, he did feel as if this plan might work. He had mulled it over for a while now, and despite the gross lack of experience in such matters, Denton felt confident. It had to work. He just needed the courage to tell them his plan. Worry now clouded his mind. What would they think of him? How would they respond? Would he feel the same way as he did when Delia, Colin, Mrs Maybury and Michael Burke saw his winky?

Suddenly, bravery took hold of him. He would stand up, there and then. He would tell them. They could only dismiss his idea. That was the worst that could happen. With an apparent lack of a conscious decision, Denton found himself stood in front of them all. He had no idea how that had happened, and yet he could not argue with the fact that he was. It was as if it was meant to be. It was as if this moment was so important, so momentous, in all of their histories, in the story of the lives, that it would have occurred whether he wanted it to or not.

Equally, of course, it could just have been that the alcohol abuse had finally caught up with him and he was losing his marbles.

Either way he was stood there.

The trouble was, he had no idea how to begin his speech.

"Look!" he found himself saying. They all stopped talking and looked at him. *Oh god,* he suddenly thought, *its like breaking up with someone. You know its going to be difficult to say and you just want to get to the part where you say 'welcome to dumpsville…'*

"Listen, there's…well…there's something I want to say to you all."

"What?" they all asked, pretty much in unison.

Denton scratched at his head, "Well…"

"You're dying!"

"You're leaving…"

"You're changing profession…"

"You're moonlighting…"

"You're heart broken…"

"You're gay!"

Everyone turned to the man who made the last comment. Brian winced awkwardly. There had been too much optimism in his observation for everyone's liking.

"No!" said Denton. "Shut up all of you!" he said masterfully. Delia purred.

"Look, over the past days, weeks, months, something has dawned on me." He spoke confidently and forcefully, his arms flailing with a purpose. "Something unites us. A common bond. A thread that links all our lives in a way that wouldn't ordinarily link the lives of such disparate people…"

Frowns formed across the group. They didn't know whether to take the last point as an insult or not.

"For whatever reason, and for whatever purpose, the common bond that links us all is that we are all unhappy. We are all unfulfilled. We all act as if we lack purpose…"

There was a general murmur of disagreement.

"Yes, we do. Don't fight it. We do. Each and every one of us has made a mistake. We all took the wrong road. What's more, we all *act* as if we took the wrong road. We act as if we missed out on doing the thing that would have made us who we are. The one thing that would have made us have that sense of purpose!"

The disagreement turned to looks of wonder, as if they might say, 'Go on…'

"All of us here gathered should be doing something else. The most miserable part of our life is the fact that we don't know what that something is."

A couple of people nodded.

"Well, I say that something has brought us here together - fate, God, a supreme being, beer - call it what you will, it brought us together. And there was a reason for that. The reason being that we should help each other - help ourselves. Together, we can do it. Alone, we're unlikely to. Alone, we'll continue wandering along in this meaningless existence without being able to find the answer. Remember the exercise in trust? OK, I know you weren't all there on the Corporate weekend away, but I was, and that exercise taught me one thing. If we all work together, and rely on each other, we can rid ourselves of the shackles that tie us down to an existence that we don't want. An existence that we don't need. An existence that leaves us unfulfilled."

"But how?" someone asked.

"Well - that's a good question. It's one I've been thinking about a lot. I have a plan. But..." he looked at Colin awkwardly, trying not to look guilty, "...for reasons that I really cannot go into right now, I can't tell you what that plan is. You just need to trust me."

There was a sigh of disappointment.

"Look, I know that that is not a very satisfactory answer. And I'm not trying to evade the question. But if there was just one chance that you could leave your lives behind. Just one possibility that you might be able to lead the life you want to lead - just one smallest, slightest, iota of a whisper that you might experience the fulfilment and happiness that you have always dreamed of, from the time you were a child dreaming of the perceived freedom of adulthood, to the day you realised that there is no such thing as freedom, would you not take it? Would you risk it passing you by? Would you??"

From no-where the sound of the A-team theme tune filtered into the room.

"Oooh, what a great ring tone this new phone has..." said Randall.

Denton scowled at him. Everyone else turned in disbelief at him.

"Sorry, you were saying?" said Randall, slightly ashamed.

"Kind of killed the mood there, Randall," Denton couldn't help but say.

"So what do we need to do to 'realise our dreams'?" asked Colin.

This was the part of Denton's plan that he knew they would all hate. It was a now or never moment. They would either embrace the idea or it would die right there and then without any of them ever knowing what the plan would actually entail.

"Quit your jobs," he said, gulping.

Their respective jaws dropped.

"What?"

"You must be joking, Denton," said Colin. "I have bills to pay, a child to support and a soon to be ex-wife to suck the life blood from me. I can't quit my job."

"Neither can I, Denton," said Delia. "In my current mood, I'd love to, but I'm a girl - do you know how much debt I have? Store cards don't pay themselves you know."

"I know it's a big ask. I do. But that is the only way you will ever be free. Let go of your jobs and do the things you want to. OK, so you lose out on your material possessions - but are they really that great anyway? Do they make you feel happy? Do they satisfy you? So you don't have that Louis Vuitton handbag,

Delia…and Colin, you'll have to let go of that London mansion of yours. But so what?"

They continued to stare at him, unconvinced.

"OK - I knew you would react this way. I have an alternative suggestion. I need two weeks of your lives. No more, no less. Each of you, get time off work for the next two weeks and come with me to the Lake District."

"The Lake District?" asked Delia. "Where's that?"

"It's north of London," said Denton and, on noticing Delia's confusion added, "yes, I didn't think anything existed out there either, but apparently it does."

Their stern expressions melted slightly. "Look, I know it sounds a little crazy, but we're all tired for our own reasons, and anyway, a holiday would suit us all. We'll go away for two weeks and stay in Colin's holiday home - well, that's assuming you'll let us Colin…"

Colin nodded, slightly stunned and unsure that he had any option but to agree with the suggestion.

"…If my plan doesn't succeed in two weeks, then you can all conclude that I'm just a mad dreamer. But if I'm right, and it works, then we'll all be a lot happier and fulfilled in two weeks time than we've ever been. Are you in?"

Colin looked at Delia. Delia looked back and then across to Randall. Randall acknowledged her glance and looked at Billy. Billy glanced at Badger. Badger turned to Brian. Brian looked back at Colin.

"Looks like it," said Colin.

"Good job I kept the receipt for my phone. If I'm soon to be jobless, I can't afford to keep it," said Randall, lamenting the fact his A-Team ring tune would soon be in the hands of another.

Denton smiled. "I love it when a plan comes together." He reached for the non-existent cigar.

Part Three

Chapter Thirty

Base Camp (The Happy Happy Hooley Holiday Home)

"What time is it?" said Denton.

"No," said Billy.

"What time is it?" said Denton again, pacing up and down.

"No! I'm not telling you!" said Billy defiantly, sat on top of his suitcase.

Denton stopped pacing.

"Why not?" he asked.

"You know why," replied Billy.

"Do not," said Denton as he began pacing again, his already furrowed brow increasing in its furrowedness by the minute.

Randall stood between them awkwardly. The three of them were on the curb outside Denton's, Randall's and recently Colin's, flat. Each one was looking out into the distance. Each with a large suitcase nearby.

Denton continued to protest.

"…I don't see the harm in…"

"NO! It's just getting ridiculous now," interrupted Billy

Randall suddenly felt as if he were at a tennis match as his eyes moved from Billy back to Denton, back to Billy again.

"Fine," said Denton.

He stopped pacing and gently rocked on his heels. None of them said a word.

"Randall?"

"Still not wearing a watch, Denton. I'm still not wearing a watch," said a weary Randall.

"Right, right," said Denton remembering.

Denton bit his lip and absent-mindedly clapped his hands together as he continued to rock back and forth.

All three of them remained waiting.

The pressure told on Denton.

"Billy!"

"Alright, alright!!" said Billy, his face flushed, "It's 9.27. OK? There! 9.27. It's now 9.27. It *was* 9.22, and before that 9.18, 9.11 and 9.05. OK. Now it's not. It's 9.27," he said emphatically.

All three waited in silence.

"He's late," said Denton finally.

"WE KNOW!" cried Billy and Randall in unison.

"He's bottled it, hasn't he? He's bloody bottled it. He's gone running back to his slapper wife. He's not coming. I knew it. I knew it. Never trust a senior solicitor with a neck brace, two largely faded black eyes, and an awkward looking nose, they said. And they were right. I knew it. I just bloody well knew it. He'll only let you down, they said. I knew it. Well that's it, isn't it? That's game over, right there. We've got no chance now. We can't make this thing work on our own," said Denton hysterically, bending over with his head between his knees, in desperate need of a brown paper bag.

Randall tapped Denton on the shoulder and stretched out a finger that pointed down the road. "He's just pulled into our street."

Colin's people carrier pulled up next to them.

"Sorry I'm late," said Colin from the driving seat through his open window. Awkwardly, he climbed out and walked around to the side nearest to them. It was only at this point that Randall, Billy and Denton could see what he was wearing. Boating shoes. A pair of pressed chino Bermuda shorts. A Ralph Lauren crystal white polo shirt, offset by a neck brace and a plaster across his nose, which was adorned by a pair of prescription gold rimmed glasses with flip up tinted lenses.

Randall, Billy and Denton stood in utter silence, completely captivated by this vision of total sartorial ineptitude. God only knew what kept them from shouting, *"Colin, you look like a twat."*

"What kept you?" protested Denton.

Colin slid the side door to reveal the largest collection of bags, boxes and suitcases ever to grace the interior of a people carrier.

"Had to load Delia's stuff on," he said in a matter of fact way, smiling politely at Denton whilst nodding his head sideways towards the Selfridges' travelling warehouse.

The respective jaws of Denton, Randall and Billy dropped in unison.

Denton glared at Delia as she emerged from the vehicle fanning herself with some papers.

"At which point did you decide that you were moving permanently?" he enquired with venom.

"Very funny," she said bluntly.

"Seriously, Delia," said Randall flatly. "What is wrong with you? We're only going for two weeks. What happened to *'let's pack light'*?"

"I did!" she exclaimed. "We had to leave the rest behind!"

"Climb in, lads," said Colin in the same way that a boy scout leader might to a pack of eager twelve year olds, off on a weekend away for the first time, "there's still plenty of room in there."

"Where?" asked Billy with a genuine sense of fear.

"Look," said Colin, "there's plenty of room over there next to Brian."

The three of them squinted into the people carrier.

"Where's Brian?" they asked.

"Hello," came a muffled voice. "I'm just here, on the third row. My face is obscured by the Donna Karen travel bag and Giorgio carry case."

A small hand poked up from behind two ridiculously sized bags.

"Are you alright, Brian?" they asked.

"What?" mumbled The Hand. "Sorry, you'll have to speak up, I have a Prada handbag wedged in one ear, so my hearing isn't as good as it used to be."

The three of them looked at each other and then back at The Hand.

"Can you breathe ok in there?" shouted Denton, still squinting.

The Hand nodded, fingers clenched straight but together like a beak.

"As long as I don't take any sharp sudden breaths then I'm laughing. Although, only metaphorically, since I have a pair of stiletto heels dangerously close to my larynx so I dare not laugh in case I puncture my throat with them," The Hand said.

"Did you forget, Badger?" Billy said turning back to Colin, who for some reason was stood with his hands on his hips admiring the view, as if secretly proud to have actually stuffed all this junk into a people carrier. Maybe it was the fact that they were using his vehicle that gave him a sense of satisfaction. Or maybe it was just the opportunity to wear the glasses. Pity that it looked as if it might rain at any second.

"No, no," said The Hand. "He's here too." The Hand turned and pointed towards the back. "He fell asleep when Delia was loading up, so we just packed over him. He's fine though. I can see he's breathing on account of the Versace carrier bag near my foot which keeps expanding and contracting," said The Hand, rising and falling to mimic the movement of the breathing bag.

"Come on, boys," said Colin, "Chop chop, get a move on, in you get."

Billy and Randall climbed in, while Denton passed them the suitcases.

"Excellent," said Colin. "Right then, we're ready to go."

"Yeah," said Denton slowly. "One slight problem though. I'm not in the car yet. Where am I going to sit?"

"Oh," said Colin, scratching his bald spot. He looked at Denton, then looked back at the people carrier (containing four grown men trapped in a suitcase avalanche), then looked at Denton again. "Mmm," he said just as Billy's face, with his eyes almost bursting from their sockets, suddenly became pressed up against the window pane - a precariously positioned bag having hit him square on the back of the head. In the front, Delia was busily filing her nails, oblivious to the chaos ensuing behind her.

Colin turned back to Denton, stood holding his back-pack, "I have the solution, but you're not going to like this."

*****

A floor sweeper's job is probably a dull one.

It can't be very satisfying to get to one side knowing full well that the other side is by now just as litter clad as it was before you started cleaning it an hour ago. It must be the case that floor sweepers, at a place like King's Cross, only do the job for that rare moment when they can be entertained by a raving loony approaching slowly up the escalator, red faced, complaining bitterly in a loud voice to anyone who will listen, about 'bloody women', 'designer outfits' and 'dead goldfish'.

"Why me?" raved the loony. "Why do I have to get the sodding train? Couldn't even give me a lift to the station. Bloody women. Bloody designer outfits. Damn you all! And the bloody goldfish." In the middle of his tirade, he stormed past the shocked floor sweeper.

With a broad smile on his face, the floor sweeper shook his head and put his mop back into his bucket.

Denton followed the masses until he was stood near enough to the overhead departure board to be able to read it. His frown slowly disappeared as a leggy blonde sauntered past him wearing a tiny pair of denim shorts. He felt sure that she gave him a cheeky smile as she did so.

This trip might not be so bad after all, Denton suddenly thought.

He roused himself from his day dream and turned his attention back to the train times.

OK, so my train goes at 12.02, he thought, *and the time is now…*

"12.01!" he shouted as he tried to jump through the crowd of people happily ambling in front of him.

Always old people! Why? he thought. *Do they wake up on a morning and say, 'Ethel, we really haven't ambled about much today - fancy going to the train station?'. 'Yes, Cecil, I've really felt lately that I'm wandering around with too much purpose - now where did I put that big empty bag? We should take that out for some exercise, you know?'.*

Denton rushed past the old codgers, who were dragging a bag behind them, and hop-skipped between a few others, at great pace, making up the time when he suddenly thought, *Shit! Which platform does the train go from? Damn it! I didn't notice! It's too late to go back. I think that it was twelve. Or was it ten? Shit! Shit!!!*

Now what are you supposed to do in this situation? There are options, although not many. First, you could ask someone - anyone. But how are you meant to treat their answer? And what exactly do you think that they are going to say when asked?

"Excuse me. Sorry. I don't suppose you know where the 12.02 leaves from?" You say to the nearest random person.

"Yes, now then. I'm glad you asked me that question. I have spent months memorising the train timetable for every conceivable destination just in case I'm running late one day. Now the 12.02 usually sets off from platform 12 on days when Frank is driving and Steve is on points. When Jason takes the early shift and Patrick mans the announcements though it usually goes from 7, and when Pluto is in ascendancy and the moss grows on the south side of the Elm in Hyde Park it departs from platform 10. However, since today is Sunday, and Venus is in the twelve house of Sagittarius, then you'd be better off running to platform 8 because they're just about to call a platform change."

"Wow, that's amazing," you might reply. *"How do you know that?"*

"Well, doesn't everyone?"

This never happens - so why is it that people will still ask random strangers if they know what platform their train is travelling from? It is as if they somehow think that the other people stood in the station have always existed there, and are just waiting to deliver their lines like extras in a bad play.

People do the exact same thing when they finally get to the train. *"Is this train going to Crewe?"* they say. *"How the hell do I know? Do I look like the driver? I don't know where it's going - I mean it's pointing the right way but that's not conclusive."*

Of course most people will say in response *'Well, I hope so since that's where I'm going.'* But seriously, what comfort is that if it turns out you're both mistaken? Do people sit there and reassure themselves by thinking, *'Well, at least if I am going the wrong way then I'll be in a strange place with someone I know.'* ?!?

Alternatively, do they expect the person they ask to have developed clairvoyance enough to be at one with the train. *"Yes, it does go to Crewe and it's getting really fed up about it. Sometimes, it just longs to go between Newcastle and Bristol. It feels so neglected and underused."*

Of course, the reality of the situation is that when you do ask someone which platform your train is about to leave from, you won't exactly be asking someone you want to strike up a conversation with either, like the fittest girl you can find. In fact, in order to disguise your own embarrassment, you are more likely than not to ask someone who is unlikely to have any social skills, and as a result there is no chance that they can report to anyone the total social faux pas that you have just made.

Whilst on the face of it your pride may seem to remain intact, the down side is that this person is likely to say *"I don't know but I'm getting that train. Why don't we find it together?"*

Great. Now you have a *'friend'*. A *'train pal'*. And you remember that fit girl that you just saw moments ago? Well, there is absolutely no way that she'll be disturbing you now. Not now you've got your own *'fit girl'* repellent. Not now you've befriended the only man in the station with a smaller IQ than the combined total of all the platforms, with his thick rimmed tortoise-shell glasses, wearing an off-green pea soup pullover with noticeable sweat patches. Alternatively, you may have befriended the old dear who hasn't spoken to anyone since 1974 and is just dying to get her views on caesarean sections off her chest.

Why did you do it? Why? Now you're done for! The only thing that you need to really top off the journey is for a gaggle of German school kids to sit just close enough for you to have to suffer their continuous drivel as they relay (in loud voices) Eurotrash songs they heard on the way through Amsterdam.

The final choice is to ask someone in uniform. Again, why? If they're not working in the kiosk, and they're just pushing a baggage trolley, then there's probably a reason.

"Do you know which platform the 12.02 goes from?" you yelp so loud that only dogs can hear you now. You flap about hysterically, looking frantically about you at every conceivable platform, just in case your blessed train lights up to point out the way.

"Erm, mmmm, well," comes the response. Slowly the baggage attendant will take off his cap and scratch his head. *"That's a good question. 12.02, you say?"*

You continue to flap about, presuming that your attempts to make this look like a question that needs an answer in a hurry had not worked. You feel exactly like a swan with its head caught in a plastic bag. Your eyes bulge and your arms flail.

Juxtaposed to this reaction, is the guard, who, instead, admires the rim of his cap and, perhaps, looks into the distance before wiping a bead of sweat from his forehead with the back of his hand.

"Well now," he might say, as if that is supposed to help, *"Well, well, well. The 12.02. Don't tell me. I know this one. Don't tell me."*

You flap around harder like the winner of the annual *'how much water can you consume'* contest, on realising that the awards ceremony follows straight on from the main event with no commercial interlude.

"Yes, it's just that I'm asking, not from a research point, or as a matter of general interest but because I have to get on it now and you see how its 12.01.48. I'm concerned by that, and in fact, to make my position clearer, my concern centres around the fact that I sincerely doubt the driver of the train knows that I have spent a small fortune on a perfectly valid ticket, and that the only reason why I'm not currently sat on his very fine train is because I'm having this conversation with you," you say, as politely as possible.

"Well now, perhaps you should just let me see that there ticket," says the guard. *"MA!"* he yelps to a store cupboard door. *"There's a crazy fella out here asking after a train, and the whereabouts of the 12.02."*

Suddenly, you notice that there is an old woman sat on a rocking chair in the background, absentmindedly knitting.

The final, final option though, which quite often seems to be the most attractive to most people is to simply wait until someone announces the platform.

Perhaps this is the most quintessentially English method. You can imagine a middle aged man in a suit, sat on his suitcase, arms folded, saying, *"No, Martha - No! I positively insist that I am not going to look for that train until someone bally well tells me where to find it. Honestly! Preposterous idea to expect me to go and find the bally thing myself! It could be parked anywhere, and I'm jolly well not going to find it! Read the platform number from the board? Is that a principle that this country was built on? I think not!"*

This option is certainly the most interesting. *"Right!"* you say checking your watch, *"twenty seconds until the train departs - I'm not worried."* All around you, people are milling around, just waiting. Some people are jumping on the spot, some limbering up, shaking their leg muscles.

Then, the moment of anticipation arrives, and you hear the crackle of the speaker as it erupts into life.

"Laaaadieeees n gntlmn'

Marks, you whisper to yourself

"Thhhheee tweeeelveee ooooooh twwwwoooooo". Why do train announcers always insist on accentuating and constricting vowel sounds when they speak? It's as if

they're about to introduce a featherweight boxing match.

"iiiisss duuuue toooooo dprt frm…"

Get set

"pppplaaaaaatfooooooorm twwwwwwwwwwwwwww…"

The announcer stops. Will it be twelve, two or twenty something?

"Twwwwwwww…"

The tension is too much for some as one or two hedge their bets and start running off in the direction of platform two.

"Tweeeellveeeee."

"Bollocks!" shouts the mistaken man from the top end of platform two.

Go go go!!

Madness ensues.

Not only is it a race to get to the train on time but now the stakes are higher, the bounty enlarged - can you get to that platform before all the airline window seats are taken, by which time you're forced to spend the entire journey facing some bucktoothed old bag who's smoked so many fags that you feel like you're passive smoking every time she breathes.

Suddenly all the previous rules are torn up. It is now a case of survival of the fittest and the fastest. Old ladies get spun around as people dash past them. Men in wheelchairs are used as battering rams by commuters before they let go of their chariot, allowing the entire cart to either run into a wall, or off the platform entirely.

Eventually, you see the train in front of you. The guard has his whistle in his pursed lips. *Will he blow?* you think. *Will he blow?* Well, no, not now you've just winded him by a quick blow to the diaphragm.

Of course, in life, there are winners, and by necessity, losers. In this case, the winners stand victoriously in the gangway of the train, admiring the fact that the train doors closed just behind them. The losers though break from their mighty stride just as the train doors close, and descend into a wimpy, limbs flailing, part dance, part tribute to Andy Pandy, which looks ridiculous enough on its own but is made worse by their feeble attempts of protestation, as demonstrated by the brief look around for a guard to complain to, or more embarrassingly for all concerned, a half-hearted attempt to press the unlit 'door open' button, even though they know deep down that that door won't be opening any time soon.

And once you're on the train, you can then partially relax and unwind as you listen to the train announcer (who is just bound to have some kind of speech impediment).

Welcum abwoard this twain sewice fwor manchesa. Calling at noowhampton, wugby, coventwy, burmingham, burmingham intewnational, staffowd and manchesa. Estimated time of a-wival in Manchesa, fowr thiwty.

Mind you, you can only partially relax because the fun is not over just because you're now on the train. Next comes the adventure of finding your seat. In this part nothing is certain. Reservations count for little. You could be sat anywhere next to anyone. The one thing that is for certain is that there is no room for the milk of human kindness on the train. It is for this reason that you won't find any in the buffet car.

"Got any milk of human kindness?" you might ask.

"Sorry, no. We do have the bottled water of human depravity, the iced tea of despair, the café au lait of pain and misery, and several thousand cans of Virgin cola," the attendant might say, probably with some cockney *sparra* accent.

Having successfully negotiated his way onto the train, the task of seating himself now befell the weary Denton. When it comes to seating, there are two natural laws in place - those relating to finding, and those relating to having found. Naturally, the two laws run neatly side by side, one being the inverse of the other.

When you're looking for a seat, all of them are taken. Possession is ownership - none of that nine-tenths stuff - there is no one tenth to play with. Someone sitting on the seat signifies that they own it. A bag on the adjoining seat equally signifies ownership. A CD player on the adjoining seat signifies ownership The corner of someone's magazine on the adjoining seat signifies ownership, and woe betide the man who challenges these simple rules. The angry eyes from every seated person towards the man looking for a seat is warning enough. You do not challenge those looks.

And yet, when you do find a seat, it doesn't seem to matter how much stuff you dump down next to you because some cheeky bastard will come up to you and say, *"is this seat taken?"*. I mean, you've got your coat there, a huge bag and they still say *"is this seat taken?"* then there's the CD player, magazines, kitchen sink, a rockery, a sub-machine gun installation and they still say, *"may I sit here?"*

On the train, it is a fundamental truth that every man is in fact an island, and just wants, more than anything else, not to have his private space invaded by an unknown. So why is it then that, even in this context, where every man, woman and child would sell his own grandmother to preserve his solitude, that people are always so honest?

"No, it's not," they say *"hang on, let me just dig up the bedding plants…"*

You don't want anyone sat anywhere near you so why don't you just lie? It's not like the person asking will say, *"are you sure? Because I'll be watching and I'll know if you're lying!"* You've never met this person before, and you'll never meet him again. So why does everyone feel honour bound to confess? Do they think that the other passengers will 'dob' them in? This is a society where no one cares about anyone else. If you fall over in the street, people are more likely than not to just step over you, tutting at the inconvenience of it. After someone has just told you that the seat is taken, they are not likely to shout *'oi! Mate! He's lying! I've been on this train from the start - I know for a fact no one's there! He's on his own! Just kick that rockery over if it's in the way.'*

"No, no," people will inexplicably say, *"no one is sat here."*

You feel like saying, *"he doesn't have a lie detector in his back pocket, you know."*

"No, please, help yourself."

People are not this honest to the taxman, the police, even their own parents.

But as soon as you ask the magic words, '*is this seat taken?*' everyone starts shopping their own grandparents.

Perhaps the police should start using this method to extract confessions from criminals.

"OK, Barry, we know you sold him the drugs, so just tell us, where did you get them from?"

"I don't know what you're on about."

"Oh, come on, Barry, tell us. Make it easy on yourself!"

"My lips are sealed."

"Oh yeah? Well tell me, Barry…is that seat next to you taken?"

"No. Dammit! Alright, I'll tell you everything I know!"

And then, of course, there is the agony of knowing that, OK, you're sat in an empty table seat now, all snug next to the window, but people are bound to get on at the next stop and pretty soon it's going to fill up all around you. The question is, who will sit there?

At each stop, you long for a twenty year old glamour puss to get on, with boobs big enough to stop cars, and a top small enough to pass for a postage stamp. And whilst it sounds far fetched, it does happen. On every single train journey, they get on and walk towards you, wink and then walk straight past to either sit opposite someone's Grandad or next to some blimp of a woman, so that you can't even eye them up and down without the human marshmallow thinking that you're coming on to her instead - thus causing her to wink back and gesture at the toilets.

Although, as time goes by, your standards drop to the extent that you'd accept any female as a seating buddy, so long as they were blonde and owned their own teeth.

Having said that though, no amount of time could lower Denton's standards to the point where he was happy sitting next to Roly's fatter brother, as he found himself now. In addition, Denton was not best pleased by the fact that the human blob was sat stuffing his face with a custard donut.

As Denton sat - squashed between the window and the beast - he regretted his earlier opportunity to change the course of his journey.

"Is anyone sat here?" the man-pudding had asked.

"No, that seat's free, but please remember I'm in this one."

Denton recoiled in horror as he remembered how the thing had oozed into the seat next to him, grunting as it squeezed into the tiny space sending a tidal wave of flab upwards, over the arm rest and into Denton's personal space. In desperation, Denton had looked up and over his shoulder in horror to note that the rest of the coach was pretty much empty.

Please don't talk to me. Please don't talk to me, he had thought.

Thankfully though, the Thing had chosen to remain silent - perhaps so it could concentrate on feeding. It had reached inside a pocket and pulled out a CD player. The earphones went in, and suddenly, the space around its vacuous mind was filled with the irritating sound of a bad bass line.

Brilliant! thought Denton, *Well how fantastic - how thoughtful of it - I get to share in its appalling taste in music. I do hope he doesn't get off until I do for fear I'll miss the ending.* Then Denton's nostrils flared. *Why!? Why do the people that sit next to me always have to smell of chip fat!*

Denton's mobile phone vibrated. He had a message. Struggling, he reached down into his trousers, battling with the flab to retrieve his phone. It was from Delia.

"Sorry u had 2 go on train. Hope it going ok. Least u can spread out unlike the boys in the back."

It was a wonder that they didn't hear his screams from the car.

*****

"Did you hear something?" asked Delia.

"What?" asked Colin.

"Nothing," she said dismissively. "So where are we?"

"Well," began Colin, "bearing in mind that we only left just over an hour ago, I'd say that we're doing quite well."

"Oh, ok, so where are we?" asked Delia optimistically.

"Cricklewood."

"Oh," said Delia, notably dejected. "But that's in the wrong direction, isn't it?"

"Yes. Kind of. But I think that it's due to the fact that Billy is navigating, and he can't really even see where he is, so I think its remarkable we're making any progress at all really."

Delia turned to look for Billy but all she could see was bags.

"I'm fine," muffled Billy from behind an Antler suitcase. "It's just taken me a while to get my bearings."

"Plus of course, we've probably lost twenty minutes through toilet stops," added Randall, even though no one asked for his opinion.

"Look! I get nervous when I'm under pressure!" complained Billy. "Everyone wants to know where we're going, where we are! Well, it affects my bladder!"

"Mmm," said Colin, "perhaps Delia should navigate since she's in the front."

Even with the benefit of hindsight, everyone would acknowledge that they thought it was a good idea at the time.

*****

By now Denton was somewhere near Manchester. His fellow companion had disembarked near Birmingham, which was something of a relief not just to Denton, but the entire train, which seemed to be travelling a lot faster as a result. Passing through Birmingham was doubly enjoyable though on account of the train announcers increasingly flamboyant, speech impediment inhibited, announcements: *"This is Burning Nun."* Denton had looked out of the window. He had seen nothing burning, nuns or otherwise.

"Change at Burning Nun, fur Nun Eating and Nun-in-ham."

The Midlands - a place where even in the twenty first century, nuns are publicly persecuted for their beliefs.

OK, thought Denton, *I have to get a connecting service once I get to Manchester which will take me to the village.* He looked down at his ticket. *The connecting service leaves at 14:42, and the time is now…* he glanced down at his non-existent watch. *Bollocks! What time is it?* He ferreted around inside his trousers and pulled out his mobile phone again. *Oh, arse! It's 14:20.*

*****

Badger was beginning to feel increasingly panicky. Covered in baggage and barely able to breathe, he felt more and more as if he was being kidnapped. What made it worse though, was the fact that he could hear himself breathing, he had no idea where he was, and all around him were angry voices, mainly emanating from Delia.

"Is there any particular reason why we're going so slowly, Colin?" Delia snapped. "I mean, you do realise that we're out of the slow moving traffic now, and the road ahead is clear?"

Colin remained oblivious, and continued to remain in the left hand lane doing sixty.

"Are you in a hurry, Delia?" ventured Randall, bravely some might say.

"YES!" said Delia. "I hate being overtaken! It makes me feel so inferior. Colin, you're doing it again! People are overtaking us, and oh, dear Lord! It was a Nissan Micra! Oh the shame! I feel so dirty."

"Good job Denton isn't here, he hates Nissan Micras," commented Randall.

"We already know that there isn't just one thing that I hate, but if there were," Denton would often say, *"then it would have to be Nissan Micra's, or more accurately, the imbeciles that drive them. I mean, what is it with Nissan Micra drivers and the motorway? Every time you see one there, you can guarantee - just guarantee - that they'll be stuck in the left hand lane or worse, middle lane, trundling along, doing no more than 55mph, seemingly without a care in the world. It's so annoying! Just get out of the way! I mean, what is wrong with those cars? Do they just not have a fifth gear or something? Or even a fourth?"*

*****

Denton ran as fast as his legs would carry him. Back-pack flailing, he threw himself towards the platform. "Must get train, must get train," he panted.

On the platform sat a battered commuter train. The kind with no onboard shop, no air conditioning, no toilets. In fact, nothing but a row of seats haphazardly bolted to the ground.

He panted up to a platform guard.

"Is this…" he gasped, "train going…to Keswick?"

Before the guard could answer the doors closed and the train moved slowly away.

The guard looked at Denton, then the train, then Denton.

"Yes," he said and then walked away.

Denton gasped and gawped at the same time (which in itself was quite painful) as he watched the train disappear.

"Boll…ocks," he panted, doubled over with his hands on his knees.

Denton stood panting, and then slowly wandered over to the electronic board in order to work out when his nightmare might finally end.

"Next train not for … twenty minutes!" he sighed.

He wandered over and sat down on a bench. The platform was deserted apart from a solitary man, sat on the same bench as Denton, reading a magazine. The guy must have been in his mid-forties. Even sat down, he looked fairly short and stocky. The sands of time had not shifted kindly. His skin had eroded and wizened in a manner that (Denton naively assumed) would not occur to Denton. His ears had sprouted tufts of wiry hair, for absolutely no reason whatsoever. His eyebrows were thick and grey. Even his head had short sprouts of wiry hair, spread out in an uneven pattern across the top of it. His thick, bushy beard was grey. The lenses in his spectacles were thick, signifying a short-sightedness of *Mr Magoo* proportions.

Poor bastard, thought Denton.

Denton enjoyed being alone for one thing, and one thing alone - the opportunity to people watch. On long journeys, there was nothing better for Denton than to sit and observe the world around him. *Who are these people that I am with? Where have they come from? Why are they here?*

Who was this old guy? What was he doing here in the middle of nowhere, waiting to go to another nowhere. What had happened to him in forty odd years that was interesting?

Denton's thoughts were suddenly disturbed. Another man was wandering down the platform. As he passed, the old man on the bench looked up. Their gaze met, and just for a moment, Denton caught a glimpse of recognition in both sets of eyes. They knew each other. Then, for an equal moment, there was hesitation, as if both men were evaluating whether the other one had seen and recognised them - a kind of *oh shit, did he see me? Well, now I'm going to have to speak to him.* Denton had long ago concluded that it was a general rule of life that people spent half of their lives, for whatever reason, trying to meet new people, and the other half trying to ignore the ones they had met before. It seemed to Denton that in every man and every woman was the instinctive reaction to conclude *oh crap, I haven't got the time to catch up with them now - I've got new people to meet!*

"Dennis," said the seated man, as he instinctively rose holding out a hand. "How lovely to see you."

"Michael, how strange that I should meet you here of all places."

"I know."

They shook hands.

Then came the moment that they had both been dreading. The moment that they both knew would happen.

Neither had the foggiest clue of what to say to the other.

Denton had seen this happen before during one of his many people watching experiences. *Now when you haven't seen someone for a while it must surely be the easiest thing in the world to find things to talk about. After all, you haven't seen them in ages. You could ask them anything about what had happened to them over the last x number of years?*

What did you do on 1 January 1987? How about 2 January 1987? 3 January? And yet, people don't. There is always a moment of hesitation from both parties as if their brain is analysing and discarding questions. What were this guy's hobbies? Was he married? Denton had, long ago, concluded that there was an easy test to work out how long it had been since two people had met. He called it his 'Universal Law of Generalisms'. The more they ask generic, non-specific questions, the longer it's been.

"So…" asked the previously seated man, "How are things?"

"Things are good. You?"

"Oh yes - no complaints here."

"Great! And work? How is work?"

"Work's good. Things are going well. You?"

"Oh yes. Things going great for me too."

"Great!"

Classic generalisms. Neither man can remember a thing about the other, and both are currently deeply regretting their misfortune at bumping into each other. Ten years without seeing each other, I'd say.

"Well. This is a nice surprise," said the standing man. "Fancy meeting you here of all places."

"I know!" said the formerly seated man. "What a surprise. I'm only passing through. I don't even live here anymore."

"Really? Wow - that is odd!"

In addition to the law of generalisms to signify the length of time both parties have been apart, is the law of evasions. If a party really does not want to renew a friendship or acquaintance, they will avoid an opening to a conversation. For example, the standing man could have asked the formerly and previously seated man, where he lived now, or what he was doing back in their old haunt, or what kind of work he was in, thus opening up the conversation. Instead, he opted for the closed route which signifies there was a reason he lost touch with this guy in the first place.

"Isn't it? Well, it must have been, what, seven years since we saw each other last?"

"Yes, it must be."

Close.

"Yes, well, how is Claire?" asked the previously and formerly seated man with hesitation. "It is Claire, isn't it?"

"Christine. It's Christine," he corrected. "Yes - she's fine," said the standing man abruptly, he reached for the formerly seated man's hand and cupped it with his left hand. "Michael - don't think me rude but I'm going to miss this train if I don't dash. It's been great, and we'll have to catch up properly another time."

"Yes," said the formerly seated man apologetically. "Yes, of course, please don't let me hold you up old boy - you go, get your train."

"Ok, great. You take care now." And with that he wandered off.

The old man sat down with a smile on his face. He shook his head and watched Dennis disappear into the distance.

"Still a wanker," he muttered under his breathe.

Denton smiled. His little laws had stood up to the test again.

*****

"Look," said Delia, "It's no good any of you raising your voice with me! I can only do my best. Map reading has never been my forte. It's not my fault I don't know where we are!"

"I'm not having a go, Delia," said Colin calmly, "I just wondered why you had suggested that we leave the M6 for the A road when I knew where I was on the M6."

"Going this way looked shorter on the map."

"But we're now going south when we should be going north," said Colin.

"Look, I said before that map reading isn't my forte."

Colin frowned.

"But Delia - why have you taken us in the wrong direction when I knew where I was going?!"

"I said I'm sorry, didn't I?" said Delia, her volume increasing. "I said that map reading wasn't my thing, didn't I? I didn't imagine that, did I?"

"Yes," said Colin, "I can hear you - but why are we going the wrong way?"

"OK! OK!" said Delia snapping, "I was holding the map upside down. OK? Happy? There - there you go. I was holding it upside down - happy now?!"

*****

Finally, Denton found himself on the local train. As expected, it was a rickety old thing and it was a wonder that it still managed to start any journey, let alone finish it. Denton was sat in a relatively empty carriage which contained just him, a middle aged man wearing a thick woolly green jumper and tweed trousers, who looked a little bit lost - presumably he couldn't remember where he'd put his shotgun and why it wasn't draped over his shoulder like normal - and a doddery old mad man who seemed to be stuck on repeat, talking out loud to absolutely no one.

"I do hope that I don't end up in Crewe. I ended up in Reading last time. They told me it was the Stockport train. Is this the Reading train? I do hope I don't end up in Crewe."

He repeated these simple, meaningless sentences over and over again. Over and over until Denton reached the point where he wished the jolly green jumper *had* brought along his shotgun if only just to shut the old bugger up.

'Oh God, this journey is taking a long time!" he silently lamented. *"Please just stop stopping at every Dingle-end station and get on with it!"*

The train trundled on towards the village of Denton's dreams.

"I do hope I don't end up in Crewe," the old man continued.

*****

"What?" asked Billy with incredulity.

"Look!" said Delia, sensing an onslaught. "It's not my fault!"

"How?" asked Randall. "How is it not your fault?"

"Well, I thought it was right, that's how."

"I knew it couldn't be right," said Colin, shuffling the map in his hands and scratching at his neck brace. They were all stood outside the now parked people carrier.

"Don't blame me!" said Delia. "It's not my fault."

"Oh really?" said Billy, quite distraught. "We've been driving for hours on end and you said we were nearly there."

"Yes, well…"

"You said," added Randall, "that we were so close that we didn't need to buy petrol because we were on the A road that led to the village."

"I knew it was wrong," said Colin distantly and to no one in particular, "I knew the road signs were wrong."

"But we were!"

"Oh really!" said Randall. "Then how do you explain this then?!" he pointed up at a town sign which read, in big black unmistakable letters *'Crewe.'*

"It was the map!" said Delia, feebly.

"The map!" scoffed Billy.

"It's getting dark, and now we don't have enough petrol to carry on!" said Randall. "Now what do we do?"

There was a noise like water leaking.

"Billy!" cried Randall.

"What?"

"You only just went!"

"I can't help it - this whole situation is too stressful for my bladder."

*****

Denton stared out of the window. It was dark now. He had no idea where he was or how much further was left. In front of him, sat the wizened old man who was so keen to avoid Crewe. He stared at Denton, and had done for the last three stops. He stared and he stared and he stared. The most uncomfortable part of it was, Denton really did not know what to say to him. What do you say to someone (who must be in their eighties) that is just staring. It's not as if you could just remark *"what are you staring at? Wanna fight?"* because there really would be no kudos in that. In any event, Denton was just relieved that the guy had finally stopped pointing out to people how keen he was to avoid getting off inadvertently at Crewe.

The train began to slow. The old man looked out of the window. His eyes gave the merest indication of recognition. He began to get up, which Denton thought brave since the train was still going at some speed. Undaunted, the man continued. Slowly, ever so slowly, he gradually got to his feet. It was so slow that Denton did not realise at first that he was doing it. It was only by looking at the man, looking away and then looking back a few moments later that Denton could recognise the change in his position. Slowly, but surely, he stood right up and lifted his stick from the seat behind him. Once properly on his feet he walked slowly down the corridor of the train, shuffling along like a tortoise carrying some heavy shopping. Finally, he reached the doors. The train came to a stand still. Denton glanced at the name of the station, and on realising that this was not his stop thought nothing of it. Further down the corridor, he could see people waiting to get off the train by the second door on the carriage. The train door lights illuminated and people departed from the second carriage door.

Not so the old man stood by the first carriage door, who simply stood staggering ever so slightly as he rested on his stick, watching the door - waiting for it to move. Denton could hardly believe what was happening - he quickly jumped up, concerned that the old man would miss his stop. *The poor old codger*, he thought. *He thinks the train doors will open by themselves - no wonder he ends up in Crewe.* He bounded down the corridor, pressing the door button, perhaps just in time. He leapt on to the platform, turning to hold out an arm for the old man.

The old man did nothing. The train doors began to emit a noise, indicating they were about to seal. Denton looked at the old man in horror.

"Are you coming?" said Denton quickly gesturing towards his own arm.

"No," said the old man calmly. "This isn't my stop."

And with that the train doors closed, and the train departed leaving Denton slightly flabbergasted on the platform edge.

"Oh, right," he mumbled feebly. "But what about my back-pack?" For no obvious reason, he waved it off.

*****

"How long did the AA say it would take for them to send someone out?" enquired Billy

"About twenty minutes," said Colin

"Well, at least there can be no dispute where we are this time," said Randall, realising that only Denton would understand what he was on about. There were blank looks all around. "You see, there was this one time when..." he said thinking of the Corporate weekend away, then he realised that he really did not have the energy or inclination to finish the story at all. "Forget it..." he said dismissively.

"Oooh!" said Delia, "what about a game of celebrity head!"

"What's that?" asked Colin.

"Well, we each write down the name of someone famous on a post-it note and then, without revealing the name, you stick the post-it to someone's head. They then have to guess who they are."

"Sounds riveting," said Randall, dripping with sarcasm.

"No, really, it is," said a needlessly excited Delia.

"OK then," said Colin. "Nothing better to do."

"Do you have post-it notes in this car?" asked Delia of Colin.

"Delia, I'm a senior solicitor in a successful law firm - of course I have post-it notes in my car. I have post-it notes in my bathroom cabinet. I have them in my sock drawer. I even keep a spare pack in the shed, just in case."

"OK, break them out, with pens!"

Delia's enthusiasm for this pursuit alone was enough to put Billy and Randall right off. It seemed that Badger and Brian were ineligible: 1) on account of being both so far away; and, 2) not being able to reach their own foreheads on account of the bags.

The players each scribbled something down on their respective post-its.

"Right, everyone pass your post-it note around to your left - without looking at it!" said Delia, which they all duly did. "Now place it on your head." It seemed to all of them that Delia had missed her vocation as a primary school teacher.

Each person now wore the post-it note on their head.

"Now what?" said Billy, who's own sticker bore the name *'Colonel Gaddaffi'*.

"Now we each ask one question in turn in order to identify ourselves," said Delia, wearing a sticker that said *'Margaret Thatcher'*.

"OK, then, who am I?" asked Randall, who's sticker said *'Michael Schumacher'*.

"I think that's cheating," said Colin bearing the name *'Lulu'*.

"I'll begin," said Delia. "Am I pretty?"

"Well, yes, you have a certain charm about you," said Colin taken aback from the forwardness of the question.

Delia sighed, "No, not me Colin! The person whose name is on my head!"

The sweat from Billy's brow became too much for the post-it note and it sailed off his head on to his lap.

"Oh, I'd have never have got him!" he exclaimed.

Delia sighed again, the game was not quite the master stroke of entertainment that she had hoped for.

"So! Am I pretty?!" she asked once more.

They stared intently at the sticker.

"No," they all said in unison. Despite her previous comment that the question was not personal to her, Delia still seemed hurt by this answer. "OK, your turn, Randall," she said, flatly.

"Am I interesting?" asked Randall.

"Erm," Colin and Delia hesitated. "No," they ventured.

"Am I the undisputed champion of the motor racing world, having won more championships than you can shake a stick at?" he asked.

Colin and Delia looked in amazement at each other and then back to Randall.

"Yes!" they said in unison.

Randall sighed, as if it were all too easy. "I'm Michael Schumacher."

"Wow!" they both said. "That's amazing!" said Delia. "How did you know?"

"Two things," said Randall. "First, that guy is *the* dullest person on the planet, even compared to Dom Peasgood - which is saying something in itself. Secondly, and more importantly, I can read backwards." He pointed to the rear-view mirror in which his reversed head appeared.

"Oh," they said, dejected.

"OK, nevertheless, my turn!" she seemed needlessly excited, in the same way that women seem to when they feel like it. "Am I a model?"

"No!" they said in unison, with a hint of disgust. Again, Delia did not seem to take this well, which also prompted Colin to remind her that this was not a personal comment. Though, in her case, it would have been true.

"Am I…" she started, but before she could finish, blue flashing lights appeared through the window and a policeman soon appeared. Colin wound down the window.

"Hello officer, can I help you?"

The policeman looked into the car and seemed to be slightly taken aback by what he saw. In front of him was an overloaded people carrier containing four people, three of which were wearing post-it notes on their head and a disembodied hand, which despite its lack of obvious visual sensory perception, was pointing straight at him in an inquisitive fashion.

He ignored the sight in front of him, and continued with his business.

"What's going on here?"

"We've broken down, and we're just waiting for roadside assistance to arrive," said Colin, adopting the position of chief spokesman and quasi-father figure.

"I see," said the policeman, not entirely able to take Colin seriously. "Well, you do realise that you're parked on a double yellow line, don't you?"

"No, I hadn't actually, officer, however, I cannot move the car because it has broken down," said Colin, repeating the information he had given previously, just in case the policeman did not quite understand it first time around.

"I see, but either way you're breaking the law," said the policeman.

"Yes, I appreciate the position that we're in, but you can see my dilemma, can't you officer? This car won't move," said Colin, as politely as he could in the circumstances.

"Look Lulu, I don't know what is going on here, but I want you moved on now!" barked the policeman.

"Oh! You've just ruined it now!" bemoaned Delia, realising too late how inappropriate the comment was.

"I see what you're saying, officer, but we really can't move on," said Colin.

"But you must!"

"But we can't!"

"But you have to!"

"But we can't!"

At this point, the AA van drove along the road, only to be flagged down by the policeman.

"Could you move this car on!" said the policeman to the driver.

"I was about to!" complained the driver.

Red faced, the policeman turned and walked away. He climbed back on to his bike and drove off.

Colin shook his head causing the post-it note to flap about. "It's hard not to feel embarrassed on behalf of someone like that when they appear so foolish!"

The rest of them shook their heads too, agreeing wholeheartedly, post-it notes flapping in the breeze.

*****

Denton wandered down the rain sodden high street. Everywhere was shut. Everywhere was dark and completely uninviting.

Baggage reclaim, my arse, he thought. *They don't know the first thing about it. The first thing!* Refusing to blame himself, he continued to lambaste the Lost Luggage counter for their needless and, in many ways, shameless histrionics as they rolled around in fits of laughter while he explained how his bag had come to be classified as lost. *Disgraceful,* he recalled.

He trudged on through the night, bag-less and, currently, homeless. *It'll turn up in two to five working days, what bollocks!* he lamented.

The rain continued to mock him.

God I need a drink, he thought. *Thirty minutes for another train to arrive. Thirty minutes! Bloody old men. Bloody goldfish! Bloody fish Sundays!*

He stopped. The rain belted down - straight down. Water ran down his face in streams. *What on earth am I doing?* he thought. *What are we doing? Chasing dreams in a monsoon. This is completely pointless. God I need a drink.* He carried on walking, hoping for a sign. Anything to show him he wasn't wasting his time here. Something to show him that there was some point to him being here. He crossed the road and randomly picked out a road to walk down. A short way down, on his left, sat a large flashing neon sign.

"Quincey's bar," read Denton. "Well, on account of the fact that this is the first thing that I've seen in this town that even resembles a bar, it gets my vote."

He pushed the door open. It was hardly lively to start with, but there was a definite sense of the music stopping and all eyes turning towards him as he wandered inside. *Great. I've just entered a local bar for local people haven't I? Is this where the tourists come never to be seen again?* he thought.

Momentarily, he felt a million miles away from London. He had been to countless bars in the City on his own. It's almost expected there. Londoners don't stare at you. They don't even notice you when you wander in. In fact, most Londoners don't even register the presence of other people - they all think that only they are real and everyone else is a figment of their drunken imagination.

The bar was long and looked like it was an extension to some other building, like a conservatory, only Denton couldn't see any other building that it was attached to. On his left were five American style booths, with two rows of seats facing inwards with a table top in between. At these, sat four or five distinctly rough looking people. More 'bikers' than 'hikers'. On his immediate right, was a pool table around which two lads stood. One of them was stood closer than Denton would have liked, chalking his pool cue whilst eyeballing Denton. Ahead of him, on his right, was a bar with a neon bar-rest around it and stools. A solitary bar man stood wiping glasses. At the bar sat one solitary female, looking mournfully into a short glass.

Denton wandered up to the bar. He sat two stools away from the girl, not wishing to crowd her space. To be honest, he really did not want to crowd anyone's space.

The bar man wandered over. "Yes?" he demanded.

"Hi," said Denton, buying himself time as he looked at the taps. "Er, what lagers have you got on tap?"

"Carling, Fosters, Carlsberg."

"Anything else?" asked Denton hopefully.

"What else is there?"

Denton shuddered. *What a backward place.*

"Oh, the agony of choice," said Denton. The barman did not appreciate the inference. Suddenly, Denton remembered where he was. "Erm, pint of Carlsberg please."

The girl next to him turned around. "Excuse me," she ventured.

Denton turned around and struggled not to stop breathing. His weary eyes were hit by a sudden visceral display of perfection that nearly caused him to fall off his chair. It was the kind of moment that should have been accompanied by the sound of heavenly music, or any kind of music other than the *Def Leppard* that was currently booming out of the tinny stereo. It was the kind of moment that your memory can never do justice to. Denton was captivated by the bright, angelic, emerald eyes that gazed into his, the soft flawless skin, the pink glistening lips, that face, that nose so perfect, so beautiful, as if an artist had carved them from marble. Denton hoped to God that his face was more composed than his beating heart and fast racing mind was. He had never experienced such an unexpected, beautiful moment before.

"Excuse me," she said interrupting his moment.

"Hi," said Denton desperately trying to remember how to speak English again.

"Hi. Sorry to bother you…"

"No. Yeah, no, that's fine," said Denton. He put his hand on his thigh. It was the gayest thing he could have done, and now, with the benefit of hindsight, he had no idea why he had done it. Trying to salvage the situation, he folded his arms and persuaded himself to shut up enough to let her finish the sentence.

She giggled nervously. "Sorry. It was nothing. Sorry." She returned to her drink.

Idiot, Denton. Idiot, he thought.

The barman placed the pint in front of Denton, which he pretty much swallowed in one go. He paid the barman, and thought seriously about leaving there and then. But then he was thirsty, and how could he, in good conscience, leave when this vision of loveliness on the pedestal next to him was present?

"Can I get another?" he asked the barman, who was in shock. He had never seen anyone drink a Carlsberg that fast, voluntarily.

"Sure," said the barman, pouring another pint.

Suddenly, Denton was incredibly self conscious. He must have looked a complete state. He was drenched. His dark black hair was so rain soaked, it was practically down to his shoulders, and he just knew it was probably curled up at the end in that stupid way that it did when it got anywhere near water.

The girl next to him seemed very awkward. She had been staring into the bottom of that glass for an age. Denton looked across, but was conscious not to make it seem like he was staring.

"Can I get you another drink?" he asked. This was a kill or cure moment.

She looked across at Denton, and seemed to take an age before answering which only served to slowly kill him. His heart was pounding and sinking lower and lower with every moment, until he felt sure it would explode out of his shoe in a way that John Hurt would have been proud of.

What is she doing? thought Denton. She was staring intently at him, as if evaluating his sincerity.

"Yes," she said without conviction. "Same again, barman. Jack Daniels. Neat. No rocks." He obliged. She took a swig of it and turned to Denton. "Thanks."

"No problem," he said. "So," ventured Denton, more confident than he had been before. "What were you going to say before?"

The girl stopped swirling her drink and looked at Denton. "Oh nothing. I was going to ask you if you were from London. You sound like you are."

"So why didn't you?" asked Denton.

"Because I realised I wasn't interested in the answer. It was just something to say. My curiosity suddenly got the better of me." She stared into the glass again. She downed her drink. Denton's heart sank into his underpants. There was no explosion out of his shoes. It just burst quietly in his bowels. It didn't want to make a fuss.

Denton felt sure that this was her cue to exit.

"Can I get another?" she asked the barman.

"Sure."

"Sorry," said the girl. "That was rude. I didn't mean it to be."

"Hey," said Denton, suddenly aloof. "Don't worry. I've had worse than that. I was just striking up conversation." He turned back to his pint.

"No, it wasn't on. Sorry. I've had a bad day. Well, a bad year really." She suddenly remembered where she was. "And now I'm telling a complete stranger."

"Would it help if I told you my name?", asked Denton.

She frowned and looked at him. "What?"

"Well, I wouldn't be a stranger then."

"No," she said, "it's fine. I should go." She shifted her weight as if about to get up. Her drink arrived.

"Denton," he said quickly without looking up from his pint. She stopped. "My name is Denton, and your drink has just arrived. Why don't you see if you can condense your bad year into the time it takes to drink your drink."

"Oh, at the rate I can drink one of these, I don't think that that is possible…Denton." she looked at him and smiled. "What an interesting name."

"All names are interesting - it's just some are used more often, and they lose their sheen as a result."

She giggled at him, or with him, he couldn't tell which.

"My name doesn't get used that much at all, so it's still shiny and interesting," he concluded.

She looked at him with interest. Her head tilted slightly and those beautiful emerald eyes gazed at him again.

"What's yours?" he asked.

"Easter."

"Ah. Well there you go. A fellow shiny name owner," said Denton, not entirely sure how much further he could go with this line of conversation.

She giggled again. "Well, yes. I should have had a dull, second-hand name, but it didn't quite happen that way."

Denton frowned and turned to face her. "How come?"

"Well, my full name is Easter Williams..."

*That name sounds familiar...*thought Denton.

"...I was supposed to be named after the swimmer, you know, Esther Williams? Anyway, my Dad was a chronic drunk and on the way to the registry office, he got a bit tipsy. When he got there his 'Esther' looked like 'Easter' and it has stuck ever since."

"Can't you change it?" asked Denton.

"Why would I want to?" asked Easter. "It's just a name. It's just a way of people identifying me from everyone else. Easter Williams, Easter Williams."

"Oh, I don't think it's your name that does that," said Denton, almost without thinking. Easter smiled and he hoped that she took the compliment the way he had meant it to sound.

"Thank you," she said in a way that did not reassure Denton that she had. He decided to let it go and move on.

"So, why has your day been bad?" he asked.

"Oh, something to do with the disgusting pigs that I work with," she sighed. She stared into the bottom of her glass again. "Look you don't want to know. I don't want to know. And I don't want to discuss it. I shouldn't even be here. I hadn't had a drink for seven months. I was trying to quit but now I've started again, apparently."

"There's nothing wrong with drinking!" said Denton.

Easter shifted her weight again. "Yeah? Tell that to my dead father, and the dead mother of mine that he killed as he drove their car off the road in a drunken stupor." She got up. "It was nice meeting you, Denton. Take care of that name."

Denton felt like an idiot. "You too," was about the only thing he could manage to say in response. He finished his pint and ordered another. He gazed at the empty stool and shook his head. He watched her as she left. The two lads at the pool table gawped at her. They sniggered to each other after she had gone.

"Well done Denton," he said into his pint glass, "You won't be seeing her again any time soon."

His mobile phone started vibrating in his trousers, and the unexpected interruption of it was almost enough to send him crashing to the ground.

"Argh!" he yelped like a girl. The barman stared at him in shock. "Sorry! I'm vibrating", he said to the barman, whilst pointing at his trousers. The barman looked at the disappearing Easter and then back at Denton with a face that almost looked like disgust. Denton sensed he had been misinterpreted but when he tried to explain, the barman just lifted his hands as if to signal that he really did not want to know.

Great! thought Denton.

"Hello!" he said, a little agitated.

"Hello, Denton - it's Randall."

"Hi mate, how are you doing? More importantly, where have you been?"

"Don't ask. It's a long story. Basically, it ends with us garrotting Delia with the strap of her Donna Karen handbag."

"Diverse," said Denton, impressed.

"Quite. Anyway, we're at base camp. Where are you?"

"Oh, I'm at some bar called Quincey's."

"He's at Quincey's - do you know where that is?" said Randall into the distance.

"Yeah, I know it," said Colin from the background.

"Yep, ok. Denton," said Randall, his voice becoming clearer again. "We're just going to unload the car, then we'll meet you. Get the beers in will you? I'll have a Peroni."

"Yeah, err, Randall?"

"Yeah?"

"They don't have that."

"Really? No Peroni?"

"Yep."

"Oh good God. Well that's just perfect. Well, anything but Carling or Fosters."

"Yeah, Randall?"

"Yeah?"

"That's pretty much all they have here."

"You're joking!"

"Nope."

"Oh, good God," Denton could hear Randall composing himself. "Your plan had better work Denton, otherwise I'll be garrotting you too."

The line went dead.

You're telling me. Two weeks to find out the missing piece of Colin's secret. It's no time at all.

With that, Denton gulped down the rest of his pint, and waited for the others.

Chapter Thirty One

The Plan

Denton awoke in a mild panic. He felt anxious. Along with the usual feeling of alcohol-induced discomfort, was a feeling of concern on realising that he wasn't entirely sure where he was.

The light cascading through the thin, flower-patterned curtains seemed to have a purity to it that, whilst he couldn't quite put his finger on the reason why he felt this way, he knew instinctively he had not experienced such a purity before. As if drawn by a curiosity of this unknown factor - like a moth around about the time before it's wings get singed and drop off - Denton rose, ignoring the throbbing in his head, and wandered over to the window to explore.

As he did so, he noticed a feather or two poking slightly through the sheet. He realised then that he had been sleeping on a soft goose down filled mattress, and had slept enveloped by a soft plump duvet, and matching pillows. Denton was struck by the fact that he had actually noticed the quality of the bed that he had just slept in. Ordinarily, he treated his bed as nothing more than a beacon to guide him to the right place to pass out. Equally, Denton knew that he could pass out anywhere but appreciated that his body would much rather he did so on the relatively soft bed as compared to the floor; wrapped around the toilet bowl; precariously balanced half out of a window; or even leaning against the wardrobe door, all of which Denton had been known to do before.

Having been struck by the nature of the bed, Denton was suddenly conscious of the room itself. It was light and comfortable. Somehow there was something about the room - the soft beech-wood - the scattering of pastel colours in the furniture - peach, cornflower blue and sea green. There was a warmth to the room that gave rise in Denton to a sensory perception that he had never felt conscious of before. It was as if he was suddenly alive to texture, colour and comfort. It was as if the gentleness and tranquillity of the place had invaded his senses in one massive attack in a way that made him feel placid, relaxed and generally at peace with the world (except for the City saunterers. He would never be at peace with them. *Magnum*). He felt soothed by it. He felt comforted. He felt strangely at odds with himself.

"Weird," he found himself saying.

He turned back to the window and flung the curtains open.

The sight that greeted him was so intense that it caused him to stagger backwards. It was mesmerising. It was daunting. It was…

"Beautiful..." he murmured.

In front of him, was a view of such beauty that he had never experienced before. It was so dazzling and so powerful that it made his skin tingle. Before him was a field of the most vibrant green grass that he had ever seen. It stretched out before him majestically before dipping down and rolling right out of view. Beyond that was the merest hint of a lake. Denton could see the tiny outline of boats floating upon it, gently bobbing up and down - peacefully - calmly. The lake itself covered the full width of the window causing Denton to crane his neck and press his face against the pane to find out if he could see how far it went in either direction. He did this despite the fact that it simply served to aggravate his hung-over condition.

Beyond that still, was a hill that rose so sharply in the distance that Denton felt overwhelmed by its sheer enormity.

Wow, thought Denton, and then, without having any clear understanding of why he might think it, he thought, *I must climb that.*

The sun shone brightly causing the sky to appear magnificently blue.

As he stared, Denton suddenly became aware of something odd happening. For the first time, perhaps ever, he felt his shoulders relaxing. In fact, all the muscles in his body seemed to be loosening. The knots in his aching back loosened and he felt his stresses and strains dissipating.

"Wow," he found himself saying again.

Without warning, an intense smile spread across his face - which almost cracked and buckled under the pressure. Since it had been so long it was a wonder that his muscles still remembered what to do with the command, *smile please.*

"This is great!" said Denton with an ecstatic - bordering on hysterical - laugh. "Woo hoo!" he cheered. "Where's Randall?" he cried out. "Where are the others? They have to see this!"

He grabbed his dressing gown and dashed out of the room, along a short corridor and into a homely-looking kitchen. As he did so, he admired the charm and beauty of the glorious cottage that he found himself in.

The others were sat around a huge pine table, and were not ready for the tidal wave of enthusiasm that was about to crash down around them.

"You guys!" exclaimed Denton, as giddy as a teenager in a 1950's B movie, "have you seen the view?"

They looked at Denton (stuffed into his blue dressing gown with his impressively unkempt hair), and then back at each other. There was definitely a discernible moment when it looked as if they did not know whether to laugh, or whether to take pity on him. Resolutely, they all chose the former. Denton, however, remained undaunted.

"Seriously! It's amazing! I'm going outside!" And with that, he dashed to the door - fighting briefly with the alien latch system - before entering the big, bright world outside. "My God!" he said, still talking out loud but now to absolutely no one. "The air! It's so clear, and clean! It feels great!"

Back inside, Billy was obviously disturbed by the incident. "Is Denton alright?" he asked Randall.

"Yeah," said Randall, not looking up from his cornflakes. "He's just not used to the countryside." He placed another spoonful in his mouth, and crunched, "or the morning."

Delia sat messing with her hair, "I'm sure that this weather is causing havoc to my hair - look at how big and frizzy it's become!"

She was roundly ignored by all except Brian. "I think it looks lovely! Gives it a much needed bit of oomph."

They all stared at him in disbelief, then turned back when he started to look embarrassed. Colin fidgeted with his neck brace. It seemed to Randall that he was uncomfortable by Brian's 'outbursts'. Randall chuckled to himself, *you're so old school Colin.*

Denton stood on the brow of the hill, admiring the view. Stereotypically, he was stood with his hands on his hips, puffing his chest out. He looked as if he was in a tampax advert, celebrating the freedom that his new found discreet tampons gave him.

"This is the life!" he exhaled in an unnecessary, self-satisfied manner.

Soon he heard shuffling, uneven steps approaching from behind him, and recognised instantly that they had to belong to Colin.

"It's a nice place, isn't it?" observed Colin.

"Colin - it's amazing!! What on earth makes you live in London when you own a place like this?!"

"The answer to that is quite simple. I would not be able to afford a place like this without London weighting!"

"But, even so, you must be tempted to just give it all up and move here, surely?"

"Maybe, especially after recent events," said Colin, uncharacteristically introspective. "True, it is very relaxing here, but it can be quite isolating as well. Perhaps I need the stress of working life to make me appreciate scenery like this."

"Really?" asked Denton. "But you'd be away from the City drones. All those suited morons traipsing along in line each day would be a thing of the past."

Colin chuckled. "I'm not like you Denton. You forget, I am one of those 'suited morons', and I have been for a long time now. I'm not so sure all my troubles would be solved just by moving out of London. There are troubles everywhere, Denton, and most of them are in here." He pointed at his head.

"I don't agree," said Denton resolutely. "You'll see when we escape the rat race. You'll see how it changes, believe me. Then you'll thank me."

Colin smiled. "Denton, you can't change the way things are. I can't change the way I am. Things happen, sometimes those experiences are pleasant, and sometimes not, but there is no way you can increase the measure of one, and limit the measure of another. You must see that, surely?"

Denton frowned. *Already dissension in the ranks.* "This *is* going to work Colin," he said firmly.

*****

Hours later, they were sat in a side room waiting for Denton to appear. The curtains had been drawn and the chairs that had been brought in all faced the far wall, where a projector screen stood. A projector whirred next to Randall's ear.

"Where did the projector come from?" asked Randall.

"It's mine," said Colin. "I forgot I had it. I'm surprised it still works after all these years."

Denton entered the room. They half expected him to be in combat gear.

"Morning," he said with self-appointed authority.

"Morning," they said, amused and intrigued by what was occurring.

"OK, it's time to reveal the plan," said Denton. From the front of the room, he grabbed a remote control from a side table and shielded his eyes from the projector. He clicked the button and an image appeared on the screen bearing the words *'The Plan'*.

They groaned. "Oh, good God, he's prepared a power point presentation," retorted Randall.

"Settle down," commanded Denton. "Thank you Randall, that's enough. Now then, as you know, you're all here on trust. That is to say, you trusted me enough to give up two weeks holiday to come up to the Lake District on this little sojourn, which I hope will bear real fruit, and not be some wild goose chase."

In true powerpoint presentation style, Denton was using six words where two would do, stating the obvious and praying to god that the slides would distract all onlookers from any and all inconsistencies and deficiencies inherent in his plan.

"Get on with it," someone heckled, probably Randall.

"OK!" said Denton, obviously nervous. "There is a man that lives in this village called Mr Gunt." He pressed a button. "This is a photo of Mr Gunt."

They all stared at a photo of Mr Gunt, taken from his company's website. It was cheesy and out of date. The slide moved on.

"My research has shown me that Mr Gunt is associated with a great number of companies. Some of them I have been able to find the link between, and some of them I haven't." He pressed another button. A slide appeared showing an incomplete group company structure.

"Now, what don't I know about Mr Gunt. Well, I don't know where he lives." An image of a house with a question mark in it appeared.

"Or who he lives with." A photo of an old lady with a question mark over her appeared.

"But I do know he has a dog," an image of a shitzu appeared. "But I don't know the dog's name." A question mark appeared over the dog. "Though I know he walks his dog at the same time every day through the village green."

"How could you possibly know that?" asked Randall.

"Because I did a google search on the term *Gunt.* It brought up forty million entries, the first of which happened to be a recent article written by Easter Williams, which showed Mr Gunt walking his dog in the village green. 95% of the other entries, as you'd expect, occurred due to spelling errors and were not relevant to my research, though that didn't stop me reviewing the odd one." He looked awkwardly at his feet. "Anyway, the story said that Mr Gunt was training his dog for entry to Crufts. It said that he always walked his dog at the same time each day." An image of the article appeared.

"However, the article did not state at what time he walked his dog." An image of a clock with a question mark on it appeared.

"I met Easter Williams randomly last night in a bar before you lot arrived."

"Did you ask her what time Gunt walked his dog?" asked Randall.

"No," said Denton, "there wasn't time and I didn't recognise her name quickly enough to remember I had read her article." Another image appeared. It said *'Conclusion'.* "In conclusion, I know Gunt is rich. I don't know where he lives or who he lives with. I know we can find him, I just don't know at what time. So we need to stake out the village green. We also need a set of walkie-talkies, and probably, some sort of separate listening device."

"For what?" asked Randall

"Listening in, of course."

Randall tutted. "OK, listening in to what?"

"You'll see," said Denton.

"OK, but what happens when we actually catch up with Gunt."

"We ask him where the buried treasure is!"

"Hang on Denton," said Colin.

Denton's heart skipped a beat. *Oh God,* he thought, his mind racing, *the bomb! He knows I've rummaged through his drawers!! He knows I know what he knows about Gunt! He's going to have me arrested. I'm a man without morals!*

"…you haven't explained why you have brought us here for Gunt. What's so special about him? After all, there are plenty of rich men in London!"

He's tricking me! thought Denton. *He wants me to reveal what I know about the bomb! He wants me to confess in front of everyone! What's so important about Gunt? Of all the people in the room, you know the most Colin! Oh shit! I knew I wouldn't be able to get away with this. I knew that I couldn't mention Gunt without him realising what I'd done!* His mind raced further. *What do I say?*

"You're right," admitted Denton. "But there is a reason why we're after him," he glanced at Colin nervously before saying the next part. "All this rests on one key thing. Being able to blackmail Gunt."

"Blackmail!" gasped Colin. "I'm a respectable solicitor! I can't go around blackmailing prospective clients!

"Neither can we!" added Delia.

Denton paused. This was not the reaction he had been expecting from Colin. It was difficult to understand what he was thinking. *What about your bomb?* he thought. This did not make any sense. He had to think fast.

"Look!" said Denton, without knowing where he was going. "We're all inquisitive people. I know that. I know you want all the answers, but I can't give them to you. I can only give you an opportunity. If we pursue Gunt, my research…" he gulped, *Please do not ask me to clarify what I mean by that*, he thought. "…suggests that we will have a hope of realising our dreams. At worse, nothing happens and we'll return to work after a nice break in the country. OK?"

They grunted.

"Isn't it exciting?" said Billy, for no apparent reason.

There were wholesale frowns across the room. They were clearly unconvinced. He appreciated that he had not revealed a reason why Gunt would want to give them money. They would have to take that part on trust. What they did not know was, Denton knew something else. He looked at Colin. There was no look of discomfort or anger emanating from him. Denton had revealed more than he had wanted to in that conversation. Perhaps he had said too much. Perhaps he had made it obvious he knew about the bomb. Beforehand he had been terrified that Colin would fly off the handle because Denton knew about it. What worried Denton more now was the fact that he had not. Why?

Chapter Thirty Two

Scouting Gunt

The dust mites were disturbed. For many years, they had lived there without interruption. Generations of them had eked out an existence living on that barren land, telling stories, passed down through the ages. Man and boy had strived and toiled through the good times, and the bad, working hard and with no reward other than to be, just be. But now that time was at an end. Their livelihood - their lives! - taken from them in one foul, unremitting, swoop. Everything gone. *Oh untimely death…*

"That's right Colin, get your wallet out, we're going to need you to pay for all this stuff. Whoa! Look at all that dust coming off it!"

Begrudgingly, Colin opened the wallet he had just fished out of his pocket. He reflected upon how easily they had all forgotten round after round of drinks he had bought them these past months.

"Well, I don't see why," he said. It made no odds. They still stood there, palms open. "What's it for, any way?"

"We're going to need to hire a second car, plus we need money for the walkie-talkies."

Colin tutted. "Fine. Here. It's all I have!" He deposited a wad of notes into Denton's outstretched hands.

"Thank you, Colin, you won't regret it!" said Randall, as he and Denton left the people carrier. With the door shut, Colin drove away, leaving Randall and Denton a lot richer, standing on the main high street.

Randall looked at the six or seven shops now presented to them. It was a quaint sight of an England that Randall did not know still existed. There was a butcher's, a baker's and a home lighting shop. "What's the name of the shop we're looking for?" he asked.

Denton unfolded the crumpled paper from his pocket - further evidence of his extensive pre-trip research. *Did he do any chargeable work the week before we left?* wondered Randall. "Erm, *Mad Louis' house of surveillance equipment.*" said Denton.

"Discreet," observed Randall.

"Yeah," said Denton, placing the paper back in his pocket. "So where is the shop then?"

They looked up and down the road. Every shop had a sign accurately displaying the nature of its contents (they assumed, though why would the signs lie?), with the exception of one. This one, a few shops from the end, had no sign at all. Just a big white gap.

"Maybe that one?"

"Let's try it. If we can't get what we want there, we can probably get it from Woolies anyway."

"Good point."

They entered the unnamed shop. It was dimly lit, a little on the grubby side, and contained absolutely nothing but a counter on the far side. Behind it stood a simple man with too many teeth, and not enough hair follicles. A bald patch at the front was off-set by a greasy jet black ponytail and a single row of short thin hair where the forehead ended and the scalp began. Presumably, they were the 'frontline' that had withstood the attack that saw off their comrades. *Ah, the fallen ones, God bless them.*

Denton and Randall approached cautiously. On closer inspection, it became apparent that the fellow behind the counter had one green eye and one brown eye.

"Are you mad Louis?" asked Randall.

The man nodded as if he were trying to throw his head into the waste paper basket behind the counter.

"Yes, yes! Yes, I am, yes. I be he." He sounded like a pirate on helium.

"Good..." began Denton.

"I am, I am. Mad Louis, yes," he squawked. "But before I confirm my identity, who wants to know?"

"But..." said Denton, confused.

Randall stepped in. There was no time to indulge the mad fool. "We are potential customers, we're after some walkie-talkies and a listening device. Do you have them?"

"Yes, yes, yes, that I do, yes," he confirmed, nodding manically. "But before I confirm I will just check."

"But?" said Denton, still confused.

Mad Louis looked both of them in the eye, perhaps with suspicion, perhaps just to demonstrate that he could. There was an uncomfortable silence before he realised what he had just said he would do. "Right," he said without further prompting. "I will go and check." With that, he left the room.

"And we thought Londoners were odd."

"Eccentricity is a way of life in the countryside - it's their right. Remember, some of these people still think dressing up and chasing a fox sounds like fun."

Mad Louis returned with a shopping basket full of products.

"Right then, I've got these for you. Yes, yes. These will do the job. Ten multi-way walkie-talkies - range of three miles. Headphone attachment extra. Fits right in the ear, just like the CIA. Got these from one of my many classified trips to America to see my mole in the CIA. Since they are classified, I obviously can't tell you anything about them. Or my mole. Not my mole, no."

"But..." began Denton, thinking *all we need now is a contact name and an inside leg measure and we'd be able to indict him.* Randall stopped him from going any further.

"They sound great, though we don't need ten. We need, what five, six?" he looked at Denton.

Denton began counting fingers. "Well, there's us two, plus the others, so that's seven? Yeah, seven."

"OK," said Randall, "we'll take seven."

"Seven, ok, seven," said Mad Louis. "They're £75 each, so for seven that would be…"

It was his turn to count fingers. That didn't work out, so he employed a pencil and a piece of paper. That proved insufficient as well, so the calculator made an appearance. Finally, Mad Louis, after consulting his implements in a huddle and reaching a consensus, delivered the verdict.

"That will be £57.50 please."

Denton and Randall looked at each other.

"Are you sure?" asked Randall. It seemed too easy.

"Yes, yes, yes I am!" said Mad Louis. "What are you suggesting? Yes, I'm sure."

Randall handed him £60. "Please, keep the change." He felt it was the least he could do.

"Fine," said Mad Louis, with a hint of aggression, "I will. Yes, yes." He inspected the notes by holding them up to the light - it was obvious he did not know what he was looking for - as demonstrated by his final check on their authenticity where he licked each note. "Look genuine to me," he said, noting the looks of disgust from Randall and Denton.

"Thank God," said Randall. "I would hate for you to have to give me them back."

"Do you have the listening device?" asked Denton.

"Yes, yes, yes," said Mad Louis. "I have it. It's here in my basket, don't ye worry about that, no worry. It be here, it be. Here. Look. Ex FBI. Fits between the legs of an agent, the mike being placed on, maybe the shirt, or maybe stapled to the chest."

"Stapled?" asked Denton, horrified.

"Yes, yes!" said Louis, "in the absence of Velcro, it would be stapled to the skin. Yes, yes, that's right!"

"OK," said Randall, quite keen to leave as quickly as possible. "So how much is that?"

"That is five thousand dollars in America," said Mad Louis.

"Oh," said Denton. "We don't …."

Randall stepped in again. "How much is it here, Mad Louis?"

Mad Louis contemplated the point. He consulted the pencil, the paper and the calculator. They gathered in a big huddle. The hole punch had wanted to join in too, but had (quite rightly) been told that it should not get above its station.

"To you, £7.92 precisely."

"Please take £10," said Randall, almost feeling sorry for the man.

"No!" shouted Mad Louis slamming his hand on the counter top. "I will take £7.92 only. Nothing else. If you do not have £7.92 then I will not take it." He folded his arms and looked away.

Randall and Denton counted their change.

"What have you got?" Randall asked Denton.

Denton counted the coins from his pocket. "£3.42."

"I've got £4.48." He turned to speak to Mad Louis. "We only have £7.90."

"Yes, yes," said Mad Louis. "I will take that. I will. Yes."

Denton and Randall handed over their coppers and took the goods. They thanked Mad Louis before departing. The door shut behind them causing a small bell to ring. Mad Louis looked around, as if an imaginary fly had just whizzed past his nose. He looked at the cash on the counter and considered his depleted stock. A look of realisation crossed his face. He sighed and looked at his feet.

"Damn," suddenly, his voice had changed. It was at a normal pitch with no hint of pirate. He retraced his calculation method, "I divided by ten instead of multiplying by ten. I cannot believe I…Oh dear me, every time! People are going to think I'm right proper bonkers," he concluded. He looked at the door and shook his head again, "B'doink," he said, as if it were a real word.

*****

"I think we just had a life experience," said Denton as they wandered down the road.

"I think you're right," said Randall holding on to their newly acquired goods.

"Right, where do we hire a car from?" asked Denton. Randall stopped. He pointed at the shop in front of them.

"How about here at *'Our hire cars are cheaper than those across the road'*?"

"What's across the road?" asked Denton, "Oh, look, it's an Avis. Let's go there."

"OK," said Randall.

They crossed the road. From the window of the shop they had not gone into, two disgruntled men sighed.

"I was sure they were about to come in," said the first.

"Me too," said the second. "What makes people always go across the road? Do they not believe that we are cheaper than Avis, because you know I've checked like a million times."

"I have no idea," said the first. He hesitated. "Do you think that maybe we're inadvertently advertising Avis with our sign?" he asked tentatively.

The second fumed before slapping the first across the face hard.

"You're right," said the first, nursing a soon to be bruised face. "I deserved that."

*****

Denton and Randall had already broached the subject of their requirements to the nice lady behind the desk. She had given them a response that not only were they unprepared for, but also they could not come to terms with.

"No," said Denton, "I can't come to terms with that."

"Well, I'm sorry but you must," implored the nice lady.

"I won't," said Denton. "There must be something else."

"There isn't," said the nice lady - though she was becoming less nice by the second.

"There must be," said Denton. "You must have more than this! Check again!"

"I don't," said the not so nice lady.

"But that's ridiculous," said Randall.

"Well, it's true," said the not quite nasty lady, but certainly getting there.

"But think of us, we cannot accept this!" pleaded Randall.

"Well you have to!" said the awful lady. "Please feel free to visit the gentlemen across the road if you are not happy, I'm sure they could help you."

The two men across the road, faces pressed against the window nodded and smiled like lap dogs in agreement with that statement.

"We came from across the road to get to here. There was nothing there but a challenge to come here," said Randall momentarily distracted. "Anyway, stop trying to fob us off, we want to see the manager."

"He will just say the same thing as me," said the nasty nasty nasty - (and might I add slightly plump) - lady, her voice raised.

"Fine, fine, fine!!" said Denton. "We'll take it."

Randall shot Denton a look, "you sure?"

"Yes," said Denton. "I can't be bothered with this. Fine, we'll take it."

"Really?" said the fat and (probably) smelly bitch behind the counter.

"Yes," said Denton. "If that is all you have left, we will take it."

"Thank you, gentlemen," said the nice lady, her nice smile returning and those additional pounds and the body odour 'situation' reducing into the background. "Here are your keys. You'll find your brand new car behind the building."

Disgruntled, they signed the documents and walked out back. In the car park was a solitary car.

They stood before it, disgusted with the car and themselves. Instinctively, they felt dirty.

It was a Nissan Micra.

"Look at it! It's not even the same size as a normal car!" said Denton tutting. "Come on, let's get in. I'll drive."

Randall got in. He looked at the floor and grunted. "I was half expecting to see foot holes to help us gain momentum."

Chapter Thirty Three

Walking the dog

"This is never going to work!" commented Randall, with just a note of unnecessary pessimism. The subtext being, *Nothing ever works when you want it to.*

"Trust me!" said Denton. "It will!" *I know, but its worth a try.*

"It won't," said Delia. *No, seriously, it won't.*

"Seriously guys!" said Denton. "It will!" *For the love of God! We could have finished it by now.*

They were stood outside a pet shop in the village. With a certain amount of trepidation, they ventured in, causing a bell to ring.

Inside were various cages and tanks. At the counter stood a man who was perhaps in his fifties, with snow white hair, and half moon glasses on a beaded chain. He was stood, bolt upright, behind a counter. He was reading a broadsheet paper. It was apparent his hearing diminished when utilising vision. He did not seem to notice them enter.

"Good morning," said Denton.

The man looked over the rim of his glasses. He fixed a look on Denton, presumably designed to convey the message that, despite his years, he could still show these kids a thing or two. Or maybe he was just contemplating a really hard sum.

Denton wanted to keep the encounter as brief as possible.

"Do you keep dogs?"

"Yes," he said with precise pronunciation. "I also sell them."

Oh I see, thought Denton, *one of those types. This is going to be hard work.*

"And do you *sell* sausage dogs?"

The man pondered the point. He removed his glasses and placed one of the arms on his crusty tongue. Delia cringed. *Eurgh!* she thought *You've just had your pickled old ear on that!*

"Dachshund?" he said, intrigued. "Yes, I do."

"And may I see one?" asked Denton, after the silence and lack of activity on the man's part became unbearable.

"But of course," he said, disappearing out back. Soon he re-emerged with a comically elongated little pooch.

"Yes," said Denton, briefly looking at Randall and Delia. "That'll do nicely. We'll rent her."

At first, the man nodded, but then his mind caught up with him.

"What?" he blurted with incredulity. "You'll rent her? I'm sorry sir, I am not in the habit of 'doing' loans, 'swapsies' or 'playing for keeps'. You buy, or you leave."

I told you it wouldn't work! thought Randall looking noticeably embarrassed. The little ears on his disproportionately small head went red.

"That's not what I was led to believe…" said Denton, mysteriously.

"What?!" blustered the old man again. "Well, I don't know who would tell you such a thing, but I can assure you, categorically, that I do not engage in such practices. I only deal in purchases, which you are clearly not in the market for. Now good day to you."

Randall turned to leave but Denton grabbed his arm.

"Sorry, Sir, perhaps I should just explain. Do you see this young lady here?" he nodded in the direction of Delia.

"Yes, why? What? What is it?" asked the man impatiently, eyeing Delia suspiciously.

"Well…" said Denton lowering his voice. "You see, she's not entirely right."

"What do you mean?" asked the man, studying Delia, his voice wavering slightly.

Yeah, what do you mean? thought Delia.

"Well, you see, she's sick."

"Sick? How? She looks alright to me," said the man dismissively.

Denton looked at Delia, and then back at the man.

"Look, I don't want us to appear vulnerable and needy. Certainly, we do not want your pity, but my sister here…"

Your sister? thought Delia and Randall at largely one and the same time.

"..she doesn't have long left…"

"Good God!" said the man, a genuine look of sympathy creeping across his crusty face.

"We want to cheer her up with this beautiful dog but honestly if the truth be known she has about two weeks left and after that…well," he said pretending to hold back the tears. "We really could not have it staying around after she's gone. It would just destroy us." He looked away, as if the tears welling up were too much, though in reality it was to hold back the giggles.

The man's face dropped. "Oh my good God that's…"

Bloody good acting, thought Randall

"..awful!" he said in horror. He stared at Delia again. "Now you mention it, she does look unnaturally pasty and painfully thin." He placed a wrinkly hand on her arm. It was uncomfortable for everyone concerned. The man looked at Delia, then Denton, then Delia.

*****

"You're awful!" screamed Delia as they marched out of the shop, a small dog tucked under Denton's arm.

He shrugged. "Told you it would work. Now let's go make this happen."

*****

"Pigeons are strange creatures, aren't they?" said Badger.

"You think?" said Brian, frowning.

"Oh yes!" he said resolutely. "The pigeon is most certainly nothing more than a flying rodent."

"Is that so?" asked Brian.

"Yes, most definitely," said Badger.

A pigeon scuttled past the Hooley people carrier. Brian and Badger were parked up next to a relatively large car park just off the main road. Apart from the several hundred pigeons, it was deserted, but for the odd man walking his dog.

Pretty soon though, even the odd man was gone.

Incarcerated as they were, Brian became thankful for the silence that descended. It was not that he did not appreciate Badger's awkward delivery of mindless trivia or that he did not like Badger - far from it - it was more that Badger was a lot easier to be trapped in a confined space with when he was unconscious.

"Also, did you know that pigeons can't pass wind?"

"Really?" said Brian, feigning interest.

"Yes! If you were to feed them paracetamol they would most definitely explode."

Brian shot Badger an uneasy sideways glance, which Badger seemed oblivious to. He just sat there and pushed the bridge of his glasses a little, careful not to upset the precarious balance of the arms on his crooked ears.

In the distance, a man sat on a bench in a large grey Mac began flapping about as if in the middle of a religious experience.

They both squinted.

"Is that Billy?" asked Brian, glad of the distraction.

Badger squinted so hard he looked like he had just followed through.

"Er, yes, I think it is."

"What on earth is he doing?"

Suddenly, Billy jumped up and started running wildly in circles.

"Quick," said Brian. "get him on the 'walkie-talkie'. He's out of position."

"Billy, come in, Billy! Over," said Badger.

There was no response.

"Billy!" said Badger once more, "You're out of position - report in!"

Still no response from the man who was now flapping about so much it looked like he was doing the Charleston whilst on acid.

"Billy!"

"Aarrgh!" came the response. "Eeee. Eeeee."

The sound was so high-pitched that it was enough to make their three collective ears hurt (Badger's other ear being too small to pick up such signals).

"Billy!" said Badger. "That really hurt! What are you doing?"

Billy stopped. "Is it still there?" he enquired, panicking.

Badger and Brian looked at each other. "Is what still there?" asked Badger eventually.

"The wasp! I'm being chased by the mother of all wasps!"

Brian grabbed the 'walkie-talkie' from Badger.

"Is that all? Look just calm down and stay still. It's just intrigued by your ginger hair. It won't sting you, I promise - just stand still."

"Well, actually…" began Badger.

Brian frowned at him and held up a silencing finger, which caused Badger to stop momentarily.

"No, I was just going to…"

Brian took his finger off the 'walkie-talkie' button. "Winston! Seriously!"

"Sorry," said Badger, a little taken aback.

In the distance, Billy started to return to his bench, occasionally flapping his hand around his head.

"Is Billy OK?" came the dulcet tones of Colin from across the airways. "It's just, he's out of position."

"Yes, we know," said Brian. "He's fine now. Where are you?"

"I'm here," said Colin, unhelpfully.

Brian and Badger looked at each other, then they looked out into the park. There was no one there but Billy, pigeons, and the odd man with his dog, who had returned from whatever it was he had left to do. Badger turned in his seat to look in the back of the car (just in case it was a trick question. It wasn't).

"Where?" said Brian once more.

"Here!" said Colin. "By the tree!"

Brian raised his eyebrows.

"I don't wish to sound as if I'm being difficult, but there are a few trees in this park. Would you mind narrowing it down?"

The sound of Colin giggling came across the airwaves.

"Billy - do you see him?" asked Brian, still looking at all the trees.

In the distance, Billy could be seen shuffling in his seat.

"Nope, I don't see him," he replied eventually.

Suddenly, Colin's position was revealed as a wave of neon orange light flooded the car from a tree just to the right of the people carrier. Colin emerged wearing his chino shorts, boating shoes and a hideous bright orange Hawaiian style, short-sleeved shirt, circa 1986.

"Aargh!" squealed Badger and Brian, temporarily blinded. Colin came scampering over to the driver's door, his neck brace bouncing slightly as he did so.

"Any sign of him yet?", enquired Colin.

Billy's voice interrupted them.

"The badger is out of the set. The badger is out of the set. Confirm. Over."

Badger looked confused. Brian and Colin looked over at Billy, and then Badger.

"What is he on about?" asked Colin.

"I have no idea," said Brian. He pressed the button on his walkie-talkie.

"Billy - what are you on about? Badger is right here."

"No!" exclaimed Billy, then his voice went quieter. "The other badger!"

"What?" Brian picked up the binoculars, and saw Gunt walking past Billy with a small yet proud Shitzu. "Oh, right! You mean Gunt."

"But where is Delia?" asked Colin, with a certain amount of concern. He grabbed the walkie-talkie. "Delia! Where are you? The madras is on the rice. The madras is on the rice!"

Brian and Badger turned to Colin.

"Seriously," said Badger. "We have got to sort out these code-words."

There was no response from Delia.

"Delia!", said Colin once more.

Nothing.

"He's getting away!" said Badger with an unnecessary amount of drama.

Then, from the distance, they could just make out the long legged figure of Delia dragging along a poor and unsuspecting dachshund.

"What on earth is that?" asked Brian.

"It's Delia!" said Colin.

"No!" said Brian. "The thing she's dragging."

"Mmm. Not sure. Looks like a dachshund…" said Colin.

"Little known fact about the dachshund…" began Badger.

"Badger, mate," said Brian calmly. "Now's not the time. OK?"

"Oh, OK," said Badger, a little deflated.

The elderly man under surveillance was now past the bench that Billy was sat on and was walking towards Delia. Delia stopped him before he walked past and engaged him in conversation.

"What are they saying?" said Badger.

"I don't know," said Brian instinctively, even though he wasn't really adding much by admitting that.

"I thought she was supposed to leave her walkie-talkie on so we could hear!" said Colin.

"Maybe she forgot?" said Badger.

The old man and Delia continued to talk. From where they were they could see Delia laughing, occasionally touching the man on the arm in an *oh, you!* type way.

"Good girl," observed Brian. "She's flirting with him!"

*****

Randall and Denton pulled up in their half-car. Randall was still grumbling as he opened the door.

"I just don't see why I'm always the one who has to accompany you in it, that's all."

"Oh, will you stop whinging about it!" said Denton.

"But it's so embarrassing. People just stare. And then there's my safety…"

"Your safety?"

"Yes, every time we go around a corner, or if you brake too hard, I'm terrified that we're just going to tip up. How embarrassing would that be? Can you imagine my family's shame if I died in one of these things? How could they look the neighbours in the eye ever again?"

"Give it a rest," said Denton, as they both wandered over to the people carrier. "You're like a little girl."

Randall sulked.

"Did we miss much?" asked Denton, turning to the others.

"Not really," said Colin. "Delia has been talking to him for a while now."

Randall turned to Colin, and gently smacked him on the arm.

"We were listening to the walkie-talkie on the way over. Madras on the rice? What is the matter with you?"

"Sorry!" said Colin. "I got a little excited. It was the first thing that came to me."

"Where's Billy?" asked Denton.

"He's over on that bench," said Brian.

"Yeah, why is Billy wearing a heavy Macintosh in this weather?" asked Colin. "He didn't come in the car with us, so we couldn't ask him."

"Oh, that," said Denton. "That's because I told him to look inconspicuous. He really does not have any idea, does he?"

Delia and Gunt were still talking.

"So what's she talking about?" said Colin. "I couldn't talk to a stranger for that length of time."

"Badger could," lamented Brian, reflecting on his earlier conversations with Winston.

"Ah, well," said Denton, oblivious to Brian's comment. "You see, her brief was to engage him in conversation with a view to going out for a coffee or something with him."

"Yes, I know that part," said Colin. "But how has she done it?"

"Well, we told her to admire his dog and tell him it reminded her of a dog that she once owned. Then we told her to get a bit teary, that way he'd feel like he couldn't just walk off."

"Oh, I see," said Colin.

"Then we told her to start flirting with him like mad," said Randall.

"How do you flirt with a seventy five year old?" enquired Colin, with interest.

"Ah, well, that's easy," said Denton, proud of what was about to be said.

"Yeah, we told her to let it slip that her husband died recently," added Randall.

Brian frowned, "I don't follow."

"Well, when you tell someone - anyone - that someone close to you has died, they always say *that's awful, how old was he?* Guaranteed."

It was Colin's turn to frown. "And how old was Delia's husband?"

"Sixty four."

Colin frowned further still. He looked across at Delia, who was showing something to Gunt. "Is she showing him a picture of her dead husband?"

"Er, yes," said Denton, a little embarrassed now on account of Colin's obvious disapproval.

"And who is that a picture of, exactly?" he ventured further, half knowing the answer.

"Erm, well, you actually," said Randall, with the smallest hint of shame. "We obtained a colour picture from the Firm's publicity shots before we left London.

"But..." objected Colin.

"Don't worry," said Randall. "He won't recognise you. Your publicity photos contain no yellow tinted eye lids, no neck brace and a very straight nose."

"And then what does she say?" said Brian while Colin stood dumbstruck.

"She's to play that one by ear," said Denton.

"But if he looks like he's going with it, she's to say *you remind me of him,* then look away briefly before giving him her best smouldering look."

"Nice," said Brian.

"Then, just to be sure, she's to flash a bit of cleavage by bending over and picking up the dog, before saying *well, it was nice to meet you - perhaps we'll meet up again soon?*"

They looked across at Delia. She was reaching for the dog. They were still chatting, and then Gunt passed her something. They parted company with Gunt briefly looking back at Delia before shaking his head in obvious disbelief. A smile cracked his face.

Denton smiled as well. "The fish is on the line. The fish is on the line."

"Really!" said Badger impatiently. "Can we please just sort out these code-words?"

In the distance, Billy jumped up and began an impromptu break dancing session in between the departing Delia and Gunt. He flapped his arms around as he screamed in the walkie-talkie: "Not my face! Not my face!"

Chapter Thirty Four

Dinner with Gunt

"Denton, I look ridiculous."

"No, you don't, you look lovely," said Denton, as he leaned against the back of the sofa, looking Delia up and down, generally admiring the view as he casually munched away on an apple. He was reminded of the weekend away and Freud's. He dismissed the thoughts as quickly as possible. Even so, he would freely admit that Delia looked pretty amazing in that red slinky cocktail dress. A little off the shoulder number, apparently from Delia's own collection, though he sincerely doubted whether she had ever been brave enough to wear it in public.

"Do you really think that?" asked Delia, as casually as she could make it sound. She was too busy brushing herself down to notice Brian busily adjusting her outfit with a mouthful of pins.

The three of them were stood in the master bedroom - it being the only room with a full length mirror. Delia stood on a small stool while Brian weaved around her, fitting the dress to emphasise her shapely body.

"Seriously, red really suits you," said Denton.

"Yes, but…" she twisted her upper body to get a better look at her derriere. "Is this recording device not going to make my bum look massive?"

Denton sighed. "Delia, we've already discussed this. The bulkiest bit of the recording device is between your legs. You know it is, you put it there."

Apparently not appeased, Delia continued. "I know it is, but still…", she twisted awkwardly again. "Are you sure my bum doesn't look bigger because of it?"

Denton rolled his eyes and shook his head.

"Mbmhn bmmffnmfh fmpnpphhh mppphmnp," said Brian.

Denton stopped chewing and pointed at Brian. "Exactly," he said.

Delia stopped twisting and looked at Brian before looking at Denton. "I'm sorry, what did he say?"

"You really didn't hear what he said?" asked Denton.

"No, I didn't hear any of it. What did he say?"

"He said that any woman who saw that dress in a shop window would dream that they looked like you do when they were wearing it."

Delia beamed at Brian. "Oh! Thank you Brian, that's so lovely. I think that's the nicest thing that anyone has ever said. Now, not wishing to ruin the moment, but I really have to go to the toilet."

"OK, but you'll have to use the second bathroom, Billy's in the main one."

Delia looked at Denton.

"Denton, that was at least an hour ago. I think he'll have finished by now."

"Oh, he'll be there, believe me," said Denton.

Cautiously, she stepped down from the stool, much to Brian's obvious chagrin. He pulled the remaining pins from his mouth as she closed the door behind her.

"I didn't say that," he said frowning. "I said that with an ass that big, who could tell if it was any bigger anyway."

Denton smirked. "I know but I wasn't about to tell her that now, was I?"

Brian smiled.

Denton turned to the en-suite toilet door.

"Right, Randall, you can come back in the room now, the recording device is out of the room."

The door opened and Randall returned to the room.

"Excellent," said Randall. "So if it goes wrong now, it's not my fault, right?"

Denton and Brian left the room and returned to the living room where Colin and Winston were sat around some electrical equipment. Randall followed them to the door and then, on noticing the electrical instruments, made a swift detour to the kitchen.

"Have you tested it yet?" asked Denton.

"No, not yet. Did you leave the device switched on when you gave it to Delia?" asked Colin.

"Of course!"

Colin pressed a couple of switches, and suddenly through one of the speakers…

"Knock knock, are you in there Billy?"

"Mpmmmh mppmhh," came the muffled response.

"That's no good, we can't hear the other person," said Brian.

"Well get a move on!" came Delia's disembodied voice.

"Hang on," said Colin, "it's probably because he's on the other side of the door."

Suddenly, there was the sound of water running, which came crackling across the airwaves.

"Sorry about that," said a voice distinctly the same as Billy's. "It's all clear now."

"That's ok," said Delia. There was a noise like a bolt being dragged across a grate and a heavy rustling sound like a beaver wrestling a vole on a log. Then came the gushing sound of water hitting water and a moment of tuneless humming before…

"Oh, you bastards!" screamed Delia. "This thing is still on, isn't it?!"

Embarrassed looks were exchanged around the room. "Successful test, I'd say," said Colin. The others nodded as he quickly turned off the machine.

*****

It was the weekend. Gunt had phoned, as he said he would, but instead of inviting Delia for a coffee, he had suggested a dinner date. Of course, Delia had reservations about this, as well as the expected comment that she had nothing to wear (at which point she was reminded of the fifteen cases she had insisted were transported up with her). Delia was driven to the restaurant in the people carrier. Someone had suggested it would be safer to use the Micra, given the fact it was rented, but for some reason Delia was not keen. And of course for "not keen", read "threatening various elaborate acts of violence". By the time she arrived, Gunt was already waiting. He stood up as she approached the table.

"Delia, you look delightful," he said as a waiter pulled out her chair.

"Thank you. You don't look so bad yourself!" she lied.

Gunt smiled. "I took the liberty of ordering wine already - I hope you don't mind?"

"Not at all," said Delia. "I like a man who knows his own mind."

*****

"I like a man who knows his own mind?" mocked Randall back at the Hooley holiday home.

"Leave her alone!" said Brian playfully. "This is not going to be an easy night for her."

"I know," said Randall, "but she should at least try to stick to the script." He held a clipboard with a list of pre-determined questions on it, ready with his biro to scribble down the answers.

*****

The first course arrived. Gunt had ordered an expensive *fois gras*. Delia followed suit. She laughed at a joke he had just made.

"Oh, that has to be one of the funniest things I have heard in a long while," she lied. There was a natural lull in the conversation, the kind that demands one party to ask a question to get it going again. "So tell me," she said, "what do you do?"

Gunt looked about her quizzically. "I do not intend to sound arrogant, but do you really not know already?"

She feigned surprise. "No, should I?"

He looked a little flustered, and almost relieved. "Well, I'm a very successful business man. I'm quite well known."

"I see," said Delia. "Well, as you can probably tell, I'm not from around here."

"What brings you here then?" asked Gunt.

*****

"Follow the script," Denton found himself saying.

*****

"Well, after my husband died, I just felt I had to get out, and, oh I'm sorry," she said, crocodile tears on standby. "I really don't like to talk about this, could we change the subject?"

"Oh, my dear, I'm sorry, of course," said Gunt.

*****

"Textbook," said Denton smiling. The others nodded.

*****

"Anyway, tell me," said Delia, "I'm dying to know. Is there a Mrs Gunt?" She raised one eyebrow seductively.

"No, there isn't," said Gunt. "There never has been." He looked quite fragile as he said it.

"Really?" she said. "I find that hard to believe." She kept his gaze. Gunt fidgeted. He smiled.

"Well, erm, that's very kind of you to say so."

*****

The main course followed soon after. Gunt had ordered pheasant. Delia, feeling less adventurous, had settled for Scottish salmon.

"So, do you live close by?" asked Delia.

*****

Randall scratched off another question from the board.

*****

"Yes, very close. You must visit."

"I would love to," said Delia raising a solitary eyebrow again.

"In fact, what are you doing on Tuesday?"

"Absolutely nothing," she said.

"Well, I would be delighted if you would attend one of my little parties."

"A party?"

"Yes, I have them on a regular basis for select local people. My house is just up the road, on the hill. You can't miss it. Bloody great big thing. Only thing up there," he chortled. Delia laughed out of politeness.

*****

There was cheering back at the Hooley home. "We have an invite to his house!"

*****

The sweet followed. Delia declined, claiming she was dieting, which sparked a wave of compliments. Gunt helped himself to a crème caramel.

*****

"That wasn't in the script, she could have had a dessert if she wanted one," said Billy.

"A typical female position, I'm afraid Billy," said Colin. "They make the comment that they are too fat so that you will tell them that they are not. It does not mean that they believe that they are. It also does not mean that you do not think they are."

"Oh, I see," said Billy, enlightened.

*****

"So tell me more about you," said Delia.

"Well, what else is there to say?" said Gunt. "You must have asked me every conceivable question during dinner, and I feel like I do not know a thing about you."

"Oh well, I'm afraid that's a lady's prerogative," said Delia, no doubt batting her eye lashes. "Tell me where and when you were born."

"Well, I was born in Pickering, North Yorkshire on 22 October 1927."

"Really?" said Delia. "Me too!" she lied.

"You look good for your age," joked Gunt. "What year were you born?"

"Oh, my goodness!" said Delia, pretending to be cross. "A lady also does not reveal her actual age!"

"Of course," said Gunt. "Please forgive me."

"I'm sure I can find a way…" said Delia.

*****

Coffee came and went. Soon it was way past everyone's bedtime.

"Perhaps you might like to visit my home tonight?" asked Gunt. Instead of sounding like a sleazy and inappropriate comment, Delia got the distinct impression that the man was asking out of sheer loneliness.

"Well, I'm afraid it's late. And of course, a lady never visits a gentlemen's house after a first date."

"Of course," said Gunt, remembering himself. "Please forgive me."

"Just this once," she said, offering her hand. He placed a kiss upon it.

"Until Tuesday," he said longingly as she departed.

"Until Tuesday," she agreed.

*****

As the taxi pulled away, she slumped into her chair.

"That had to be the hardest thing I ever did," she said, knowing the microphone would pick her comments up. "So did I make a convincing Bonnie Belcher tonight?" She smiled with self-satisfaction. All that was left to do was reel the fish in, and hope there was a big fat cheque stuck to it.

Chapter Thirty Five

Bread Roll Play

"Do you want some?" asked Randall, with menace, to a poor, unsuspecting Japanese businessman. Clearly not familiar with the English language, he was at an obvious loss as to what to say. He did, however, make a grab for the keys in his pocket, just in case things 'got ugly'. "Well, do you?" Randall asked again.

Denton appeared.

"Leave it, Randall, it's not worth it," he said, firmly grabbing Randall with his spare hand.

"Really?" asked Randall, the tone in his voice softening. He turned his head towards Denton, body still facing the Japanese businessman, just in case.

"Yeah," confirmed Denton. "If they don't want any canapés, you don't have to force them to have some."

"Oh," said Randall, surprised. "But I thought, you know, since we're on commission and all."

They were stood, dressed in smart white uniforms, each holding a plate of delicate savoury pastries with a white gloved hand. The Japanese businessman scurried away quickly whilst Randall was distracted.

"Yes, but it's not on the basis of the number of snacks we offload. Anyway, what does that matter? Remember, we're here to do more than waiter service."

Randall winked knowingly, but resisted the temptation to make reference to the fact they were expected to serve wine as well. It would have added nothing to the conversation.

They stood under the main staircase at *'Chateau Gunt'* surrounded by everyone from Z list celebrities to foreign dignitaries, and pretty much everything in between. In amongst the throng of people were Denton and Randall. Not far from them were Billy and Brian, similarly dressed like penguins in camouflage gear. Somewhere amongst them was Delia, wearing a new dress this time (though she had been reminded of how ridiculous the 'need' was, considering the mountains of cases she had transported up), pretending not to know them. Colin was sulking in the kitchen, pretending to wait for more delights to be baked, but instead still annoyed that he had had to foot the bill for Delia's latest excursion to the boutiques of the Lakes (being Colin who had reminded and reminded and reminded Delia of her excess baggage). All of them had decided early on that Badger should sit this one out for 'health and safety reasons'.

It had not been easy to gain access in the manner they had. The idea that

Delia should go alone had been mooted, but ultimately dismissed. How could Delia learn anything at an event where she would be observed intently by the other guests? They had concluded that the only people who could walk freely without suspicion at these kind of 'do's' were the waiters. From there, the flawless plan was born.

Of course, the execution of a plan like that was less than flawless. How the hell do you rock up pretending to be waiters at these kind of things? Surely someone would catch you out? Surely?

Colin appeared. There was still a slight look of annoyance between those yellow tinted eyelids and crooked nose.

"You alright?" asked Denton.

"Chef sent me out." He was carrying a full tray of edibles. "Don't let him catch you without a full tray. He'll go mad."

"Really?" asked Randall. "Well, he should try coming out here himself to get rid of these things - no one is buying."

"Too busy chatting and drinking," commented Denton. They nodded in agreement.

"We're so unappreciated," said Colin. "It's so depressing when you've no authority in your position."

Both Randall and Denton resisted the temptation to let Colin know that he had never had any authority at the Firm either.

"I don't know though," said Denton. "Brian seems to be enjoying himself."

Not too far in front of them Brian was twirling around guests, plate held daintily aloft, spinning it down whenever a guest expressed an interest in his goods. "Entrée, canapé, *amuse bouche*?" he asked with genuine interest.

"There is something definitely not right about that boy," said Colin shaking his head.

"Come on, let's disperse so we don't attract unnecessary attention," said Denton. "After all, we told Mr Gunt we were here to work hard."

*****

On Monday night, Delia had telephoned Gunt. Nothing too fancy or suspicious, just a quick call to say thank you once again for a 'splendiferous' evening (yes, it is a word. No, no one actually uses it in real life), and to express excitement at the prospect of attending the party. Delia stated, not enquired, in order to bring up the topic of waiters by saying that she had not been to a party with outside catering in a long time. "Test the water," they had told her. "Test the water delicately without arousing suspicion."

Gunt had played straight into her hands by confirming that there would be waiters.

"Who do you use?" asked Delia.

"Oh, erm, do you know, I don't know," said Gunt. "Anyway, I can't wait to see you again. I had such a lovely time, it was quite refreshing to spend an evening with someone like you."

*****

Delia had made the phone call from the main bedroom whilst the others listened to the conversation in its entirety from a second unit with a loud speaker in the living room. They had ensured the mute button worked on no less than three trial runs.

"Bring the conversation back round," shouted Billy. "Bring it back round!"

*****

"Really?" said Delia, secretly flattered. Well, not that secretly. "Don't you just say the nicest things? Do you really mean that?"

"Oh yes, I do, absolutely!" replied Gunt. Delia smiled. No one had ever said anything as nice as that before.

*****

"You're losing the opportunity!" screamed the masses in the living room. It was as if they were watching a football match.

"Get on with it!"

"Don't mess it up!!"

*****

"Well, that is kind," said Delia. Then she remembered herself. "I hope your waiters are as nice."

"I don't!" said Gunt. "I don't want you to disappear at the end of the evening with one of them!"

*****

"Ironic he should say that," noted Randall.

The others nodded.

*****

"Well, if they're anything like the waiters we used, you will have no problem on that front!" said Delia.

*****

"Oh, genius!" cried Denton, genuinely impressed.

*****

There was a pause. "Really?" enquired Gunt. "Who were they then?" His interest had been piqued.

*****

There was a small round of applause from the living room. It was well deserved.

*****

"Oh, I forget," lied Delia. "I think we were told about them from a friend, I could find out their number if you are interested?"

There was another pause. And then finally, with heart breaking predictably. "No, do not trouble yourself my dear, I don't want to send you the wrong signals," he chortled. Delia was not laughing. "I am sure I can trust you with a lot of fairly good looking students from Germany. What would you think of me if I couldn't?"

"Well," said Delia biting her tongue. "Quite!" *Arsehole, wanker, fucking great big…loony…with a stupid fucking…aaarrrggh!!!!!* she screamed in her head.

*****

There was a sigh and general stamping of feet in the living room, much akin to that time in Italy when Chris Waddle thought he was playing rugby.

*****

Holding a tray of savoury pastries aloft, Denton stood motionless for a moment. At first, he did not know whether it was a day dream or whether it was real. *The girl from the bar. Easter was here!* He was not sure if she had seen him but then it became clear she had. She was talking to someone and kept looking out of the corner of her eye at Denton. He was convinced that she had smiled at him on at least two, no wait, three occasions. The conversation had obviously petered out. She moved away from her former 'conversationee' and made straight to Denton.

"Oh, sweet Mary and Jesus in his bed," whispered Denton, a tad unprepared for the whole event.

She looked amazing in a little gold and burnt sienna Jane Norman number. It was the most perfect vision he had ever seen of a women. Her blonde hair straightened, probably painstakingly. Her eyes radiant, mascara neatly applied, emphasising their natural beauty - emeralds lulling him into submission. Her figure, a picture of womanhood arousing every sense he had, and some that he had not even been aware of previously. As she approached, she smiled - a smile that broke him in two. It was a smile that seemed as if she had kept it in all these years just for him. A smile that conveyed warmth, understanding, kindness and undeniable sexuality of proportions he probably was not even ready for, but he was prepared to take his chances on that front.

"At last a friendly face - it's Denton, right?" she beamed as she approached.

"Yes," croaked Denton, barely able to co-ordinate his vocal chords.

"Hi, it's Easter - you remember, we met at the bar?"

"Yes," spluttered Denton again. *Stay cool!* he begged himself *Stay calm and cool! Please for the love of God!*

"Have I disturbed you at a bad time?" she said, her enthusiasm to speak to him waning fast. It was obvious he had no interest in her.

"No," he blurted. *Get a grip man!!* "No, not at all - just a bit embarrassed, that's all."

"Embarrassed?" said Easter. "What on earth for?"

Because you are the single most beautiful creature on the planet and I'm dressed like a nun in a snow storm?

"Because... because..." he mumbled. She looked inquisitively at him. "Because, you are..." She tilted her head to one side. He bit his tongue, or the bullet, one or the other. "...are the single most stunning vision of natural beauty I have ever been blessed to witness, and I am finding it hard to form coherent sentences..."

Oh God! said a voice inside his head *Tell me I did not just say that out loud.* Denton's brain appreciated the enormity of what he had just said, and in order to avoid (or maybe just dilute) the embarrassing silence that was sure to follow, replayed clips of how he had ended up in this situation in the first place.

*****

"I tried!" protested Delia. "I tried."

"It wasn't your fault," said Brian, trying to be of some comfort.

Randall frowned. "Who's was it then?" he enquired, arms folded defensively, head shaking as he asked. Brian tutted dismissively at him.

"I don't mean to sound harsh," ventured Denton, "but if we don't all gain access to the house, then the game is over. We're not playing the long game here. If we are going to do this in the limited number of days remaining, we have to be there at that party."

Colin disagreed. "Well, what if only Delia can get in. That's not so bad, is it?"

Denton shook his head. "No Colin, it is. Delia is going to be a guest. Generally, guests get noticed if they just wander aimlessly around someone else's party."

"But, why?" asked Billy, tending to agree with Colin. "Delia could just make out she was drunk and forgot which room she had just come out of. She could find what we're looking for all on her own!"

Denton shook his head again. Maybe he was trying to dislodge a nit. "Look, you don't seem to understand at all. The point of the exercise is not for Delia - or any of us - to commit a felony there and then."

"Really?" asked Randall.

"Yes," said Denton - still shaking his head (which was confusing in itself). "The point is simply this - reconnaissance. We are going in to find out what is there."

"But…" said Colin, obviously confused.

"Look!" said Denton. "None of us - to the best of my knowledge - are professional criminals. If we are going to break and enter, we need to know the lay of the land. We cannot 'break in' at a party. None of us have the requisite experience, or, frankly, the balls, to just attend a party, and potentially rob the guy. We can only do it when we're on our own and in total silence. We cannot be disturbed. We need to know where the stuff is, how we get it, and when we can get it without him being there. Agreed?"

They all considered the point. They nodded.

"And we all agreed that Delia, on her own - a newcomer - cannot go mooching around without risking Gunt becoming suspicious and blowing her cover altogether?"

They all considered the point. They nodded.

"And so, you must all agree that if Delia did lose her cover, then we have no plan 'B' at all. The only plan 'B' we have relies upon the fact that Delia has Gunt's ear."

They all considered the point. They nodded.

"Right then," he said, breathing a sigh of relief. "Then we cannot do this until we are in the house. It's game over otherwise. Admit it."

They all considered the point. They sighed with disappointed realisation.

*****

Delia sipped more of the exquisite pink champagne on offer. "Really, senator? No, that is a funny story. I had no idea that tales of American legislation creation could be so entertaining." She giggled, girlishly, much to the senator's amusement. *Oh, God help me!*

She looked around and instantly wished she had not.

*****

"Canapé, madam?" asked Brian. The lady shook her head then, when her husband wasn't watching, grabbed two and wolfed them down. "Sir?" asked Brian, distracted by the act he had just witnessed. He saw Delia out of the corner of his eye. He looked up. There was something haunting about her. Something in her eyes - a sorrow he had not seen before. What was it? Longing? Regret? *Don't stare!* he thought. *Don't give the game away. Remember, you're not supposed to know her!*

He wandered over in her general direction. "An entrée, madame?" he enquired of her.

She smiled thinly. "No thank you, I could not stomach anything right now."

Brian saw the hurt in her eye. It was brief and she hid it well, but it was there.

In the distance, Denton stood talking to Easter.

*****

"Oh screw this!" Randall had said. "If we're going down, let's go down with a raging hangover - to the nearest pub!" The sullen silence in Colin's front room had been disturbed. Randall raised a non-existent sword, and led the charge for the door. Denton followed, Billy next. Then Brian.

Colin turned to Delia. "You coming?"

She looked at him. "You know what? I don't think I will."

He was only half listening to her. He felt so alive. He felt so accepted. He was part of a gang! A group. A meeting of like minds. He was respected. He was involved. He was 'it'. *Things are looking up,* he heard himself saying. "I'm coming!!!" he bellowed.

"Good!" someone shouted back. "Don't forget the car keys - you're the designated driver, old timer."

"And pick up your wallet too!"

"Bollocks," he winced as he reached for the keys on the table, and charged out of the door.

*****

Randall returned to the kitchen. Colin was already back there, ready to gather more of the delicacies. He was chatting to the chef.

"You know, I've worked here for seven years now?" he exclaimed.

Randall did not know what to make of the situation he was now witnessing. The chef was sat on a stool with a short glass in one hand and a bottle of expensive whiskey in the other.

"Seven years, I've given this man! Seven!" It was quite apparent that he had already seen off most of the bottle.

"Really?" said Colin. "You must be able to tell me some stories about him?"

Oh, Colin! You beauty! thought Randall.

"Well, I don't know about that," sighed Chef. "I mean, there is such a thing as loyalty."

Colin sighed. "Well, I should probably get back to it. There are people out there without nibbles."

The chef nodded.

"Although, I don't know how many I can shift. I mean the old man did not help things by spitting his on the floor," said Colin, mischievously.

Chef looked up - suddenly attentive. "He did what?"

"Oh yes," said Colin. "Right on the floor. I had to pick it up."

"Oh, that man!" said Chef, guzzling another slug straight from the bottle. "He would be nothing at these events but for me. Me who looks out for him. Me who reminds him about his house maintenance. He would have been burgled a million times over if it were not for me! How dare he! How dare he!"

Colin frowned, Randall listened. "What do you mean?" said Colin intrigued.

"Well, I mean, all the times I tell him about broken locks and fallen fences."

"Really?" said Colin, giving the man more rope.

"Yes!" said the Chef. "Look! Look at this door, right here." He led Colin to a door at the rear of the house, through the scullery. "Look! Always broken it is. The lock does not work. Not at all. It is permanently unlocked."

"My God!" said Colin, with no genuine concern whatsoever. "So how come he has not been broken into before?"

"I have no idea!" said Chef. "Seriously, anyone could get in. It does not bolt at all. Anyone could get in to the house."

Colin frowned again. "But surely that is not right, there is an alarm?"

Typical solicitor, thought Randall, *always concentrating on the problems.*

"Well, that's right. But then, this alarm is very old. The panel to deactivate it is in the hall, the motion sensor there is very old and not very sensitive. If you walk slowly enough on the left hand side, hugging the wall, then you can get right up to the panel without it going off."

Genius! thought Randall, *you're challenging the man to demonstrate his plan is plausible and he is falling for it!!!*

"Yeah, right!" said Colin.

Chef looked hurt. "No really! It's true. I wouldn't lie."

"Oh really?" said Colin, acting even more mischievously. "Prove it!"

"What?" said Chef, sobering up slightly.

"Prove you can do it."

"I can't!" said Chef. "I can't put the alarm on with a room full of people!"

"Course you can," said Colin.

"I can't," protested Chef. "I can't. I'll get the sack!"

Colin pondered. "No, that's not it," he said confidently. "You won't do it because you can't. You don't know the code, do you. Admit it!"

Chef looked visibly hurt. "I do!"

"No you don't!" said Colin, dismissively.

"I do! I do!"

"You don't. Don't waste my time! I have things to do."

"I do, I do!"

"Oh yeah?"

"Yeah!"

"Well, what is it then?" asked Colin.

Chef hesitated.

"See!" said Colin, turning to Randall to use as a prop. "He doesn't know at all. Just a load of big talk!"

"It's 1234!" blurted Chef. He clamped a hand across his face as soon as he had said it. "I should not have said! I should not have said! Please do not tell anyone!! Please!" He gulped down two or maybe even three slugs of whiskey.

Colin and Randall looked astounded that Colin's plan had even worked. "Of course we won't!" said Colin. "Get the man more whiskey!" he said to Randall. Two more bottles quickly appeared. Chef would have no trouble making them disappear again.

*****

They had been disenchanted and only the prospective of beer (even that of a truly mediocre variety) could offer some solace. As conscripted designated driver, Colin had had them at the pub in no time. This was only because the others had had his right foot pinned to the ground for the entire journey.

"What can I get you all to drink?" asked Randall.

There were general murmurings that five pints of lager would be in order. Randall conveyed this message to the bar. "OK," he said. "I arranged the beer, who's going to pay for it?"

All eyes turned to Colin. He winced, and submitted a piece of plastic. The barmaid smiled, and his account duly shrunk.

"To a shit outcome!" cried Denton as he raised a beer to the sky. They cheered.

"So near, yet so far," said Billy, echoing the sentiment. They cheered.

"To a dream lost!" said Randall. They cheered.

"To the fading opportunity of recouping the money I wasted!" said Colin. They sneered. *Tight fisted old…*

"To a return to dreary life!" said Brian. They cheered once more.

Randall became a bit careless and stumbled back.

"Aeie! Guten tag, meine shaftengelister!" (or something like that) screamed a blonde fellow.

"Sorry!" said Randall.

"Zat iz fine," zed ze gemannen.

A thought struck Denton. "Are you, by any chance…" he sighed deeply, "…German?"

"Ya begutten ve are all German. All zeven of us are ze Germanbeschitzmal."

Denton looked at the others and smiled an even larger smile. "And…by any chance…", his amused smile was almost causing his face to burst at the seams, "…are you also waiters by profession?"

"Ya!" cried another geblonden, "Ve are all vaiters veschamalenbine und ve are all vorking in dis tuun as de vaiters if you vould like to hire us, maybe, gebingendingen, mmm?"

Denton smiled. The rest of them had caught up with his thinking. They also smiled.

"We'll get to that," he said. "But in the meantime, are you…by any chance…interested in a challenge to a drinking game?"

The seven of them looked at each other, then back at the five men in front of them, then the seven of them again.

"Vell, fur surr. Ve love ze drinking wid ze bubbles und ze churning of ze stumuch, ya gehailer-hailer."

They smirked, perhaps in the same way their football team smirked at the start of that game in Autumn 2001.

*****

It was Tuesday. Delia was slightly annoyed. Despite the fact that it was after eleven in the morning, it had only been three hours ago that she had managed to nod off, having been woken up at 4am by a bunch of mindless drunken imbeciles. Her mobile was ringing. She answered.

"What?" she barked.

"Hi," said the voice. "It's me." She looked at the display, it was Gunt.

"Hi," she said, her tone softening. "What's wrong?"

"It's my waiters for tonight," he sounded distressed.

"Oh," she said, mildly intrigued.

"Yes, it's the strangest thing. All of seven of them have called in sick. Food poisoning or something. What am I going to do?"

"Well…" said Delia.

Chapter Thirty Six

Break in

It seemed to Denton that the idea of breaking and entering into someone else's property, even if it was to save their own souls, had the strangest effect on some people, which manifested itself in their choice of attire.

Randall, as one might expect from his brief foray into the territorial army, obviously felt that the part required something from the Schwarzenegger/Stallone wardrobe. He had pitched up wearing fatigues, which presumably had been given early parole from the moth prison they had once inhabited. At least, Denton hoped that was the case, briefly shuddering at the idea that Randall regularly wore this get up. Denton did, however, feel that Randall had gone a little too far though. Certainly, the war paint was a nice touch but Denton thought, as they all did, that the bandanna was a bit much. It seemed that it was only Randall who couldn't be convinced this situation was not akin to Vietnam.

Brian, as you'd expect for a security guard, was reliably dressed in black, which was good, and it would have been perfect if it wasn't obvious from further inspection that he was, in fact, wearing a silk kimono. Even this would have been acceptable if it wasn't for the large, white dragon symbol on his chest and back. This let him down. Well, that and the sandals.

Next to Brian stood Colin. The old Hooley.

It had become clear to all of them now that Colin had allowed the whole episode to play on his mind too much. The absolute terror that he must have been experiencing at the time of dressing had evidently caused him to experience temporary, perhaps even permanent, paralysis of the common sense part of his brain. This was the only explanation to account for the fact that he had arrived in a pair of khaki corduroys and a bottle green, chunky knit sweater. Even his grey splashed, wiry haired mop seemed disturbingly at odds with its usual self.

At least Tapman was reliable. He had definitely dressed for the occasion having chosen to wear a black jumper, black trainers and black loose fitting jogging bottoms - presumably for easy access should nature call.

As for Badger, it was difficult to tell what clothes he had on since he had gone to a lot of trouble with camouflage. He had covered himself entirely in leaves and branches, possibly having raided the shrubbery outside Colin's cottage on the way over. But you had to hand it to him, even at a time like this, when danger was breathing down their necks like a supervising partner eyeing a blonde trainee's cleavage at an appraisal meeting, when a lifetime in jail was becoming more a probability than a possibility, Badger was cool…Badger was calm…Badger was ice cold…in fact…on closer inspection…Badger was snoring…

"Badger! Wake up!" snapped Denton. *Honestly,* he thought. They all glanced quickly at the startled Winston, and then looked back at the house.

Not one of them has my own brand of sartorial elegance, thought Denton, scoffing in his head at his colleagues and soon to be cellmates. *All black is the way forward. Black trainers, black trousers, black jacket, black beanie. As smooth as Bond, as cool as Shaft, as prepared as Ethelred.*

And so they crouched there. Six men with a mission. Six brave souls willing to risk all for their dreams. Six heroes ready to do what was necessary, to lead by example for their children's sakes. Six blokes hiding in a rockery like a bunch of wankers.

"So, are you ready, guys?" asked Denton, not sure of the answer himself. There was a murmur of agreement. "OK, sound off…"

"Is that really necessary?" asked Colin. "I mean you can see that we're all here."

"Yes, it is!" said Denton, despite the fact that he knew it probably was a bit of overkill. Still, he was nervous, and it delayed the inevitable for a while. "Right, Rumpole."

"Yes," said Randall.

"Flower."

"Yes," said Brian.

"Stopcock."

"Yes," said Billy, slightly humiliated.

"Egon."

"Yes," said Colin, "Even though I still have no idea who that is."

"Back chat not necessary, thank you," said Denton with all the humour of a Colonel Major.

"Zebedee," said Denton.

There was no response. "Badger, wake up!", he bellowed. Badger stirred, which was good enough. "Rat? You there?"

"…"

"Rat…you hear me?" Denton said, tapping his ear. They all looked at each other, slightly concerned at the mutual thought that maybe Rat had been captured…well, all of them, except…

"Badger! For the love of God, will you wake up!"

"Rat!! You there?" asked Denton, with a certain amount of desperation in his voice. *Oh God! What if Gunt was at home after all, spotted the van, called the police and now she's been arrested?*

"…"

Well, that's it then.

"…"

Game over.

"…you call me Rat just one more time, and I'm going to drive this people carrier straight through the fence and over your fucking feeble little bodies."

She was still there.

"Sorry, but it's important that we all have a call sign, including you!" snapped Denton, perhaps as a reaction to the terror she had just put them all through.

"So, why couldn't I have one like, Princess, or Fairy, or Angel, you know, something pretty like that."

"She's got a point," said Colin. "You could have given her a nicer name."

"Rat is less gender specific though," said Randall, trying to explain. "Makes it harder for anyone who is listening with surveillance devices to establish the exact make up of the group."

Denton turned a nasty shade of purple. "Do we really have time for this now? Do we?" he barked with obvious annoyance. "I mean, do you not all recognise that the time to raise these kind of queries was prior to the event? Hmmm? Or would you now like to conduct a mother's meeting in the woods to establish which tag names you all think would flatter your looks and compliment your star signs!!!!"

There was silence.

"OK, right then. That's better," said Denton, noticeably calmer. "Now, let's just stay frosty and alert."

"You're damned right. It's freezing in here. This people carrier got a heater?" said Delia. I mean Rat. God, I hope no one overheard that.

Denton raised his eyebrows. Randall moved up to Denton as they moved out. "Denton," Denton frowned, "I mean, Petrocelli, a little late to be raising a practical question at this late stage I know, but did anyone check to see if Gunt had guard dogs - in addition to the Shitzu?"

Denton paused. "Rumpole, the answer to that question would be 'sort of'."

"And by 'sort of', you mean…"

"No."

"No," said Randall, needlessly repeating the answer, "OK. Glad I asked."

Denton and Randall stopped and looked nervously around.

Like trained animals of stealth - squirrels, for example, - they moved across the huge lawn that lay between the road where Delia had parked up, and Gunt's enormous house.

"Obviously, making up for what he lacks elsewhere…" said Denton, with no jealousy at all. None whatsoever.

Randall brought up the rear while Denton took the lead, as Brian, Billy and Colin ran in between. The whole time they moved low, occasionally stopping to make sure they hadn't been spotted. Badger lagged behind the group. The whole camouflage thing now seemed like a ridiculous idea, since he couldn't move very well in it at all, and, for this, he really had to hang his head in shame. Of course, he blamed his tardiness on the outfit, though everyone else suspected that it was on account of the quick naps he was having.

In spite of this, everything seemed to be going to be plan. They were nearing the house and their earlier reconnaissance efforts would hopefully bear fruit if Gunt really wasn't at home.

In fact, it was all going really well, until…

"What was that?" said Denton as he stopped and crouched down. The rest of them stopped where they were and crouched.

"What?" asked Randall.

"What?" said Brian.

"Petrocelli, can we hurry this up? I think I'm getting rheumatism from being out in the damp air for so long…" said Colin

"…yeah, and I really need the loo," added Billy.

"Shush! I can definitely hear something. Zebedee - you're further back - you hear that?"

"Hear what?"

There was a definite noise.

"That noise! Did you not hear anything?"

"Oh. Sorry, I was asleep. I did wonder why you had all stopped though."

They all looked back and saw what looked like a big shrub in a place where no one in their right mind would plant a big shrub. It was a good fifty metres behind them, all on it's own, looking highly conspicuous.

"Petrocelli! You're imagining it! Let's go, we're wasting time," said Randall.

"…yeah, you're right. Just a bit jumpy I gue…" but not quite as jumpy as he inevitably was when he heard the barking start.

"Ruuuuunnnnn…" squealed Denton.

After turning back to spy four huge Alsatians bearing down on them, they all shot up and began to run as quickly as possible towards the wall surrounding the house. Their odds of making it across the wall alive improved when one of the Alsatians stopped to take a leak on a nearby bush.

"Urgh…guys!" whispered a terrified Badger. "There's a dog taking a piss here and…urgh…that just went in my mouth."

As Denton and Randall reached the wall, they couldn't help but glance at each other with a look of disgust tinged with sympathy at Badger's plight. Billy, Brian and Colin soon caught up.

"My bladder's too full for this," said Billy as he vaulted over.

"Ooh, my back's too old for this," muttered Colin on his turn.

"My, my, would you look at those beautiful roses," purred Brian.

Just as the dogs reached the wall, Denton managed to scramble safely over to the other side.

Randall, unfortunately, didn't.

From the safe side, they crept slowly to the side utility door, which, of course, they knew, from their earlier surveillance, would be unlocked and not covered by the alarm sensors.

Once inside, Denton ventured over to the connecting door to the rest of the house.

"OK, now remember, the panel to switch off the alarm is just inside the door. I will go in and de-activate it while you lot stay here. Remember though, touch nothing. Not a thing. Let's make this operation quick and painless." He had no idea where the last part came from. It sounded like the type of thing that James Bond would say in a similar situation if he ever found himself surrounded by morons.

"Yeah, yeah, yeah…you did the whole frosty and alert thing earlier," snapped Randall as he rubbed his leg, still resentful at the fact the dogs had attacked him.

"…and did we listen?" said Denton like a mother scalding a child. "No, instead we got sloppy and just thought we could saunter through the entire thing like a child in a playground, hence the reason you got bitten like a frog carelessly hopping onto a bread board," he concluded, using one strained simile too many. *Definitely something Bond would say,* he thought.

Randall continued to feel resentful. "Yeah, yeah, but it was a big dog," he said like a sulky infant.

"It was a poodle," said Colin.

"Could have had my leg off!" protested Randall.

"Yeah, it wasn't a poodle…" said Billy. "More like his shitzu."

"Hope my tetanus is up to date," said Randall, now seemingly oblivious of the other conversation taking place.

"OK, now, I'll deactivate the alarm system," began Denton, now apparently convinced that he was James Bond. "When I give the all clear, we'll split up, but remember, and I cannot stress this enough, this guy is likely to have CCTV cameras everywhere so stick to the shadows people. We don't know what auxiliary security systems this guy has, and we don't want any of them to go off from spotting us, so stay sharp, look real and play the game. OK?"

The others looked understandably baffled.

"Denton? I mean, Petrocelli?" ventured Billy.

"What is it, Stopcock?" asked Denton, a little miffed by the lost looks on the faces of the others.

"We've already de-activated the alarm and the cameras."

It was Denton's turn to look baffled. He looked around. "How? I was stood by the door the entire time - how could you have turned the alarm off? And how did you turn off the cameras, we weren't told how to do that?!"

"Well, when you were doing your whole 'shadows' speech, me and Randall were stood by this wall…"

"Go on," said Denton impatiently.

"…and then Randall did something and this panel here went from saying 'active' to 'inactive' before changing to 'permanently inoperable, call technician immediately'."

Denton looked at Randall with accusing eyes. How dare he steal his thunder.

"I only looked at it, I swear!" said an embarrassed Randall, no longer able to maintain eye contact with anyone through the shame of his technological ineptitude.

"My God, you're good," said Denton, the look on his face changing from contempt to what seemed to be a genuine sense of awe.

"You stay away from all the electrical stuff in my cottage, you hear?" said Colin.

"But, anyway, why didn't you just say that you'd deactivated it?" asked Denton.

"Well, you seemed to be enjoying yourself so much with your whole little speech. Well, it just didn't seem right somehow," said Billy.

"Right," it was Denton's turn to be embarrassed. "OK, well, in any event, listen out for Zebedee's call. He's on lookout. And Zebedee, this is a pre-emptive wake up. So wake up!"

"Roger that, Petrocelli," said Badger, seconds before passing out again.

"Right, let's split up. Stopcock and I will take the upstairs. Rumpole and Flower take the downstairs portion to the west. Egon, take the east side."

"But, I'll be on my own," protested Colin, lamely.

"Egon. You're a grown man, what's the matter with you? You scared of the dark? Ghosts? What is it?"

"Don't worry, Egon," said Randall trying to reassure the big baby. "If you see anything scary get it with your photon pack."

The others sniggered. Colin just looked confused and annoyed.

"I keep telling you, I don't know what an Egon is. I don't understand the youth of today."

"Can we hurry this up?" asked Billy. "It's just, I need the loo. You know the thing, with the dogs. It really affected me."

"What are we looking for, Denton?" asked Randall, seemingly oblivious to Billy. "You still haven't told us." Despite the fact that he had a very good point, Denton couldn't help but feel a little put out by Randall's particularly pointed question.

"I told you before, we're looking for anything that we can blackmail this guy with."

"Like what?" asked Randall. "We've been here for a week and a half now and we haven't seen anything about this bloke that's evenly remotely suspicious."

"Look, we haven't time for this," said Denton, trying to hide his frustration at what he perceived to be criticism. "You'll just know it when you see it," he said knowing full well they wouldn't. He just hoped he saw it first. "If you see anything suspicious, let me know and I'll come to have a look. That OK with everyone?"

They nodded, though he suspected they were not at all convinced with the merits of this plan. Denton didn't mind so long as they found what he was looking for. Once they had that, everything would fall into place and they would never have to waste another day of their lives again.

"OK," said Denton, trying to maintain a certain sense of order. "Let's go."

Denton and Billy cautiously climbed the stairs as the others made their own way to their designated area. All around them were grand vases, impressive statues, magnificent paintings, luxurious carpets and rugs.

"Look at this place," said Denton agog. "It's amazing!"

"I know," said Billy.

They wandered down a corridor. Denton illuminated the long hall by a discreet torch, careful to ensure the light remained pointed at the floor.

"Look in this room first," he said nodding to a door on their right.

"OK," said Billy pulling up his gloves. He tried the handle.

"No good," he said. "It's locked."

"Good sign," said Denton.

Denton crouched down and peered through the keyhole. It took his eyes a while to adjust. When they had, he could see that there was an upstairs living room behind the door. There was a sofa, a lamp and a TV. More importantly, in the far corner, was a safe.

"Bingo," whispered Denton.

"Really?" asked Billy. "What do you see?"

"The answer to our prayers," said Denton distantly.

"Is it the bathroom?" asked Billy.

Denton returned abruptly from his day dream. "What? No! Do you still need the loo?"

"Well, did you see me go?" asked Billy, now beginning to hop up and down.

"Oh for goodness sake - try down the hall."

As Billy disappeared, Denton grabbed his walkie-talkie.

"OK, anyone find anything yet?"

"Nope," said Randall. "We haven't found a thing, apart from some lovely artwork and a floral display that Flower has become rather attached to."

"Well tell him we're not stealing anything - that will only attract attention."

There was a pause.

"No, you don't understand. He's become attached to it. It has a special kind of cactus or something in it, which has got tangled up in his kimono. I'm trying to get it off him now."

Denton rolled his eyes for his own benefit.

"Oh, for pity's sake. Egon - what about you?"

There was no answer.

"Egon? Where are you?"

"I'm in the kitchen," said Colin mumbling. "I'm not on my own."

"What, did you actually find ghosts?" chortled Randall into everyone's earpiece.

"Not exactly," said Colin distantly. A young girl was stood in front of him making, what appeared to be, a large G & T.

Startled by what Colin had just said, Denton sprung up and ran to the nearest window. Outside maybe fifteen to twenty cars had pulled into Gunt's driveway. Denton's first reaction was to think that the cops had just arrived, and yet on closer inspection it was obvious that these were nothing more sinister than party goers. Gunt was holding an impromptu party.

"Shit," said Denton. "Shit! He's having a party! He's holding a goddamn party!"

"Bollocks!" said Randall. "But he's just had one - why is he having another so soon?"

"I don't know!" said Denton. "Would you like me to ask him?"

"There's no need for sarcasm!" snapped Randall

"Ow!" said Brian.

"Now look what you made me do. I've caught Brian's hand on the cactus."

"Is he loose?"

"Yes," said Randall. "He's fine now."

"Is the display intact?"

"Oh, don't you start!" said Randall. "It's bad enough wandering around with Flower, commenting on every set of bloomin' flowers we see."

"No," said Denton through clenched teeth. "I mean, is it obvious that someone has messed with them!"

"Oh," said Randall. "No, they're fine."

"Then get up here. All of you."

"Why?" snapped Randall. "How are we going to escape from up there?"

"I don't know, but how do you plan to escape when those people are all down there with you?!" retorted Denton.

"OK, OK," said Randall. "We're coming up!"

"Is everything alright?" asked Billy, who had now appeared next to Denton.

"Yes, it's fine. They're all coming up now. I can't understand this though, I mean why is he having a party now? I just. I," Denton looked across at Billy. "are you jigging, Stopcock?"

"Yes," said a slightly embarrassed Billy.

"Do you still need to go? I thought you'd gone?!"

"I couldn't. All the commotion in my ear gave me the stage fright."

"Oh, for the love of God! Well, now really isn't a good time. Just stay where you are while we wait for the others." Denton ventured closer to the stairs and tried to peer down over the banister to the floor below.

"Any one got any bright ideas on how we get out of here?"

"Not me," whispered Randall. "We're not far from the stairs now, but there are people in rooms all around us. I don't want to sound unhelpfully pessimistic, but we're going to get caught."

"OK, Rumpole, that isn't helpful. Remember your legal training, 'problem - solution'."

"Thanks for reminding me of my failed career. We'll be up in a mo."

"Egon, you got any ideas?"

"…"

"Egon? Are you alright?"

"…"

"There must be some way for us to get out of here. What's up here anyway? There seems to be a lot of rooms, paintings, expensive looking vases, hideous huge plant pots, the odd cabinet…Maybe if we…" Denton was suddenly distracted. "Stopcock! Are you peeing in the plant pot?!"

"Don't talk!" retorted Billy concentrating intently, "you'll distract me!"

If Billy felt any kind of embarrassment, then it was certainly matched if not bettered by Colin. Colin found himself in the kitchen surrounded by people that he didn't know, and equally, who didn't know him.

This, to anyone else in his position whose experience of breaking and entering was either based purely on professional experience (so, in other words, none) or else limited to mindless television police shows, would be the part where the hands should go up and the immortal words 'it's a fair cop guv' should spring forth from one's mouth as the right thing to say. And yet not here. Colin's arms did not spring up. They couldn't. For one, he was partially paralysed with fear. For another, he was holding a large G&T and a handful of assorted nibbles.

"Are you enjoying your G&T," said the stranger in front of Colin. "Sorry, how rude of me, I should introduce myself, I'm Rita, although you already knew that."

Colin didn't. There was a pause. Presumably for admiration to follow. It didn't. The woman looked almost annoyed, though on noticing Colin's startled look, presumed it was due to him being overwhelmed.

"Yes, well, anyway, I'm sure we've met before. I never forget a face you know. You were at that thing with Charles and Olivia where it all kicked off and we thought the police would be called but they weren't. All a big stunt, you know. All a big stunt. Anyway, it's Maxwell, isn't it."

Colin took his chance. He nodded with more than a hint of sheer, unadulterated fear in his eyes.

"Anyway, you'll know all about these stunts just like me. After all, we're both in PR, we know the score, you know you know."

"…not really…" squeaked Colin.

The woman took a long stare before laughing out loud.

"Ha ha! How very post-modern of you. Yes, of course you do. Anyway, you'll remember how it all back-fired with Joel and Sylvia standing in the way of that rollocking from Joan. Oh, yes. Anyway, and can I just say, I love what you're wearing. They do say that old man is now 'old school cool'. I love it, just love it."

Colin looked lost.

"My God Maxwell, you've still got it," she said, leaning in close. "Do you remember Toulouse? How could you forget? I still think about that night, how we almost… My God, I love the way you just listen so intently. I love a man who is so sure of himself he doesn't need to say a word. How 'bout it?" She was rubbing her thighs needlessly.

She winked.

Colin put his drink down. "I think I need the toilet." He walked off patting his brow with a hankie.

"OK, darling," she called after him. "I'll see you later."

She turned back to the others. "My God, I love a man who plays hard to get. Just look at those buns of steel. Meow!"

A group of revellers had moved from the hallway, presumably back to the kitchen to re-charge their glasses. Randall and Brian took the opportunity to ascend the stairs to the waiting Denton.

"What now?" whispered Randall.

"We get out of here!" whispered Denton back. "Did you manage to find anything downstairs?"

"No," said Randall. "We didn't have time. You?"

"No," said Denton, beginning to feel the pressure. If they left the house empty handed they might as well admit defeat and leave the Lake District now too. "Look, you two keep guard while I try and get into this room. It's locked."

"So?" said Randall, almost petulantly.

"So, I take that to be a good sign! Plus I think there's a safe in there!"

Randall looked at the door. "It's not locked." He said.

Denton studied the door. "Yes, it is."

"No it isn't."

Denton tried the handle. The door did not budge. "Yes, it is!"

"No, it is not!" said Randall. The whole exchange was becoming painfully circular.

"Look, it won't open!" said Denton. "What makes you say it is not locked."

"Look, the bolt is not across. It is not locked. It must be just stuck." He stood up and heaved his body weight into the door. It opened, causing a loud bang. They all stood silently, terrified the noise would alert someone. After a painfully long pause, there came the sound of cheering.

They all breathed a sigh of relief. "Probably think it was a champagne cork popping," said Randall.

Denton moved into the room. Randall followed. *Here it is!* thought Denton, distracted. *The answer to our prayers!*

"So, where's the safe?" asked Randall, puzzled.

"What?" said Denton, recoiling from his thoughts. "It's there!" He pointed at the safe.

Randall looked at Denton dumbfounded then at the safe. He pulled the handle, releasing the door. "This is your safe?" he said sarcastically. He pulled something out from inside. "How many people do you know who chill white wine in their safe?"

Denton looked inside and suddenly felt stupid. His safe was a refrigerator. "But…"

"Come on, we're wasting our time here," said Randall. "It's time to leave."

"Hang on," implored Denton, grabbing his arm. "Look, just wait while Billy and I search the rest of the floor. Then we'll leave, ok?"

Randall sighed. It was worth a go at least. "OK, but we don't have long."

Outside the room, Billy was waiting. "Come on, Billy," said Denton. "Keep a look-out for us, Randall."

Randall nodded.

"Oh, and keep an eye out for Egon. God knows where he's disappeared to."

They wandered to the far end of the corridor, occasionally checking the rooms around them. Mostly, they found bedrooms and the odd bathroom. There was nothing until they stumbled upon a study.

"Interesting," noted Denton. He studied the walls, which even in the darkness, he could see were covered in walnut panelling - no doubt, very expensive walnut panelling. Everything in the room felt big and heavy. The desk set in the middle of room was huge and probably weighed a ton. There were full bookshelves, and a solitary painting on the wall to the right of the door. It was illuminated by a spotlight.

Denton pointed at the painting.

"There," he said. Billy wandered over. He tried to lift the painting but seemed to be struggling. Denton wandered over. He paused a moment before taking the right side of the painting and pulling it towards him. The painting swung out, attached to the wall by a hinge on the left hand side. Behind it was the absence of a refrigerator. Instead, there was a safe.

"Very interesting," commented Denton. "Rumpole, we've found something."

"What?" came the response.

"A safe."

There was a pause. "You sure?"

Denton frowned. "Very funny!"

"You sure you don't want me to come down and look at it."

"No, thank you," said Denton flatly.

"OK, so you've found a safe, well done," said Randall. Though clearly he was not impressed.

"What?" asked Denton.

"And the combination is?" asked Randall.

Denton paused, before looking at Billy despondently. "Good point."

"Look, I don't want to ruin your moment but it's getting very busy downstairs. Not much of a 'problem - solution' comment, I know, but I think our time here must come to an end very shortly."

"Noted," responded Denton. He looked at Billy. Billy looked at Denton. It was clear both appreciated that the solution to their current misery was not more than a few inches away. Neither, though, had any idea how to get through the inches of steel in the way.

"Dynamite?" suggested Billy. Denton scowled at him. "I don't know! I can't think straight! I'm terrified! My brain is all over the place."

Denton put a firm hand on his shoulder. "Then just calm down and think.

If you owned a safe, what would your combination be?"

"The date that I bought Happy on," he said instinctively.

"Jesus, Stopcock, we need to get you some help," said Denton shaking his head. He put a hand to his ear. "Rat - any ideas from you?"

"None at all, though I suggest you hurry up. It's getting busy out here. I've had to move the car three times to avoid being boxed in."

"What did he say at the meal? Was there anything he said that could help us?" asked Denton despairingly. They were so close!

"Like what, Denton? Like *'by the way if you ever feel like breaking and entering the combination is 31-22-14. In the meantime, would you like more wine?'*"

"Not helpful, Rat," said Denton impatiently.

There was a pause.

"Sorry," came the reply. "I'm just a little edgy. We're going to get caught. Plus, your repeated use of the term 'Rat' is making the situation worse. You know I hate that!"

"OK, maybe we could discuss this later. In the meantime, try to be helpful," said Denton looking at Billy and shaking his head. Billy rolled his eyes. "Women!" he mouthed.

"I don't know. Try his birthday."

There was a further pause.

"Of course! He told you his birthday! What was it again??" asked Denton. He was slightly resentful that this information had not followed automatically without the need for prompting.

"Erm…" said Delia.

"Hurry up!" said Randall.

"Err…"

"Come on, Rat," said Denton, impatiently.

"Oh no," she said finally, "I can't remember!!"

"Anyone?" said Denton. He could feel time ticking away.

"Come on!" said Randall. "People are coming this way."

"I think it was October," said Billy. "Or was it November?"

"That's right!" said Brian. "It was October"

"OK, great, October the what?" asked Denton.

"Err, erm…" said Delia. "Twenty something? I don't know! Why did no one write it down?!"

"I did!" protested Randall.

"So, why don't you remember?" screamed Delia.

"I wrote it down so that I would not have to remember!" said Randall through gritted teeth.

"22 October 1927," said a voice over the airwaves. They all looked up at the ceiling. Why? Only they knew.

"Egon?" asked Denton.

"Yes, it's me," said the voice.

"Where are you?" asked Randall.

"I'm hiding in a toilet on the ground floor," said the voice. "There is a woman out there trying to get in here with me!"

"Egon!" hissed Randall. "Stop messing around and get up here. Petrocelli - will you just open the safe! We're going to get caught!"

Denton nodded, and refocused his attention to the safe.

"It'll never work," muttered Billy unhelpfully.

Denton sighed. "Remember, this is the man who's alarm code is 1234."

"Good point," said Billy nodding.

Nervously, Denton twirled the dial to the numbers 22-10-27. He had never used a safe before, having only seen them in films. How long were you supposed to wait between numbers? Once he had twisted all three numbers, he stood back and waited. Nothing happened.

What am I doing here? he thought.

His shoulders slumped and he turned his back on the painting. He began to move away when he heard an audible click. He turned back to find that he could see the contents of the safe.

"It worked!" he hissed loudly. He almost kissed Billy before thinking better of it. Billy looked relieved.

"What's in there?" asked Rat.

"Yeah," added Randall. "What do you see?"

What did he see? Denton shuffled through the various papers.

"Nothing," he said finally. "There's nothing here. A few important looking documents - deeds to his house maybe, bearer bonds or something - we can't take them - and lots of porn magazines. Who keeps porn magazines in a safe? He lives on his own for God's sake!"

Denton stood despondently looking at the papers in his hand. They were so close! Somewhere in this house there had to be the evidence he needed. Somewhere. But where?

"Petrocelli, we've got to go!" said Randall. "We have to go now! We're out of time."

"Ok," mumbled Denton, accepting his fate. He placed the papers back in the safe, closed the door, and placed the painting back against the wall.

Denton and Billy wandered back to Randall and Brian.

"How's it looking?" asked Denton.

"Hard to say," said Randall. He advanced down a few stairs before turning around sharply. "Quick, hide! Someone's coming!"

They dispersed quickly.

Without quite knowing how, Denton found himself in a small cupboard with Brian. A *Dyson* separated them. In any other set of circumstances, Denton would have found the situation unnerving, however, there was something comforting in having a co-conspirator with him.

The door to the cupboard had slats in it. Through them, Denton was able to see a shadow pass by. He could feel himself holding his breath. And then, without warning he heard a voice in his head.

"Where are you all? Are you hiding? I thought you said that you came upstairs."

Denton's heart stopped before he realised that he recognised the voice.

"Is that you, Colin?" he said, the trauma of the situation causing him to forget to use the correct moniker.

"Yes. Where are you?"

Noticeably breathing a sigh of relief, Denton and Brian emerged from the cupboard like guilty schoolboys. At the same time, Randall emerged from behind a particularly tall vase.

"Where's Stopcock?" asked Colin. They looked around. Billy was nowhere to be seen.

"I'm a bit busy at the moment," came a voice accompanied by the sound of falling water. "I'll be with you shortly."

"What have you been doing all this time?" Denton whispered to Colin in a manner which indicated he would have screamed had he not been keeping his voice down.

"I told you, I've been hiding!"

"Where?" asked Denton and then on getting slightly closer to Colin added. "Have you been drinking?"

"Yes," whispered Colin. "This lady made me a strong gin and tonic downstairs and then chased me to a toilet."

"You were spotted?!" said Denton with incredulity.

"Yes, but it's alright. She didn't question it. She thought I was someone called Maxwell." Colin noticed that Denton, Brian and Randall all looked stunned. "In fact," he added, "before being chased into the toilet, I had been wandering around the party. Gunt is in one of the rooms down there. Turns out the party he was at was a bit average, so he invited everyone over here."

"Did he see you?" asked Denton.

"No, he was too busy talking to people. I did try to see him to re-introduce myself but there was such a queue, I decided against it."

Denton stared at Colin then Randall, then Brian and back to Colin.

"You decided against it because of *the queue?!*"

"Yes," said Colin. "Anyway, I think we should probably make a move. Things are starting to tail off and the other guests will no doubt be leaving shortly."

Denton could hardly believe his ears.

"We know! We want to leave but we don't know how."

Colin looked at the three of them with a distinct look of confusion.

"Why don't you just use the door?"

Denton didn't know whether to laugh or cry.

"Because we'll get spotted, won't we?!" he screamed in a whisper.

Colin laughed. "No one will even notice, I promise."

"What?"

"Come on, let me show you." He started to walk off. Billy returned buttoning up his flies.

"Sorry about that. You know how it is with the nerves. Are we leaving?"

"Apparently," said Randall.

They wandered down the stairs. The hallway was crawling with people drinking and laughing. Not one looked at them with anything even resembling suspicion. A couple of people even said goodbye.

"See!" said Colin. "I told you."

"This is surreal," noted Randall.

Outside it was quiet. The gravel drive was filled with cars as they crunched their way out of the estate. In the distance they could see Colin's people carrier. As they trudged towards it, Delia turned on the lights. Denton reached the car first and opened the sliding door.

"You're missing someone," Delia commented.

"What?" said Denton looking back at the others. Then it clicked. "Oh right, yeah, Badger."

"Yes, Badger," said Delia needlessly repeating in the same annoying fashion that mediocre secondary school teachers have made a career out of.

"Don't worry about it," said Denton. "We'll get him in the morning. I can't be bothered to go and fish him out now, he'll only stink the car out with the smell of dog piss."

The rest of them climbed into the people carrier. They were despondent, but not quite to the same degree as Denton. Tonight had not just been a failure, it had been a personal failure for him. They had trusted him on his promise. He had not delivered. Come Monday, they would all be back at work. More importantly to Denton, he would be sat back at his desk in a world where he had no future. The thought of that made him distinctly uneasy.

Worse still, the same thought ran over and over in his mind. Why, throughout all of this, had Colin not volunteered information about the bomb? Why did he not confirm what he knew about Gunt? He must have concluded by now that Denton knew all, so why had he not reacted in the way that Denton had imagined? Why had he shown no reaction at all?

There was nothing left for it. Desperate times and all that. He had no choice. He had to confront Colin.

He had to know the truth about the bomb.

Chapter Thirty Seven

Confessional

It was the Saturday before the return of Sunday inevitability and Monday monotony.

There was distinct sense of gloom around the kitchen table that morning. As Denton stood at the doorway, examining his failed cohorts, it seemed to him that no one was actually blaming him for wasting their time. Instead, there was a tangible sense of, well, disappointment. If there was any positive to take from this failed adventure, then it was the fact that Denton had correctly identified that these people were ready to give up everything they had worked hard to achieve - to cheat, steal, lie, break in, con, hide - in search of the one thing their lives did not give them. Fulfilment. Denton had revealed to them that they were prisoners in their own lives. He had helped them to dig the escape tunnel. He had got them under the fence. He just couldn't get them to Switzerland. *Ah, the Great Escape,* thought Denton, *one of the biggest film title misnomers in history.*

OK, so I couldn't lead them to the promised land, but I opened their eyes. They are bound to be thankful for that.

The others noticed Denton loitering at the doorframe.

Look at them, ok, they're disappointed but in time they will come to understand, respect and be thankful for what I have done. I have helped them turn the corner. I have helped them to see the light. Some of them may even name their children after me…

"There he is!" screamed Delia like a banshee. "Get him!"

A look of horror crossed Denton's face. This was not his idea of being revered for leading the way. He had no chance to escape before they all pounced upon him, dragging him to the study. He was slung onto the chair behind the desk. Brian stood directly behind him, pinning him down.

Delia sat down directly opposite him.

"OK, we've been talking. We have some questions, Denton. Randall, close the curtains!" She grabbed the table light, turned it on and shone it into Denton's eyes.

From the darkness, Denton heard Colin's feeble voice.

"I just want you to know, Denton, that I do not approve of this militia action."

"Shut up, Colin!" shouted Delia as if they had been married for the past twenty years.

Denton was in shock.

"Explain yourself, Denton. Why are we here?! Why did you bring us here?!"

Denton sighed. It was more out of fear than anything else.

It was no good. He was going to have to tell the truth. He would have to suffer the consequences, whatever they would be. At worst, he feared prison. At best, he feared the sack.

"OK. OK," he said slowly. He sighed again. "Colin, tell them about the bomb."

They all looked at Colin, the pacifist, stood in the corner.

"What?" he said, slightly startled. (This was probably because Delia was now shining the light at him.)

"Colin. I know about your bomb. I know that you were going to blackmail the firm with what you knew about Gunt. I couldn't say before for fear of the consequences, but I know. I know, Colin. Tell them."

"Denton, what are you talking about?" asked Colin with a genuine look of confusion on his face.

Denton looked pale. *Why does Colin genuinely look like this isn't ringing a bell?* he thought. Alarm bells began to sound.

"Colin. Your bomb. In your desk drawer. Project Maybury."

Colin looked mildly angry. Well, as angry as you could look in a neck brace.

"How did you get into my personal things? How dare you?" He fumed. "For your information, Project Maybury is the name of the first deal that I ever worked on and I keep that file to remind myself of where I came from and as a useful reminder of the capabilities and limitations of trainees as inept as you! And the nature of my 'bomb' is nothing to do with you!"

They all stared at Denton.

"Is he telling the truth?" asked Delia, looking intently at Denton. Denton was speechless. She turned back to Colin. "What is he talking about, Colin? What is your 'bomb'?"

"It's nothing," said Colin.

"Denton obviously knows Colin," said Delia. "Look, why are we bothering with this posturing. Denton, get your photocopy of the evidence. You must have done one otherwise you would have had no evidence to blackmail Gunt with and hence you would not have brought us all up here."

"Yeah," added Randall. "After all, Colin, he is a trainee. You might call him inept and you may be right, but if there is one thing he knows how to do and do well, it's photocopying."

"OK! OK!" said Colin. "Fine. My bomb has nothing to do with Project Maybury. I have no idea what Denton is rambling on about. There is nothing in Project Maybury to blackmail any one with! I promise. My bomb is in fact a signed memo from the senior partner to all the other partners, which I got hold of by slightly devious means. It confirms the firm's practice of over-billing clients. The bomb is my protection from the sack, Denton. If they sack me, I go public. It's the reason why they did not get rid of me after Muftny left."

Denton felt quite small. The comment about him being inept had not passed him by. Of course, he now knew that it was true. He was inept. This was partly evidenced by the fact that he had not taken photocopies of any damning materials. There had not been time. Some solicitor he would have made.

Denton did not speak. He did not dare move. What had he done? All this time he had been working from a complete misassumption. But then he remembered. *The Project Maybury file had contained evidence to justify the plan,* he thought feebly. *It could have worked!* Clearly, he was the only one who believed that now.

"Oh, well, that's just brilliant!" snarled Delia. "We have trusted you throughout this little charade. You promised us that this little plan of yours would lead to 'buried treasure', I think was the exact term. What we want to know is, what was it all for, Denton? This non-existent bomb? What have we risked our careers, our integrity, our lives, and more importantly, some of my best clothes for?"

Denton mumbled something. It was incoherent. He had to think quick.

"What?" asked Delia. "Because let me tell you, Denton, none of us are impressed. We all trusted you. Do you understand that? We trusted you when we came up here. We believed in you. You showed us the deficiencies in our lives…"

I knew I had! thought Denton with a misplaced sense of self-satisfaction.

"…but you also promised us all the answer. Where is it?! Is this it?!"

Still, the power of speech was beyond Denton. Besides, the light was blinding him.

"I risked my integrity on so many occasions, Denton, just for you. Do you even have the slightest idea how embarrassing and difficult it was trying to flirt with that old man? Do you have any idea how disgustingly awful it is for me - for womankind - to play up to old men's fantasies? What was it for, Denton? Answer me!"

"Yeah, answer her!" they all cheered, apart from Colin, returning to his role as pacifist.

"Right," mumbled Denton.

"Pardon?" said Delia. "We didn't hear that."

"Alright!" screamed Denton, shaking Brian's hands from his shoulders. It was their turn to looked slightly shocked. He grabbed the table lamp from Delia. "You want answers? I'll give you answers. I'll give you answers you'll wish you did not hear." He pointed the table lamp to Delia.

"Delia, when Randall and I first met you, you were just a stuck up cow whose chip on her shoulder had grown to such an extent that you wanted to prove your point so badly that you could no longer even remember your point."

Delia looked a bit taken aback.

"Do you remember the point you were making, Delia?" asked Denton. "You were trying to show the world something, weren't you? You were trying to show them how impressive you - womankind - could be in the field of law. You were trying to show them all that women could get to the top. The only problem was that in your narrow-sighted search of this pinnacle, you had lost touch with the entire world. You had no friends, you had no lovers, you drove people away with your constant battle to out do them. We…" he pointed at Randall, and himself, "…gave you back your sense of perspective. We gave you back your hope. We showed you what life is all about!"

Delia looked a little less forthright than she had done.

"…We showed you how to enjoy your life. What did you get out of all this? What was it all for? If nothing else, Delia, I showed you what was going wrong in your life. I showed you how it could change. I showed you what you really wanted. Not a career. Not backstabbing. Not getting ahead for the sake of being 'the best'! I showed you fun. I showed you friendship. I showed you what to do!"

Delia looked visibly dishevelled. None of them looked quite as comfortable as they had done. He wheeled the light around into Brian's eyes.

"Brian! You! Think of where you were months ago. You were a security guard who couldn't express himself. You couldn't even look at a flower arrangement without a tangible sense of discomfort. Look at you now! You dress how you want to dress. You are not afraid to talk about flowers. What have I done for you? I have helped you 'out' your dirty little secret!! I have helped you win back your self respect!"

Brian looked forlornly at the ground. He nodded timidly.

"Billy!" shouted Denton shining the light towards Billy. "What have I done for you? How could you ask that? Before all this, you were living in the past. You had all these deep-rooted psychological issues born out of your parents' death, which you just didn't deal with. You looked to a goldfish for the support and love that was missing when your parents died, for God's sake."

Billy nodded. It was true.

"I helped you through that. This whole little adventure has been the longest time I have ever known you not to retreat back into the hiding place that you call your flat. You're dealing with things, Billy, you're moving on! What did you get out of this? You got your life back!"

He flashed the light towards Randall.

"Ow!" said Randall, as the light blinded him.

"Randall! You, I'm most disappointed about. You, I expected to be on my side, no matter what. You let me down, Randall. You, of all people I expected to see how their life has changed."

Randall looked slightly guilty.

"We're best friends, Randall. That must have meant something to you? You stand there, conveniently ignore all that, and then ask me what I have done for you? I've given you the choice, Randall. You had real doubts about whether the law was for you. Hasn't this break from it all given you the chance to choose? Hasn't it given you the chance to look at your life, out of context, to see if the pursuit of a dream is worth giving everything up for, for the chance to start again? Hasn't it shown you whether you want to stay in the law?"

Randall nodded.

Denton flashed the light to Badger.

"Badger!" said Denton. He hesitated. "I'll accept that I haven't done a lot for you, but then it did give you the opportunity to pass out in new places."

Badger reflected. "Yeah, I'd agree with that."

Denton turned the light back so that it was flashing up underneath his chin. "What was all this for? It was for all of you! It was for all of us! It was to show you the trap you had all fallen into! None of you were happy with your lives before. I took you away from all that. In our wild goose chase, you have had the chance that no one else does. You had the chance to look at things in a new light. Where you go from here is up to you. Whether you speak to me again is up to you, but do not ever suggest that I have let you down."

They all looked at Denton with a look of new found realisation. Slowly they all nodded. One or two said thank you. Denton smiled, now with an appropriate sense of self-satisfaction.

Good bullshitting, Denton, you'll go far, he thought.

"So was this really just a wild goose chase, Denton?" asked Billy. "Was there really no plan to get us out of our lives? Was there ever a real bomb?"

Denton paused. He looked up and saw Colin still stood in the background. *Would it ruin the mood if I mentioned the part that Colin has obviously forgotten? Would it help if I explained how it could have worked if we had found the missing piece?* he thought.

They all looked at him in expectation. He was about to speak and then paused again. *If I do mention the missing part and nothing comes of it, surely I will just undermine all the good bullshitting, I mean, work that I've just done. Surely no good will come of me mentioning it. Or would it?*

He looked at them a moment longer. *No bomb does any good anyway - it only creates agony. It only prolongs the pain.* "Billy," said Denton, wondering how to phrase his thoughts, "the world is full of plans, full of ways to go. Just reflect on the way you have gone, and where you go from there."

Chapter Thirty Eight

Conflicts of interest

The light cascading through the thin curtains blinded Denton in a manner he did not appreciate. It seemed so intense that he could not even open his eyes, and yet, he desperately wanted to, if only to relieve the muscles that were currently scrunching up his face. His head ached. More generally, there was a feeling of nausea and malaise.

It was Sunday.

Groaning, he sat up and pushed four fingers and a thumb through the knotted mess of dark hair on his head. It didn't help. He still felt dreadful. More so than usual, he also felt distinctly uneasy. He no idea how the evening had ended.

He did remember that they had all decided to go out for one last round of drinks. He remembered that there had been more than one round. He could not remember how many though. There had been loud music. There may have been dancing. They had spoken of what they would do with their lives. They had laughed at their belief in Denton's plan. They had (finally) acknowledged that Denton had been right. Their view of life had changed. Their perspectives had been altered. Denton could remember that feeling of pride as they thanked him. He had changed their lives. He liked that feeling. He couldn't remember much after that.

He looked down at the floor. Amazingly, there was a pint glass full of water on the floor.

"Thank God for the water," he choked. Reaching down, he noticed that his knuckles were almost purple. Then the flashback hit.

Easter had been there.

He had not spotted her at first. It was her who had approached him. She had looked amazing. Her face beaming as he spoke to her. They had laughed. It had been nice.

Denton's head pounded. He placed the glass of water to his temple. As expected, it did not help, but it was vaguely comforting.

"You seem like a really nice guy," she had giggled.

"Yeah, well, you seem like a good laugh yourself," he had said.

"No, really," she said, placing a hand on his arm. "I really like you. You make me feel really comfortable. I'm not used to that."

"Well," said Denton, praying that she never moved her hand again. "I do my best."

"What are you doing here, anyway?" she asked. "What are you, a travelling waiter?"

Denton laughed. "No, I'm a lawyer."

"Wow," said Easter. "That was an unexpected answer. You don't act like one!"

"Thanks," said Denton, pretending to be hurt.

"Oh, sorry!" said Easter, holding one hand to her face, and stroking Denton's arm with the other. "I just mean, I always thought they were really stuck up. It's weird seeing one getting as drunk as you are!"

"Oh, they all do that!" said Denton. "Well, most of them anyway. They're just not all as much fun as I am!"

She giggled. "Are you planning to move on soon?" she asked.

Denton looked at her. Both of her. "Well, yes actually. I'm going back to London tomorrow. That's where I'm based."

Easter swayed slightly as the words sunk in. "That's a shame," she said. The words hit Denton like knives. He thought she would walk away at that point. She certainly looked like she would. She hesitated, as if weighing something up in her mind. "Well, before you do, would you like to go to dinner?"

"Really?" asked Denton, betraying his childlike enthusiasm at the idea. "You serious?"

"Yeah, why not?"

Denton's brain struggled with the instruction to be cool. "Because you're so beautiful - look at you - why on earth would you want to go to dinner with me??"

Brilliant, thought Denton. *Thank you brain cells for a truly inspired answer.*

"Thank you," said Easter, smiling. "No one ever says that to me."

"Really?" he asked.

"Yeah, I normally just get innuendos not compliments. You know that thing you said at the party."

Denton winced. What was she about to say?

"It was very unexpected. A little unnerving…"

You're killing me here! he thought.

"..but, definitely, the most beautiful thing that anyone has said to me." Her eyes sparkled as she said the words.

"Oh," said Denton, unsure what to say next. Over Easter's shoulder, he saw two men scowling at him. "Who are those men staring at me?"

Easter turned around then turned back. "Those are the two assholes who normally give me the innuendos. I work with them. They disgust me to the bone."

"Oh," said Denton, still unsure what to say. "Are they bothering you now?"

"Not really."

"What are they doing here then?"

"We all came together. I work with them. They are slimy, hideous little men to whom bad things should happen." She stared at Denton. "I used to think all men were like that. Now, I know they're not." She beamed at him again. She gave him a peck on the cheek. "I'm leaving now, but I'll see you tomorrow. You've got my number." With that she left.

Denton was beaming. Then his brain kicked into gear. "No, I don't have your number!" he said, too late. She was gone. He continued to beam though.

*****

Denton's hangover was one of the worst he had had in a while. After that point in the night, there had been no stopping him. He was bouncing off the ceiling with enthusiasm. Now, in his miserable state, he took a sip of water, then a large gulp, then two more, all in quick succession. He almost retched. He recollected further: at least to start with, he had been bouncing with enthusiasm. Then Delia had spoken to him.

"What are you doing!" she bellowed, her words slurred, her eyes all over the place.

She was hammered.

"What?" asked Denton, not much better off himself.

"I saw you!" she shouted. "I saw you! You were talking to that slut!" Her words would have been heard by the entire pub had it not been for the Heavy Metal being played at ten times the recommended level. Denton's ears rang.

"What are you talking about, Delia?"

"That little fucking bitch you were talking to before. The one from the party. I thought you were different, Denton. I trusted you!" She was red in the face.

"Delia, seriously, what is wrong with you!"

"I love you!" she blurted. "I fucking love you, and this how you repay me. You're the only man I ever trusted and loved, and you do this to me? You flirt with someone right in front of me? How could you?"

Denton did not know quite how to react. Everything was getting a little bit too weird. First, there was Easter's revelation, now Delia's…

"Delia, I…" he had no idea what he was about to say next.

She stared at him expectantly as if she were thinking, *don't break my heart, don't break my heart.*

"I'm sorry," he said finally. "You're a nice girl. You're very attractive, but you're not for me. You're for someone else. I was curious about you. I just wanted you to see how beautiful the world is - how beautiful you are." Her eyes filled with tears. She slapped him hard across the face.

"You sanctimonious little prick."

She turned and ran out of the pub. Colin looked over. He saw her leave and followed.

*****

I need more water, thought Denton. It was pointless though, he was too disorientated to leave the bed. He lay back down and rested his bruised fist on his chest.

*****

Denton remembered that he had then spoken to Randall. Randall could not believe what Delia had done. He told Denton to follow her to make sure she was ok. Denton said he thought Colin had gone, but couldn't be sure. He had left the pub.

Outside though, neither Delia nor Colin were anywhere to be seen. It would be three years before he found out what happened.

Instead though, he saw Easter again. She was not on her own. Those two guys were there. They were stood hovering. Easter was against a wall.

I'm going on a date with that girl tomorrow! he thought. He was unbelievably happy despite all that nonsense with Delia. Denton looked back towards the pub - Randall was beckoning him inside. "Your pint's getting warm!" he shouted.

Denton looked back towards Easter one last time. *Beer!* thought Denton. He went back inside the pub.

"What the fuck is wrong with you?" asked Macey. "Are you a fucking lesbian or what?"

"Get lost, Macey," she said.

"Don't talk to me like that, young lady, or I'll have you fired. I'll have you down that alley in a moment to discipline you good and proper using my belt!!"

Malcolm chuckled. "Do it anyway!" he said.

Macey sneered. He stared down Easter's top. "Perhaps we should take a quick trip down the alley, there's something I want you to see."

Easter felt scared. She knew what was about to happen. She looked at her feet. What else was there to say or do?

"Anything you have to say to her, you can say to me!" said Denton.

Macey turned around. He looked Denton up and down. "Look, Malcolm, it's that prick that was messing with our Easter earlier."

Malcolm towered over Denton. "Oh yeah, so it is. You looking for a peck on the cheek from us as well, you little prick?"

Denton's heart was beating fast. It was a bloody good job he was too drunk to be scared otherwise he'd have been bricking himself.

"All depends on how much you faggots charge," said Denton. It seemed like an appropriate response.

"We haven't got time for this," said Macey. "Sort him out while I take care of business," he said, sneering at Easter. There was a yelp followed by a crash. Macey laughed and turned back to Malcolm. "Well done," he said. "No more distractions…" His face dropped.

Denton planted a fist straight into his face. There was a crack of bone. Macey collapsed into a heap.

Easter was shaking. Denton wasn't doing much better. He held out a hand to her. "Can I escort you home?" he asked.

"Where? How?" she asked. "Where did you come from?"

"Well, I was looking for someone and saw you standing here. Then I went back into the pub for beer. Then when I got back inside, I realised you were in trouble, so I came back out."

Easter was dumbfounded. "You're like a guardian angel, or something," she said. It was almost a whisper. She looked down at Macey and Malcolm. The anger kicked in. So, in turn, she kicked Macey in the stomach as hard as possible. "You are a little shit! And I resign!! No career is worth this!!! Wanker!" she screamed, spat on both of them and then, composing herself, she took Denton's arm and walked away. "Thank you," she said, wiping away the tears that were forming.

"It was no problem. Besides, I had to. I didn't have your telephone number."

*****

Denton rubbed his aching temples once more. He smiled. Lying on the floor next to his bed was a business card. *Easter Williams, Journalist,* it said. He fell asleep again and dreamt of Easter Sunday.

Chapter Thirty Nine

A change of plan

It took ages for him to find her house. It was down several streets off the main road. A rabbit warren of houses. He had driven past her place, parking the Micra a safe distance away so that she saw him before the vehicle. Timidly, he stood in front of her door.

"Please let this be the right place. Please let this be the right place!" he mumbled to himself.

Easter opened the door. Denton was lost for words. Initially he thought he was at the wrong house. A thousand words and thoughts passed through his head. The words *gorgeous* and *beautiful,* were prominent as was the phrase *perfect vision of loveliness* and *sex on a fucking stick,* but none of those words or phrases did justice to how she looked. Recreating the image to others later would have involved a host of clichés bound together. What he saw was original. It was pure. She was perfect, and there were no words to describe that vision to others because he knew no one else would see her the way he did. He didn't care though. He didn't want any one else to feel this way about her.

"Hi!" she said.

Denton, slightly lost for words, floundered. "Hi!" he said after a short time of gawping.

"Come in!" she said, with enthusiasm. "Listen, I'm not quite ready yet." *You look gorgeous!* thought Denton. *What else is left to do?* "Come and make yourself at home while I just finish off."

Cautiously, Denton entered. *Am I imagining all this is happening?* he wondered. "Thanks," he said. He moved into the living room. The whole house had looked tiny from the outside, and like an anti-Tardis, he discovered that that was because it was.

"Your place is lovely!" lied Denton.

"Well, I like it," said Easter in the way that people are always defensive when they live in small homes. "It's more than enough for me."

There were photos all over the place. *Please, dear God, don't let it be rows and rows of images of ex-boyfriends she hasn't got over yet.*

"You have a lot of photos," said Denton, in the way that people always state the bleeding obvious when they first see other people's places. *You have a big kitchen, you have a tidy front room, your dining table seats eight.*

"Thanks," said Easter from a bedroom. "They're photos of stories I've covered."

Denton breathed a sigh of relief. Now he knew they were safe, he examined them more closely. He was attracted to one in particular. It was a photo of a man he felt as if he had come to know intimately those past few weeks.

"You have a photo here of Mr Gunt, what story was this?"

"Erm, which photo is it?" asked Easter.

"Well, it's one of Mr Gunt with a ribbon and a pair of scissors outside a building."

Easter entered the living room.

"Have you seen my house keys?" she said. Denton shook his head. She saw him holding the photo. "Oh right, yeah, that was him opening up a new wing of a hospital. Paid for it himself. Everyone knows he has a chain of restaurants, but did you know he was in hospital catering as well?"

Denton pondered the point. "Do you know him well?"

"Yeah, I know Gunt," said Easter as she searched for her house keys. "He's nice. He's very lonely though, up in that old house. Real shame."

"Must be," said Denton staring into the photo, willing it to reveal Gunt's secrets.

"Yeah, just goes to show, doesn't it?" said Easter, "All that money he made, it did not buy him happiness."

"Suppose not," said Denton. "Maybe he just didn't appreciate it. I mean, if you've always been rich, then you never know any different."

Easter stopped.

"Oh, no, Gunt wasn't always rich. He worked for his money. He started off with nothing, then became a millionaire overnight. Got into restaurants first, and then hospital catering. Real boom area for him. Never looked back."

Denton's heart exploded into life. "What did you say?"

"What?" asked Easter, still running around looking for keys. "I said, Gunt made his fortune in hospital catering. Yeah, there's always been murmurs about how he made so much so quickly. I thought there was a story there, but there wasn't. Did you see where I put my keys?" she asked.

"No, have you tried your kitchen, that's where mine usually migrate to?" murmured Denton. Easter disappeared into the next room.

It all makes sense! thought Denton, his mind racing away from him. *The hospital restaurant in this photo! Of course. Colin's bomb!!! It's all linked.*

Suddenly, Denton found himself back in Colin's office. Colin's top drawer, contained an A4 paper file, which was annotated *Project Maybury: Duplicate file of Colin Hooley, trainee solicitor.* In it were several pieces of paper, presumably bits of research and forms that Colin had done as a trainee. Of note though was the attendance note that Colin had written. This is what Colin had forgotten about. At first, Denton had dismissed it, until he realised that bombs do not always tick.

Project Maybury was one of Gunt's first deals. He had acquired a restaurant - 'The Maybury' from some old boy in Stockport. Colin had raised a query over the fact that he could not find much information on how Gunt was financing the deal. The partner in charge had dismissed Colin out of hand, telling him not to ask too many questions - the fact they had got the deal in the first place was enough, and that he shouldn't rock the boat. Colin had no evidence but suspected that the deal was dodgy. He mentioned money laundering, and had been told to keep quiet.

Colin's note! He had mentioned money laundering! Colin had no evidence, just a suspicion. A suspicion of a man who had suddenly acquired a lot of money very quickly.

Denton had searched for weeks to find out which companies Gunt controlled and whether he could see a link to dodgy businesses. Then he realised the exercise was pointless - organised crime is, by it's nature, organised. People don't tend to leave around that many clues, and they certainly do not file them at Companies House.

But it all makes sense. Restaurants! Hospital catering! All those types of establishments take a lot of coinage and notes in the course of trading and no one bats an eyelid! Denton's mind was falling over itself with ideas. *Of course, if he had become 'connected' back in the seventies he could have taken notes and coins from drug dealers, prostitution, racketeering, anything, and processed it neatly without anyone becoming suspicious. All he would have to do was process the money as transactions. He could set up all kinds of restaurants, have the money go through the till, then pay it into the bank and pass it back to the crooks as dividends. Surely, there was something there to blackmail him with. We could go to the house tomorrow morning - we could blackmail him into submission and insist that he give us a cut of his profits otherwise we'd ruin him.*

Denton was almost giddy. *It would all work. It would fall into place. We could all escape our dull and boring lives. We could escape our Fish Sunday thinking!!*

Easter returned to the room. Just for a moment, Denton's thoughts were interrupted. He chuckled. There was an ease about her. There was almost a child-like innocence about the way she seemed so puzzled by the loss of her keys. It gave her a real warmth that Denton admired.

I don't want to go setting bombs off, he thought. *I just want this.*

She caught the odd look on his face. "What's wrong?" she asked.

He beamed. She had such a graceful, calming way about her. Maybe it was those beautiful eyes. Nothing was a problem when she entered the room. Everything seemed to dissipate and resolve itself in his mind. He shook his head and smiled. "Nothing," he said. "I was just thinking about things. Stupid, ridiculous things."

A frown crossed her face. "Don't go getting all introspective on me!" she warned with a wink.

"No, I wouldn't!" he said. "But I have decided something."

"Oh yeah?" she said, slipping her shoes on.

"Yeah, I've decided I've had enough of London." He looked into her eyes. "I'm not going back."

"Wow!" she said. "That sounds like a life-altering decision to me. It's a lot to throw at a girl on a first date."

It was Denton's turn to frown. "Is this what this is? A date?"

She stopped and placed her hands on her hips. "Well, what did you think it was? Come on, we're going to be late for dinner."

"I really like this place," said Denton as she took his arm and led him out of the flat.

"Good," she said, closing the door as they left.

The photograph of the hospital restaurant opening remained on the table. It's potential unused. In the distance came Denton's voice…

"Will you help me set up home here?"

"OK," came Easter's giggling voice.

"Thanks," he said. "Would you mind if I kissed you?"

"First things, first, Denton." she said. "Let's eat, first, I'm starving. Then we'll think about afters…"

Chapter Forty

The end. And also the beginning.

"Three years and the odd month had passed since the journey to the Lakes.

The group, such as it was, if it ever was, had largely split. They had all gone their own ways to do their own thing.

Randall, now a qualified solicitor, had left that large multi-national firm with delusions of grandeur and visions of world dominance. Instead he had joined a nice West End boutique firm where the hours were good, the pay was excellent and everyone knew everyone else's name. He was living with a bubbly blond girl he had met at a party. She was charming and pretty. He thought the world of her. They would no doubt marry, and have beautiful blond babies with perceptively smaller than normal heads.

Badger had done very well for himself. He had set up his own business in London where he had installed a small booth near Liverpool Street station. It looked almost like a confessional. You paid your pound to enter, and were invited to air all your frustrations and anger with the world to Badger who was sat listening through a small grate in the wall. He made a fortune. The concept appeared in all the newspapers. People said that they found that it genuinely helped them to relax more. There are currently plans to set up more of them. Of course, what was never reported was that Badger was unconscious for most of the time.

Billy had become a counsellor of sorts himself. By night, he was the chairman of a 'coming to terms with grief' group. I always knew he had never come to terms with the death of his parents. By day, he was a guinea pig, and loaned himself out to the local university, where he helped scientists better understand the limits of the human bladder.

Brian had quit his job as a security guard. He had opened up a flower boutique in Kensington with a new business partner, Quentin. At least, I think it's his business partner.

Colin had left the firm and had moved to Leeds where he was a partner at a mid-tier firm. His ex-wife had run off with the pool boy, and had originally tried to take him to the cleaners in a messy divorce. She had not succeeded though, mainly due to her unexpected death. That put a spanner in the works and certainly caused her to re-evaluate her priorities. Colin didn't care, he led a happy little existence. By day he worked hard making deals happen. By night, he managed his boy's rock band as well as taking care of his new baby boy, who was about two years old, getting on for three. This was by his new wife. Delia.

After running out of the pub that night, Colin had found Delia crying in the car park. The rumour is that he helped Delia realise that she was not a failure at all, but a very beautiful young lady. Then he shagged the arse off her. I never knew he had it in him.

Bonnie Belcher had been on the fast track to partnership. Having sucked most of them off, it was inevitable. Unfortunately though, she was the principal cause of a twenty three million pound negligence claim against the firm. Apparently, Campbell had failed to supervise her at all. Probably too busy knocking her off over the files to actually read them. Last I heard, she was stacking shelves at Tesco's. Her little Cambie is her manager there.

As for me. Well, things worked out well. I work at the local CAB in a small village to the north of the Lake District. Easter is no longer my girlfriend. She's my wife. She never did return to work for Macey. She works as a journalist in our new village instead. We have very little money - so little in fact that I hardly drink at all any more. We spend the weekends cuddled up on our battered old sofa watching films on our black and white TV. Neither of us is ambitious. You may think it sounds slushy, but we've achieved all that we wanted to just by being together. Not only that, but the sex is incredible - who cares about a career after that?

And Gunt? Well, he died of a broken heart. I heard that he left message after message for Delia, but she just didn't return them. His suicide note said that all he wanted was to be with her forever. After his death, they found out he had been involved in money laundering for years, which caused a certain amount of embarrassment to the Government that helped him do it in his later years through their PFI hospitals.

I sometimes think about what would have happened to me if we had blackmailed him. I sometimes wonder what would have happened if I had qualified with the firm. I would have been a lot richer, but a lot worse off. All that time spent worrying about where I was going, what I was doing - it would have driven me mad. Now my days are spent thinking of Easter. I know she does the same. We spend our Sundays talking and laughing. We spend our time together. We spend our time fulfilled.

And as a result, I'm no longer troubled with Fish Sunday thinking."

The End.

And they all lived happily ever after.

(Apart from those that didn't, for the reasons described above, the repetition of which would be pointless at this juncture.)

(You should always obtain independent legal advice before applying anything you have heard to any specific set of facts.)

(Now wash your hands.)

Printed in the United Kingdom
by Lightning Source UK Ltd.
106310UKS00002B/43-408